About the Authors

Caroline Anderson's been a nurse, a secretary, a teacher, and has run her own business. Now she's settled on writing. 'I was looking for that elusive something and finally realised it was variety—now I have it in abundance. Every book brings new horizons, new friends, and in between books I juggle! My husband John and I have two beautiful daughters, Sarah and Hannah, umpteen pets, and several acres of Suffolk that nature tries to reclaim every time we turn our backs!'

Carol Marinelli recently filled in a form asking for her job title. Thrilled to be able to put down her answer, she put writer. Then it asked what Carol did for relaxation and she put down the truth—writing. The third question asked for her hobbies. Well, not wanting to look obsessed she crossed the fingers on her hand and answered swimming but, given that the chlorine in the pool does terrible things to her highlights—I'm sure you can guess the real answer.

Margaret McDonagh can't remember a time when her nose wasn't buried in a book. She read avidly, but always knew that she had to write. In 2005, after twenty years of writing novellas for *My Weekly Story Collection* and Linford large print, plus serials and magazine short stories for *The People's Friend*, her manuscript was accepted by Mills & Boon. She has been writing novels ever since! You can contact Margaret via her website: www.margaretmcdonagh.com

Finding Forever

Finding Forever:
An
Unexpected
Bride

CAROLINE ANDERSON

CAROL MARINELLI

MARGARET McDONAGH

MILLS & BOON

First Published in Great Britain 2021
by Mills & Boon, an imprint of HarperCollins*Publishers* Ltd,
1 London Bridge Street, London, SE1 9GF

www.harpercollins.co.uk

HarperCollins*Publishers*
1st Floor, Watermarque Building,
Ringsend Road, Dublin 4, Ireland

FINDING FOREVER: AN UNEXPECTED BRIDE
© 2021 Harlequin Books S.A.

St Piran's: The Wedding of The Year © 2010 Harlequin Books S.A.
St Piran's: Rescuing Pregnant Cinderella © 2010 Harlequin Books S.A.
St Piran's: Italian Surgeon, Forbidden Bride © 2012
Harlequin Books S.A.

Special thanks and acknowledgement are given to Caroline Anderson,
Carol Marinelli and Margaret McDonagh for their contribution to the
St. Piran's Hospital series

ISBN: 978-0-263-30300-1

MIX
Paper from
responsible sources
FSC™ C007454

ST PIRAN'S:
THE WEDDING OF
THE YEAR

CAROLINE ANDERSON

CHAPTER ONE

'OH, DR TREMAYNE, Kate left this for you.'

Nick stopped by the reception desk and took the sealed envelope from Sue, glancing at it in puzzlement. How odd...

'Is she still here?'

'Yes, I think so, but she's about to go. She has to pick Jem up from holiday club. Do you want me to find her?'

'No, it's OK.' He gave the envelope another glance, and with a curt nod to his patients as he passed them, he went into his room, closed the door and slit the flap open with his forefinger as he dropped into his chair behind the desk.

He drew out a single sheet, handwritten in her elegant, decisive script, and as he smoothed it out with the flat of his hand he stared at it in disbelief.

Monday 12 April

Dear Nick,

I've written to the PCT, and will tell Chloe and all my other colleagues and friends over the next few days, but I wanted you to know first that I've decided to leave Penhally and my post here as midwife. I'm putting my house on the market and Jem and I will move away from here over the summer, in time for him to start secondary school in September. It's the right time to go, as far as his education is concerned, and I thought we could move closer to my mother in Bristol.

I'll miss the practice and all the people in it, but it's time for us to move on. There's nothing here for me any more.

I would just like to thank you for all the support and kindness you've shown to me over the years.
Yours,
Kate

Stunned, Nick scanned the letter again. She couldn't leave. Where the hell did she think she was going? And taking Jem away…

He pushed back his chair and crossed to the window, pressing his hand against the cold glass and staring out numbly at the sudden squall that had sprung up. The rain was streaming down the pane in torrents, bouncing off the roofs of the cars outside, and people were running for cover.

Including Kate. She wrenched open her car door, and as she got in her head lifted and she met his eyes, holding them for a moment through the lashing rain, then with a tiny shake of her head she slammed the door, started the engine and drove away, leaving him staring after her.

He sucked in a harsh, juddering breath and turned on his heel, moving away from the window before he put his fist through it in frustration. The letter was lying there on the desk, taunting him, and he crumpled it up and hurled it at the bin. It missed, and he picked it up, crushing it tighter in his fist.

Why? Why now, of all times, when he'd begun to feel there might be a chance…?

There was a tap on the door and old Doris Trefussis popped her head round and came in with a smile.

'Cup of tea for you, Dr T., before you start,' she said brightly, 'and a couple of Hazel's fairings. I saved them for you.'

'Thank you, Doris,' he said tightly, and held his breath until she'd shut the door. The last thing he could do was eat, it would choke him, but there was no way he could tell Doris that. She'd kill him if he didn't eat Hazel's biscuits, he thought, dropping down into his chair and dragging his hands over his face before flattening out the crumpled page and reading the letter again.

It didn't make any more sense the second time. Or the third.

Maybe the tea would help.

He cradled the mug in his hand and stared blankly out of the window. It was slack water, the boats in the harbour swinging every which way in the squalling wind. He knew the feeling. He'd been swinging at anchor himself ever since Annabel had died five years ago, unsure of what the future held, of which way the tide would turn.

For a time he'd thought Kate was getting married, but then he'd heard on the grapevine that it was over now, and with Rob out of the way, he'd thought that maybe now, with both of them widowed—but then this, out of the blue. He'd never expected this. Never expected that she'd go...

She couldn't leave. She couldn't. She'd lived in Penhally for ever, her entire life. He'd known her since she was twelve, dated her when she was fifteen and he was seventeen, left her at eighteen to go to university, intending to come back for her—but then he'd met Annabel, and everything had changed.

Except Kate. She'd stayed the same—sweet, funny, kind—but those soft brown eyes had held reproach and disappointment ever since. Or maybe he'd imagined it, but all he knew was that every time she looked at him, he felt guilt.

He shut his eyes and sighed. God knows, there was enough to feel guilty about in the past thirty-odd years.

He folded the crumpled letter and put it in his pocket. He could go round there this evening, see if there wasn't a way he could convince her to stay—but there was no point, he thought grimly. She'd made up her mind, and maybe it really was for the best.

He'd miss them both, but especially Kate—Kate he'd depended on for her kindness and common sense when he'd been in turmoil, Kate who'd managed the practice for years before she'd returned to midwifery and become a firm favourite with the mums.

Kate he'd loved, all those years ago.

Had loved, and lost, because of his own stupid fault. His chest felt tight just thinking about it, and he stared out of the window again, trying to imagine the practice without her. His life, without her. She couldn't go. He couldn't let her.

There's nothing here for me any more.

Particularly not an emotionally bankrupt old fool like him. He had no choice but to let her go. No power to do anything else. The least he could do was do it with dignity.

He pushed the tea aside, strode to the door and yanked it open. 'Mr Pengelly, would you come in, please?'

He tried to concentrate, tried to give the man his attention while he described his symptoms, but the letter was burning a hole in his pocket and judging by the feel of it the acid was doing the same thing to his stomach.

'Sump'n's goin' on out there,' Mr Pengelly said, jerking his head at the window.

'Hmm?' Nick dragged his mind back into the room and listened, and then he heard it over the rain and his clamouring thoughts. The sirens wailing, the rapid footsteps as Oliver Fawkner ran to his car outside Nick's window and shot off up the road. He was on call today, acting as First Responder in the event of a serious accident as part of those duties, and he'd obviously been called out to the emergency.

'The sirens,' Mr Pengelly said unnecessarily.

'Yes,' Nick said, blanking it out of his mind as he examined him, weighed him, checked his blood pressure, listened to his chest. He was a heart attack waiting to happen, and if he had one, it wouldn't be Nick's fault. He'd given him sage advice for years, and it was time to lay it on the line.

More sirens. It was a big one, he thought, and eyed his patient firmly. 'Right, Mr Pengelly, I think we need to have another look at your lifestyle. You're overweight, you're unfit, you don't take your drugs regularly, and then you come in and tell me you have chest pain, but you don't seem to be prepared to do anything about it and if you go on like this you'll kill yourself. We need to check your cholesterol level again. It was high last time, and you're still smoking, aren't you?'

'Ah, but I've cut down, Doc.'

'To what?'

He hesitated, then under Nick's uncompromising stare he sighed and came clean. 'Only twenty a day now.'

Only? 'That's twenty too many. Make an appointment on your way out for a fasting cholesterol test first thing one morning, as soon as possible, and then we'll review it, but you need to start exercising and attend the stop smoking clinic—'

'Must be a big'un. There's the chopper coming now,' he said, gesturing at the window again, just as the phone rang, and Nick frowned and reached for it, irritated that the man didn't seem to be paying any attention.

'Excuse me a moment—Tremayne.'

'It's Sue. I'm sorry to disturb you, but Oliver rang. Kate's had an accident, and they're airlifting Jem to hospital. He said you'd better get over to St Piran's.'

He felt the blood drain from his head, and sucked in a breath. 'What's wrong—? How bad is he—is he—?'

'Head and pelvis, he said, but he was quite insistent that

you should go, Nick. Kate's going to need you. And he said to tell her not to worry about the dog, he'll sort it.'

The dog? He mumbled something and cradled the phone with a clatter. 'Um—Mr Pengelly, I have to go. I'm sorry. Make the appointment, if you wouldn't mind, and we'll talk again when we get the results.'

'So—do you want those biscuits?'

The man was a lost cause. 'Help yourself,' he growled, and got to his feet and went out to Reception, his legs moving automatically. 'Right, Mr Pengelly needs a fasting cholesterol ASAP with a follow-up appointment,' he told Sue. 'I'm going to St Piran's—can you get Sam to cover my surgery for me?'

And without waiting for her reply, without even pausing to pick up his coat, he strode briskly out of the doors into the lashing rain.

The drive to St Piran nearly killed him.

His stomach was in knots, adrenaline pouring through his veins, and with no one to distract him his thoughts were free to run over all the things that could be wrong, and all the things that could go wrong as a consequence.

The list was hideous, and just thinking it all through made him want to retch.

He called Ben's mobile from his hands-free. His son-in-law would be there today, in A and E, and he'd give him advance warning. He drummed his fingers on the steering-wheel, waiting impatiently for Ben to answer, and when he did, Ben got there before he did.

'It's OK, Nick, we're on it. I can hear the helicopter now, we're going out to meet it. Just drive carefully and meet us in Resus. I'll get someone to look out for you.'

'OK. Ben—check Kate over, could you? Or get someone to? She was in the car with Jem and I don't know if she's hurt. And tell her I'm coming.'

'Sure. Got to go. See you soon.'

The phone went dead, and he sliced through the traffic and in through the hospital gates, abandoned the car on the kerb and ran in. It would probably be clamped but he'd worry about that later.

He was met at the door and ushered straight through to Resus, and as the door swung open he froze for a second. He was assailed by memories, his emotions suddenly in turmoil. He couldn't do this. Not here, not this room, of all the places.

He had to. On autopilot, he looked around at a scene of organised chaos, Ben snapping out orders and the team anticipating him like a well-oiled machine. A machine that held the boy's life in its hands?

The same machine—and the same man—that had held Annabel's—and lost it?

Dear God.

They were cutting Jem's clothes off, slicing through the sodden fabric, peeling it away so they could get a proper look at him, talking reassuringly to him all the time, and it could have been any of his boys lying there, all skinny limbs and ribcage with only the pelvic binder left to hold his pelvis stable.

Don't let him die. Please, God, don't let him die…

'OK, let's cross-match for ten units and get five units of O-neg to start with, and some packed cells, and let's get some X-rays—a full trauma series, starting with head, spine and pelvis. What about pain relief?' Ben asked. 'What's he had already?'

'Three milligrams of morphine IV, but his blood pressure's dropping. Want to try—?'

The voices washed around Nick, only two things really registering. One was the bruised little face scarcely visible under the mask, most of Jem's head concealed by the padding of the neck brace; the other was Kate, sodden and bedraggled, standing a few feet away watching as they worked on her little son, her eyes wide with fear, her lips moving soundlessly.

Praying?

Probably. There was little else to do. He crossed over to her, and she gripped his hand and gave a tiny sob.

He squeezed back. He wanted to hug her, to say, 'It's OK, it's going to be all right,' but he wasn't sure it was, wasn't sure she'd want him to hold her, wasn't sure she'd believe him—and anyway his tongue was glued to the roof of his mouth.

He freed it with effort and concentrated on the facts. 'Have you done a FAST exam?' he asked, sticking to something safe, and Ben shook his head.

'No, we're just about to.'

'Fast?' Kate murmured.

'Ultrasound, basically,' Ben said. 'It might show what's going on.'

Such as free fluid in the abdomen. Blood, most particularly, from torn arteries, sheered bone ends...

Nick felt the bile welling again, and dragged his free hand over his face.

The radiographer was setting up the X-ray machine as Ben quickly ran the head of the ultrasound wand over Jeremiah's thin, slightly distended abdomen, and Nick watched the screen, wincing at the image. Free fluid. Lots of it. Damn.

They were handed lead aprons. Ben must have realised they wouldn't leave, and as the X-rays appeared on the computer screen a few moments later, Nick sucked in a breath.

Even across the room, he could see the fractures on the left side of Jeremiah's pelvis, the bony ends displaced, the damage they'd caused all too easily imaginable.

'OK, this needs fixation before he goes anywhere,' Ben was saying. 'Are the orthos free?'

'No. They're just finishing off so they're ready for him,' the charge nurse said. 'Want me to get Josh?'

'Please—and fast-bleep the anaesthetist, we need to get on with this.'

'Who's Josh?' Kate asked, her face white.

'New guy,' Ben said. 'He's good—don't worry, I've known him for years. He's done a lot of this—he's a bit of a trauma specialist. But we need to get this pelvis rigid before we move Jem and he needs to go straight up to Theatre if we can't stop the bleeding here. You need to sign a consent form for that. Why don't you do that and then get a cup of tea—?'

'His pressure's dropping.'

Ben frowned and bent over the boy. 'OK, Jem, stay with us, come on, you're doing really well. Let's give him a 250-mil bolus of O-neg and we'll see if he stabilises. Kate, I don't suppose you know his blood group, do you?'

She shook her head, her face terrified. 'No. No idea. I'm O-positive, if that helps.'

'Cross-match results are up,' someone said. 'He's B-negative.'

B-negative? Through the roaring in his head, Nick heard Ben sigh harshly. 'Damn. We used all our stock this morning. I don't know if it's been replaced yet.' Ben's eyes flicked questioningly to Nick's, and he swallowed.

'I'm B-negative,' he confirmed, the last traces of doubt obliterated from his mind with this one small fact. 'So's Jack. We're both regular donors.'

Ben didn't miss a beat. 'OK. Nick, contact Jack and ask him if he's able to donate today, then we'll get Haematology to sort it. That'll give us two units, and we'll salvage his own in Theatre and recycle it and give it back to him, and we can use O-neg if necessary until we get more, but if we get the ex-fix on, the bleeding may well stop anyway.'

Or it might not. 'You can take two units from me,' Nick said, and he saw Kate turn towards him, heard the hitch in her breath as she waited for what he was going to say. Not that. Not out loud, but he met his son-in-law's eyes squarely, and Ben gave a brief, imperceptible nod of understanding.

A door flapped shut behind him, and Nick turned and looked straight into Jack's eyes.

'Kate, Dad—hi. What's going on?' he asked. 'I was out in cubicles—they said Jem was in here.'

'He is,' Nick said, and Jack looked at the X-rays, winced and glanced down at the child on the trolley.

'Hell,' he said softly. 'Poor little chap. What's the damage?' he asked Ben.

'Pelvis, for sure, and maybe abdominal and head injuries. We were about to contact you,' Ben told him. 'We're short of B-negative. Have you given blood recently?'

'Um—about three months ago? No—just before Christmas, so nearly four.' Jack sighed harshly and glanced at the clock. 'I've got a meeting I should be at and I'm already late. Can you call me if you definitely need me?'

'We definitely need you,' Nick said, his voice deliberately low so that only Jack could hear. 'He's your brother, Jack,' he added, and watched the disbelief like a shockwave on his firstborn son's face.

'Jeremiah? Kate's son? He's—?'

'My son,' Nick said softly, voicing the words in public for the first time, and beside him he felt Kate squeeze his hand. His words hung in the air between them for a moment, and Jack's face was suddenly expressionless.

'Well, we'd better roll our sleeves up, then, hadn't we?' he said after a long pause, and Nick let out his breath on a shuddering little sigh.

'Thanks,' he said, but Jack turned to him, his blue eyes like chips of ice.

'Don't thank me,' he said, his voice deadly quiet. 'I'm not doing it for you.' He turned back to Ben. 'Give me five minutes. I just want to make a couple of calls.'

'That's fine, we're using O-neg for now. You've got a little while. We'll save cross-matched blood until he's stable.'

He nodded curtly and walked out, slapping the door out of the way with his hand, and Nick closed his eyes and swallowed. He'd known it would come out at some time, he'd known it would be hard, but like this, with Jeremiah's life hanging in the balance—

'OK, what have we got?' a new voice asked, and a man strode in, a man they'd never seen before, with a soft, lilting Irish brogue and that dangerous blend of rakish charm and lethal good looks that would leave trouble in his wake.

Nick knew all about that. He'd been like that in his youth; it had gone to his head, and look where it had got him. He almost felt sorry for Josh O'Hara, the new A and E consultant, but maybe this man wouldn't make the same mistakes he had. He'd have to try hard to do worse.

He was bending over Jeremiah now, smiling at him. 'Hello, Jem, I'm Josh. I'm just going to have a quick look at your X-rays, and then we're going to send you to sleep and fix you, OK? That'll take away a lot of the pain for when you wake up.'

Jem made a feeble sound of assent, and beside him Nick heard Kate give a little sob.

Nick tightened his grip on her fingers. 'It's all right,' he said, reassuring himself as much as her. 'He'll be all right,' he repeated, and hoped to God it wasn't a lie.

Josh looked up and met their eyes. 'Are you the parents?'

They nodded, the irony of it striking Nick like a hammer blow. Of all the ways—

'OK. You need to sign a consent form, and then I think someone needs to take you to the relatives' room and give you a cup of tea.'

'I don't want a cup of tea, I want to be here with my

son!' Kate said adamantly. 'I'm a midwife, you don't need to mollycoddle me.'

'We don't need to scrape you off the floor, either, and it's a sterile procedure. You can stay till he's out, then you go.'

Nick put an arm round her rigid shoulders, squeezing them gently. 'He's right,' he said, fighting his instinct to argue, to stay. 'You shouldn't be here. Not for that. And someone needs to take a look at you.'

'I'm fine.'

'We don't know that. Nick's right, you need your neck checked, Kate,' Ben said gently, lifting his head to meet her eyes. 'And your feet. I gather they were trapped. Let us sort Jem out, and then while he's in Theatre I'll come and have a look at you, hmm? And in the meantime, go and have something hot to drink, and some biscuits or something. You're in shock.'

She'd signed the form by the time the anaesthetist arrived a minute later, and Kate clung to her son's hand, pressing it to her heart and murmuring softly to him as he drifted off, then Nick ushered her away, leading her out of the room and down the corridor to the relatives' room, his reluctant feet tracing the familiar path.

'You can wait in here—I'll bring you both some tea,' a nurse said with a kind smile. 'How do you take it?'

'Hot and sweet, isn't it?' Kate said shakily, trying to smile back, but Nick couldn't say anything, because the last time he'd been in this room had been in the horrendous minutes after Annabel had died, almost exactly five years ago.

It came flooding back the shock, the horror, the guilt. He should have realised she was ill, should have done something, but he'd been so tied up in the practice he'd scarcely noticed she was alive. And then, suddenly, she wasn't. She'd had a ruptured appendix, and Ben hadn't been able to save her.

And yet again the guilt and the senseless futility of it threatened to swamp him.

CHAPTER TWO

KATE cradled the tea in her hands and tried to force herself to drink it.

'I hate sugar in tea,' she said, and looked up at Nick, trying to smile, trying to be brave, but his face was shut down, expressionless, devoid of colour and emotion, and she felt the fear escalate.

'Nick? He'll be OK.' He had to be, she thought desperately, his stark expression clawing at her control and threatening to destroy it, but Ben had seemed confident, Josh also, and there was no talk of ifs or buts or maybes, so he would be OK. Wouldn't he?

'Nick?'

He sucked in a breath, almost as if he'd forgotten to breathe for a while, and turned his head to meet her eyes. 'Sorry, I was miles away.'

Miles away? When his son was under anaesthetic, having his pelvis stabilised with an external frame so they could try and stop the bleeding that was draining the life out of him? Where on earth had he been, miles away? And with that look in his eyes...

He scanned the room, his face bleak. 'I haven't been in here for years. It hasn't changed. Still got the same awful curtains.'

And then she realised. Realised what he was seeing, what

this must cost him, to be here with her, and her heart went out to him.

'Oh, Nick, I'm sorry,' she murmured, and he tried to smile.

'Don't be, I'm all right. It was five years ago.' And then he frowned. 'More to the point, how are you? Were you hurt? What was Ben saying about your feet? I didn't realise you'd been trapped in the car.'

'It was nothing—just a pedal. I'm fine.' Her smile was no more successful than his, she supposed, because he came over and sat beside her, searching her eyes with his.

'So what happened?' he asked.

She shrugged. 'I was picking him up from outside the high school. It was my fault—I parked on the right, hitched up on the kerb and rang him, and he ran up and got in, and I pulled back out onto the road. I couldn't see a thing—the rain was sheeting down, but there were no lights coming, and I remember thinking only a fool would be out in this without lights, so it must be clear, and I pulled out, and there was an almighty thump and the car slammed sideways into the car I was pulling out around, and the airbags went off and—'

She broke off.

It had been over in an instant.

There had been nothing she could have done at that point, no way she could have changed it, but for the rest of her life, with the stunning clarity of slow motion, she knew she would hear the sliding, grinding crash, the scream of her child, and the thump as the airbag inflated in her face...

'Ah, Kate,' he murmured, and she looked up, into dark, fathomless brown eyes that normally hid his feelings all too well. But not now. Now, they were filled with sympathy and something else she couldn't quite read. 'I'm sorry. It must have been horrendous.'

She nodded, looking away because if she didn't she'd lose

her grip on her emotions, and she couldn't afford to do that, couldn't afford to succumb to the sympathy in his eyes.

'I can't believe I didn't see him coming.'

'You said there were no lights.'

'I didn't see any, and I was looking, but—'

'Then it's not your fault.'

She gave a soft snort. 'Tell it to the fairies, Nick. I pulled out in front of a big, heavy off-roader when I couldn't see, and Jem could have been killed. How is that not my fault?'

His mouth firmed into a grim line.

'He must have been speeding, Kate.'

'Very likely. It doesn't absolve me of blame.'

'Don't,' he warned, his voice strained. 'Believe me, don't take on the blame for this. It'll destroy you.'

As his guilt over Annabel's death had nearly destroyed him? She bit her lip, trapped the words, looked at the clock. It had hardly moved, and yet they seemed to have been in there for ever.

'He'll be all right, Kate. He's in good hands.'

'I know.'

She gave him another little smile, and reached up to touch his cheek fleetingly in comfort. The day's growth of stubble was rough against her fingers, ruggedly male and oddly reassuring, and somehow his strength centred her. She had to stop herself from stroking her thumb over his cheek, backwards and forwards in a tender caress, the way she would with Jem. With anyone she loved. She dropped her hand hastily back into her lap. 'Are you OK?'

His smile was crooked. 'I'm the last person you should be worried about,' he said gruffly, but it wasn't true. She always worried about him—always had, always would, and running away wouldn't change that, she realised. And even though it was tearing him apart, he was here for her now, when she needed him the most, just as he had been on the night her husband James had died. And he needed her now, too, every bit as much as he had then. So, yes, she was worried about him. She could never rely on him, not in the long term, but she worried about him.

'Don't be silly,' she said with a little catch in her voice. 'I'm really grateful to you for coming. I know it's really hard for you, being here. All those memories. It was such a dreadful time for you, and I'm sorry to have to put you through it again.'

'It just caught me by surprise, coming in here again, that's all. All a bit too familiar.' His smile was crooked and didn't quite reach his eyes, and he rested his hand over hers. 'He'll be all right, Kate,' he murmured, his eyes reassuring, his touch steadying her tumbling emotions.

The unexpected tenderness brought a lump to her throat, and gently she eased her hand away before she crumbled. 'I'm sorry about Jack.'

He shrugged slightly. 'I knew he'd hate me for it, but it's not a problem. He's hated me before, I can live with it.'

It was a lie, even if he was trying to make himself believe it, and she felt herself frown. 'He's a good man, Nick. He'll come round. And he'll be good to Jem. They all will.'

He nodded, sighed, and stood up, thrusting his hands into his pockets as he crossed to the window and stood staring out into the rain. 'Oh, they will. They'll close ranks round him and take him into their hearts, all three of them. They're like that. They take after Annabel.' He glanced down at the table, at the mugs sitting there, the tea growing cold.

'You haven't touched your tea,' he said, and she let him change the subject and picked up the mug, giving him room, not crowding him. He hated emotion, and he was awash with it today, trying hard to hang together through all the horror of it. It was all right for her, she thought, her eyes welling. She could cry her eyes out and everyone would sympathise, but Nick—Nick had to stay aloof and distant, hold himself back, because for him, today was judgement day.

And, boy, would they be judging, and talking, and there would be plenty to say. Nick had been well and truly married twelve years ago, at the time of Jem's conception, and the good people of Penhally held no truck with infidelity. When they found out...

Not that it mattered now. The only thing that mattered now was that her son—their son, she corrected herself—survived this, and lived long enough for Nick to build a relationship with him. She wondered what they were doing to him at this precise instant, and decided she'd rather not know. Midwife or not, there were things one didn't need to see.

She pressed her hand against her heart, and realised it hurt. It was tender where the seat belt had tugged tight in the accident, pulling on her lumpectomy scar and the still fragile skin where the radiotherapy had burned it, and she suddenly felt very uncertain. Dr Bower had given her the all-clear from her breast cancer in January, but it was very much an 'it's OK for now' result, and there were no guarantees for the future.

And if anything happened to her, Jem would need Nick. Assuming he survived—

'Nick, drink your tea,' she said, slamming the brakes on that thought, and he sat down beside her again and picked up the mug and took a mouthful, toying with the biscuits, crushing them to dust between his fingers, crumbling them all over the table.

'Josh O'Hara's a friend of Jack's from London,' he said out of the blue. 'I gather he's red hot. Ben used to work with him as well. That's why he sounded him out about the vacancy. And Ben won't let anything happen to Jeremiah—'

The door opened and Ben came in, and she dropped her mug onto the table with a clatter, fear suddenly closing her throat.

'How is he?' she asked, barely able to find the words. 'Is he—?'

'He's stable, his blood pressure's low but holding, so Josh and the anaesthetist have taken him to CT now to rule out any other injuries, then he'll be going straight up to Theatre. And we need to check you over. Come on.'

She tried to stand, and suddenly realised how weak she felt, how uncooperative her legs were, how very long she'd been holding her breath. She wasn't really listening any longer. All she'd heard was 'He's stable', and her mind had gone blank, unable to take in any more than this one, most important, fact.

Relief was crashing through her, scattering the last shreds of her control; she sucked in some air, but it wouldn't come, not smoothly, not sensibly, just in little jerky sobs, faster and faster, until at last the dam burst and she felt Nick's arms close around her, holding her firmly against a broad, solid chest that felt so good, so safe that she wanted to stay there for ever, because if she leant on him, if she stayed there, then surely it would be all right…

Nick stood there for a second—scarcely that, but it felt like an age before he came to life again and his hands gentled, cradling her head against his shoulder, holding her against his heart as he rocked and shushed her.

She must be going through hell, he thought, and then it hit him that this wasn't just her son, but his, too. Emotions slammed through him one after the other, but he crushed them down. There'd be time for them later. For now, he just had to be here for Kate, for as long as she needed him.

'Why don't you go and let them take the blood?' Ben suggested, once Kate had stopped crying and been mopped up and taken through to X-Ray. 'I'll keep an eye on her.'

'Isn't Lucy expecting you home?'

He smiled again. 'She was—two hours ago. Don't worry, I've told her what's going on.'

'All of it?' he asked, his heart jerking against his ribs, but Ben shook his head.

'No. I thought I'd let you or Jack do that.'

'She'll be disappointed in me.'

'I don't know,' Ben said thoughtfully. 'Maybe a little, at first, but she's said before how well you and Kate get on, and she knows you went out with her before you met Annabel, so I don't think she'll be exactly surprised to know you had an affair. In fact, she said only the other week that you ought to get together, now you were both free.'

His laugh sounded hollow to his ears. 'I hope she's not holding her breath for that. Kate's going. She's handed in her notice—she's leaving Penhally.'

'Wow.' Ben frowned. 'That's a big step.'

He shrugged. 'She told me today—well, she left a letter for me.'

She hadn't even told him to his face. That hurt, but he put it on one side, like all the other feelings that were swamping him.

'I'm sorry,' Ben said, and Nick blinked in surprise and met his eyes.

'Why should you be sorry?'

'You tell me,' Ben said softly, and Nick looked away from eyes that saw too much.

'She's blaming herself. She said she didn't see any lights, and she pulled out.'

Ben accepted the change of subject without a murmur. 'Visibility was awful, apparently, and I gather the other guy not only didn't have his lights on but he was speeding significantly, according to witnesses. He wasn't wearing a seat belt, either, and the car wasn't taxed. He's in overnight for observation, and the police have been in to talk to him already. It definitely wasn't Kate's fault. I need to check her out. You go down to Haematology and I'll see you when you come back.'

He nodded, and walked quickly down to Haematology to give the blood they would process and give to Jeremiah later, after his surgery, after he was stable. God willing. Jack was standing at the reception desk waiting, and turned to him, his eyes raking over Nick's face.

'Are you OK?' he asked, and Nick nodded.

'Yes. Ben's taking a look at Kate.'

'Have you eaten recently?'

Nick nearly laughed. For a moment there, he'd thought his son was enquiring after his emotional well-being, but, no, he was checking that he was OK to donate.

'Lunch,' he said, trying to remember and recalling a sandwich of some sort. He'd left half of it, and it seemed a long time ago. It had been a long time ago. He should have eaten Hazel's fairings instead of leaving them for Mr Pengelly. 'They gave us tea and biscuits in A and E, but I didn't have them.'

'Here.' Jack handed him a small packet of biscuits from his pocket. 'Eat those, and get a drink from that water cooler, otherwise you'll pass out when they take the blood from you.'

And without another word Jack turned back to the desk and spoke to the haematology technician who'd just come to find him. Nick followed them, grabbing a cup of water on the way, and then lay in the next cubicle to his son, the curtain between them firmly closed, while the technician set up the intravenous line and started collecting his blood.

'Can you be quick? I need to get back,' he said, and she smiled.

'It's a good job you're a regular donor, Dr Tremayne,' she said tolerantly. 'Saves all the screening. I take it nothing's changed since the last time?'

'No, nothing.' Nothing except his youngest son nearly

dying and Kate deciding to leave the county. 'Take two units,' he insisted.

She tried to argue, but Jack's voice cut across them both.

'Just do it. It might keep him quiet. You can take two from me as well.'

'Are you sure? I don't like to, but our B-neg donors in the hospital have all been called on recently and there isn't any available until tomorrow. Stocks are really low at the moment; we've got O-neg but obviously this is better. You're not still working this evening, Mr Tremayne?'

'No. I've finished for the day and I've got a light day tomorrow. My registrar can cover me if necessary,' Jack answered.

'And you, Dr Tremayne?'

'I'm not leaving the hospital until I know Jem's all right.' Nick replied.

If he was all right. Hell, he had to be all right. There was so much to say to him, so much lost time to make up for. It would be the bitterest irony if now, when he was finally beginning to accept that Jem really was his son and realise what he meant to him, he lost him before he could tell him.

Nick rested his head back, closed his eyes and prayed as he hadn't prayed since the night Annabel had died.

He couldn't lose another member of his family, and neither could Kate. It just wasn't an option. He pumped his hand to speed up the flow, so he could get back to her side as quickly as possible...

'She hasn't got any fractures, but she's sore,' Ben said softly, taking Nick to one side when he returned to A and E. 'Her right ankle's got a nasty bruise, and she's whiplashed her neck slightly, and her chest is a bit tender where the seat belt cut in. The skin's still a bit fragile anyway, after the surgery and radiotherapy last year.'

He realised he didn't even know if it had been the left

or right breast, and asked—not that it made any difference, or was anything to do with him, but he just wanted everything straight in his head, trying to make order of the chaos of the day, and this was another brick in the wall he could straighten.

'Left,' Ben said, not even questioning his need to know that stupidly irrelevant fact. 'I wanted to keep her here for a bit, let her rest, but she won't hear of it. She's very shocked, though. I've given her some pain relief, but she wouldn't let me give her a sedative.'

'No. She wouldn't. Stubborn woman.'

Ben smiled tolerantly, and Nick gave a short, ironic laugh.

'Pot and kettle?' he said, and Ben chuckled.

'Go in and see her, she's waiting for you. And give me your car keys, I'll get it moved. It's obstructing the entrance and the ambos are getting cross.'

He handed over the keys, thanked Ben and went to see Kate.

How long could he be?

Ben had insisted she should lie there for a while and wait for Nick, and frankly she didn't have the strength to argue. Anyway, there was nothing she could do for Jem now except will him to be alive, and she could do that lying down in A and E as well as she could hovering outside the scanner room in Radiology.

Once Nick was back, she'd get up and go and sit there, waiting for news, but for now, she was lying wide-eyed, alert, her adrenaline running flat out, her pulse rapid, her throat dry.

'You're a mess, Kate Althorp,' she told herself, and closed her eyes. She wouldn't sleep. No way. But she could shut out the light.

* * *

She'd dozed off.

Or so he thought, but as Nick stepped into the cubicle, her eyes flew open.

'Is there any news?' she asked, her face worried, and he shook his head.

'No. I've just spoken to Ben, but they haven't heard anything. Josh is with him in CT. Are you OK to go down there now?'

She gave a humourless little laugh that cut him to the bone, and tried to smile. 'Sure. My right ankle hurts, but I've got some arnica gel in my bag, I'll put it on later. Let's go.'

'Want me to do it now?' he asked, wondering how he'd cope with touching her, smoothing his hand over her skin, feeling her warmth beneath his fingers and knowing she wasn't his to touch, to hold—to love?

Would never be.

'Not now. Later, maybe. I need to be with Jem.'

'I'll get a wheelchair,' he told her. 'Stay there.'

'Don't be ridiculous, Nick,' she said, swinging her legs down and wriggling her feet into her damp shoes with a grimace. 'I'm perfectly capable of walking. I'm fine.'

She wasn't. She wasn't fine at all, but she had guts. He tried to smile, but his own guts were strung tight. He tucked her hand in his arm so she could lean on him, and walked with her to Radiology, glad they were moving fairly slowly. He was feeling a little light-headed and wondering if his stubborn insistence on giving two units had been such a good idea after all. It was a quarter of his circulating blood volume—enough to crash his blood pressure into his boots. He ought to get something to eat and drink, but now wasn't the time.

'He'll be out in a minute, he's nearly done,' the receptionist told them, and they sat and waited, Kate suddenly even more nervous because of what the CT might show up.

She thought her stomach was going to turn inside out it was churning so hard, and the painkillers Ben had given her didn't seem to be helping. Well, they were helping, but not enough. She rolled her neck slightly to ease it, but it didn't work. It was because she was tense, coiled like a spring, poised for bad news.

'I can't sit here, I'm going to have to walk around,' she told Nick, pushing herself to her feet just as the doors opened and Jem was wheeled out by Josh and the anaesthetist. The radiologist came over to them, nodded to Nick and then turned to her.

'Mrs Althorp?'

'Yes,' Kate said, trying not to fall down and feeling Nick's firm hand on her waist holding her in place. She dragged her eyes from Jem and the gap in the blankets showing the frame holding his pelvis rigid, and leaned against Nick, grateful for the support, both physical and emotional, wondering what was coming, hardly daring to ask. 'How is he?' she managed, her throat tight.

'Stable. No damage apart from the fracture—he's been lucky, and there's no sign of a bleed from the head injury, so they're taking him straight up to Theatre now. You'll need to go up with him and sign the consent forms, if you haven't already done it, and I imagine you'll want to wait up there for news?'

She nodded and looked at Jem. She wanted to talk to him—touch him, just touch him so she could reassure herself he was still alive, but he was unconscious, still under anaesthetic. She leant over the trolley anyway, and rested her hand on his cheek briefly, reassured by his warmth but frowning at the bruises as they walked towards the lift.

'Jem? It's Mum,' she said softly. 'You're all right, my darling. You're going to be OK, can you hear me? I'll be waiting for you, OK? I'll be here, all the time. I love you—'

She cracked, and Nick hugged her to his side as they followed the trolley to the lift and went up with him. They watched him go through into Theatre, and then Nick guided her to the chair-lined recess, and the long wait began...

'So that's your father-in-law?'

Ben grunted in confirmation, and Josh watched him. 'Interesting undercurrents between him and the woman. I thought he was the kid's father at first. It took me a minute to work it out. He seems OK—bit distant, but supportive. I take it they're friends?'

Ben sighed and put down his pen, and Josh propped his hips on the back of the other chair and raised an eyebrow.

'She's a colleague as well. He's known her for years.'

Josh nodded. 'I know you didn't always get on with him. Jack mentioned that he could be...'

'Difficult?' Ben supplied, his smile wry, and Josh grinned.

'He probably wasn't quite as polite as that.'

Ben gave a grunt of grudging laughter. 'Yeah. But that's all behind us now.'

'Is it? I passed Jack on the way into Resus, and he was steaming down the corridor with a face like the Grim Reaper. I take it they'd had words?' Josh waited, but Ben obviously wasn't being drawn. He capped his pen and pushed his chair back, changing the subject.

'Nice job, Josh,' he said. 'The ex-fix. Very neat. You're going to be an asset to the department.'

He took the hint. 'Thanks. Let's hope I can convince them all.'

'Giving you a hard time?'

He shrugged. 'Some of them. Not all. I'm the new boy. They're suspicious.'

'Well, they don't need to be. I'll have a word.'

'No, leave it. I'll win them round—I'll bring in doughnuts and smile a lot, work a bit late, you know the routine. A little of the blarney thrown in for good measure...'

'Well, don't expect it to impress me, I know you better than that, and they won't be fooled by it. Stick to what you're good at. Save a few lives—that'll win them round.'

'I'll do that for an encore,' Josh said with a lazy grin, happy that Ben, at least, seemed pleased to have him there. Shrugging away from the desk and putting the Tremayne family out of his mind, he went off to conquer some of the sceptics.

How could the time pass so slowly?

Kate watched the hands crawl round the clock face—a minute, two. She shifted yet again on one of the padded plastic armchairs, resting her head back against the wall with a fractured sigh.

'He'll be all right, Kate,' Nick said, for the hundredth time, and she just nodded slightly and flexed her ankle.

It was enough to make her wince, and she felt him shift beside her.

'Give me the arnica gel.'

She handed it to him and pulled up her trouser leg a little, kicking off her shoe, and he squeezed a blob onto his fingers and crouched in front of her, so she could rest her foot against his lean, hard-muscled thigh. That was all the running and walking he did, mile after mile over the moors, trying to outrun his demons. She could feel the muscles flex beneath her sole as he shifted his position slightly, and the open neck of his shirt gaped so she could see the pulse beating in the hollow of his throat, hard and fast, driven by the adrenaline that must be coursing through his body as it was through hers.

She lifted a hand and laid it against his shoulder, and he went still. 'Thank you, Nick,' she murmured. 'For everything.'

'Don't be ridiculous.'

'I'm not. Nick, we need to talk.'

He squeezed more arnica gel onto his fingers and smoothed it gently over the top of her other foot where a small bruise was starting to show.

'About?'

'Did you get my letter?'

He said nothing for a moment, just kept rubbing her foot, round and round until the skin was all but dry, then he stood up again and washed his hands in the sink in the corner.

She wriggled her feet back into her shoes, wondering how long the leather would take to dry, how she could have got so wet. Standing in the rain, of course, watching while they'd cut Jem out.

'Nick?'

He dried his hands, then like a caged lion he started pacing, from one side of the small waiting room to the other, then back again, ramming his hand through his hair and rumpling it further. It suited him, she thought randomly. The steel grey threading through it made him look distinguished, setting off his strong features—the features Jem had inherited from him. He was going to be a good-looking man, her son—their son.

Nick's son.

Finally he stopped pacing, sucked in a long, slow breath and turned back to her, scanning her face for clues, but there were none. Her warm, golden-brown eyes met his calmly, giving nothing away, as usual. She never gave anything away unless she meant to, and then it was usually disappointment in him. 'May I ask why you're going?' he asked, his voice carefully expressionless.

'Why? I would have thought it was obvious, Nick. I can't just be here for ever waiting for you to sort yourself out. Did you think I would? That I'd stay, to let you see your son a few times a year, in carefully arranged, apparently casual circumstances, so you can keep in touch without having to tell him you're his real father? Or, more to the point, so you didn't have to rock the boat and tell your other kids that we made love while their mother was still alive?'

'Once,' he said flatly. 'Just once. It's not as if we had an affair, Kate.'

'No, you're right. It was nothing so premeditated, was it?' she acknowledged gently, as if he needed reminding about anything that had happened that hellish night. 'We just reached out, to someone we could trust, someone who could trust us. But we were married—well, I suppose technically I was probably widowed at that point, but you weren't. And we did make love.'

And they'd made a child. Until Ben had told him about the blood group, there had still been an element of doubt in his mind, of disbelief. But not now. Not any more.

He looked away from the shrewd, understanding eyes that saw too much. 'Neither of us was thinking that night.'

'And you've done your level best to avoid thinking about it ever since,' she murmured. 'So I'm going to make it easier for you. Easier for all of us. I'm taking Jem away, and we're starting a new life.'

'With Rob?' he made himself ask, even though he'd heard it was off, but maybe it was back on, maybe that was why. 'Is he going, too?'

A flicker of distress crossed her face. 'No,' she said quietly. 'He deserves better than me. I'm like you, Nick. Scarred, broken, emotionally bankrupt. I'm no good to anyone. He's a good man. He was very kind to me, and to Jem.'

He said nothing. After all, she was right. Rob Werrick was a good man, a decent man, who'd stood by her last year during her treatment for breast cancer, who'd supported her through the most dreadful days of fear and uncertainty, a role Nick had sorely wanted to play, but all he had been able to do was sit, isolated from her, and pray for her. And Rob was the man who'd taken Nick's son to his heart and made room there for him, when the man who was his father had found he was unable to do so.

'So was it you or him who called it off?' he asked in spite of himself.

'Me. He asked me to marry him, and I said no. I don't love him—I can't love him, not in the way he deserves to be loved.' Her brown eyes were reproachful, her voice tinged with sadness. 'So I'm going, and we'll start again, and we'll be fine.'

His heart felt as if it was being crushed in a giant fist, but if this was what she wanted, to go, to leave, then maybe she was right. Maybe it was for the best. Easier all round. And away from the shadow of this guilt they both carried, perhaps she'd find happiness with another man.

He ignored the little twist in his chest and nodded. 'You're right. If that's what you want, then go, Kate. I won't stop you—'

'You can't stop me, Nick.'

'True. What about Jem? Will I ever see him?'

She gave a mocking little laugh that gave his heart another little wrench. 'What about him? He'll be fine. He doesn't know you're his father, it hasn't done him any harm not to know, so it won't in the future. I'll tell him when he's eighteen. I can't stay here so you can ignore him at close range. Anyway, you don't see him now—why would this make any difference?'

'Don't be ridiculous—of course I see him,' he denied. 'I see him a lot.'

'Only if you can't avoid it. Seeing him reminds you of your human frailty, and you don't like that.'

He didn't. He hated the constant reminder of what they'd done that night, of how he'd betrayed Annabel, tarnished the memory of James. But that didn't mean he didn't want to watch the child grow up, make sure he was all right—

'How the hell am I going to explain it to my children? They won't understand.'

'You could tell them you're human?' she suggested softly, her eyes so wise, so—so damn knowing.

He gave a quiet snort. 'Oh, they know that.'

'And this is about what they think of you?' she said, her voice heavy with reproach. 'What about what Jem will think of you when he finds out that he doesn't matter as much as your other children—your proper children, all respectably born in wedlock? They're no different, Nick' she reminded him, her words still soft and yet flaying his skin off with their accuracy. 'Conceived in haste, every single one of them. Story of your life. Well, I don't want to be a part of it any more, of the carefully constructed illusion of reality you fool yourself with every day,' she said wearily. 'I'll work my notice, once Jem's better, but then I'm off, Nick, and you won't hear from me again. It's better that way.'

Was it? He wasn't sure. He was suddenly filled with a cold, nameless fear for the future—a future without Kate, and without the boy, this last, unacknowledged and yet still infinitely precious child who, it seemed, he'd managed to love in spite of everything.

He sat beside her, the chairs so close he could feel the warmth radiating from her body, feel the air move with every shallow breath as her chest rose and fell.

'I thought you wanted me to be in his life?'

'I do—but not like this, giving him fragments of yourself from time to time. He deserves more from you.' Her eyes suddenly filled with tears. 'I can't do this any more, Nick. I'm leaving, and that's an end to it. Please. Just let me go.'

Let me go...

He held her eyes, watched the threatening tears well, watched in despair as one slipped down her cheek and fell to the floor. She never cried. Before today, the last time he'd seen her cry had been the night he'd taken her into his arms and held her. The night Jeremiah had been conceived.

Swallowing the bitter taste of regret, he stood up and turned away.

How could he let her go?

He couldn't—but how could he make her stay?

CHAPTER THREE

HE SAT down again a while later, but not for long, pacing restlessly, ramming his hand through his hair again and again until she thought he'd tear it out.

And then the doors swung open and Lucy and Jack came down the short corridor towards them.

'How is he?' Lucy asked, looking at Kate, avoiding Nick's eyes as if she wasn't sure how to do this.

None of them, in truth, knew how to do this. They'd just have to feel their way through.

'Still in there. They stopped the bleeding, they're just plating his pelvis. He's been lucky, apparently—'

She broke off, wondering how on earth what had happened to her son could in any way be considered lucky, but then she felt Nick move closer, his hand on her shoulder, warm and reassuring despite their earlier words. Unable to resist the pull of that warmth, she dropped her head against his side, listening to the steady thud of his heart, and above it, the tension coming off them in waves, she could hear their quiet, fraught conversation.

'I'm glad you came,' Nick said, and she saw Lucy tense.

'I had to, Ben asked me to give you back your car keys. It's in the staff car park.' She dropped them in his hand, then shook her head. 'I'm not here for you, anyway, I'm here for a little boy who's apparently my brother. I don't know what to say to you. All that fuss when Mum died, but all the time you'd been carrying on behind her back—'

'Lucy, it wasn't like that. It was just once, right after the storm. Kate was distraught, I was distraught. It just—'

'Happened?' she said, her voice a little hard, unlike her usual self, but then she would be, Kate thought. None of them were themselves.

Nick let Kate go and moved away a fraction, and she lifted her head and looked up at Jack and Lucy.

'It wasn't just his fault. It takes two, remember. I was as much to blame. And just as married, really. James had only just died. There was no decent interval, believe me. It was inexcusable, but it never happened again.'

'Not with you, maybe, but were there others?'

Jack's question made Nick suck in a sharp breath.

'No,' he said firmly. 'There were no others. Apart from that one occasion when we were both beside ourselves with grief and I didn't really know what I was doing, I was never unfaithful to your mother. I loved her.'

Jack snorted. 'Strange way of showing it.'

'Jack, leave it,' Lucy said. 'It's irrelevant to this. But what I can't understand,' she went on after a slight pause, 'is why you've never told us he's our brother—why you've kept it a secret for, what, eleven years or more?'

'Two. I didn't know about Jem until two years ago,' Nick said, and their eyes swivelled to Kate.

'So, did you know?' Lucy asked incredulously. 'Before then, did you know? I mean, you are sure about this? That James wasn't his father? Have you had a DNA test?'

'James isn't his father. You've only got to look at him, Lucy. Look at his eyes. Look at his mouth. He was just like Jack's little Freddie when he was three or four, just like Jack and Edward at his age now. And, anyway, James and I had been having fertility investigations. We were talking about adoption. Why would I need a DNA test? Besides,' she added, 'if I needed any other proof, I have it now. James was A-positive.'

Lucy sat down hard, her eyes accusing and filled with tears. 'So—for eleven and a half years you've been convinced he was Dad's child, and you didn't tell him until two years ago?'

Kate reached out a hand, but Lucy snatched hers away, and she gave a fractured sigh and dropped her hand back in her lap. 'How could I? He was happily married, he had three other children—who was I to throw all that into chaos?'

Jack gave a short, hard laugh. 'The mother of his child?'

She met his accusing eyes. 'Exactly. I wasn't Nick's lover, I wasn't his wife—I was the mother of a child. And I did what I could to protect my child, and you, his other children, and his marriage. There was no point in upsetting all of that. Two wrongs don't make a right. And we've been fine. Jem's had a good life, settled, and I've given him all the love he could ever need.' Her voice cracked. 'And now he could be dying…'

She felt Nick sit down beside her again and slide his arm around her, there for her, giving her his strength and support—at least for now. 'It's OK,' he said softly, turning her head into his shoulder and cradling it gently. 'Don't cry, Kate. He'll be all right. It's going to be OK.'

Was it? She hoped so, but she couldn't for the life of her think how she'd cope if it wasn't.

She felt Lucy sit beside her, felt the gentle touch of her hand. 'Kate, I'm so sorry, I didn't mean to upset you, I'm just— It's a bit of a shock, that's all. And I'm so worried about him.'

'I know,' she whispered, patting Lucy's hand reassuringly. She loved Nick's daughter, she'd delivered her babies—she hated it that Lucy thought less of her now because of this, but it was only what she deserved. She'd given Lucy's father the means to commit adultery, and it was every bit as much her fault as his.

But for now her guilt was directed towards her son, lying there on the operating table, his life hanging in the balance, hoping that when they opened him up they didn't find anything unexpected.

She concentrated her mind on him, focused all her thoughts, willing him to pull through, to make it, to be all right. And then the door opened, and her heart stopped in her chest, eyes locked on the surgeon as he approached.

Nick got slowly to his feet, and Kate held her breath, unable to move until she knew he was all right, but he was, she could see that from the surgeon's smile as he pulled off his mask, and with a leap her heart started to beat again, the slow, dull thud threatening to deafen her.

He acknowledged Jack with a nod, then crossed to her, his hand extended.

'Mrs Althorp—I'm Martin Bradley. I've just finished operating on your son.'

She shook his hand on autopilot. 'How is he?'

'He's OK.' He perched on the chair beside her, taking Nick's place. 'I'm sorry I didn't have time to talk to you before we started, but I was already scrubbing in and I'm sure Ben Carter will have explained what we were going to do. Under the circumstances I didn't want to make him wait. Anyway, he's fine, he's come through the operation well, we've managed to fix the fractures and I think he'll get a very good result. He's broken the two bones at the front of his pelvis on the left, hence all the bleeding, but the pubic symphysis, the cartilage joint between the two halves at the front, wasn't disrupted so he'll be back on his feet quite quickly. We've sorted out the vascular damage, plated the fractures, and in fact it's all come together very neatly. It shouldn't give him any problems once it's healed in a few weeks.'

'So—he'll be all right? He hasn't got any nerve damage?'

'Not that we know of. His left sacroiliac joint might be sore for a while, but it wasn't displaced and I'm confident he should make a complete recovery. We'll know more later, but it's looking good at the moment. We're running whole cross-matched blood into him now, and we salvaged the free blood in his abdomen—that's gone off to the lab to be cleaned up so it can be returned to him if necessary, and then we'll do some tests and balance the blood components over the next twenty-four hours, but that's all pretty routine stuff. Any questions?'

'No. I just want to see him.'

'That's fine. If you think of anything, don't be afraid to ask. I'll be around for the next couple of hours, just in case there are any problems. Jem's in Recovery now, so you can come and talk to him. He's very drowsy, but he's come round and he's fine. I'm sure he'll be pleased to see you.'

Kate nodded, her body suddenly turning to jelly, and she was glad she was sitting down. Nick helped her up, his arm around her as they went through into Recovery, and it tightened as she stood by Jem's side, sucking in her breath at her first sight of him.

He was linked up to a mass of tubes and wires and drips, a monitor blinking on the wall behind him, and his poor bruised little face was so chalk-white against the pillow he almost disappeared on it.

She took his hand in hers, wondering at how small and fragile he looked—somehow so much more vulnerable, with his eyes shut and all the tubes and wires. Where was her lively, vibrant boy, his gangly limbs and eager enthusiasm carrying him through life at a hundred miles an hour? Where had he gone? She stroked his hair back from his bruised forehead with a shaking hand and bent to kiss it.

'Jem? It's Mum. I'm here, my darling, right next to you. You're going to be all right. You sleep now, OK?'

There was a small sound that could have been acknowledgement, and his fingers flickered in her hand. She squeezed them back, and he seemed to sigh and go off to sleep again, and she felt her legs start to buckle with relief.

But Nick was there, holding her up, giving her moral and physical support. She didn't want to rely on him, but there was something about him, like a rock, an anchor in a world that had gone mad, and she leant against him and let him hold her. Just for now, just while she stared at her son and let herself believe he might live.

'You won't get much out of him,' Martin Bradley murmured. 'He's heavily sedated, and we've given him some pretty hefty pain relief, but he should be more comfortable now his pelvis is stable.'

'So what happens now?' Nick asked, staring down at the injured child who looked so fragile amidst the plethora of tubes and wires and technology, and he shrugged.

'He'll stay here for a while—an hour or two? Just until we're quite happy that he's stable and we don't have to take him back into Theatre. Then he'll be in PICU—Paediatric Intensive Care—for the night. He doesn't really need to be there, but they've got the bed available and they'll be able to monitor him more closely overnight while we balance his bloods, so we might as well take advantage of it. He'll probably move to the ward tomorrow, and then he'll be there for a couple of weeks, I expect, while we get him up on his feet again, and then it's just a case of getting slowly stronger. We'll have to see. The plates and screws will have to come out at some point, as he's still got a lot of growing to do, but we'll worry about that in a few weeks or months. Anyway, I'll be around, so we'll talk again tomorrow if I don't see you later. And try not to worry. He's going to be all right, you just have to give it time.'

Kate wanted to smile, but her muscles didn't seem to work. She realised she was still leaning on Nick, and she straightened up, moving away a fraction, distancing herself. 'Thank you,' she murmured, and held out her hand. 'You've been very kind.'

He shook it firmly. 'My pleasure. I'm glad to see you've got someone with you—the whole Tremayne clan, no less, including Lucy. I haven't seen you for a while. Are you well?'

'Yes, very,' she said with a smile, but Kate could see it didn't reach her eyes. 'Busy. I've got two children now.'

'Yes, so Ben tells me. Well, it's good to see you again, and it's nice that Kate's got so many friends around her supporting her.'

Nobody contradicted him, and he left them alone, nothing to break the silence but the soft beeps and hisses from the instruments, and the distant ringing of a telephone in another room,

Lucy broke the silence first.

'Um—I ought to go. I've left Ben with the children, and Annabel's had a cold, so she's a bit fractious, and Josh is teething, but keep in touch.'

'Yes, make sure you do that,' Jack agreed. 'I should go, too, I haven't seen the kids at all today, and I've only seen Alison under the edge of the duvet, so I'd better go home before they can't remember who I am. I'll come up tomorrow and see Jem, but if there's any change in the meantime, Kate, give us a ring, OK? Or if there's anything we can do?'

'Of course I will,' she promised, and they walked out, shoulder to shoulder, Jack putting his hand against Lucy's back to escort her through the door. And then it swung shut behind them and Nick let go of some of the tension that had held him for the last few hours and looked down at Kate with a fleeting smile.

'I told you he'd be OK.'

She dredged up a smile. 'Of course you did. I just didn't dare believe you.'

'Do you believe me now?'

'I might be starting to,' she admitted, and looked back down at Jem, her face drawn and fraught. 'You don't have to stay, Nick.'

Was she mad? 'Of course I'm staying. You can't believe I'd leave you alone now.'

'Why not? You heard the surgeon, he's out of danger. You don't need to be here, you've got to work tomorrow.'

'No. I'm not leaving you, Kate. I'm here for you, for both of you, for as long as you need me.'

She met his eyes, and they seemed sincere, but she'd thought that thirty-something years ago, and he'd left her. Left her and married Annabel when she'd become pregnant with the twins. 'I can't lean on you, Nick. I won't let myself. Every time I do, every time I think I dare, you let me down.'

'I won't let you down. I promise you, Kate, I won't walk away from this.'

She stared at him, at the serious expression on his face, the conviction in his eyes, in his voice. Dare she trust him? 'You always walk away,' she said at last.

'I didn't the night James died.'

She gave a soft huff of laughter and shook her head. 'No, you didn't, did you? Maybe it would have been better if you had.' But then she wouldn't have had Jem, and her life would have been empty and pointless. And she needed him now.

'I know I've let you down,' he said softly. 'I know I've let Jem down. But I'm here now, and I'll stay here for as long as you need me, and I'll do whatever I can to help you. Just give me a chance.'

She shrugged and looked away. 'I can't stop you. But I can't lean on you, either. I have to do this on my own.'

'No, you don't,' he said, trying to inject something into his voice that she could believe in. 'And I'll prove that to you.' Even if it took years. A lifetime.

Her shoulders were drooping, and his heart went out to her. Poor Kate. She was exhausted, he thought, exhausted and shocked and traumatised, and it was late. 'You ought to eat,' he coaxed gently. 'Keep your strength up.'

She shook her head. 'I can't eat. Not when he's like this. Maybe later. I could murder a drink, though. I wonder when they'll move him to PICU?'

'An hour or so? Shall I go and get you something? Tea, coffee?'

'Tea would be lovely. Do you mind? I really don't want to leave him.'

'On one condition—you sit down beside him and rest, and you eat something if I bring it back.'

'You're a bully, do you know that?' she said, but she was smiling, an exhausted, rather watery smile that in a heartbeat could have morphed into tears, and she sat obediently in the chair he put there for her.

'I'm looking after you is what I am,' he said, and headed for the door. 'Any special requests?'

'Tea. And a sandwich, if I must, but no cheese. I'm going to have nightmares as it is.'

'OK. Back in five.'

He went through the door and down the stairs, pausing halfway because he felt suddenly light-headed. Damn. That was giving two units of blood, not drinking anything like enough to replace the lost fluid or taking in any food—apart from Jack's biscuits, he'd had half a cup of tea, a cup of water and whatever he'd had in A and E in the relatives' room, and that was all since his miserable half-sandwich and instant coffee at lunchtime. And it was—good grief—a quarter past midnight.

And the café, when he got there, was shut, with a sign directing him to the main canteen some distance away.

There was a vending machine, and he pulled some coins out of his pocket with fingers that were starting to shake violently, and put them into the machine, pressed the button for a bottle of sports drink to boost his fluids and blood sugar, and twisted the cap to loosen it. And it sprayed him.

He swore, twisting it shut again, and suddenly it was all too much. He dropped his head forwards against the vending machine and resisted the urge to slam it into the gaudy metal case. Head-banging wouldn't cure anything.

'Is it broken again?'

The voice was soft and feminine, and he lifted his head and stared vaguely at the woman.

'Um—no. Sorry. Did you want the machine?'

'No, it's OK.' She tilted her head on one side, looking at him keenly. 'Are you all right?'

He opened his mouth to say yes, and then stopped. The woman was slender and delicate, but curvy in all the right places. She was probably younger than Lucy, her dark hair twisted up into a clip, and there was compassion and understanding in her emerald-green eyes.

'A friend's little boy's just been admitted,' he said, gagging on the half-truth. 'They had a car accident. His pelvis is fractured. I was getting us something to eat, but...'

She frowned. 'I'm so sorry. Has he been to Theatre?'

'Yes—yes, he's had an op to plate it, and he's OK, he's in Recovery at the moment and then he's going to PICU, but he shares my blood group, and it's B-negative, and stocks were very low, so they took two units from me, and...'

'And you haven't eaten or drunk anything because you've been too stressed, and the café's shut, and now the bottle's got its own back on you.'

He smiled. 'Something like that.' He held out his hand, then looked at it ruefully and smiled again as he withdrew it. 'Sorry—it's a bit sticky. I'm Nick Tremayne.'

She flashed him an answering smile. 'Jack's father—of

course. You look just like him. I'm Megan Phillips. I'm a paediatrician, so I'll be looking after your friend's son. What's his name?'

'Jeremiah Althorp. Jem.'

'I'll keep an eye out for him.'

'Thanks.' He tried to unscrew the drink again, but his fingers were shaking so much now he fumbled the lid and it fell to the floor. She picked it up and handed it back to him.

'Come on, you need to sit down. Let me go and get you something to eat.'

'No, I couldn't.'

'Well, I'd rather you did, otherwise I'll have to pick you off the floor on the way to the canteen. I'm going to buy myself some sandwiches. Why don't I get you some? I can bring them up to you, I'm going that way.'

'I couldn't ask you to do that.'

'You didn't ask, I offered.' Her smile was gentle. 'Chicken salad? Ham and cheese? Tuna? There isn't a fabulous choice, I'm afraid.'

'Anything. One without cheese for Kate, and I don't care what I have, whatever's going. And two teas, if you've got enough hands. You're a star. Here, take some money.' He pulled a twenty-pound note out of his wallet and handed it to her.

She took the note out of his hands and smiled. 'I'll come up in a minute. Drink some of that before you go back up there, and I'll come and find you.'

He took her advice, downing half the cloyingly sweet drink, and after a moment he began to feel better. Less shaky and light-headed. He made his way slowly back upstairs, and when he pressed the buzzer a young woman let him back in, waving goodbye to Kate as she left the room.

'Oh—were they shut?' Kate asked, eyeing his all but empty hands in surprise.

'Yes. I was going to the main canteen, but I met someone. A paediatrician, of all things. She's gone to get something for us. She said she was heading that way anyway, so I gave her a twenty-pound note. At least I hope she was a paediatrician.'

Kate chuckled softly. 'Nick, you're so cynical.'

He gave a weary smile and offered her the bottle.

'Do you want some of this? I saved you some.'

Kate eyed him thoughtfully. 'No, I loathe it, thanks, you have it. What was her name?'

'Megan Phillips. Who was that, by the way, who let me in?'

'Jess Carmichael. She's a counsellor. She heard I was here and she's been working late so she popped in. I saw her for a while after my lumpectomy. She was lovely. Really kind to me. She gave me a lot of support when I needed it the most.'

He felt a little stab of pain to accompany the familiar guilt. 'I'm glad.'

Kate met his eyes, her own holding that particular brand of gentle reproach that she reserved for him. 'I could have done with your support then, too, Nick.'

He looked away, swamped with regret, but what could he have done? 'You had Rob,' he reminded her.

'That didn't exclude you.'

Oh, it did. 'I didn't want to get in the way,' he said. 'He seemed genuinely decent, very fond of you—I thought you might stand a chance of happiness, a future for you and Jeremiah with a man you loved. A man who could love you back. I didn't want to get in the way of that.'

'You wouldn't have done,' she reasoned, remembering how it had felt when he'd kept his distance—Nick, the only man she'd ever really loved, keeping her at arm's length when all she'd really wanted was for him to hold her and tell her it would be all right. Tell her that if it wouldn't, he'd be there for their son. 'You wouldn't have been in the way,' she told him, realising, even as she said it, that of course he would have been.

'You know that's not true,' he said gently, and she shook her head.

'Nick, I needed you—even if you weren't with me, I needed to know that you cared, but you never said a thing.' She laughed, but it came out slightly bitterly with the re-membered hurt. 'I thought you'd brought me flowers, but they were from everyone at the practice, you were just the messenger.'

He gave her a wintry smile. 'Would you have accepted them if they'd been from me?'

And then she knew—realised, with sudden insight, that they had been from him—been his idea, his choice, probably even paid for himself. And him bringing them had been the nearest he could get to telling her that he was thinking of her, worrying about her.

That he cared.

He hadn't let her down, he'd just given her space, stepped back out of Rob's way. And she'd misunderstood.

Her eyes filled, and she nodded, just once. 'Yes,' she said. 'Yes, I would have accepted them. Thank you.'

'Don't thank me,' he said gruffly. 'I did nothing—just as I always do nothing. If I'd acknowledged Jeremiah sooner, if I'd done what I should have done, then I would have been supporting you financially, making sure you had a safer car, a car with side impact protection instead of a little tin box that crushed like an eggshell—'

'No!' she said, reaching for his hand, clutching hold of it so he couldn't avoid her, her voice no more than an urgent whisper in the quiet room. 'I won't let you do that! This is not your fault. This is my fault, my guilt, and I'm damned if I'll let you have it and add it to the endless layers that you hide behind! I had the crash, I bought the car—'

'Because of me,' he returned stubbornly. 'Because I didn't accept that he was my son. Because I was letting you down again, hiding from the truth, hoping it would go away, but it won't, will it? But you are, and you're taking my son with you.'

And he didn't want her to, he realised. He really, really didn't want her to.

He turned his back on her, and saw Megan Phillips at the door, beckoning to him. 'Looks like our food's here,' he said curtly, and went out.

Kate followed him, and the woman smiled at her.

'You must be Nick's friend. I'm Megan Phillips, one of the paediatric registrars,' she said. 'I'll be looking after Jem when he's in PICU and on the ward later. How's he doing?'

'He's all right. He's going to be all right. Mr Bradley said it's just routine now,' she said, trying to inject some conviction into her voice, and as she did so she realised that for the first time she believed that he might be all right, that he might turn the corner, might actually make it, and the relief nearly took her legs out from under her.

Megan handed over the food she'd brought up for them, gave Nick his change and then left them to it. Nick opened Kate's sandwich and handed it to her, pushing her into a chair.

'Eat that before you collapse,' he ordered gruffly, ripping open another packet and demolishing the contents, then he drained his tea and dropped his head back, rolling it towards her with a sigh. 'You're not eating, Kate. Come on. You need to keep your strength up.'

'I can't eat.'

'Come on, you promised.'

She nodded. She had, and he wouldn't give up until she'd eaten the darned sandwich, she knew that, so she took a bite, and he stopped watching her like a hawk and glanced at his watch.

'I need to make a call.'

'A call?' she asked, realising she hadn't told her mother yet. Or Chloe, or Rob. She ought to tell them Jem was all right—but not now. Not in the middle of the night. She'd call them tomorrow—except…

'Oh, Nick, the dog. I need to make arrangements. I hadn't even thought about it.'

'It's OK. Oliver said not to worry, they'll sort it.'

'Bless them. They're so kind.' She sighed with relief, then looked at her watch. 'Nick, it's awfully late. Who are you ringing?'

'Edward.'

His other son, currently in South America and still, presumably, unaware. 'Oh. Oh, Nick.' She reached for his hand and he squeezed hers reassuringly.

'Hey, I'm fine. I'll be back in a minute. Eat, and have some tea. It's just the right temperature.'

She nodded, and forced herself to finish the sandwich and drink some of the tea before going back into Recovery to sit by Jem's bedside.

They'd been monitoring him constantly, checking him every few minutes, and as she went back in, they told her he was ready to go through to PICU.

'We'll find you a bed if you like—are you staying?' the nurse who was moving him asked her, and she nodded.

'Yes—if I can. I'll sit in the chair beside him, though. I don't need a bed.'

'We'll see. Let's take him and get him settled, and you can decide then, but he's stable now and he'll sleep all night; if you take my advice, you'll get your head down, because he'll need you when he wakes up and being the parent of a sick child is very wearing. You'll need your rest if you're going to be any good to him.'

Sensible advice, but she wasn't happy to take it. She wanted to be beside Jem, couldn't bear to leave his side, and even if she did, she didn't think she'd sleep.

'Kate, you were in the accident, too, you need to rest,' Nick said firmly when she continued to protest to the PICU nurse after he was settled. 'I'll sit with him. Go and have an hour, at least.'

'Half an hour,' she conceded, giving in because she knew it made sense and she was at the end of her tether. And the nurse was right—if she was going to be any use to Jem, she needed some sleep. 'I could do with lying down. What about you? Are you feeling better? Less shaky since you ate?'

'I'm fine,' he said, telling her nothing, as usual.

'Did you get hold of Edward?'

He shook his head. 'Go on, go and lie down. I'll get you if there's the slightest change.'

'Promise.'

'I promise,' he said, and she didn't know why, but she believed him. Maybe because she had no choice. Or maybe because this time, at least, she knew she could trust him?

So she went, escorted to a tiny room nearby just big enough for a chair, a little bedside locker and a bed made up with crisp white hospital linen. She'd never been more pleased to see a bed in her life. Her neck was a little sore, she had a killer headache, probably from the stress, her ankle was aching where the pedal had been squashed into it and she was emotionally exhausted.

She took some of the painkillers Ben had given her, then crept under the covers with a shaky sigh. Oh, that was better. Half an hour of this and she'd be able to cope again. Rolling to her side, she closed her eyes and lay there in the quiet room, and as the tension drained out of her, the only thing that had held her together up to now, she gave a tiny sob and tears leaked silently out of the corners of her eyes and dribbled down onto the pillow as she lay there.

Jem was all right. He'd be all right. He would.

She told herself the same thing, over and over again like a mantra, and gradually she fell into a shallow, restless sleep.

CHAPTER FOUR

NICK closed the door softly and stood looking down at her.

He didn't want to wake her, but he'd promised her he would, and she'd had over three hours, not just the half hour she'd agreed to.

But she was sleeping so deeply, curled on her side with one hand tucked under her cheek, and she looked defenceless and vulnerable. He perched on the hard plastic chair by the bed and watched her sleep for a moment, then with a quiet sigh he leant forwards and stroked her hair. She didn't stir, and he let his hand fall to the pillow.

And frowned. It was wet, and in the soft glow from the bedside light he could see a damp stain under the edge of her cheek, below her eye. Salt trails had dried across her temple, and down over her nose from the other eye, and he realised she'd been crying in her sleep. He closed his eyes and took a slow, steadying breath, then touched her again.

'Kate?'

Her eyes flew open, and she started to sit up. 'What is it? What's wrong?'

'Nothing,' he said hastily, kicking himself for scaring her. 'It's all right, he's fine. He's asleep, but you asked me to wake you.'

She let her breath out on a shaky little sigh, and dropped

back against the pillows. 'Oh. Sorry. I must have dozed off—
What time is it?'

'Twenty to five.'

'Five!'

She sat up again, pushed back the covers and slid to her
feet, swaying slightly. 'Steady,' he murmured, standing up
and putting his arms around her to support her, and she rested
her head against his shoulder with a sigh.

'How's your neck?' he asked, and she gave a little
shrug.

'OK.'

He was pretty sure it wasn't. A bang hard enough to do
that to Jem must have shaken her up, and he slid his hand
carefully around the back of her neck and massaged the taut,
tired muscles under the soft waterfall of dark hair. She shifted
so her forehead was propped against his chest, just above
his heart, and if he'd bent his head a fraction he could have
dropped a kiss on her hair.

But he wouldn't. Of course he wouldn't. She wouldn't
want it, and he wouldn't embarrass her by doing anything
so stupid, but he held her head, his hand curved protectively
round it, steadying her as his fingers worked slowly, gently
on the muscles.

'Better?' he asked, and she nodded slightly, so he eased
back and let her straighten before he moved away. 'Go and
sit with him and I'll get us a coffee. Do you want anything
else?'

'Tea. Tea would be lovely, and maybe a pastry or something. Thanks, Nick.'

'Any time,' he said, and backed away, leaving her to
straighten her clothes and freshen up while he made the round
trip to the canteen. He could do with stretching his legs, and
a change of scene wouldn't hurt after hours of staring at his
son's bruised and swollen face and wondering how the hell
to tell him he was his father.

More to the point, wondering what Jeremiah would make of the news. He suspected not a lot. All in all, it was probably shaping up to be another thoroughly bloody day...

She sent Nick to lie down when he got back with the hot drinks and pastries, and he nodded and went without a word. He looked exhausted, she thought. Drained and stressed and emotionally threadbare.

She'd never seen him like this, even when he'd lost Annabel. He desperately needed a shave, and for a man who usually dressed so fastidiously, he was falling apart. His shirt was creased and open at the neck, the tie long gone, and his usually immaculate suit was crumpled and weary.

And despite it all, he was still the best-looking man she'd ever seen, the only man she'd ever really wanted. Apart from necessity he hadn't left her side since he'd arrived in Resus, and she didn't know how she would have got through it without him.

Although, of course, even though the biggest hurdle had been overcome in that Jeremiah was still alive, there was still the next obstacle to deal with, the one they'd been avoiding now for years, and she had no idea how Nick would be when the time came. One thing she knew for sure, he couldn't bottle out now, and maybe it wasn't the right time to go away. Her letter to the PCT was still in her bag, waiting for her to post it after she'd picked Jem up, only of course that had never happened, and now...

Oh, what on earth should she do? It had been complicated enough before this, but now...

She sipped her tea, hands cradling the paper cup, fingers tracing the ribbed cardboard holder round it, chafing it rhythmically as she sat with glazed eyes fixed on her sleeping son, watching the slow rise and fall of his chest, the occasional flutter of his eyelids, the trace of his heartbeat on the monitor, and prayed that when the time came, he could forgive them both for what they'd done to him.

They woke Jem at six, when they came to check his obs, and he smiled at her a little wanly. She'd never been so pleased to see his smile in her life.

'Mum,' he croaked, and she felt her eyes well with tears.

'Hello, darling. Good morning.' She leant forwards and took his free hand, the one that wasn't wired up to the drip, and kissed his bruised cheek gently. She'd studied his notes, and he'd had several units of blood overnight. She wondered if any of them had been Nick's, if his father's blood was now circulating in his veins. Or Jack's.

Like blood brothers cutting themselves and swapping blood, but on a grander scale and one-way. Would it bring them all closer? She hoped so. Apart from her mother in Bristol, and James's brother, the man Jem called Uncle John, there was no other family. It would be nice for him to have the family he should have had all along, but she wasn't going to make assumptions. Maybe they wouldn't want that level of involvement. She couldn't blame them. And there was still that hurdle to overcome, of course.

She stroked her thumb lightly over the back of his hand, and his fingers tightened a little. 'What time is it?'

'Six in the morning.'

'Oh.' He thought about that for a moment, then gave a tiny sigh. 'Can I have a drink? My throat's sore and my mouth's really dry.'

She glanced up. He was still nil by mouth, but she could give him a mouthwash. She spoke to the nurse, and a minute later she was swabbing his lips with the cool liquid, wiping away the dried secretions so he'd be more comfortable. 'Better?' she asked, and he smiled and nodded.

'Mmm. I'm sore all over, Mum.'

Her heart contracted. 'I bet you are, my love. You've

been through the wringer. Do you remember what happened yesterday?' she asked him softly.

He shook his head. 'No. The last thing I remember was making you a pot.' He frowned. 'Did I tell you I'd made you a pot?'

She nodded, thinking it might have been the last thing he'd done, the last thing he'd said to her, and she struggled not to cry. 'Yes, you did. A yellow one. I'm looking forward to seeing it. Do you remember me picking you up? Or the helicopter?'

He shook his head. 'Helicopter? No. I don't remember anything after making the pot. Did I go in a helicopter?'

'Yes. The air ambulance brought you here.'

'And I don't remember,' he mumbled, looking disgusted. 'I've always wanted to go in a helicopter. So what happened to me? Why am I so sore? Did we have a car accident?'

'Yes. I pulled out, and—'

She broke off, just as Nick appeared on the other side of the bed. 'Someone was going too fast,' he said firmly, 'and ran into the side of the car. It was his fault.'

'Oh,' he said, but she could see he was flagging. 'I can't believe I don't remember the helicopter,' he mumbled drowsily, and then looked at Nick and his brows clumped together in a little frown. 'Uncle Nick, why haven't you shaved today?'

She heard the quiet rasp as he scrubbed his hand over his jaw. Emotions chased across his face, and he pressed his lips together briefly. 'I haven't had a chance, I've been here all night,' he said. 'We both have.'

'Really? Why?'

Because you were sick. Because we thought you were going to die—

Kate met his eyes, and Nick reached out and brushed his knuckles over his son's thin, pale cheek and tried to smile. 'We were worried about you. You've been pretty sick. You had to have an operation.'

'Why did I need an operation? I don't really understand. I'm just really sore all over and I can't move, it hurts too much.'

Her fingers tightened involuntarily. 'I know. The surgeon will come and see you later—he'll explain. You had some broken bones, and they had to fix the ends together, to keep them still so they can heal and stop them hurting.'

He frowned. 'I can remember it hurting,' he said slowly. 'Much worse than this. And Ben—was Ben there?'

'Ben was there,' Nick confirmed. 'Don't worry about it, it's all over now and you're on the mend. You just need to rest and get well again, and then you'll be able to go home.'

'When?'

Kate swallowed. 'Not for a little while.'

His face fell. 'I'm going to miss the rest of holiday club, aren't I?' he said, looking worried, and she nodded.

'I'm afraid so. You could be in here for a few weeks.'

'Oh. Can Matt get my pot for you? Will you ask him?'

'You can ask him yourself. I'm sure he'll come and visit you soon.'

She saw Nick stiffen, but she couldn't pander to his feelings. Rob and his son Matt were an important part of Jem's life, and although she wasn't going to marry Rob, she wasn't going to avoid him, either, or his son. For Jem's sake, he needed to keep some continuity in his life.

Nick would just have to get over it.

Martin Bradley came to see Jem just before eight, and decided he could be moved into a side room on the paediatric ward just down the corridor as soon as it was cleared.

'You're doing really well, we're very pleased, so you can have a nice room to yourself for a few days so you can rest quietly until you're feeling a bit brighter, then we'll move you down into the other ward with kids of your own age, to give you some company. I'm going to increase your pain relief, because you're obviously quite sore, and once you're a bit more comfortable you'll feel a lot better.'

'Thanks,' Jem murmured, and his eyes flicked past Kate to the door, and he grinned weakly. 'Hey, Ben,' he said, and Ben came into the room and perched on the end of the bed.

'Hi, tiger. So, how is he, Martin? Will he live?'

'Oh, I reckon. Nice work, that pelvic fixator, made my job a lot easier. Did you do it?'

'No, that was Josh O'Hara. He's going to be a real asset. I had a look at the X-rays—it's looking good.'

'Mmm. It went back nicely. I'm pleased. Well, I'll leave you all to it. I'll catch up with you later, Jem.'

'So, how's it feeling, young'un?' Ben asked, and the boy shrugged.

'Sore.'

'Yeah, I'll bet. Still, you'll soon be up and about. Look on the bright side, you won't have to go to school for a few weeks.'

Kate frowned. Of course he wouldn't. And that meant she wouldn't be able to go to work, because there was no way she was leaving him with anyone else until he was better.

'Kate, don't worry, they'll get cover,' Nick said softly, reading her mind. 'I'm going to have to go in and sort it all out shortly, but you're not to worry, it'll be fine.'

She nodded. Of course it would be, but there were so many patients she wanted to be there for—Gemma was a few days overdue now and she didn't want to hand her over at this stage; she was one of their own, a practice nurse who was married to one of their GPs, Sam Cavendish, and Kate hated the fact that she'd have to bail on them at this stage. And there was a woman she'd seen—heavens, only yesterday—who she'd been a bit worried about. She couldn't even remember her name, but Chloe would sort it for her. As the only other midwife based in the practice, she'd have to.

'Nick, I need to speak to Chloe. There's a patient—'

'I'll get her to come and see you. She'll want to, anyway. They all will.'

Of course they would. They were a fabulous bunch of people, and she didn't know how she would have got through the last year without their support. She nodded, and turned back to Ben, who was making Jem laugh weakly with a dreadful joke. She smiled at him, and he winked and stood up.

'I need to get back to work, but I just thought I'd come and touch base. And Lucy'll be in later. She's going to leave the kids with me at lunchtime and slip up for a minute. You might want to shave by then.'

His teasing eyes met Nick's, and Kate thought she could read reassurance and support in them. Had Lucy come round? Maybe Ben had been able to listen to her and let her talk it all through last night, and maybe she'd softened her stance a little. Goodness, she hoped so. She didn't care if Lucy never forgave her for her part in it, but that she shouldn't forgive Nick—that was unthinkable.

She was his little girl, the apple of his eye, and he adored her. He'd be gutted if there was a permanent rift between them.

And then, when Ben had hardly left the room, Jack came in and grinned at Jem and perched on the end of the bed where Ben had sat.

'Hi there, kiddo. How're you doing?'

'OK. Bit sore.'

'I'll bet.' Jack glanced up at his father, and winced at the state of him. 'Dad, you look like a tramp. I think you need a shower and a shave. I've got a clean shirt here—do you want it?'

'No, it's OK, I'm going to go shortly and sort some stuff out at the surgery, so I'll have a shower then. Thanks, anyway.'

'Don't thank me, I just didn't want you scaring the children,' he said, but this time his voice was kinder, less condemnatory than the last time he'd told his father not to thank him, over the blood donating issue, and Nick gave a wry smile.

After a few moments of banter, Jack, too, left them alone, and it wasn't long before the nurses came to move Jem through to the paediatric ward.

'All ready to go?' the staff nurse asked cheerfully, and he nodded as they kicked the brakes off the bed and wheeled it through the door, down a corridor and then into a bright, sunny room off the children's ward that looked out over the gardens below.

'There are ducks down there,' Kate told him, peering out of the window and trying to find something normal to talk about as they sorted out his oxygen and monitoring equipment and pushed his locker back into place. 'A mother duck and some ducklings. You'll be able to see them when you can move around a bit more.'

'How many ducklings?' he asked, but she couldn't really tell.

'At least five. Not sure. We'll count them together later. They can't go anywhere, they're in a courtyard.'

'What, trapped?'

'Until they can fly. I expect someone's looking after them, but they'll be safe from any cats and foxes, at least.'

'Mmm.'

His eyelids were wilting, and it was obvious he was still very far from well. The move from PICU to the little side room had been more than enough for him, and Nick glanced at his watch. Ten-fifteen, give or take.

'I need to go to the surgery, sort a few things out, and if you're staying, you could do with some clothes and wash things, and some stuff for Jeremiah. Give me your keys, I'll sort it.'

She stared at him blankly. 'I haven't got my keys,' she said slowly. 'They must be in the car still.'

'Has anyone else got a key?'

She nodded. 'Yes. Chloe. Take her with you, she'll know what to get. And tell her I'm sorry about Bruno. If she can't manage, then I'll have to—'

'I'm sure they can manage the dog between them,' he said reassuringly. 'They said you weren't to worry. I'll be as quick as possible, ring me if you need to or if you think of anything specific you need.'

'Thanks.'

He found his car in the staff car park, and drove straight to the surgery, even though he was desperate for a shower and a change of clothes. There was a tie in his jacket pocket, and for a moment he contemplated it, but he was in a hurry now. He probably should have gone home, but for some reason he just needed to be here, amongst his friends, and it was nearly eleven, so with any luck the patients would have gone by now so they didn't have to see him looking like this. He walked in, straight up the stairs past a couple of waiting patients and the startled receptionist, ignoring their concerned questions, and into the staffroom.

It was crowded, and they all turned and stared at him, Sam Cavendish getting to his feet and breaking the silence first.

'Nick! How is he?'

'He's…' He couldn't finish, couldn't find the words, and Chloe gasped and covered her mouth with her hand. 'No! He can't be—'

He shook his head. 'No. He's all right,' he said hastily, and there was a collective sigh of relief. 'He's stable now and out of Intensive Care. It's been…um…'

He didn't know what to say, but they were clustered around him, gathered there as if they'd been waiting, and he lifted his head and met their eyes, seeing the love and concern and support there for him, for Kate, and for Jeremiah. And there was only one thing that mattered, one thing he needed to tell them, these people who were his friends, first and foremost, although they might well not be when they knew.

'It's been a bit of a worry, but it looks like he's going to be all right,' he said, and then he added, 'Actually, we're both going to need some help in the next few weeks with cover. There's something you should know, something I'd rather didn't leave this room. Jeremiah's my son.'

If he'd expected a shocked reaction, he didn't get one.

There was no condemnation, no gasps of horror, just acceptance and support.

It turned out that most of them had worked it out—some, like old Doris Trefussis, cleaner, tea-lady and general all-round good egg, years ago. Sam Cavendish knew, certainly, and when everyone had dispersed and left them alone, Sam put a mug of coffee in his hand and sat down at right angles to him, his bad leg stretched out and propped on the other ankle, a mug cradled in his hands and his eyes thoughtful.

'You can do it, you know,' he said, surprising Nick.

He frowned. 'Do what?'

'Be a good father to him. You were more of a father to me in my teens than my own father had ever been, and I know you've been good to my brother in the ten years I was away. And you love the boy. That means more than anything else.'

Nick gave a soft huff of laughter, and smiled tiredly at Sam. He'd been fond of him since he'd been a boy, and he'd been more than happy to take him on at the surgery when he'd come home wounded after a run-in with insurgents in Africa. And he was glad he had, because Sam had ended up back with Gemma, one of their nurses and his childhood sweetheart, and their baby was due any day. 'When did you get to be so wise, Sam?' he asked softly, but Sam just smiled back and ignored his remark.

'We need to sort the rota out, because Gemma can't go on

much longer. She's been having contractions off and on for days and every morning I wake up and think, How can she still be pregnant? So it won't be long, and we'll need another locum if you aren't going to be here.'

'Why not? I can still work most of the time.'

'No—because you'll be at your son's bedside,' he offered gently. 'Does he even know yet?'

Nick felt emotion well in his chest and cleared his throat. 'No. We're going to tell him when he's a bit stronger. To be honest, I'm dreading it and I'm happy to put it off as long as possible.'

'Don't leave it too long,' Sam advised, as if he hadn't already done that very thing, then he tilted his head on one side and raised a brow. 'You look like hell, by the way,' he said conversationally, and Nick growled softly under his breath.

'If one more person tells me that today I'm going to—'

'What? Go home and shower? Good idea, Nick. You could do with a seriously close shave, a shirt that's seen an iron in living memory and trousers that haven't got more wrinkles than an elephant's hide.'

He looked down at himself and remembered what he'd looked like less than twenty-four hours ago. How could that be? It seemed a lifetime ago. Nearly had been…

'We'll sort out the rota,' Sam was saying. 'I'm booking myself off now for a fortnight, because Gemma was looking iffy this morning, and I'll make sure they book you off, too, and we'd better have open-ended cover for Kate. I think Chloe might already have organised that, but I'll check. Kate's dog is being looked after, so all you need to worry about is your family. Go on, go and sort yourself out and get back to them. Have you had any sleep at all?'

'I had an hour this morning.'

'You might want to get your head down as well, then.'

He shook his head. 'No time. I can't leave Kate without back-up. Oh, and I'll need Chloe to find some stuff for them both. She's got a key to Kate's place. Kate's house keys were on her car keys, and they got left in it. I expect the police have taken them. I need to follow that up.'

He got to his feet with a sigh, put his mug on the draining board and paused at the door. 'Sam—thanks.'

'What for? I owe you more than I can ever repay, Nick. You go and look after your son, and leave the practice to us. We can manage.'

He laughed. 'Easy for you to say, you're booking yourself out on paternity leave as of now!'

'The others can cope. They love a challenge. Go on, shove off.'

He shoved. Half an hour later, after a rapid shower and a desperately-needed shave, dressed in clean trousers and an open-necked casual shirt and feeling a little more human, he headed back to the hospital, armed with Chloe's love for Kate and Jeremiah, the spare key to her cottage and a bag of toiletries and clothes for each of them, which Chloe had kindly picked up while he had been sorting himself out.

He got back at a little after one-thirty, and found Kate sitting by Jem's bed, her face exhausted.

'How is he?' he asked, putting the bags down by the chair, and she shrugged.

'The same, really. He's in a lot of pain—they've just given him more painkillers, and he's gone to sleep at last. Jess came and sat with me for a while, she's very kind. Oh, and Lucy popped in a little while ago—she's going to come back later when you're here. She sends her love. And Jack's been up again.'

He nodded, his eyes welling up. Lucy had sent her love. And Jack had been back, too, giving up his time to a brother he hadn't known he had. It didn't surprise him. His twins were both kind and generous to a fault, and he was immensely proud of them.

'Have you had lunch?'

She shook her head. 'I didn't like to leave him. Have you?'

'No—but he's asleep now, so why don't we pop down to the café and grab something while the going's good?'

She nodded, and got stiffly to her feet, easing out the kinks and giving him a wry smile. They told the nurses where they were going, then she fell into step beside him as they headed for the café.

'Oh, it's nice to move. I've been so afraid to make a noise in case I disturbed him.'

He smiled ruefully. 'I'm sorry I was so long, but I had to sort out the fallout at the surgery, and I got sick of everyone telling me I needed a shower. So, do I look better?'

She smiled up at him. 'Just a bit.' Actually, she'd quite liked him with the roguish stubbled look, but it was better to have him back with her—much better. She'd missed him. He'd been gone what felt like ages, and it had been a bit of an emotional roller coaster watching Jem in pain. It was good to step off the ride for a moment now he was comfortably asleep.

Nick looked up at the menu, then glanced at her. 'What are you having?'

'Oh, I don't know. Vegetables! All I've had in the last twenty-four hours is sandwiches. I'm sick of bread.'

'They've got salads.'

'Perfect.'

'I'll get you one. Go and sit down over there by the window and relax,' he ordered, so she went, and a few moments later he set a laden tray down in front of her.

She tried to summon up some enthusiasm. 'That looks nice,' she lied. 'What do I owe you?'

'Owe me?'

'For my lunch.'

He scowled at her. 'Don't be ridiculous. I got you a fruit

smoothie as well as the salad because I know you like them and I thought you were probably sick of tea and coffee, too.'

'I am.' She gave him a tired little smile, all she could manage. 'Thank you, Nick.'

He scowled again. 'Don't keep thanking me. I've made a complete fist of everything I've ever done for you. It's high time I started balancing the books.'

If only. She gave a quiet sigh and picked up her knife and fork, wondering how long she was going to be based at the hospital and when she'd be able to go home and lie down in her own bed, just for an hour or two. She was so tired, so very, very tired...

'Kate?'

She pushed her plate away. 'I'm sorry. I'm not really hungry.'

'You're exhausted. You should be in bed.'

'I can't, Nick. I have to be here for him. Tomorrow. I'll go home tomorrow—maybe in the morning, once we've seen Martin Bradley and we know if he's happy with him. I could go home then and have a rest.'

'OK. But if you're doing that, you're eating your salad now. Come on, you can do it.'

And so, with him coaxing and cajoling her, she finished most of it, drank the smoothie and then realised she was feeling more human. 'You're so sickeningly right always, aren't you?' she said with a smile, and a fleeting frown crossed his face.

'Now I know you need sleep,' he said gruffly, and stabbed his fork into the last slice of tomato on his plate and put it in his mouth.

She laughed at him. 'That's better,' she said softly. 'You sound more like the old Nick.'

He pushed his plate away and thought about it, realising

she was right. 'I feel better. It's amazing what a shower and a square meal can do. I've brought you some things, by the way. Chloe sorted them out—she sends her love. Well, everyone at the practice sends their love,' he amended with a smile that felt distinctly crooked. 'I told them he's my son,' he added, his voice low. 'I hope you don't mind. I asked them to keep it quiet.'

'How did they take it?'

He shrugged. 'It was odd. They didn't seem at all surprised. In fact, they were incredibly supportive. Chloe had arranged cover for you for the rest of this week already, but I've told her I'm writing you off sick for four weeks—'

'Four? Why?'

He smiled again, this time a little wryly. 'Because you've got whiplash,' he reminded her.

'No, I haven't.'

'I'm sure you have. You're having four weeks to get over it, whatever,' he told her, and, actually, she found she didn't mind his high-handed approach this time, because she needed the time to devote to Jem, and it wasn't entirely false. Her neck was a little sore.

She rolled it, wincing slightly, and he found himself aching to ease it for her, to massage it gently until it relaxed so she could get some relief. 'Sam's signing off on paternity leave—and, no, Gemma's not in labour, as far as I know, but he wasn't quite sure if she was on the verge this morning so he's booked a locum anyway.'

'She's a week overdue,' Kate said, biting her lip. 'I should be there for her.'

'Don't worry. Chloe's there, she'll look after her. And Sam is a doctor. They should be able to cope without you. And Sam's getting a locum to cover me for the next week at least, unless they really can't manage without me. I want to be here for you both,' he added, when she started to protest.

She said nothing for a moment, then sighed softly. 'Thank

you. I don't know how I would have coped without you yesterday and last night.'

'I would have been here anyway, Kate,' he told her quietly. 'Even if he wasn't my son, I would have been here for you.'

She nodded. 'Yes, I know you would. That's the funny thing about you, you're so generous, so kind, so helpful, but if anybody dares to realise it, you get so uncomfortable—look, you're doing it now.'

She shook her head slowly, carefully folding her paper napkin for something to do with her hands, because it would have been so easy to reach out to him, to take the hand lying on the table, fiddling with the little sugar packets.

'We ought to tell Jem, I suppose,' he murmured. 'Nobody in the hospital apart from Jack and Ben knows, so it shouldn't leak out, which means we can tell him when the time's right.'

He carried on fiddling, piling up the sugar packets and pushing them into straight lines with his fingertip. 'I'd just like to do it when I've had a chance to build a relationship with him—made friends with him, got to know him a bit better. You're right, I haven't ever really talked to him, or spent meaningful time with him, and it's time I did. Time I gave him a chance to get to know me, too. And it'll give you a bit of a break as well, if we're sharing the visiting. It's going to be a long haul.'

She nodded. 'Yes. Yes, I know. It should be better once he's on the mend, though. They have lessons and activities and he'll be doing physio, and there will be other kids for him to talk to. And his friends'll be able to visit in a few days' time, so that'll take the heat off us, too.'

And who knew? They might even find some time to be together themselves. That was a novel thought, but probably not one that would lead to anything. She'd do well to keep reminding herself of that fact, because it would be all too easy to fall into the habit of relying on him only to find he wasn't there when it came to the crunch.

She was sure he meant well, and maybe this time he really thought he could do it, but she wasn't holding her breath.

CHAPTER FIVE

MEGAN PHILLIPS, the pretty young paediatric registrar who'd been on call overnight, was waiting for them at the nursing station.

'We've got his blood results,' she began, and Nick felt his heart stall.

Don't let him have a problem. Not thrombocytopenia, he thought. Please don't let it be that, don't let him have DIC.

'He's OK now, but the biochemistry was a bit skewed. We needed to tweak some of the components, but it probably explains why he was feeling a bit rough. We've started an infusion and he should be fine now. We'll check it again in a while, OK?'

Relief hit him like a wall, and he smiled and thanked her, wishing, as a doctor, he didn't know so much. Ignorance would be bliss, he thought as he ushered Kate back into the side room where Jem was still sleeping. She stopped in the doorway and put her hand over her mouth for a second, sucking in air, and he squeezed her shoulder.

'He's all right,' he murmured.

'I know, but he looks so vulnerable, so fragile lying there like that,' she murmured.

'He'll be fine. You heard Megan,' he said firmly, and watched as she perched on the edge of the armchair by the bed.

It was upholstered in a hideous pink—wipe-clean vinyl, of course—and he found himself wondering how many parents had sat on it and watched their children.

He sat on the arm, laid his hand on Kate's shoulder and watched his son sleeping...

Megan reached out her hand to pick up the phone, and it fell back to her lap, nerveless with shock.

No!

It couldn't be him! She'd heard there was an O'Hara starting in A and E, but it had never occurred to her it was him, that he'd be here in Cornwall, of all places! She'd thought she'd be safe here, never have to see him again, never have to be reminded...

Her heart raced, and she shrank back into the chair, trying to get away, retreating from the sight of him. She must be mistaken, she told herself. It wasn't Josh. It couldn't be.

But it was him—tall, lean, more attractive even than he'd been eight years ago. He was the most good-looking man she'd ever seen, so sure of himself, so at home in his own skin that he exuded an almost tangible aura of confident masculinity. Alpha man. A man that women couldn't resist. A man who only had to crook his little finger and stupid, senseless little girls would abandon all their brains and follow him to the end of the earth.

He glanced over and caught sight of her, his body arresting momentarily, then excusing himself he walked towards her, resting a hand on the top of the counter and looking down at her with those extraordinary indigo-blue eyes, and she couldn't look away, for all she wanted to.

'Megan?'

His voice was shocked, his eyes dark with a host of emotions she couldn't even guess at, but it wasn't his emotions she was worried about, it was her own, tumbling in free-fall as she stared back at him, mesmerised, horrified, memory after memory crashing through her and robbing her of speech.

She unglued her tongue from the roof of her mouth and tried to remain professional.

'Hello, Josh.'

Just the two words. It was all she could manage, all she could force out through lips that were stiff with shock.

His hair fell over his forehead, and he threaded his fingers through the glossy black strands and raked it out of the way, making her suck in her breath. She could still remember the soft, silky feel of it between her fingers. 'I didn't know you worked here,' he said, that soft Irish brogue rippling over her nerve-endings like little tongues of flame. 'How are you?'

He looked vaguely stunned, his eyes wary now, concerned. As well they might be after what he'd done...

'I'm—I'm fine. Busy. Excuse me, I need to make a call.'

'That's OK, you can do it in a moment. I'm looking for a patient who's had surgery for a fractured pelvis—Jem Althorp? I put on the ex-fix in A and E.'

'He's fine. There's a minor problem with his bloods, that's all. He's in that room there. Now, I need to deal with this, Josh, and I don't need to deal with you. Excuse me.'

And picking the phone up again with shaking hands, she rang the haematology department, conscious all the while of Josh standing there, until with a quiet sigh he turned on his heel and walked away.

She nearly wept with relief.

The rest of the day dragged for Kate and Nick.

Josh O'Hara had popped in briefly, but he'd seemed distracted and hadn't stayed long. Just long enough for them to thank him for the procedure that might well have saved their son's life.

Jem's blood was quickly sorted, as Megan had promised, and he was feeling better, but by the evening Kate was at the end of her tether, and Nick sent her off to bed at nine, when Jem had drifted off to sleep again.

'I'll sit up with him.'

'But you haven't had any sleep either,' she protested. 'I've had more than you.'

'I haven't been in a car accident,' he said firmly. 'Go on. I'll get you if there's the slightest thing to worry about, but there won't be.'

'But how will you know?' she asked, fretting. 'You don't know him—you don't know how he sleeps, and what's normal—'

'Kate, he's just a child, like any other,' he said gently. 'If he's sick, I'll know. He'll be fine. Go to bed before you drop to pieces.'

So she went, reluctantly, and he settled down in the hateful pink chair and watched the monitor blinking steadily, watched the nice, even trace of Jem's heartbeat through the night, while the staff came in and did hourly obs and brought him endless cups of tea.

And then at three Kate came and took over, sending Nick off to grab some sleep, and he went into the little room where she'd been sleeping and lay down on the still-warm bed, her scent all around him and the residual heat of her body seeping into him like a soothing balm, sending him into a deep, restful sleep.

Jem woke shortly before six, and Kate could see at once that he was stronger.

'Morning, soldier,' she murmured, and, leaning forwards, she stroked his hair back off his forehead and smiled at him. 'How are you?'

'I feel better,' he said. 'I don't hurt so much, and I don't feel so sick. I'm hungry, though.'

He'd graduated from nil by mouth to sips of water, and so Kate poured a little into the beaker and held it to his lips.

'Maybe they'll let you eat something light later on. I've got some wash things for you. You'll feel better after we clean your teeth and wash your face with nice hot water,' she said soothingly. 'Grandma sends her love, and so does Chloe and everyone at the practice.'

'Where's Uncle Nick?' he asked.

She stroked his hair. 'He's here. He spent the night next to you in this chair, and then I got up and swapped over. I expect he's still sleeping. Why?'

He shrugged his skinny shoulders. 'Just wondered. I thought he might have gone home.'

She shook her head. 'No. He wouldn't leave you,' she told him, and she watched something terrifyingly like hero-worship dawn in his eyes.

But all he said was, 'Oh,' and then his eyes drifted shut again and he lay quietly for a while.

Behind her the door opened and closed, and she knew it was Nick without turning round.

'How is he?'

'Awake. Better. He was asking where you were.'

'I'm right here, son,' he said softly, the irony of it catching her in mid-chest as he perched on the foot of the bed and laid his hand lightly on Jem's ankle 'How are you?'

Jem opened his eyes. 'OK.'

'Good.'

Kate saw Nick's shoulders drop a fraction, and knew he'd been worried. 'He's hungry.'

'That's a good sign,' he said, and his shoulders dropped a little further.

'My bruises hurt,' Jem mumbled from the bed. 'My leg's really sore, and my side hurts, and my elbow's sore, but it's not like it was yesterday.'

'It'll feel better soon.'

There was a tap on the door, and a nurse popped her head round. 'We were going to give Jem a bit of a wash, if you two want to get some breakfast,' she said, and so they went down to the café that was fast becoming their second home, and had bacon rolls and pastries and lashings of coffee.

'One day I'll get home and start eating proper food,' she said, pushing the last crumbs around the plate. 'I never have anything like this for breakfast. I have yogurt and fruit.'

'You could have had yogurt and fruit,' Nick said with a frown, but she just smiled.

'I know, but I wanted a bacon roll, and I couldn't resist the pastries.'

He laughed, and, reaching out his hand, he covered hers and enfolded it in his warm, gentle grasp. 'Crazy woman,' he said, his thumb stroking slow circles over the back of her hand, and she felt the ice inside her starting to thaw, replaced by a strange heat that warmed her from deep inside, somewhere in the region of her heart.

'You need to go home this morning,' he went on gently. 'You're exhausted, and you need a shower and just to get out of here. Once the doctors have been round and they're happy, I'm going to take you home—and don't argue.'

She smiled a little unsteadily. 'I won't. It sounds wonderful. I could really do with a change of scenery, just for a little while. I ought to sort my car out, too, really. I need the keys.'

'We can phone the police, get that organised,' he said. 'I'll contact them. And you'll need another car.'

She rolled her eyes. 'I have no idea how long that'll take.'

'We'll get you one today,' he said. 'What do you want?'

She frowned at him. 'Why should you do that?'

'Because he's my son? Because you need it to transport him? I'll get you a bigger one, a stronger one.'

'No! I'll get it, and, besides, it can't be big, I have to be able to park in tight spaces.'

'So I'll get you a small stronger one.'

She sighed. 'Nick, that other driver must have been going at well over forty. Nothing's that strong. And I need it to do my job as well. Maybe I'll have to get a contract one through the PCT after all.'

'They can't do it that quickly. I can get you a car today—or at least organise it.'

She sighed again. 'Nick, it's very kind of you, but I don't really need it in a tearing hurry if I'm going to be stuck here for days.'

He shrugged. 'So you can have one in days. Just tell me what you want.'

She gave up. Sort of. 'I'll think about it,' she told him, and changed the subject.

The doctors were pleased with him. The blood setback seemed to have been resolved—routine, as Martin Bradley had said—his wound was healing well, and he was happy for them to leave the hospital—for a short while.

'Don't be too long,' Jem said, having a little wobble just as they left, and she hesitated, but Nick's hand on her arm was firm, and she promised they wouldn't be long and let him lead her out.

They went via the police station to pick up her keys and the items that had been in her car, and Nick put the bag in his boot and drove her home. It was the first time she'd been back since the accident, and it felt like for ever. She walked inside, picking up the post as she went, and then looked around.

The place was littered with Jem's things. A book on the stairs, his sports bag in the hall, a jumper dropped on the floor in the sitting room.

It caught her totally unawares, and she stared at the things numbly. What on earth would it have been like to come back to this if he'd died?

'I need a shower—put the kettle on and make yourself a drink,' she said, and hurried upstairs, needing to get away from Nick, to hide herself away in the shower where the sound of water might drown the threatening sobs that were rising in her throat.

She stripped her clothes off, the sobs starting to break free, and stepped into the shower, turning her face to the wall and slumping on it, her hands pressed over her mouth to hold in the pain that had been bottled up for days, the pain she couldn't hold inside any longer.

She could so easily have lost him. Just another couple of miles an hour…

A wrenching sob ripped through her, and she folded over, propping herself up under the pounding spray.

She was crying.

He'd heard the sound before. She'd done the same thing when James had died, and he'd brought her home from the headland and sent her to shower and warm up.

He couldn't go there again—not in the shower with her, holding her—but how could he leave her? How could he have left her then, torn apart by grief?

He went up.

She hadn't locked the bathroom door, and he opened the shower cubicle and turned off the water. She was huddled in the corner, and he reached for a towel and crouched down, draping it round her as he lifted her out, sitting down on the floor with her curled into his lap, her tears giving way slowly to fractured sobs that tore at his heart.

'He could have died,' she said at last, her voice fragmented by emotion. 'I came in and saw all his things, and I thought, What if I'd come back here, like I did when James died, and his things were everywhere—and…'

She broke off, fisting her hands in his shirt, and he held her closer, rocking her gently, hot tears scalding his eyes again as she clung to him, sobbing. 'Shh. He's all right, Kate, he's getting better now. He's going to be all right, sweetheart, he really is. You have to believe that.'

She nodded and sniffed, the sobs dying away to random hiccups. Every now and then there was another little bout, but he just held her close and let her cry, let her get it out of her system until at last she lifted her head and let go of his shirt, then swiped the tears from her face with shaking fingers.

'I'm sorry.'

'Don't be.'

'I always do this, don't I? Hide in the shower to cry.'

He shushed her again, smoothing the damp strands of hair back from her face and pressing his lips softly to her tear-stained cheek.

'All right now?'

She nodded slowly, and he eased her out of her arms, rescuing the towel as it slid down and tucking it back round her.

'I'll leave you to wash. I'll be downstairs,' he told her, and, standing up, he pulled her to her feet and kissed her cheek again. 'I'll make you a cup of tea.'

'Thanks.'

She came down a few minutes later just as the kettle boiled, dressed in clean clothes, her hair still damp and combed out over her shoulders and her smile wry.

'Sorry about that,' she said, looking a little sheepish. 'I just lost it.'

'Don't apologise, you've had a hell of a couple of days. You needed to get it off your chest. And talking of which, I'm a little underdressed. There's a bag of clean clothes in my car that I keep there for emergencies—could you do the honours while I shower? Since I'm already drenched?'

He'd taken off his sodden, crumpled shirt, but the trousers clung to his legs and her eyes scanned his body. Comparing him to Rob? He wouldn't come off well. He took care of himself, but Rob was a fitness fanatic and a PE teacher. And an ex, he reminded himself, and took small comfort from that.

'Sure,' she said, and took the keys, and he went upstairs to the bathroom. When he emerged from the shower a few moments later, the bag was there, just inside the door, with a clean, dry towel. She'd come in, and he hadn't noticed. Just as well, he decided, because when that towel had slipped he'd had a whole plethora of inappropriate thoughts and frankly he wouldn't trust himself with her at the moment.

He went back downstairs and found her sitting at the kitchen table with a cup of tea, and she ran her eyes over him again and smiled.

'It's a good job you keep spare clothes in your car,' she said, pushing a mug of tea towards him, and he gave a rueful laugh and sat down.

'Well, more or less. Trousers and shirt, at least, for predictable accidents. I don't tend to carry underwear.'

She chuckled, then sat back and eyed him thoughtfully. 'Are you telling me you're going commando, Dr T.?' she asked softly, raising an eyebrow and trying to stop her mouth from twitching, and the inappropriate thoughts leapt into his head again.

'That depends who wants to know,' he murmured, feeling the smile tug his own mouth, and the twitch got worse.

'Are you flirting with me?'

He felt his smile fade and searched her beautiful, teasing brown eyes. 'Would that be such a bad thing?' he asked softly.

The teasing look vanished, and there was a moment of breathless silence. 'I don't know—would it?'

'I'm not sure. It might be fun. It would make a change—we haven't had fun like that since our teens.' He glanced down at the mug, lined the handle up carefully exactly at right angles and then met her eyes. 'How about it?'

'How about what?' she asked carefully, and he thought she was holding her breath.

'Us.'

'I'm not sure that would be a good idea,' she said, after a seemingly endless pause. 'Maybe we'd just better concentrate on Jem for now.'

She'd hesitated, and in that time he'd held his own breath. He let it out now and gave a little shrug. 'If you want.'

'I want. Things are complicated enough.'

He nodded, and she gave a quiet sigh of relief. She didn't want to rush into anything. There was, however, another worry that was playing on her mind, a more immediate problem, and she raised it now.

'Nick, how am I going to manage when he comes out of hospital? I don't have a downstairs bathroom, or even a cloakroom, and stairs could be really difficult at first.'

'You could come to mine.'

She shook her head instantly. 'No. Not to Annabel's house,' she said softly, and watched the guilt flash across his eyes before he looked away.

'No. You're right, it wouldn't feel appropriate and, anyway, it's not exactly off the beaten track. So—perhaps we could rent somewhere? A bungalow or something, neutral ground. Just for a while, until he can manage the stairs again. I'm sure there are things out there. It's only April. It might be harder in August with the tourists, but I'm sure we could find something now and it needn't be for long. A few weeks, maybe.'

A rental property? 'It's worth a try,' she said, feeling the weight of that worry lifting from her shoulders with relief. 'I would never have thought of that.'

His smile was a little crooked. 'You see? I can have my uses, slight though they might be. I'll call the agents now.'

He made a couple of calls while she dried her hair,

and when she came down he was fizzing with suppressed excitement.

'There's a single-storey barn conversion. They've been trying to sell it, but it hasn't gone because it's quite pricy and the owners have been unrealistic, but they've now decided to let it, but only to people who don't want a long lease, which we don't.'

She nodded slowly. 'OK. Where is it?'

'On the way to Ben and Lucy's, so only about three miles out of the village. It's got a distant sea view, apparently—it's U-shaped, two-storey in the central section, with a courtyard garden and surrounded by farmland. Worth a look?'

'Definitely,' she said, then hesitated, not sure how to ask but just knowing that she had to, that this needed to be set out in black and white. 'Nick—is this just for me to stay in, or were you thinking of being there, too?'

He gave an enigmatic shrug, his eyes veiled. 'That depends.'

'On?'

'You, Jem? I don't know. If you want me there, I'd like to be there, but I don't want to confuse him or pre-empt any decision you might make in the future. I know Rob lived with you, but—'

'No,' she corrected hastily. 'Rob didn't live with us. He and Matt came to stay after I came out of hospital, but the boys shared Jem's room and Rob was on the sofa bed downstairs. We didn't share a room. It didn't feel right, when it came to it.'

He wasn't sure why, but that made him feel better. Not much. He knew they'd had an intimate relationship, because he'd gone to talk to her one night about a year ago and seen them through the window. He could still picture Rob bending his head to kiss her in the kitchen, and then the lights going off and coming on upstairs. Not that there was any reason why they shouldn't, but that had been before her surgery. Maybe that had changed things. Was that what she had meant about it not feeling right?

'I don't have any ulterior motive, Kate,' he told her. 'There are four bedrooms there. Two upstairs, each with en suite, and an en suite guest room, another bedroom or snug and a study downstairs in one of the sides. It's got a big open living space with a sitting room one end, a kitchen at the other and an open vaulted dining hall in the middle, with the stairs off it, and the third side is utility, workshop and garaging, apparently. We'd have plenty of space.'

She blinked. 'It sounds amazing.'

'That's what I thought. I've asked the agent to meet us there in twenty minutes.'

Her eyes widened. 'Wow. OK. You don't hang around, do you?'

'Is that a problem?'

'No. No, no problem, it's been worrying me to bits. It would be great if it was any good. The only thing is, how much is the rent, because I can't afford a fortune.'

'You let me worry about that.'

'Nick, I can't—'

'You can. It's not for you, it's for our son, and God knows I've done precious little for him in the last eleven years. Just let it go, Kate. Please. Don't argue.'

She opened her mouth, thought for a moment and then gave in. 'OK. But don't get in the habit of doing this.'

'What? Caring for my son? Why the hell not?'

There was a look in his eyes she hadn't seen for years, a purpose, a passion, and it was as if this whole course of events had brought him back to life.

She smiled. 'Shall we go and look?' she said, and he grinned and tossed his car keys in the air.

'After we've been via mine and I've got some underwear

on,' he said with a mischievous twinkle that gave her heart an unexpected lurch, and he ushered her out, closing the door firmly behind them.

It was fantastic. Perfect.

Built of granite, it was solid, tucked down in a fold of the land to shelter it from the prevailing south-westerly wind, and he couldn't find a single thing wrong with it.

It was to let fully furnished with every necessity and equipped to a very high standard, with king-size beds in the main bedrooms, lovely battered leather sofas in the sitting room and invitingly luxurious bathrooms with showerheads like dustbin lids.

He hadn't felt so excited about anything for years. He'd made his mind up after the most cursory walk-through and an exchanged glance with Kate, who was looking slightly stunned. It was wonderful, and he couldn't imagine why it hadn't sold instantly.

He said as much to the agent, who just shrugged. 'I don't know, either. It's been a second home and their circumstances have changed and they want to sell it, but they want a lot for it. The only thing I can assume is that it's too expensive for a holiday cottage and there aren't enough people living around here who can afford to buy it. As far as I can see, there isn't a single catch apart from the price, but the market's been a little odd recently. Maybe that's it.'

Maybe. And it was expensive, but Nick was doing some quick calculations. He wasn't a big spender. He'd been careful over the years, he was sitting on the cash he'd got for his parents' house when Ben had bought it at auction for Lucy, and if he sold his own house, he'd have enough to buy it.

Not that he was going to do anything rash just yet, but it might be worth having a word with the agent to see if he could have the option on it as they were renting. And maybe, if things went well…

'What do you think, Kate?'

Her smile was enigmatic. 'I think we need to talk.'

He frowned, as if he couldn't see what on earth they might need to talk about, and then with a slight shrug he turned to the agent.

'Can we have another wander around for a few minutes, talk this through?' he asked, and the agent nodded.

'Sure. Take your time. I've got a few calls to make, I'll be in the car.'

He left them, and Nick turned to Kate.

'Well? Come on, let's hear it, you've obviously got something you want to say.'

She smiled at his impatience, but she wasn't going to be railroaded, no matter what she thought of the house. 'I think it's wonderful,' she told him honestly. 'Absolutely gorgeous. I also think it'd be impossible going from this back to my house when he's better.'

He gave her a level look. 'Maybe you won't have to.'

'Because I'll sell up and move away?'

'I wasn't thinking of that. I was thinking you might stay on, live here.'

'Nick…' She gave a little, despairing laugh and shook her head. 'We can't just live here for ever.'

'Why not?'

She felt her eyes widen. 'Why not? Because it's outrageously expensive! I can't even afford to rent it, let alone buy it—'

'But I can. I could buy it, and you could stay here.'

'No.' She backed away from him a step, shaking her head again but in denial this time. 'Nick, no. Don't try and buy me, please. Or Jem. Especially not him. I'd rather carry him up and downstairs or put his bed in the sitting room with a commode beside it than let you do that. Please. I mean it.'

He sighed and rammed his hand through his hair. 'Kate,

I'm not trying to buy you, don't be silly. I'm just talking through the possibilities.'

'Well, how about possibly finding a simple, small bungalow somewhere with three bedrooms while he recovers?' she suggested bluntly, not sure she could picture him in that setting but pushing him just to see if he'd go for it, for his son's sake. For hers.

He stabbed his hand through his hair again and gave an exasperated sigh. 'Look, forget the money, forget the value, because it's not about that, it's not about impressing you, or Jem. It's about giving us somewhere to get to know each other, all of us, somewhere calm and safe, tranquil, somewhere we can all heal, because I'm under no illusions about it. When we tell him I'm his father there will be some wounds that need healing, Kate, and we'll need somewhere to do that in peace.'

He was so right—of course. He took her hands, meeting her searching gaze with troubled eyes, eyes that were filled with sincerity and pain. 'That's why I've held back, Kate, why I haven't involved myself with Jem, not because I didn't want to rock the boat with my other kids, but because of what it would do to him. I thought, when there was a possibility that you'd marry Rob, that he might not ever need to know, that he could have a stepfather who'd love him and keep him safe, and the knowledge that his father had died a hero. But now you aren't going to marry Rob, and it was only with the blood group thing that I realised there was no question that he was mine, and that he had to know.'

He dropped her hands and turned to the window, gesturing at the courtyard garden. 'Look at it, Kate. It's warm, sheltered, with flat paths where he can walk safely while he heals. Your garden's terraced at the back, your drive slopes up to the house and there are steps to the front door. My garden's the same, and it's so public there—so many people who'd make it their business to have an opinion and to express it.

If I'm ten minutes late taking the milk in, there's someone there with it in their hand, ringing the bell and checking up on me.'

'And you don't want people to see us together? Is that it?' she asked, a hideous sinking feeling in her chest. 'Are you ashamed of him, Nick? Because if you are, this stops now. I'm not having my son thinking you're ashamed of him—'

'Kate, no!' he exclaimed, his face horrified, and she knew instantly that he wasn't lying. 'Of course I'm not ashamed of him! I think he's a great kid—and I'm really proud to be his father. I just dread the impact it'll have on him when it gets out, and if there was anything I could do to protect him from that, to prevent it happening, I would do it, believe me, but I can't. I can just be there for him, to fend off the gossips, and the easiest way to do that is to avoid them. At least here we'd be free to explore our relationship in peace, and can you think of a better place to do it?'

He was right, of course, but even though she was reassured about his motives, she still had doubts.

'I don't want him to know you're thinking of buying it, Nick,' she said slowly. 'Not at first.'

He lifted his hands in a shrug. 'Why not? I'm still his father, I still intend to be part of his life, and maybe it's time to move on from the home I shared with Annabel. He can come and stay here with me. And if you move away, he'll be staying for longer—weekends, weeks…' He broke off and rammed his hands in his pockets.

'I don't know if I am,' she said slowly. 'Moving away.'

His eyes narrowed. 'I thought you'd handed in your notice to the PCT?'

'Not yet. I didn't get round to posting it. And now—well, now, maybe I should stay. That depends on you, on your relationship with Jem, on how you get on once he knows you're his father. We'll have to see.'

'But—'

'Nick, don't push it,' she warned, too emotionally fraught to make sensible decisions about their future right then. 'I need time to think this through, and I don't want to feel under pressure.'

'I know. And I want to give you that time. Please don't feel pressured, Kate. I don't want to do that. I'm just trying to give you all the options, and this might be one of them, if you think you'd like it to be.'

'You obviously would,' she murmured, watching his face, and he turned and gave her a crooked little smile.

'I would. I love it here. The moment I stepped inside, I felt it wrap itself around me. I know it sounds crazy, Kate, but I felt as if I'd come home, for the first time in my adult life. And I want it—the whole package. All of it.'

The whole package? Did he mean them, too? Or was she reading things into his words that didn't exist? Whatever he meant, when she searched his eyes she found nothing but a burning sincerity. For all his flaws, Nick Tremayne was nothing if not honest and honourable, and she knew he was only telling her the truth. If he said he'd give her time and not pressure her, he meant it. Whatever his ulterior motives.

And so she nodded. 'OK. We'll try. We'll tell Jem it's just rented, that it's only till he's better, so there are no carrots dangling in front of him, nothing to influence him in any way, and we'll see how it goes. All right?'

His mouth quirked into a wry smile, and he nodded.

'Sure. Sounds good. Let's go and tell the agent he's got a deal,' he said, and she followed him, wondering if it would work, hoping that it would and that it wouldn't all turn out to be the most hideous mistake...

CHAPTER SIX

THEY shook hands on the deal, agreed they could take possession of it as early as the next day and went back to the hospital, Nick still with that air of suppressed excitement about him, Kate assailed by doubts.

Their track record wasn't great. What if this was just another disaster in the making?

Think positive! she told herself, and walked with him up to the ward.

They found Lucy at her new-found brother's bedside, Jem propped up a little, a games console in his hand and an intent expression on his face. Lucy looked up at them with a smile. 'Hi.'

'Hi. Everything all right?'

'Fine.'

'OK, I'll see you in a few minutes, I've got some calls to make,' Nick said, and headed for the door. 'I won't be long.'

Kate perched on the chair by the bed and leant over towards Jem. 'So what's this?'

He grinned at her. 'Lucy's lent it to me—it's Ben's, and it's really cool. And I made her cry.'

Lucy looked a little sheepish. 'He was so sweet—he said he'd wanted one for ages, and it just got to me.'

'Oh, Lucy.'

She shrugged, smiled and carried on watching him as he got to grips with it, and moments later Nick came back in and sat on the chair beside her, perching on the arm with his hip against her side and the subtle scent of his cologne drifting over her, carried on the warmth of his body.

She thought of sharing the barn with him, and a little shiver of anticipation swept over her skin.

'So what's that?' he asked, and she looked up at him and smiled.

'Lucy brought him in a games console,' she said softly. 'He was so thrilled, he made her cry. He's wanted one for ages and we just haven't been able to afford it.'

Jem caught sight of Nick then and grinned excitedly. 'Hey, look what Lucy's lent me, Uncle Nick,' he said.

'I'm looking,' he said, deeply touched that his son wanted to share his excitement, but—Uncle Nick? 'That looks cool.'

'It's not just cool—it's awesome,' he said, stretching the word and making Nick's lips twitch. 'Absolutely epic! Lucy's lent it to me. You can do all sorts of things with it.'

'That's kind of you, Lucy,' Nick said, feeling a little choked and also inadequate because he'd been in such a hurry to get back yesterday he hadn't brought him in anything, and today he'd been so preoccupied with the barn that a simple thing like a present for his child hadn't even entered his head.

Lucy tutted. 'Don't be silly, Dad—it was lying around at home and we hardly ever use it, but don't imagine you're keeping it, half-pint, because it won't happen.'

She ruffled his hair gently, and he grinned and ducked slightly out of her way as she bent to kiss him, but she followed him and blew a raspberry on his forehead and made him laugh and grimace.

'You be good, and no giving the nurses trouble, or I'll set Ben on you, OK?'

'OK,' he agreed, and smiled at her a little shyly. 'Thank you for bringing it in. It's really nice of you.'

'My pleasure. You take care. I'll see you soon.' She hesitated by Nick, and then, going up on tiptoe, she kissed his cheek. 'Bye, Dad. I'll see you later. We need to talk,' she added, and he gave a brief nod.

'Yes, we do. Soon. Bye, Lucy. And thank you.'

'I want to try the face thing later,' Jem said as she went out. 'It's got a really cool thing where you can take pictures of people and it shows how they're the same, like eyes and stuff. And Lucy says you look like Jack, so we're going to try it when he comes to see me again.'

Nick swallowed. It wasn't only he and Jack that looked alike, he realised now that he was able to admit it, and Lucy had obviously thought of that, too. 'That sounds really interesting, I'll have to have a look at it some time. You seem much better,' he added, quickly changing the subject and relieved that he was sounding so much perkier, even though he could see he was beginning to flag now Lucy had gone.

'It doesn't hurt so much any more. They gave me some stronger painkillers just before Lucy came. My leg still aches a lot, though.'

'I'm not surprised. It got thumped pretty hard.'

'Is the car completely trashed?' he asked Nick.

'I don't know. I haven't seen it.'

Kate thought of the state it had been in by the time they'd cut the roof and the doors and the front wing off.

'Completely,' she said, shuddering inwardly. 'The boot was full of stuff, and it all got wet when they cut the roof off.' She laughed and felt herself colour. 'The boot's always full of stuff, but I'd sorted out all kinds of things for the charity shop, and I hadn't got round to dropping them off. And it'll be getting mouldy, it's still in the back of your car in a bag, Nick. I ought to deal with it.'

'Don't worry,' he told her, wondering how she could get

worked up about something so incredibly trivial in the face of her son's injuries. Or maybe it was because it was trivial that it was safe to worry about it. Safer than thinking about Jem? 'We can sort it out tomorrow.'

She smiled at him and agreed, and then looked at her watch.

'Have you had lunch, Jem?'

'Yes, there was shepherd's pie and peas and jelly and ice cream, but I could only have toast and jelly and ice cream, but I'm having pasta bake tomorrow 'cos I can eat properly then, they said. The jelly and ice cream was nice, though.'

'Good, I'm glad. And it's good news you can eat properly tomorrow, but you should be resting now. Why don't we leave you to sleep, and Uncle Nick and I—'

She broke off, hesitating over the Uncle Nick thing, and looked at him in mute distress, but he just smiled and said, 'We'll go and grab some food while you have a bit of a zizz, and we'll be back. OK, Jem?'

'OK,' he said, and he held the game out to Kate, his eyelids drooping. 'Can you stick that in my locker so it's safe? I don't want it to fall on the floor. I promised Lucy I'd look after it.'

'Sure. Sleep well,' she murmured, and bent over and brushed her lips over his forehead, her stumble over Nick's name reminding her all too forcibly of the conversation that was to come.

'I don't care if you both still call me Uncle Nick,' he said quietly as they walked down to the cafe. 'I don't care what he calls me. It's not what matters.'

Kate felt a little stab of pain for him. 'I know. I'm sorry, it's just—you've been Uncle Nick for years, and—'

'Kate, it's all right,' he said, squeezing her fingers with his free hand. 'I don't need to be anything else. I was happy being a surrogate uncle, and if that's what he wants when we've told him, I'll carry on. All I ask is the chance to be part of his life.'

'You are part of his life, Nick. You always have been, I've made sure of it. And you always will be.'

She heard him sigh softly, and paused on the stairs, her hand on his arm. 'Nick, it'll be all right. We'll get there.'

'Will we?' he asked doubtfully. 'I hope you're right, Kate, because I've suddenly realised how much I want it, and the thought of losing it all now is untenable.'

The day dragged slowly by.

Jem slept for most of it, still not allowed any visitors apart from family, and Jack and Ben came in turn during the afternoon, when they had a moment.

He was sleeping when Jack arrived, and Kate excused herself for a moment and left the men to talk. God knows, they had enough to say to each other, she thought.

'I'll be back in a few minutes, I just want to make a few phone calls,' she said, and slipped out of the door, pulling it ßbehind her.

Jack met his father's eyes, his own guarded, and Nick sighed quietly. It had taken him a while to rebuild his relationship with Jack once he'd returned to Cornwall, and he was desperately sad that it now seemed in peril again.

'Jack, I—'

'I'm not stopping. I've just come to tell you we want to see you. Tonight, Lucy's house, eight o'clock. Be there—and no excuses.'

And without giving him a chance to argue, he walked out, and Nick sat down heavily on the awful pink vinyl armchair beside the bed and stared unseeingly at his son's face until Kate came back.

'He didn't stay long.'

'Long enough to say what he came for. I've been summoned,' he told Kate softly, standing up again and giving her the chair. 'Eight o'clock tonight, Lucy's. Will you be all right if I leave you to go there?'

She smiled sadly. 'Of course I'll be all right. I've just heard Gemma's been admitted. I might take a walk up there and see how she's doing. You go and see them, Nick, and try and build some bridges.'

He nodded, wondering how he could be in two places at once and only really wanting to be here, by this injured child he was beginning to realise he loved more than life itself...

Ben came by on his way home after his shift finished, by which time Jem had woken up in pain again.

'I've got the most amazing bruises,' he told Ben, but although he was trying to sound as if he was showing off, Kate could tell he was frightened by them, and she wasn't surprised. When he turned back the blankets and showed his side to Ben, she winced yet again, the sight making her curl up inside.

'That's impressive. I'm not surprised you're hurting. I'll go and find someone.'

He went out, coming back a few moments later with Megan Phillips. They consulted the chart together, and she chatted to Jem about his pain, and then she turned to Kate.

'We want to get the pain under control because we don't like him hurting, but also because we'd like to get him up soon. We might start sitting him up on the side of the bed tomorrow and see how it goes, and if he tolerates that we'll move to the chair, and so on. It'll be slow, but you'll be in control of what you can manage, Jem. We'll let you guide us. And Mr Bradley wants your physio to start properly from tomorrow, so all your muscles don't forget how to work, but very gently at first, so nothing to worry about. Anyway, I'll talk to you in the morning, and I'm on all night if you're worried about anything, Mrs Althorp. Just get them to call me.'

'Thank you,' she said, smiling at the lovely young woman,

her dark hair held back in a clip out of the way, the thick curls trying hard to escape. She was kindness itself, but there was something lurking in the back of her eyes today, Kate thought, that hadn't been there yesterday. Something sad and desperate and a little lost. Her heart went out to her.

'I'll go and update your notes right now, Jem, and get someone to come and give you the extra pain relief shortly, OK? And if you're still really uncomfortable, press the bell and they'll get me and we'll have another look at things.'

'Thanks,' he said, looking relieved, and after she'd gone out he looked up at Ben again. 'Thanks for asking her, Ben.'

'Any time. Right, I'd better go home. Apparently I'm cooking tonight. I'll see you later, Nick?'

'Yes. I'll be there.'

Ben gave him a fleeting smile, murmured, 'Don't worry,' and left them alone with their son.

'Here you go, my gorgeous—jelly and ice cream,' a nurse said, putting it down on his bed table with a smile and helping him sit up a little.

Nick glanced at his watch, and realised it was suppertime. He looked at Kate. 'Why don't you go and have a rest for an hour or so while I sit here with Jem?' he suggested gently. 'Or you could go and get something to eat, as I'm eating at Lucy's.'

For a moment he thought she was going to argue, but then she smiled slightly and went out, and he settled himself on the edge of the pink chair and looked at the instructions for the games console while Jem ate the jelly and ice cream and told him how to work it.

'I don't know how you guys work these things out,' Nick said, frowning at it, and Jem laughed and took it from him.

'It's easy, Uncle Nick, but don't worry, Rob couldn't work out how to use Matt's, either. It's because you're too old for this kind of thing,' he explained innocently.

'Is that right?' he asked, taking the machine back and

having another go. So Rob couldn't work it? He ignored the voice that mocked him for his childish urge to be better than the other man, and got Jem to show him once again. And finally, finally, he cracked it.

After that, dealing with Lucy and Jack didn't seem nearly so daunting...

He left Jem's bedside at seven-thirty, just after Kate came back to sit with him. She'd had a rest, and something to eat, and she looked more like herself.

'I'll come back later and update you,' he promised. 'And I could stay, if you like—take turns, like we did last night.'

'We'll see. Have a lovely time,' she said, but her eyes were saying, Good luck, and he gave her a fleeting smile and left.

It took fifteen minutes to get there, and he parked the car outside and went in through the kitchen door, the way he'd always gone into his family home. He braced himself for the reception committee, but it was only Ben in the kitchen and he greeted him with a smile and a glass of wine. 'Here—I thought you might need this.'

'I'm driving.'

'Not for a while, and it's only a small glass. They're in the sitting room, go on through. And, Nick? Don't worry. They aren't going to skin you, they just want to understand.'

He nodded, and, taking the wine with him, he walked through the familiar house, feeling like a condemned man going to the gallows. Crazy, because in many ways this was none of their business, it was between him and Kate and Jem, and the only other person he owed an explanation to was Annabel, and she was dead.

But he supposed they felt they were acting as her representatives, and of course there were financial implications. Jeremiah, as his son, was entitled to an equal share of his estate, so each of them would lose a percentage of their stake.

Maybe that was what they wanted to discuss. Although he doubted it. His children weren't like that.

Shaking his head slowly, he straightened his shoulders and went through into the sitting room, and the conversation stopped dead.

'Well, don't mind me,' he murmured, and Lucy coloured.

Not Jack. He stood up, looked his father in the eye and said, 'You'd better sit down. We've got Ed on the webcam.'

He nodded, glad that he'd be able to talk to his other son at last, and sat down opposite the laptop on the coffee table, with Jack and Lucy across from him, visible over the top. So he could see them all, and they could all see him. It was like an interview panel, he thought. Or a jury.

I swear by Almighty God…

'Dad.'

He glanced down at Edward, his face moving a little jerkily but still very recognisable.

'I've been trying to ring you,' Nick told him.

'I know. I didn't answer because I don't know what to say to you,' Ed told him, his voice puzzled and hurt. 'I can't believe it—what the hell were you thinking of?'

Nick sighed and ran a hand through his hair. 'There's nothing I can say or do to change what happened, and I'm not going to make excuses,' he told them all, 'but I meant my vows to your mother, Edward, and I swear it was the only time.'

I swear by Almighty God…

'It's not that. That's between the two of you. I just hope she never knew. It's him I'm thinking about, a boy who thought for years that his father was dead when you could have been taking an active role in his life. Sure, it would have hurt Mum, but we were grown up, it was none of our business, and we could have spent time with him and made him feel wanted.

That's what's so gutting, that he didn't have any brothers or sisters there for him when we could have been, so easily.'

Nick shook his head. 'I didn't know. It was Kate's decision not to tell me, and she made it for good reasons. Wrong ones, maybe, but still out of consideration for everyone involved, and there weren't any right ones—'

'Don't palm it off on Kate. You've known for two years,' Jack retorted, cutting in. 'That's two lost years he could have had a father. You should have said something sooner, Dad.'

'How?' he asked. 'And when? She was with someone all last year, and she's been ill. You know that. She's had breast cancer. We could hardly tell him then, could we, with his life in turmoil and another man there ready and willing to act as his father? And before then, well, I guess I was still coming to terms with it—still in denial. I'm sorry you're so angry with us, but the only person I can worry about at the moment is your little brother, and I'm afraid he's taking all my time and thoughts right now.'

Edward frowned. 'How did he take it?'

'He doesn't know yet. He's still in a lot of pain. We're going to tell him later, when he's stronger, and when we've had some time to get to know each other. I'm hoping that with time we'll be able to get to know each other better and he'll learn to forgive us both, but I'm going to be part of his life now, come hell or high water, so I'm glad you've all accepted that, at least.'

'Don't worry about us. We're big enough and ugly enough to take care of ourselves. It's Jem we're all worried about.'

He pinched the bridge of his nose, pressing his thumb and forefinger against his eyes before dragging his hand down his face. 'Who the hell do you think I'm worried about?' he asked hoarsely, scanning all their faces. 'At the end of the day, I've done my bit for you lot. I haven't even started with him. I owe him so much I don't know where to begin—'

'That's what we want to talk to you about. You need to

change your will, to make provision for him,' Lucy said, and he glanced across at her and wondered if this had been her idea, his little girl, his peacemaker.

'I already have,' he said quietly. 'I did it yesterday, as soon as I found out—as soon as I was sure. The amendment to the will is with my solicitors in St Piran waiting for my signature.'

'And what about his schooling? We all went to private school. Where will he go?'

'Wherever he wants, Jack. I would think the high school in Penhally, with his friends. I don't want to change his life, I don't have the right to interfere.'

Jack snorted, and he met the condemnation in his eyes with new understanding.

'Is that how you saw my involvement in your lives? As interference?'

'Somewhat,' Edward said bluntly. 'It was "My way or the highway". No middle line, no grey areas, just black or white.'

Nick frowned. 'That's not how I see it at all. I did my best to be a good husband and father. I gave you guidelines. I thought that was what being a father was, but this—I don't know how to deal with this, how to be a father to him now.'

'Is that why you haven't?'

He looked at her and let his breath out on a long, ragged sigh. 'Yes. Yes, that's exactly why. I want to be a good father to him, to all of you, but I just—I can't seem to do it right, apparently. And with Jem—I didn't even get the chance until recently, and it was so nearly too late...'

He broke off, squeezing his eyes shut, pinching the bridge of his nose again, determined to hold it all together in front of them, but it was all still so raw, the image of Jem lying there in Resus while they cut his clothes away and poured fluids into him etched on his memory in acid.

'I still don't understand how you ended up sleeping with Kate when you were married,' Jack said, sounding so like him that at any other time it might have been funny. 'All the morals you rammed down our throats as kids, and yet you could do that—and you ended up with a child you won't even acknowledge! It's just so damned unfair. At least we knew you loved us—and we thought you loved our mother.'

'I did—and I love Jeremiah,' he told them earnestly. 'Don't imagine for a moment that I don't, and I fully intend to show him that, given a chance.'

'You're changing the subject,' Jack said. 'I want to know how the hell you came to have a random one-night stand with another woman totally out of the blue!'

'I don't think that's any of your business,' he began, but then he sighed and sat back, giving up the unequal struggle. If he ever hoped to make them understand, he had to explain at least some of it. He looked up and scanned their faces in turn.

'You want to know? All right, I'll tell you.'

'Dad, you don't have to,' Lucy protested, but he shook his head.

'I think I do—because it wasn't totally out of the blue at all. Kate and I go back thirty-five years.'

'We know you dated her.'

He smiled gently at Lucy. 'It was rather more than that. I'd know her since I was fourteen, but I was seventeen when I first really became aware of her; she was only fifteen, though, so we took things slowly—walks up on the moors, swimming, surfing, going for picnics. We went to the cinema, I took her to a rock concert—all pretty innocent stuff. And we fell in love.'

He hesitated, remembering those halcyon days, and then he sucked in a breath and carried on. 'I was in my last year at school, and I'd got into med school in London. We talked about me going away, and I promised I'd come back for her.

She was sixteen by then, I was eighteen, and although we still weren't sleeping together, that was pretty much a technicality. By the end of that last summer, I knew Kate's body as well as I knew my own, and I cherished it. But I was going away, and people change, and I didn't want to do anything that might hurt her later, so we held back from that last step. And then I met a girl during Freshers' Week, a beautiful girl with stunning blonde hair and the most incredible blue eyes, while we were being dragged round on some crazy pub crawl in fancy dress, and somehow we ended up in her room. I woke up in the morning feeling sick and ashamed and appalled at what I'd done, but it was too late. She came to me a few weeks later in floods of tears and told me she was pregnant, and I didn't know what to do. I just knew I had no choice but to ask her to marry me, and to make it work.'

'And Kate?' Lucy asked softly. 'What happened about Kate?'

'I came down and saw her, and for the first time ever I lied to her. I told her I'd met someone else and fallen in love, and I was going to marry her. I told her she was pregnant—and Kate was devastated. So was I, because I loved her so much—I never had to explain anything to her, I still don't. She still understands me as no one else ever has, anticipates me, and somehow forgives me. She actually sent us a card, saying she hoped we'd be very happy together. And I did everything I could to be fair to Annabel, to be good to her, because it wasn't her fault I'd got her in that mess, and she was lovely. It was no hardship being married to her, and if I didn't think about Kate, it was OK. But even though I did everything I could to make it feel right, I couldn't, not entirely, because my heart was with Kate and always has been. And even though I was with your mother, I always knew what was going on in Kate's life—we went to her wedding to James, we saw them socially from time to time, and I managed to convince myself that we'd both moved on. Only I never really did, of course, and I don't think she did.'

He tried to smile at them, but his mouth felt frozen. 'I don't know that I can explain what happened that night—the night of the storm. It was a few hours after my father and your Uncle Phil had died, and Kate's husband had been washed out to sea.'

He filled in the details of the day, the rescue that had gone wrong and led to the death of three men, the horror of it. 'Later that night your mother told me to find Kate, to see if he'd been found, and he hadn't. She was still on the clifftop, so I took her home and tried to look after her, but she was falling apart, devastated, and so was I, and we just reached out to each other. We've never needed words, and we didn't need them that night. We just hung on while the storm raged all around us, and afterwards I put her to bed and left her, and went back to your mother and tried to carry on.

'And that's what I've done for the past twelve years,' he said, 'tried to carry on, to keep going, keep putting one foot in front of the other and not hurt too many people along the way. And then I find I have another child, a son, and we're going to have to tell him, and yet again I'm going to hurt someone I love.'

He stopped, unsure what else, if anything, he could tell them, but there was nothing more of any relevance, so with a long, deep breath, he sat back and waited.

He'd told them things he'd never told anyone, not even Kate, and there was a long silence until Lucy knelt up beside him, put her arms round him and rested her head on his shoulder. 'Dad, I'm so sorry,' she whispered, and he could feel a wet patch forming on his shirt from her soundless tears.

He hugged her back, and she dragged in a shuddering breath and sat up. 'Ed, are you OK?' she asked.

Nick looked at Edward, clearly moved even on the jerky picture.

'I'm sorry,' he said. 'We had no right to make you go through that. You were right, it was none of our damn business. Look, I'm going to go. Just—look after him, could you, and send him my love? I'll write to him. You can give him the letter when you think he's ready.'

'Thanks.'

The screen went blank, and Lucy shut the laptop and leant back with a sigh, and he glanced across and saw Jack, stony-faced and silent, but he was far from unmoved, however tight his control.

'Well—I suppose we ought to eat,' Lucy said at last, and, unfolding her legs, she got off the sofa and went out. Seconds later, they heard her crying, and Ben's voice murmuring quietly as he soothed her.

'I'm sorry, I probably shouldn't have told you all of that,' Nick said softly, but Jack made a dismissive noise and shook his head.

'No, I'm sorry. I owe you an apology. I thought—'

'That it was some dirty little affair? That we'd gone out and got drunk? Believe me, that would have been easier to deal with.'

'I'm sure. How's Jem doing?'

'Oh, he's all right, I suppose. Still sore, still got the drain and the catheter, and I don't think that pleases him, but maybe he'll have them out tomorrow.'

'Probably,' Jack agreed. 'Are they going to get him up?'

How odd, Nick thought, that Lucy could hug him and then go and cry, but Jack was here talking about his treatment, hanging onto normality. So like him, so ready to push his emotions aside if they became inconvenient or embarrassing.

But this business with Jem was teaching him a lot about

his emotions, most of it uncomfortable, and he was learning to deal with them.

Ben appeared in the doorway. 'Supper's ready when you are. There's no rush.'

'It's OK, we're ready,' Nick lied, because his guts were so knotted with tension he didn't think he could possibly eat again.

'So—what happens now?' Lucy asked, and he shrugged.

'I don't know. We're taking it a day at a time. I've found a converted barn to rent—it's near here, you probably know it. St Adwen's. It's been for sale, but they haven't managed to shift it, so they're letting it, and it's mostly single storey, with two bedrooms upstairs and two down, so when he comes out of hospital we're going to stay there for a while until he recovers. It'll give us a bit of privacy and time to be together as a family, without the pressure of having to buy anywhere.'

'What about your house?' Jack suggested. 'That's got a room downstairs he could use as a bedroom, and a shower room next to it.'

'Neither of us would feel comfortable there, under the circumstances. It's very much your mother's house, but maybe it's time I moved on.'

'Meaning?' Lucy asked, looking at him keenly.

He set his fork down, very precisely, and met her eyes.

'I'm thinking of asking Kate to give me another chance. We're going to see how it goes with Jem, but if I think we could make a go of it, I might ask her to marry me.'

Her eyes flooded again, and she got up and came and hugged him. 'Oh, Dad. I'm so pleased. I've been so worried about you on your own, and Kate's so lovely, and now we know how much you love her—'

'Hey, hey, don't jump the gun, I haven't asked her yet and she certainly hasn't said yes. It could all fall apart if Jem throws a hissy fit at the idea of us living together.'

She sat down again and propped her chin on her hand. 'Do you think he will?'

He shrugged. 'I really have no idea. He doesn't know I'm his father yet, we still have to cross that hurdle, and I have no idea how he'll react.' He sighed. 'Although with my track record maybe he'd be better off not knowing—'

His children both chipped in then, contradicting him, telling him he was a good father, the best...

'What about "My way or the highway"?' he quoted back at them from one of their recent conversations. 'What about all the morals I stuffed down your throats?'

'Well, at least you had principles, even if you weren't always strong enough to stick to them,' Jack said reasonably.

'And you've always loved us, even if you were a bit tough and uncompromising, and we've always known that,' Lucy said, reaching out and squeezing his hand. 'Don't worry. Just give him time. And we'll be there, too. Once he's better I'll take the kids in to visit. They love him, and he's their uncle, of course. I think he may find that a bit of a shock when he works it out.'

'I hadn't even thought of that,' Nick said, and picked his fork up again, suddenly hungry. 'This is good chilli, Ben. Thanks.'

'My pleasure,' Ben said, giving him a wry smile. 'There's plenty more.'

'D'you know, I don't mind if I do,' he said with a grin, and handed Ben his plate.

Kate waited for him, lying awake on the top of the bed they'd given her at the hospital, and when he called her, shortly before midnight, she told him to come up. He tapped on the door and came in and perched beside her, and she reached for his hand and held it.

'How was it?'

'Oh, pretty much as expected. They were angry at first,

worried about Jem, about the impact this would have on him—you were right about them, they've taken him to their hearts, he's part of the family now whether he likes it or not. Curiously it wasn't that much about the fact that I was unfaithful to their mother, although that didn't thrill them. They seemed more concerned for him—about my provision for him in my will, about his education and what I intend to do to take care of him, and about you.'

He hesitated, then went on, 'I told them about us, about how we met, and a bit about that night—not all of it, but enough. I know you didn't want me to, but they didn't understand, and how could they, without being there, without understanding how devastated we were that night, how bonded together by our grief we were. So I tried to explain.'

'And did they understand, in the end?'

He gave a low laugh. 'I think so. I was pretty graphic. Not about us, but the rest. They apologised for making me dredge it all up—they were pretty shocked. They hadn't realised what it had been like that day, and I didn't pull any punches. I even told them about their Uncle Phil and how he died.'

'Oh, Nick,' she said, squeezing his hand tighter. 'I'm sorry you had to go through it all again.'

'It's all right. It was important that they understood, and I think they do now. I also thought they should know that Annabel sent me to make sure you were all right.'

She stared at him. 'Annabel sent you?'

'Yes. I thought you knew that?'

'How would I know, Nick? We've never talked about it— never discussed the night of the storm. I'm not sure I even know fully what happened. Will you tell me?'

'Really?'

'If you can bear to go over it all again.'

He shrugged. 'Sure. If you really want to know.'

'I do,' she said, and then, because he was still clearly running it over in his head, still chock-full of emotion, she patted the bed and shuffled over. 'Come here. You need a hug.'

For a moment he did nothing, but then with a tired sigh he lay down beside her and drew her into his arms. She put her head on his shoulder, and wrapped her arms round him and held him.

'So tell me,' she urged softly. 'Tell me how it happened.'

'Well, you know the school kids were stranded down on the rocks at the foot of the headland—that's where James was, of course, and my father was on the top of the headland, helping with the children that had been brought up the cliff while my brother was abseiling down the face and rescuing the ones still stranded. The last child's helmet had fallen off on the way up, and so Phil took his off and gave it to her, and then a huge wave—the same wave that swept James off the rocks—picked them up and threw them against the cliff and shattered his skull. My father helped pull them up, and failed to tell anyone he'd had a heart attack three weeks earlier.

'I hadn't been there at first, I was in my surgery over in Wadebridge, but I was called to help and I arrived to find my father collapsing with another heart attack, and my brother lying on the grass in the lashing rain with the back of his skull caved in. There was nothing I could do for Phil, he'd died instantly. My mother was at home, unaware of what was going on, but Annabel was in the church hall, making tea for everyone, so I told her to pick my mother up and meet us at the hospital, and I went in the ambulance with my father, trying to keep him alive when he arrested. And by the time we set off, we knew that James had been washed off the rocks by the same wave.

'I managed to keep my father going until we got to the hospital, and my mother was with him when he died, although he never recovered consciousness, and after she'd said goodbye to her husband, I had to take her down to the chapel of rest to say goodbye to her son.'

He broke off for a moment, reliving it, and beside him he heard Kate suck in a shaky breath. 'Nick, you don't have to do this.'

'It's OK,' he said softly, taking her hand and squeezing it. 'It's time we talked about it, because otherwise it's too damned easy to say we should have known better. Anyway, I took them back to the house, Annabel and my mother, and we had tea.' He gave a shaky laugh. 'It's funny how tea always seems to come into this equation. I can't tell you how much tea and coffee I've drunk in the last couple of days. Anyway, after a while Mum started to cry—that terrible sound of grief.'

'Oh, Nick. Poor, poor woman. How on earth did she cope, losing both of them on the same day?'

'She didn't. It broke her. And on that night of course we couldn't leave her, but I couldn't stop thinking about James, and neither could Annabel. She told me to go and find you and see if there was any news of him. I think we both knew he was dead, and afterwards I wondered if she knew what she was doing when she sent me. I suspect she did. She wasn't stupid.'

It had been a bizarre conversation, most of the words unsaid, he remembered. And he could remember, too, the look in her eyes. The understanding, the quiet resignation. The blessing. He gave a quiet sigh and went on.

'The rest you know. I found you on the headland, with the wind and rain lashing your clothes, and you were so cold— chilled to the bone.'

'I was waiting for you. I knew you'd come.'

'I don't know how. I just knew I had to.'

He'd undressed her and put her in the shower, and put the kettle on, just like the other day. And just like the other day, he'd heard her crying, like his mother, with inconsolable grief, and he'd gone to her. The woman he loved, the girl he'd fallen for. The woman, he realised, he still loved with all his heart. He closed his eyes and swallowed.

He paused, remembering that he'd already stripped off his saturated, blood-stained shirt, and he'd taken off the rest and gone into the shower and put his arms around her and held her, and she'd clung to him, just as she'd clung to him that morning, and they'd cried together. He had no idea how long for. Ten minutes? An hour?

He wasn't really sure what had happened then. He hadn't understood it at the time and he still didn't understand it now, but they'd needed each other in a way so deep, so elemental that there had been no denying it. They were both angry, furious that something so crazy had happened to kill two young, healthy men with years ahead of them and an old man who should have lived to enjoy his retirement and instead had been snuffed out like a candle.

Maybe it was just defiance, and the fact that people they'd loved had died so senselessly, and it was almost as if they'd had to prove to themselves that they were still alive, but there had been no stopping it, no reasoning, just a soul-deep need that had driven them half-crazed into each other's arms.

Afterwards he'd turned off the water and dried her and put her to bed and then he'd gone home and showered and changed and gone back to his wife. They'd never spoken of it again, but after that, nothing had been quite the same...

'Nick?'

He started a little and stared at Kate, then shook his head to clear it of the unwanted, haunting images.

'I'm sorry that night was so awful for you all,' she whispered. 'Thank you for telling me. And I'm sorry the kids were hard on you.'

'It's OK. It's over now, and I'm glad it's out in the open. I think they realise now that it wasn't a premeditated decision to betray their mother, or that Jem was conceived as a drunken result of some sordid little date, just two people, who had always cared about each other, on the edge of despair and reaching out to each other that night.'

'We weren't ourselves. No wonder we didn't think about contraception, not then and not afterwards.'

'I did, but not till weeks later, when you told me you were pregnant, and I asked you if it was my child, and you said no. And I accepted it without question, with relief, even, because I didn't ever want to have to think of that night again. But you knew, didn't you? You knew he was mine because of the fertility problems.'

'Yes. Yes, I knew. James's notes had gone back to the PCT when he died, so I'd had to ring the clinic and ask them for the results, and they'd told me that James was sterile. But I couldn't tell you. Not then. It wouldn't have achieved anything and so many more people would have been hurt. But maybe now we can move on.'

'Maybe.'

He turned his head, and she lifted her face and their lips met in a gentle, tender kiss that made her heart skip a beat. He shifted, turning towards her, and their legs tangled, their bodies hard against each other.

'Nick, we can't,' she whispered, and he sighed, his breath soft against her cheek.

'I know. I just need to hold you.'

But he kept on kissing her, his lips tracing soft circles over her cheeks, her eyes, her throat.

'Nick…'

'Shh. It's all right,' he murmured, drawing her closer again and settling her head on his shoulder once more. 'I'm going in a minute.'

Except he didn't. He was asleep in seconds, emotionally exhausted, and although her arm had gone to sleep, she didn't have the heart to wake him. So she lay there for an hour, until he stirred and gave a sleepy grunt, and she murmured his name.

'Sorry—I didn't mean to doze off. Are you all right?' he asked, sitting up and shifting out of her way.

'I'm fine. My arm's dead, though.'

He tutted and took it in his hands, rubbing it briskly until the pins and needles had gone and she sighed with relief, and then he stood up. 'I ought to go home. How's Jem been? Did he go to sleep all right?'

'Yes, he's fine. And Sam and Gemma have a baby boy. They're calling him Archie—Archie Nicholas, for you.'

She heard him suck in his breath, and then let it out again, obviously touched by the gesture. 'That's great. How are they?'

'Well. Fine. The baby's beautiful, and Gemma's OK, it was a nice, straightforward delivery. It was lovely to see them. A bit of normality, really. They send their love.'

'I'll pop up tomorrow, take them something. And I ought to bring Jem in something, but I have no idea what. I don't want to look as if I'm trying to buy him,' he said with a wry grin, and she laughed.

'So bring him grapes. He adores grapes, and he needs fruit on all these opiates.'

'Grapes? Lucy gives him a games console that probably cost well over a hundred pounds, and you suggest I bring him grapes?' he said, laughing softly.

'Or you could look as if you're trying to buy him,' she said reasonably, and he sighed.

'OK. Grapes it is. And I suppose the games console's only on loan.'

It was, although of course he could always buy him his own, she thought, but she didn't suggest it. Time enough later for extravagant gestures, and she'd rather he didn't get into the habit of playing on a games machine as a regular thing.

He bent and kissed her cheek, then lifted his head slightly, stared into her eyes and slowly lowered his head again, touching his lips to hers once more. Just briefly, very lightly, but it was like being stroked with fire.

'Sleep tight. I'll see you in the morning,' he murmured, and he went out and closed the door softly behind him, leaving her lying there with her fingers on her lips, and her body tingling with anticipation.

CHAPTER SEVEN

NICK didn't arrive until ten the next day, to her surprise.

By the time he came in, Martin Bradley had been round, and as Jem seemed comfortable, the surgeon said he could try sitting up a little in bed, instead of just having his head and shoulders being propped up.

It ached a bit, Jem said, but Kate could tell he was happier. He was getting so bored lying down, and sitting up properly he was able to play with the games console to his heart's content while she sat beside him with a magazine and let it all go on around her.

Her presence was less essential now than it had been. He was no longer in danger, and he was used to the staff, familiar with his surroundings and happier about being left.

She'd already decided the night before that it would be the last time she stayed, and she was getting desperate for her own bed.

Or at least one that didn't have a plastic mattress.

If Nick would only arrive, she thought, she could talk to him about the barn. She hadn't told Jem yet what their plans were, she wanted to do that with Nick, preferably before he signed on the dotted line at the letting agent's, but when he arrived he dangled a bunch of keys in front of her with a smug grin, like a magician pulling a rabbit out of a hat.

'Your keys, ma'am,' he said, dropping them into her hand. 'You can move in whenever you like.'

She was at the nurses' station, out in the ward, talking to the ward sister and Megan Phillips about what was to happen next, and she stared at the keys in slight consternation.

'What's the matter?' he said, his voice dropping. 'I thought that was what you wanted?'

'It is,' she said. 'But—I thought we were going to talk to Jem first? What if he says no?'

'What if he does? He's ten years old, Kate. There are some decisions that aren't his to make. This is a temporary fix, for a few weeks initially, to cover his convalescence. His friends can come and visit, he can treat it as a holiday—and if it doesn't work out, if he doesn't want me around, then I can go home. It doesn't change anything. It's just for now.'

He was right, of course—he was always right, she thought, except when he was wrong, and then it tended to be on an epic scale. But this—this was just common sense, and she let her breath out on a little huff of laughter and tried to smile.

'You're right. I'm sorry, it's not as if it's a permanent thing. I'm being silly.'

And she'd been letting herself get carried away with all the possibilities. A temporary fix, she reminded herself. Just that, nothing more, for a few weeks, and it might be a total disaster on several counts.

'This might be more long term,' he said then, pulling another set of keys from his pocket, and dropping them in her hand too.

She glanced down, and blinked. 'Car keys?'

'Mmm. I wasn't sure what you wanted, so I asked Chloe if you'd said anything. She mentioned a model you liked.'

She stared at the keys, confused. 'You've got me a car on the PCT contract this quickly?' she said. Surely she had to sign something…

'No. I've bought you a Golf—a nice economical little diesel. They're delivering it to the barn this afternoon.'

She stared at him as if he'd gone mad. 'You bought me a new car?'

'No. It's not new. It's two years old. I thought you'd shout at me if I got you a new one.'

She opened her mouth to shout at him anyway, and to her horror a little sob came out instead.

'Kate?'

'Sorry,' she said, flapping her hand and blinking hard. 'I— It's just— Oh, Nick, you didn't have to do that. I could have got myself another car. Renting the house is one thing, this is quite another. You're doing too much, going too fast.'

'No, I'm not.' This one's got a much better NCAP crash rating. I'm not trying to bribe you,' he said grimly, 'I'm trying—too late—to make sure my son stays safe.'

She swallowed, unable to argue, filled with guilt that her car had contributed to his injuries, but he misunderstood her silence and sighed.

'I'm sorry. I know I interfere. It doesn't matter, you can use it for the moment and once you get yourself the car you want, I'll give it to Lucy or something, make it a pool car for the practice maybe.'

'No!' She closed her hand around the keys, reached up and kissed his cheek. 'Thank you. I was just stunned, that's all. I've had to rely on myself for so long, and— Oh, damn.'

Her eyes were welling up, and she rummaged for a tissue in her pocket. He got there first, plucking one off the top of the nurses' station and handing it to her, and she blew her nose and sniffed hard. 'Sorry. It's been a bit of a roller-coaster.'

'I know. How is he?'

She filled him in on the day's events, and he went in to see Jem while she packed her things in the little room she'd been using and gave herself a thorough talking to. She handed the key back to the staff nurse and thanked her, and went into Jem's room to find Nick perched beside him on the bed, leaning up against the backrest and watching him with the games console while he ate grapes.

'You could put that down for five minutes, you know,' she pointed out, but Jem just grinned.

'Uncle Nick wanted to see how I was doing. I was just showing him. I've been teaching him how to use it.'

She stared at him, realising how easily these two had slipped into an easy relationship, almost as if Jem knew Nick was his father. He must have been so desperate for a father all these years, she thought, and he'd never said a word about it; perhaps he didn't realise it, even now. She'd thought he was all right, that they were fine on their own, but maybe she'd been deluding herself and all the time there'd been a void.

A void that should have been filled by Nick.

'We've got something to talk to you about,' she said, determined to get the barn out into the open. 'Could you put that down and listen, please?'

He looked up at her, his eyes wary, and then looked down again. 'Oh, no, it killed me!' he wailed, and put the console down on the locker, then looked up at her again a little worriedly. 'What did you want to talk about?'

'You. When you come out of here, you might not be able to walk up and down stairs for a while, and we've got no bathroom downstairs.'

'Oh. Does that mean I'll have to stay in here longer, till I can go upstairs?' he asked miserably. 'I don't want to. I want to go home as soon as I can. It's not the same here.'

'I know. And, no, it doesn't mean that. It means we'll have to stay somewhere else for a little while. Uncle N—' She broke off, met Nick's eyes ruefully and went on, 'Uncle Nick's found somewhere for us, somewhere he can stay, too, just outside Penhally, near Ben and Lucy. It's a barn, and it's got a downstairs bedroom with doors out to the garden, and an en suite wetroom—'

'What's a non-sweet wetroom?'

'En suite—it's French. It means it's a bathroom attached just to one bedroom. And a wetroom means it's got a tiled floor and you just walk into it and shower, so you wouldn't even have to step up to a shower tray.'

'Wow. And we can stay there?'

'Yes.'

'And you're coming?' he asked, swivelling his head round to look at Nick, and he nodded.

'Yes—so I can help out, and I can do stuff for you that you might not want your mum doing, like help you shower and so on, if you need help at first.'

He nodded. 'Can the dog come?'

'Yes.'

'OK. So was that all you want to talk about?'

She met Nick's eyes and they were full of relief and wry humour. She smiled. 'Nothing else. Just that.'

'Oh. Well, can I try and get to the next level, then? I was nearly there and then it killed me.'

'Kids.'

'Don't. I can't believe he took it so well.'

'Of course he did,' Nick said as if it was obvious, and put the tray down on the table. 'He trusts you to take care of him. You've done it—made it possible for him to be discharged as soon as it's practicable. Why should he take it any other way?'

'Because we always talk everything through. Before I do anything, we talk it through. We're not impulsive like you.'

He looked at her as if she had two heads, and she thought of Lucy and Jack pointing out to him that he interfered, and stifled a smile.

'Don't laugh at me. I'm not impulsive, I'm decisive. It's different,' he protested.

'Actually, you're both,' she pointed out gently, reaching for her coffee. 'Nick, you're going to have to get used to him. Jem likes to see all sides of a thing before he'll commit to it. If I say jump, he doesn't ask how high, he asks why. And I know it's an alien concept to you, but it's the way I've brought him up.'

'It's not an alien concept,' he disagreed, stirring his coffee with huge concentration. 'It's just that some things are as they are. He has to know that there isn't always an answer, that sometimes you have to take some things and some people on trust.'

'And you know what he'd say to that?'

'"Why?"' they said together, and then laughed, reaching out and linking their fingers on the table.

'Did you get anything for Gemma's baby?' she asked, and he nodded.

'Yes. I found a lovely pop-up book of farm animals. It's not for now, obviously, but I thought he might like it later.'

'That's a lovely idea, and it goes really well with my present. I've knitted him a little jumper with fluffy sheep on the front.'

He frowned quizzically. 'Really? You can knit?'

She laughed. 'Of course I can knit! All women can knit.'

'Annabel couldn't knit.'

She felt her smile die. 'Nick, I'm not Annabel,' she reminded him gently. 'And that's not a criticism of her, it's just a fact.'

He closed his eyes for a second and sighed. 'I know you're not Annabel. I'm only too aware of who you are. I just didn't know you could knit. It's one of the very many things I don't know about you, that I've never had the chance to find out. I didn't mean to offend you by comparing you to Annabel.'

'I'm not offended,' she said quickly. 'Not at all. But we are—were—different. You need to realise that if we're going to live together.'

'Well, then, isn't it a good job that I've already noticed?' he said softly, and, draining his coffee, he got to his feet. 'There's Lucy—she said she'd try and pop in. Come on, we'll go up with her.'

He held out his hand to help Kate up, and then tucked her hand in the crook of his arm. 'Hello, darling,' he said, kissing his daughter's cheek, and she took his other arm and walked with them to the ward.

'I've got something for you, from Ben. His chilli recipe. He says you can look after Kate, spoil her a little. Here.'

He grinned and tucked it in his pocket, and vowed to make it for her soon.

They left Jem with Lucy, telling him they were going to see the barn and would be back later, and twenty minutes later they'd pulled up outside and unlocked the door.

'Welcome home,' he said softly, pushing the door open, and she stepped inside, a little bit of her disappointed that he hadn't carried her over the threshold. But how stupid was that? They weren't married—far from it, and they might never be. This was just about Jem, and if she'd expected more because of his tenderness with her last night, she was deluded.

The entrance was in the single-story section on the left-hand side, between the living space and the bedrooms, and they walked through to the sitting room with its low beamed ceiling and comfortable furniture grouped around the log burner, and into the central section where a battered old oak refectory table sat in pride of place.

It would be the perfect setting for family get-togethers, she thought—all Nick's children with their spouses and families gathered around, the air filled with their laughter. She could hear it now, as she looked around her at the great vaulted space of the dining hall. Its huge, soaring window faced the courtyard, with its flat, winding paths and low shrubs giving structure to the sheltered little garden, the wings of the house wrapped round it like arms, protecting it from the elements, and then beyond it were the fields and then the sea.

And like Nick had the first time he'd stepped inside, she felt the house welcome her, as if those arms had folded round her and gathered her to its heart.

Romantic nonsense, she thought, and yet...

'You were right, it is calm and tranquil here,' she said softly, feeling the tension drain out of her. 'It'll be so good for him. Thank you, Nick.'

And going up on tiptoe, she kissed his cheek.

For a long moment he stared at her, their eyes locked, and then he seemed to pull himself together and looked away, and they walked around the rest of the house slowly and had their first real, proper look.

'It's amazing,' she said, standing on the galleried walkway above the dining hall and looking out over the courtyard to the sea in the distance. 'Beautiful. I could stand here all day and look at that view.'

'There are plenty of chairs you could sit on,' Nick pointed out with a smile, and she laughed softly and turned away from the window, looking up at the vaulted ceiling with its heavy beams. The gallery spanned the space, leading to a bedroom at each end, and they were both amazing.

'Which bedroom do you want?'

She glanced at him. 'I don't know. Maybe I should be downstairs with Jem. He could call me then, if he needed me in the night.'

And she'd be further from temptation.

'It doesn't have its own shower.'

'There's a bathroom almost next to it. I'm sure I'll manage.' She went back downstairs and round the corner to the wing with the two bedrooms and the study in it, on the other side of the entrance hall. The bedroom there which she would take was a small room in comparison to the ones upstairs, but big enough for her, and most importantly it was close to Jem's.

'It'll be fine,' she said firmly, and he nodded. She wasn't sure, but she thought he looked a tiny bit relieved. 'What about you?'

He gave a wry smile. 'If there's no competition, I'll have the one with the sea view from the window by the bed.'

It also had a view of her bedroom window, she realised, glancing out of it and looking up at the taller section of the barn. 'We ought to get some food in,' she said, trying to be practical and not think about his bedroom.

'I've done it. I ordered it on line last night. It's being de-livered in the morning between seven and nine.'

'Will you be here?'

'Yes. I thought I'd stay here tonight, start moving some things in. I ought to go into the practice tomorrow, too, and catch up on some admin. I can't just bail on them, and Jem seems to be improving steadily. I'll take you over there when-ever you like so you can be with him, if you don't feel ready to drive yet. Just tell me when you want to be picked up.'

'After the shopping arrives?'

He nodded. 'Sure. I'll come and get you from your place once it's here.'

'Or I could stay here, too,' she said rashly, and his eyes locked with hers.

'You could.'

But their eyes remained locked, both of them trapped, like rabbits in headlights, transfixed by the prospect of being alone together in this house.

Nick dragged his eyes away. 'Of course you could move in, start getting settled, and I could stay at home. And you could get the dog back from Chloe and Oliver. He must miss you.'

'But I can't really leave him alone here, he's not used to it. He'd be better in our puppy crèche until Jem's out of hospital, at least for the days. And I'm not sure how safe the garden is. I don't want him getting out.'

'There's a fenced area—I had a look at it this morning on my way to the agents. I couldn't get into the house, but I walked all round the garden, and the back of it's entirely enclosed to about four feet in height with sheep netting. He'd be quite safe. He could just run around and let off steam when you're here, and he could go to the puppy crèche when neither of us is around. And I can come over and help you walk him.'

'But you've ordered food. It should be you here, not me.'

'I can eat with you. You have to eat, too, Kate. As Ben said, I can wait on you,' he said with a wry smile, and she chuckled.

'I can just see that.'

'Let me try. You never know, I might be good at it. One of my hidden talents.'

She gave a splutter of laughter. 'Very successfully hidden. You've kept it from me for thirty-four years,' she said drily, and went back to the kitchen to acquaint herself with it.

She heard a quiet sigh behind her, and turned back to him, shocked by the sadness in his eyes. 'Oh, Nick...'

'I'm sorry,' he said, his voice bleak. 'It wasn't the way it was meant to be, was it?'

'What?'

'Life. Our plans.'

'We don't always get what we're expecting in life,' she said gently. 'I always thought you'd come back from university and marry me and I'd have your children. Instead you married Annabel, and I married James, and we couldn't have any, and you ended up with loads.'

'Was that why you gave up midwifery? Because it hurt too much not being able to have your own?'

She smiled. 'That and watching you and Annabel bring the children down here on holiday year after year when they were little. All the children I might have had if I'd been with you, and yet there I was with James, banging our heads against a brick wall. And then you moved back down here close to your family and got a job in Wadebridge and bought the house on Harbour Road, and I was falling over you all the time, a constant reminder of what I'd lost.'

He sighed heavily. 'Kate, don't. We can't turn the clock back.'

'No. But even if we haven't gone home together every night, I've worked with you for years now in the practice. I've seen you every day, spent time with you, so it hasn't all been bad,' she pointed out gently. 'You've still been part of my life. And I have Jem. You can have no idea what that's meant to me, over the years.'

'I can imagine. My children are infinitely precious to me, even though I haven't always seen eye to eye with them, so you don't have to try and explain.'

She smiled sadly, wishing that Jem had been one of those precious children, that she'd been their mother, but, as he said, they couldn't turn the clock back and if they did, it would all be very different. And so she couldn't wish it undone, no matter how hard it had been at times.

He came over to her, standing just inches away, and with the tip of a long forefinger he tilted her head up so she met his eyes. 'Don't be sad, Kate. We've got a chance now, if we choose to take it. Let's not waste it.'

A chance? For them? So maybe she hadn't misunderstood. 'I still don't know how good you could be at waiting on me,' she said lightly, and he laughed.

'Oh, I'm good,' he said, his eyes twinkling with mischief, and she sucked in a tiny little breath and turned away, before she did something silly, like kiss him. He'd kissed her last night, but that had been in the safety of the hospital, where anyone could have come in. They were alone here, and awareness of that and of him made her tingle with nerves.

'I'm looking forward to finding out,' she said lightly. 'So, are you moving in here tonight, or am I?'

'Do you want to?'

'Not alone. It makes me feel a bit nervous,' she admitted. She held her breath for a second, then said, 'We could always be grown up about it and share.'

His mouth twisted into something that could have been a smile if it hadn't been so touched with sadness.

'Grown-ups sleep together, Kate,' he said softly. 'And I'm not sure you're ready for that yet.'

Her heart hammered against her ribcage. 'Can't we have a little restraint?'

'Oh, yes. We can have a little. I just think it might take rather more than that.'

She looked away, his eyes too revealing suddenly, full of feelings that had been locked away for very many years. Her tongue flicked out and moistened her lips, and he groaned.

'Kate, don't,' he whispered, his voice almost inaudible.

The air was vibrating with tension, almost solid, as if she could cut it with a knife, and it seemed to have set all around them, holding them in place, their eyes locked again.

The sound of the doorbell was shocking, dissolving the air so they could move again, and Nick walked to the door as if he was in a trance.

He opened it and looked past the man standing on the broad flagstone path. There were three cars outside. His, and two others.

Of course. Kate's new car.

'Delivery for Mrs Althorp?' the man said, brandishing a clipboard and some keys, and he gave himself a mental shake and breathed in.

'Yes—thank you. Kate?'

'I'm here,' she said, coming to stand beside him. 'Is that it?'

'The metallic grey one,' he said, his voice sounding strained. 'You have to sign for it.'

'You'd better check it over,' the man said.

It could have had square wheels, for all the attention they gave it. Kate could see nothing but the look in Nick's eyes, he could see nothing but her tongue flicking out to lick her lips.

'It's fine,' he said, and she signed the sheet with trembling fingers and the delivery driver handed her the keys.

'Enjoy your car, then,' he said, and drove away in the other vehicle, leaving them standing there.

'So, will it be all right? The car?' he asked, trying desperately for normality, and she nodded.

Not that she was really able to concentrate on it, but it was exactly what she'd wanted, top of her wish list, and she was thrilled with it. She would be thrilled with it, just the moment she could get that look in his eyes out of her head.

'It's wonderful. Thank you, Nick. I'll look after it, I promise.'

'No. I'll look after it. I've bought a service package with it. It's got the next three years of servicing paid for. All you have to do is book it in.'

Her eyes filled. He seemed to have thought of everything, and she ought to pay a bit more attention to it after all his trouble and expense. She sat in the driver's seat, and rested her head back with a sigh.

'All right?'

'Lovely. Really good seat. Gosh, it's nice to rest my head. My neck's still a bit achy.'

He gave a short sigh and held the door for her. 'Come on, you need to lie down, and I'm going to massage it for you,' he said firmly, and, locking the car, he ushered her back inside and down the corridor to her bedroom.

'We'll need to bring bed linen,' she said, clutching at normality.

'Yes. What have you got on under that top?' he asked, and she swallowed.

'A vest top and a bra.'

'Right. Take the top off, leave the vest top on and lie down on your back with your head at the foot of the bed,' he instructed in a businesslike doctor's voice, and then he covered her with her top so only her shoulders were exposed, put a pillow under her knees, knelt down on the floor by her head and slid his warm, hard hands under her shoulders, running his fingers gently but firmly up the columns of muscle each side of her spine and up into her neck.

'Oh, that's amazing,' she groaned, and he said nothing, just kept on with the gentle, rhythmic movement until the tension had eased out of her neck and shoulders and she was utterly relaxed. Then he got to his feet and stood looking down at her, an odd expression in his eyes.

'Stay there for a while, have a rest. I won't be long.'

'What are you going to do?'

'Get us some milk from the Trevellyans' farm shop, and something for supper. I'll only be a few minutes, it's just up the road. Try and have a sleep.'

She heard the front door close behind him, and then the sound of a car driving away, crunching on the gravel. Odd, how they hadn't heard the other two arrive, but, then, she'd not been able to hear anything over the pounding of her heart.

She got up and pulled her top back on, lay down the right way up with a pillow under her head, and curled on her side, staring unseeingly out of the French doors at the courtyard beyond.

There. They'd managed it—been in a bedroom, had their hands on each other, even, and survived it.

They could do this. Behave like grown-ups.

Grown-ups sleep together, Kate.

'Not if they choose not to,' she said out loud, and closed her eyes determinedly. Before she knew it, she'd drifted off to sleep.

He wasn't long—just long enough to give himself some much-needed sea air and take Kate's new car out for a spin. He drove to the Trevellyans' with the windows open and the wind in his hair, and by the time he'd returned with the shopping, he was almost back under control.

He pottered round the kitchen, putting everything away while the kettle boiled and investigating the contents of the cupboards. It was such a blessing that the place was furnished as a holiday cottage and equipped with everything. It meant they only had to bring clothes and bedding, and they could pick them up later. Or whoever was staying would. He still wasn't sure who it would be.

The kettle boiled, and he made a pot of tea, left it to brew and tapped on her door.

There was no reply, and when he opened the door he saw she was fast asleep on her side, her hand lying open, relaxed, the fingers loosely curled. He stood there for a few moments, watching the slow rise and fall of her chest, and as if she'd become aware of him she opened her eyes and looked up.

'Oh. You're back,' she said softly.

'I've made tea. It's in the kitchen. And Mike Trevellyan sends his love.'

'Oh, you saw him.'

'Yes. And he'd heard a rumour about me and Jem. I told him it was true. He won't spread it further, but I thought he ought to know. And, anyway, they're Ben and Lucy's neighbours.'

'Yes, of course. So it's out, is it?'

She sat up on the edge of the bed and ran her hands through her hair, lifting it away from her neck and letting it fall, and he felt heat slam through him.

'It seems that way.' He walked away, heading back to the kitchen before he did something he'd regret. 'I've poured the tea,' he called over his shoulder, 'and I bought one of Fran's lemon drizzle cakes.'

She followed him, tugging her top straight and reminding him of what was underneath it. Not that he needed reminding, after kneeling by her head and staring down her cleavage for ten minutes. 'That's my favourite,' she said with a smile.

'I know. That's why I bought it.'

He slid a plate towards her with a generous slice on it, and followed it with a cup of tea, and she sat down at the table overlooking the courtyard and the sea and smiled again.

'I could learn to love it here,' she said.

He sat down beside her, propped his elbows on the table and looked out at the view while he bit into the cake.

'Good. Me, too. So, who's moving in when?'

'Both of us. Tonight,' she said firmly, and he nearly choked. He couldn't blow it, he reminded himself. It was too important, there was far too much at stake.

He could do this. He could.

Even if it killed him.

CHAPTER EIGHT

WATCHING Jem slowly recover his strength was both a joy and a relief, but unbelievably draining.

Every hour brought further progress—sitting up in bed, then sitting out, then standing for a moment on his right leg as he swivelled onto the chair for himself. It was like watching a time-lapse sequence of a baby turning into a toddler, but Kate was more than happy to sit through it. She was looking forward to seeing him walk again, to seeing him run, but for now, she was just glad he was alive and making progress.

And to know she'd be going home to the barn every night with Nick. She felt that if she pinched herself, she'd wake up and find it was all a dream, and the thought was frightening.

They'd moved in last night, collecting just enough clothes and linen to see them over the next few days, and then he'd cooked for her—not Ben's chilli, but a cold chicken and ham pie from the farm shop, with a lovely fresh salad and boiled new potatoes, followed by some utterly delectable honey and ginger ice cream made on the farm.

And they'd talked about telling Jem. Today. Later, after Nick arrived. He was at the surgery now, doing a clinic and seeing a few patients, and then he was coming over and they were going to tell him.

Somehow. She still had no idea how.

She went for a walk up the corridor to see Gemma and her baby while they took out Jem's catheter, to his relief, and then they moved him to the ward downstairs, which was for the children who were on the mend; it had access on one side to a courtyard with seats and toys and lots of things to look at, and on the other side, right near his bed, was the courtyard with the ducklings.

Five of them, they finally concluded, watching them peck about amongst the moss and bark chips, brown and yellow and fluffy and very cute. They watched them for ages, until at last the mother tucked them back under her wings for a rest, and he went back to his games console.

He was allowed other visitors now, and the first people to come in the afternoon were Rob and Matthew.

The boys had plenty to talk about and they left them to it. Rob took her hand and squeezed it fleetingly. 'How are you? It must have been hell—have you coped OK?'

She nodded. 'Yes. It's been pretty awful, but Nick's been great. Rob—there's something you need to know.'

He shook his head and smiled. 'I know already—I can see it in your eyes, and I'm really pleased for you. You go for it. I know how you feel. Your heart will never really belong to anybody else, just as mine won't, but at least you've now got that chance, and you have to take it.' He glanced at Jem, his head close to Matt's, bent over the games console. 'Does Jem know yet?' he asked softly.

'The paternity thing?' she murmured. 'No. Or about Nick and me. That's so new I'm not sure I know about it, really.'

He smiled. 'I think Jem will be fine with it once he's used to the idea. Is there anything I can do, anything I can get you?'

She shook her head. 'No. Just bring Matt to see him sometimes. He's going to be horribly bored. Oh, and we've taken a rented barn up near the Trevellyans' farm, with some bedrooms and a shower room on the ground floor, in case he can't manage stairs for a while. I'll give you the directions. Matt can come and stay later on, if you like. It'll give Jem something to look forward to when he comes out.'

'That would be really nice. Look, is Nick all right about this? He does realise I'm just bringing Matt to see Jem?'

'Yes, he does. And he's fine with it. He likes you.'

Rob laughed softly. 'That's good of him. I'm not sure I'd be so generous in his shoes. I hope you can make this work.'

So did she, but they still had the hurdle of the great reveal, as she was beginning to call it in her head, and she couldn't really think past that.

They didn't stay long, and Nick appeared soon afterwards. She wondered if he'd been lurking somewhere, waiting until the coast was clear, giving them space.

She didn't know. He'd been a little odd with her that morning, maybe because of the barn and being there alone together. She'd gone to bed early, closing her door quite firmly, and he'd gone up a short while later. She'd seen his light come on, seen it go off shortly afterwards, and she wondered if he'd slept as well as her. They were both tired, both drained, and he'd looked better at breakfast, but he'd been quiet, a little distracted.

'So, how's it going?' he asked Jem. 'Worked your way up another level yet?'

'My battery's flat again,' he said. 'I had to ask the nurses upstairs to charge it, but I don't know any of the nurses down here so I don't know who to ask.'

'I can charge it for you,' he said. 'We've got to go soon—we're going to pick Bruno up from Chloe and take him back to the barn and settle him in, so it can be charging while we do that and we can bring it back this evening.'

'Great—and then can we do the face thing on it, Uncle Nick?'

'Yes, I'm sure we can,' he said, and there was a flicker of

emotion in his eyes, just as there always was when Jem called him that. And Kate got a stupid lump in her throat, just as she always did. But maybe not for much longer. She felt a shiver of dread, and stifled it. It would be fine. It would.

He found the charger in the locker, and packed it up with the console and put it in her bag, and they went back to the barn, put it on charge and collected Bruno. He was so excited to see her, she thought the young dog was going to wag his tail right off, and her eyes filled with tears.

'Oh, sweetheart, have you missed me? I'm so sorry,' she said, getting down on the floor with him and hugging him, but he was too excited, and bounced around barking, and Chloe laughed and let him out into the garden so he could race round like a lunatic and have a mad five minutes with Chloe and Oliver's little bitch from the same litter of flat-coated retriever puppies.

'It's been a bit hectic on the puppy-sitting front this last week,' Chloe admitted when Kate thanked her yet again for her kindness. 'I haven't even had time to see Gemma yet—how's the baby?'

Kate smiled. 'Gorgeous. He's absolutely gorgeous. I had the nicest cuddle yesterday morning. One of the advantages of being a midwife—I can pull rank and sneak in outside visiting hours! But they were coming home today, so you should be able to pop over there anytime over the weekend.'

'Oh, I will, don't worry!' Chloe laughed. 'I'll give her ten minutes to settle in, and I'll be there. Right, young man, back inside and settle down, and then I think you're going to go to your new home. That'll be a bit exciting, won't it?'

Bruno wagged and leant up against her leg, tongue lolling and a big smile on his face, and Kate clipped his lead on.

'Come on, you big hussy. That's enough flirting,' Nick said, and put him in his crate in the back of his estate car—much, much easier to transport him in—and they drove back to the barn and introduced him to the house.

'It's a good job they don't mind pets here,' she said, wondering how much damage he would do, but he hadn't wrecked anything at home yet, and she hoped if he settled here quickly, there wouldn't be a problem.

'Can you put him in the crate, if necessary?' Nick asked, reading her mind, and she nodded.

'Yes, but I hardly ever use it, he's been so good. And I've got him a new rope toy to play with. That might keep him occupied.'

They took him out and let him run around in the garden, and he christened a few of the bushes and came back inside, flopping down in a patch of sunshine on the wooden floor of the dining room and watching them from under his eyebrows as they made a pot of tea.

'We mustn't forget to take this back,' Kate said, checking the charge on the games console while Nick poured the tea, and while she waited for it to cool and stared at the view, he cut them thick slices of the lemon drizzle cake and put one down in front of her.

'I'll be like a house,' she protested, but he just smiled.

'You haven't put an ounce on in years,' he told her. 'You work too hard.'

'Well, I'm not working now.'

'No, but you haven't been eating in the hospital.'

'That's rubbish, I've been eating junk food! Except for the pie last night, and that was hardly low calorie.'

'It was good, though, and let's face it, a little weight on you won't hurt. You'll just get curvier, and there's nothing wrong with that. You've got a beautiful body, Kate. Be proud of it.'

She met his eyes and saw the heat flicker in them before he banked it, and she felt tears clog her throat. He didn't know what he was talking about. Maybe once, but not any more. Not since her surgery.

She looked away. 'I'd rather not gain if I can avoid it,' she said, 'so I hope you're planning something low calorie for supper.'

'Not tonight,' he said with a wry laugh. 'Tonight is Ben's chilli, but I'll cut down on the oil and it's extra-lean steak mince. And kidney beans are good for you. Anyway, you'll love it, it's a great recipe—assuming I can pull it off.'

She raised an eyebrow. 'Isn't it a bit ambitious for you?' she asked, glad to get off the topic of her body. 'I mean, I know you're trying to spoil me, but we all know you're the king of the ready meals aisle.'

He laughed and picked up his cake. 'I don't know. We'll see, won't we?' He took a bite of the cake and put it down, then stared back out of the window, his smile fading. A quiet sigh eased from his body, and he turned to her, his eyes troubled.

'How are we going to tell him, Kate?' he asked softly.

She gave a helpless little shrug. 'I have absolutely no idea.'

In the end, it was easy.

Jem was sitting up in his bed when they arrived, waiting for them. They gave him the games console and settled themselves down, Kate on the armchair by the bed where he sat during the day when he was allowed out, and Nick on a hard plastic chair facing them, so they could both see him.

There was a child in a bed near Jem who was having a blood transfusion, and he looked around, his eyes tracking to his drip and up to the bag of blood running slowly into him. He watched it drip for a moment, then said thoughtfully, 'I wonder who my blood came from?'

She saw Nick stiffen slightly, and their eyes met. Was this it? The time? She felt her heart thump against her ribs, and he gave her an imperceptible nod.

'It could have been Uncle Nick,' she said quietly. 'Or Jack. They took some from both of them. You're B-negative—it's a fairly rare blood group and they'd run out, and you have to have the same otherwise it makes you very ill.'

'And you're the same as me?' he asked, looking straight at Nick.

She saw his jaw clench. 'Yes.'

'That was lucky. Are you the same, Mum?'

She shook her head. 'No.' His head swivelled back to Nick. 'So how did they know we were the same?'

'They tested you. I know mine, because I give blood regularly. So does Jack.' He hesitated, then said carefully, 'You inherit the genes that determine your blood group from one or other of your parents,' he said, and then waited.

Jem frowned. 'So—my dad must have been B-negative, too, then?'

'Yes.'

It wasn't strictly true. His father could have been AB, but they both knew he wasn't, and thankfully Nick didn't complicate it any more than it already was. Because the essence of it was already registering, Kate could see.

'And it's rare?' Jem was saying, a little frown pleating his brow, and she saw the muscle in Nick's jaw flicker again.

'Yes. Yes, it's rare. Less than three in a hundred people.'

The frown deepened, and his eyes swivelled to Kate's. 'That's weird.'

'Not really.' She could feel her heart pounding, and she swallowed before continuing, 'Jem, there's something you need to know, something I should have told you before.'

She saw the light dawn in his eyes, and he turned his head slowly back to Nick and stared at him hard. 'Are you my father?' he asked, his voice flat.

She saw Nick's throat work, and he nodded slightly. 'Yes,' he said, his voice gruff. 'Yes, I am.'

For an endless moment he just stared at Nick in silence, and Kate could see the pulse beating in his throat.

'But—how? I thought— Why didn't you tell me? Why

did you tell me my dad was dead?' he asked, turning back to Kate and spearing her with accusing eyes. 'I thought I didn't have a father, but if Uncle Nick's my father, I could have had a dad all my life! Why didn't you tell me?'

Her stomach knotted into a ball at the look in his eyes. 'I couldn't. Nick was married, he had a family, and I didn't think making them all sad would make us any happier, and it wouldn't have helped us. We had each other, Jem. We were all right—'

'No, we weren't! I didn't have a dad. I wanted a dad—I've always wanted a dad. But I thought he was dead, and all the time he was alive and you didn't tell me! If I hadn't had the accident, if I hadn't needed his blood, would you have told me? Ever?'

She swallowed down the tears. 'Of course I would. I always knew I'd have to tell you one day when the time was right, I just didn't know when that would be. We've been trying to work out how to do it without hurting you.'

He stared reproachfully at her, then at Nick again, and asked him a question she'd asked herself over and over. 'Why don't you want to be my dad?'

Nick flinched as if he'd been kicked in the gut. 'I do.'

'You don't,' Jem said firmly. 'When we were on the beach flying the kite, ages ago, after Christmas last year, that American lady said I was like my father, and I laughed, and you said you couldn't do this and stormed off. I didn't understand, but that was it, wasn't it? She realised you were my dad, and you didn't want me to know, so you walked away, because you don't want to be my father.'

'I do.'

'No, you don't!' he said, his voice rising, a catch in it. 'If you did want to, you would have stayed, you would have told me then. But you didn't want me.'

'I did want you, Jeremiah,' Nick said hoarsely. 'I do want you—more than you can ever imagine. But I didn't think you'd want me. The man you've always thought was your father was a hero, a brave man. How could I be as good as that?'

He stopped abruptly, turning to the window and propping his hand on the frame, staring out into the courtyard. Kate could see the muscles working in his jaw, see the tears tracking down his cheek, and she reached out a hand and laid it against his side in comfort. He closed his eyes and swallowed, and she dropped her hand and turned back to her son.

'Don't blame him, Jem,' she said softly. 'It was me who lied to you, me who let you believe my husband was your father. And Nick didn't know. I didn't tell him for ages, because of Auntie Annabel. It wouldn't have been fair to her. He's only known for two years.'

'So why didn't you tell him before? After Auntie Annabel died, why didn't you tell him then? You could have told him then,' he said, his voice accusing.

'I didn't know how,' she said softly. 'He was very sad and angry when she died, and he was very busy at work sorting out the practice. It wouldn't have been a good time. There was never a good time. I thought there would be, I kept waiting, but then—when he did know—'

'I tried,' Nick said, turning back from the window again, his face taut. 'It may not seem like it, but I did try. But James was a hard act to follow. I thought maybe you'd be happier with things as they were, with me just as Uncle Nick, just as I've always been. And I tried to spend more time with you, quality time, to get to know you and let you get to know me, and I thought we might be getting somewhere, but then that woman commented on us looking alike, and I panicked. I wasn't sure the time was right, and I was so worried I'd make it worse. And just when I thought we ought to try again, your mother met Rob, and they seemed to be getting on so well. He's a good man, and I thought he'd make you a good father, a much better father than I would. You all seemed to be so happy together, and I didn't feel I had the right to destroy that. What good would it have done, Jem? I could have ruined it for you, for all of you. I didn't want to do that. I didn't have the right—'

'But you're my real father,' Jem sobbed, his bruised face anguished. 'You should have told me! I should have known. I don't care if you're complete rubbish. It's better than being dead!' And he turned his face into the pillow and sobbed brokenly.

Kate leant forwards, resting a hand on his shoulder, but he shrugged her off, and she bit her lip and tried to stop the tears, but they fell anyway, coursing down her cheeks and dripping off her chin, and then she felt Nick's arms round her, cradling her gently against his side as he perched on the arm of the chair.

'Shh. Come on, he'll be all right,' he murmured, his voice ragged. 'He'll come round.'

'No, I won't,' Jem sobbed from the depths of the pillow. 'I won't be all right. Leave me alone! I hate you both! Go away!'

And then she felt Nick shudder, felt the pain tearing through him, and she slid her arms around his waist and hung on.

'Come on, let's give him some space,' he muttered after a few seconds, but she wouldn't leave him.

'I can't go. Not now. You go, leave me with him. I'll talk to him.'

'Will you be all right?'

She lifted her tear-stained face to him and tried to smile. 'I'll have to be, won't I? I have to do this, Nick. He's my son.'

A tremor ran through him, and he stood up. 'I'll see you later—I'll give you an hour. Call me if you need me to come back,' he said, and, closing the curtains around the bed, he walked swiftly away.

* * *

She watched him go, listened to the sound of his footsteps retreating, and then she turned back to Jem, biting her lip and wondering how on earth she could unravel this sorry mess of hurt and lies and broken trust that they'd created.

She had no idea. She just knew she had to find a way.

Tentatively, with nothing but love on her side, she reached out her hand and touched him.

'I'm sorry. I'm so, so sorry,' she said unsteadily, and after a moment he opened his eyes and turned his head to look at her.

'Why?' he asked, his voice breaking. 'Why didn't you tell me? I could have kept a secret. All these years, I thought I didn't have a dad, that I'd never have a dad. And then you met Rob, and I thought maybe he could be my stepdad, but all the time I had a real father, and I didn't know!'

'I know. But you do at least know him, even if you didn't realise he was your father. I've made sure you see him regularly, and he knows you, and all about you. I did everything I could under the circumstances. Don't blame him, Jem. It was my fault, too, and he didn't have any choice. I kept it from him too. And I'm so sorry we've hurt you.'

He sniffed, but the tears still welled, and, unable to bear it, she got up and leant over, taking him gently into her arms, and he burrowed his face into the side of her neck.

Nick held it together just long enough to get out of St Piran, and then he pulled over on the coast road into a parking area, got out of the car and sucked in a lungful of the fresh, salt air.

If he'd been that sort of man, he could have wept bitter, anguished tears for the son he'd let down and all the years that had been lost. Years he couldn't give him back, years that were gone for ever. But he wasn't, and so he shoved it all aside and concentrated his efforts on the future.

If it took him till the end of his life, he vowed, he'd do his best to build a relationship with this child.

He got back in the car and drove to his house. There were some things he needed to pick up, and he could be alone there, think things through.

Except he wasn't alone. Sam Cavendish was there, just coming out of his mother's house next door, and he propped himself against the fence and frowned at Nick.

'You look like hell. Fancy a drink?'

'No, I'm going back to the hospital. We just told him.'

Sam winced sympathetically. 'Ouch. How did it go?'

'Pretty much as expected. Why don't you come in? I don't really want to talk about it here.'

So Sam followed him into the house and propped himself up on the worktop while Nick put the kettle on, for something to do as much as anything.

'So—what happened?' Sam prompted.

Nick sighed and rammed a hand through his hair. 'There was a kid in there having a blood transfusion, and Jem was asking about where his own blood transfusion had come from, and it sort of followed from there. He's the same blood group as me.'

'Yeah, Jack told me,' Sam said. 'And how did he take it?'

'Badly. He's angry. He said he'd spent nearly eleven years thinking he didn't have a father, and all the time he did, and he said…' His voice cracked, and he coughed again and flexed his fingers. 'He said he didn't care if I was complete rubbish, it was better than being dead.'

Sam snorted. 'Well, I'd agree with him if my own wasn't so useless he might as well be dead, but what made him think you'd be rubbish?'

'I did. I told him James was a hard act to follow, that he might have preferred a hero. Apparently not. I didn't realise Jack had told you about the blood group thing.'

'Mmm. He was angry, but he's not really surprised.'

Nick's head snapped up and he stared at Sam, stunned. 'What makes you say that?'

Sam laughed softly. 'Oh, come on, Nick, everyone knows you've always loved Kate.'

They did? Well, why the hell hadn't they all reminded him of that in Freshers' Week when he'd been busy drinking himself senseless and making love to the first pretty girl who'd had enough alcohol to make her forget her common sense and sleep with him—the pretty girl who'd told him four weeks later that she was pregnant, and nine months later had presented him with twins, and then a year later with another son, while he'd worked his way through university supported by their parents and tried not to think about the girl he'd left behind. Had Annabel known she wasn't his first choice? Had she known he'd only done the decent thing and made the best marriage he could with the hand fate had dealt him? He sincerely hoped not, but if his feelings had been so obvious to everyone else, then why not to her?

And she'd sent him into Kate's arms, the night of the storm, almost as if she'd known that only Kate could comfort him.

'I tried to love her,' he murmured, as much to himself as to Sam, then he lifted his head and met Sam's eyes. 'I did love her, and I tried to be a good husband, and I think we had a good marriage, but maybe I was deluding myself.'

'I don't think so. I remember her—I grew up next door, don't forget. I spent a lot of time in this house. It was like a second home to me at one point. And she always seemed very happy, contented. At peace. She had a good life with you and a lovely family. I don't think you let her down, Nick. And she's been gone five years now. I think if anything you let yourself down, cheated yourself, and Kate, for too long. And maybe now it's time to do something positive about that.'

Sam shrugged away from the worktop, clapped Nick on the

shoulder and headed for the front door. 'I'm going home to my wife and child. And tomorrow we're going house-hunting.'

Nick followed him through to the hall.

'Why?'

Sam laughed. 'Because my ankle doesn't like the hill and Gemma can't lift the buggy up the steps into the house. And we need to be nearer my mother.'

'How much nearer?' he asked, an idea dawning. 'Like— next door?'

Sam's eyes narrowed and he tilted his head on one side. 'Next door? As in, here?'

He nodded. 'There's a barn. I've just moved into it with Kate, so that when Jem comes out of the hospital in a few days he can live on the flat for a bit until he's got his mobility back—assuming he's speaking to us by then. And it's for sale. We're renting it at the moment, but I think it's time to move on, time to lay Annabel's ghost to rest, whatever happens with me and Kate and Jeremiah. So I'm going to sell this house, and buy the barn, and then if it works out…'

Sam's jaw sagged slightly, and then he laughed. 'Really? You're selling? How much?'

He shrugged. 'I have no idea. It's the least of my worries. I won't cheat you, Sam.'

Sam grinned. 'I'll make sure of it. Talk to the agents—let me know. And I'll go and sound Gemma out, but I know what she'll say. She loves this house, and so do I.'

Nick felt himself smile as the weight lifted a little. 'I know you do,' he said. 'And it needs another family.'

And if Sam and Gemma bought it from him, it would bring his dream a little closer…

CHAPTER NINE

HE FOUND Kate in the deserted café, sitting nursing a stale cup of coffee and looking like death.

He sat down opposite her and took the cup out of her hands. It was stone cold, and he tutted softly and wrapped her hands in his to warm them. 'How is he?'

She shrugged. 'They had to give him some more morphine and something to help him sleep. I think it was all the upset…'

She trailed off, and he sighed, stroking his thumb over the back of her hand. 'What did he say? After I left.'

She shrugged again, a helpless little gesture that made his heart ache for her. 'He's just really shocked, I think. It's a lot for him to take in. I explained to the staff—the night sister and Megan Phillips. They were really nice to him. Megan, especially, was really lovely. She's such a nice girl. And I rang Jess Carmichael, and she came up and talked to me for a minute while he was asleep, and she makes so much sense. She's going to come and see him when he's feeling a little better and let him talk it through with her.'

'Do you think he will?' Nick asked, not sure about the idea of unburdening to a counsellor, but Kate nodded.

'I think so. He likes her. He talked to her before, when I was ill.' She sighed. 'Nick, I'm really tired, can you take me home?' she asked, and his heart contracted.

'Sure,' he said softly, and, helping her to her feet, he wrapped an arm round her shoulders and led her out to the car.

'So much for Ben's chilli,' she said as they went into the house, and he just pulled her into his arms and held her while the dog sniffed and wagged around their feet. She was exhausted, and she had to be hungry. He was—or his body was. His heart wasn't in the least bit interested in anything as trivial as food, but for her sake, he'd fix them something to eat and make sure she ate it.

'I'll cook us something quick,' he said, giving her a last little hug and letting her go. 'We can have more of the cold pie, or toast, or anything you want.'

'Toast,' she said. 'Toast and a nice, hot cup of tea. And it's cold—I know it's April, but do you think it would be possible to put the heating on?'

'Want me to light the fire?'

She glanced at the big woodburner and sighed longingly. 'Oh, that would be lovely. Is there any wood?'

He nodded. 'There's a pile out in the cart lodge, I'll get some while I'm taking the dog out. I'll put the kettle on, you go and sit down. You look done in.'

'Do you think we could have done things any differently?' she asked later, as they lay side by side with their legs stretched out towards the fire and its living hearthrug.

Nick stared at the dog and wondered what it must be like to have no responsibilities. 'In what way?' he asked. 'Do you mean the way we told him now, or if we should have told him years ago? Either way, I don't know. I don't think there was a right way, under the circumstances, but I wish you'd told me sooner, Kate. I wish I'd known, right back at the beginning. I would have made sure I saw more of him.'

'How?' she asked, turning her head to face him, searching his eyes and finding only confusion that mirrored her own.

'You were working in Wadebridge, living in Penhally, and I can see your house from mine—I could look across sometimes and see Annabel hanging the washing out! How were you going to spend time with him, under those circumstances, without arousing suspicion? And I didn't want to do that to you, to put you under that sort of pressure for something that hadn't been your fault.'

'Of course it was my fault!' he said. 'I heard you crying and I walked in when I knew you were naked, when I'd seen you, I'd undressed you—dammit, Kate, I knew what was going to happen if I opened that door.'

'Nick, I was falling apart, and so were you.' She lifted her hand and cradled his jaw, feeling the muscles clench beneath her palm. 'You needed me, every bit as much as I needed you. We were on autopilot—we didn't set out to make love, and if I hadn't got pregnant, nobody would ever have known.'

'I would have known. I never forgot, Kate. It haunted me—it still haunts me. And things with Annabel were never quite the same after that. I don't really know why, if it was because I'd changed, or because she sensed what happened between us that night. Maybe she even knew Jem was mine. I'll never know. But I knew when I walked through that door how dangerous it was, and I should have stopped myself.'

'And left me there alone, in that state? How was that right?' She leant over, closing the gap and touching her lips lightly to his cheek, then rested her head on his shoulder. 'I needed you, Nick, and you needed me, more than we'd ever needed anyone before. It wasn't your fault, it was just one of those things—part of being human. And you can't take all the responsibility for the fact that I got pregnant.'

'Why not? I know how the system works, Kate, and God knows I'd had enough object lessons in it!'

She eased back so she could look at him. 'Was Annabel on the Pill?'

'Yes.'

'So it wasn't unreasonable that you didn't think about contraception, because it wasn't a normal part of your sex life at the time. Nor was it mine. I didn't even think about it. James and I had been trying for three years, and we'd finally admitted that there might be something wrong and gone for tests, just a week before. We were still waiting for the results when he died, and maybe I should have told you, but how? Who would have gained?'

He sighed, and his arm around her back tightened a fraction and eased her closer.

'You're right,' he murmured as she rested her head back on his shoulder. 'It was an impossible decision, a no-win situation. There was no right way to deal with it, we've just got to make sure we do it right now. Maybe you'd better give me a script.'

'You don't need a script. Just rely on your instincts, Nick.'

'My instincts are fatally flawed,' he said drily. 'If we rely on them, it's a sure-fire recipe for disaster. And talking of my instincts, before I do anything else I'll regret, I'm going to take the dog out, and then I'm going to bed.'

She tilted her head and stared up into his eyes, held motionless by the sensual message in their rich chocolate depths, and with a ragged sigh he eased her closer and touched his mouth to hers.

She parted her lips, and he growled low in his throat and took instant advantage, the hot, silken sweep of his tongue plundering her mouth, sliding one hand around the back of her neck and threading his fingers through her hair to steady her as the other hand curled around her bottom and hauled her closer. Her legs parted at the pressure from his knee, and one hard thigh lodged between them, sending need shooting through her, turning her body to fire.

'Nick,' she moaned, but the sound of her voice seemed to

stop him in his tracks, and he pulled back, lifting his head and staring down at her, his chest rising and falling rapidly. She could see the hammer of his heartbeat in the hollow of his throat, and after an endless moment he got to his feet and walked away, calling the dog.

'Nick?'

'Leave it, Kate. For the love of God, just leave it,' he said rawly, and she heard the door shut behind him, the lights coming on automatically as he walked out of the back door from the utility room into the garden, the dog at his heels.

For an age she sat there, staring after him, her eyes fixed blindly on the closed door, and then with a fractured little sigh she got to her feet, put their glasses in the kitchen and went to bed.

They were supposed to be being grown up about this, she reminded herself, and so far it was only Nick who was sticking to the plot. How long that would last, she had no idea, but as she lay down in her bed, her mind went back to Jem.

How on earth had she forgotten about him? He was lying there in hospital, distressed and heartbroken, and all she could think about was making love with Nick, which was what had got them all in this mess in the first place!

It was a long, long time before she went to sleep.

The next day was very hard.

Jem refused to talk to Kate at first, and he refused to let Nick visit. After he'd got over his crying spell the night before, he'd withdrawn into himself, and the only thing he showed any interest in was Lucy's games console. It took him out of himself, she thought, gave him something to concentrate on, something to hide behind while his subconscious sorted out the wood from the trees.

So she just sat beside him, reading a magazine and waiting, and finally he cracked.

'Why did you lie to me?' he asked suddenly, and she put her magazine down and made herself meet his hurt, accusing eyes.

'I didn't—well, not really. I tried very hard not to, and I never actually told you that James was your father, because I knew it was a lie, and it was more a case of letting you believe something than telling you something wrong. So when you asked about your father, I told you that if he'd known he had a son, he would have been very proud of you, and that, at least, is true. He is proud of you, and he loves you. He always has.'

'But you let me think that James was my father. That was a sort of lie.'

It was. A lie of omission, and she nodded. 'Yes, it was. But it seemed like the best of some not very good choices, and I wanted to do the best I could for everyone. I didn't really know what else to do without hurting innocent people.'

'I'm innocent,' he said, and her eyes filled.

'I know. I'm sorry. It's a mess, and it's my fault, not your father's. You shouldn't blame him, he had no say in it.'

'Where is Uncle N—?' he asked, and then frowned. 'Mum, what do I call him now?' he asked fretfully.

She stroked his hair. 'I don't know. You'll have to ask him that. Whatever feels right. What do you want to call him?'

He shrugged. 'Dunno. I mean, he's my dad, isn't he?'

She nodded, blinking back the ever-ready tears. 'Yes. Yes, he is, but you must do what feels right for you both. I can't tell you that, darling, it's up to you. And he's here—I expect he's in the café. Why? Do you want to see him now?'

He shrugged his skinny shoulders again. 'Just wondered if he'd gone. He went home yesterday.'

'Because you told him to.'

'But I didn't think he'd go,' he said perversely. 'Not if he really cared.'

'Oh, he cares, Jem,' she said softly. 'He was really upset. He went because you asked him to, not because he wanted to, and that's why he's not here now, but he is in the hospital, in case you want to see him. And he'll be here, waiting, until you're ready.'

'Really?'

She nodded. 'Really. However long it takes. He wants to see you,' she told him, and she watched that sink in, watched the realisation that Nick did care, that he wanted Jem. Was here for him, any time he asked.

He didn't ask, not then, but later, when he'd obviously been thinking about it for a while, he lifted his head and said, 'This face-merging thing. Do you think it would work with him and me?'

She took a second to realise he was talking about the games console, and lifted her shoulders. 'I don't know. Probably. Do you want to try?'

'Maybe. If he's still here.'

She felt a great weight lift off her chest, and smiled. 'I'll find him.'

He was in the café, in a litter of torn sugar and salt packets, pushing a pile of white crystals around on the tabletop.

She sat down next to him, and he lifted his head and gave her a weary smile. 'Hi. How is he?'

'He's OK. He wants to see you.'

His eyes widened, and she could see hope flickering in them. 'Really?'

'Really. He was talking about the photo-merging thing. I think he wants to try with your faces.'

'Ah. That might need Jack or Lucy.'

'It might not. You might be able to work it out. You've got the instructions.'

He nodded slowly. 'I could try. Any tips or hints? For him, not the game.'

'Give him time. He's still angry with us, but more than that, he's confused and he needs time to adjust to the new reality of having a father. We all need time to adjust to it, but we'll get there.'

'Will we?' he asked doubtfully, as they left the café and walked along to the ward. 'I hope you're right.'

She sent him in on his own, and Jem looked up and gave him a wary smile.

He smiled back just as warily and sat down on the chair. 'Hiya. Your mum says you want to try the face-merging thing.'

'Mmm.' Jem fiddled with the games console for a moment, then mumbled, 'Uncle Nick? Can I call you Dad? 'Cos that's what you are, really, and it's what Jack and Lucy call you. But I'm still mad with you, though, for walking off and not explaining,' he added hastily, just in case he wasn't aware of it.

No chance of that. Nick's throat closed, and he swallowed hard. 'That's fine, I deserve it. You can call me whatever you want. And if you want to call me Dad—well, that would be awesome.'

His son rolled his eyes and grinned, looking so like Jack that Nick couldn't believe he'd never seen it. 'You can't say that, Dad, you're too old, you sound silly. And I am still mad with you.'

He gave him a wry smile. 'That's OK. We can talk about that,' he agreed, and blinked hard. He'd called him Dad—as if he'd been practising it in his head all day, and finally felt brave enough to try it out. Brave enough, and trusting enough.

He sucked in a deep breath, and picked up the games console. 'Right. Instructions?'

'They're here. Where's Mum?'

'I think she's having a drink and a bit of fresh air. Why?'

He shrugged. 'Just wondered. I thought she'd like to see this.'

'We can show her later when she comes back, if we can work it out. Or I can go outside and phone her,' Nick suggested, realising Jem was still scared. Still scared, and still needing his mother, but the man who'd been Uncle Nick all his life didn't have the power to fill that gap, and maybe never would. He realised that he was jealous of her relationship with him. So stupid. Of course he needed his mother, he was a little boy, still not quite eleven years old, for all his courage.

'Want me to call her? She could come now, I'm sure. She's not far away.'

Jem shook his head. 'No, it's OK. We can show her later, like you said,' he agreed, and Nick felt himself relax a little. One step at a time…

'We did it, Mum, it was amazing,' their son said by way of greeting, and she felt the tension ease out of her.

'Did you make it work, then?' she asked him, and he nodded.

'Yeah—come here, let me show you. And I'm going to look so like him when I'm older. It's awesome, isn't it, Dad?' he said, and Kate's eyes widened slightly and then filled with tears.

'Yes, you will be like him,' she said, looking at the games console as Jem switched from one face to another, the similarities striking. Her voice wobbled slightly, and she swallowed hard and avoided Nick's eyes. But he'd seen, and his hand came out and squeezed hers in support.

'Lucy sent me a text. She's invited us for supper. Want to go?'

She shook her head. 'No. I ought to let the dog out and I could do with putting some washing on before I come back here this evening, but you can go, if you like.'

'No. That's fine. I'll drop in and have a cup of tea with her after I take you home, and I could go and pick up my post—yours, too.'

'You can go now, Dad, if you like,' Jem said. 'Mum and me'll be all right.'

'Mum and I,' she corrected automatically, and turned in time to see the flicker of pain on Nick's face.

'Sure. I'll do the dog and the post and have tea with Lucy, and I'll come back this evening and take you home after visiting, then, if you're both sure?' Nick said gruffly, and then, after a fractional hesitation, he bent over the bed and dropped a kiss on his son's bruised forehead. Just a fleeting one, the sort of kiss he'd given his other boys in their youth, but he wasn't sure of his reception and when Jem slid his arms round him and gave him a quick hug, he felt the love swell in his chest and threaten to choke him.

'You take care,' he said gruffly, ruffling his hair with a gentle hand, and because he didn't want to leave her out, he stooped and kissed Kate's cheek, as well, in passing, and he was rewarded by her smile.

At least supper was sorted out, he thought as he headed back to Lucy's—fresh sea bass from one of the fishermen in the harbour. He'd been spotted turning into his drive when he'd collected his post, and Toby Penhaligan had pulled in behind him and given him two beautiful, plump fish straight from the sea.

'How's the lad?' he'd asked, and Nick wondered if he'd heard the rumour, too.

'Doing well, thanks,' he'd told him. 'He should be out of hospital by the end of next week.'

'I hear you've taken the barn for the summer.'

So the jungle drums were working overtime. No surprises there, then. 'For a while, anyway. I'm giving Kate a hand to look after Jem—he can't manage the stairs, so it seemed to make sense.'

He'd felt Toby's eyes track to the more-than-adequate family house behind him, and was hugely grateful that the barn was out of the way and might afford them a little much-needed privacy.

He'd gone straight there, put the fish in the fridge and walked the dog, then gone to Lucy's.

'So, how is he?' she asked.

'OK,' he told them. 'Good. He called me Dad today...'

His voice cracked a bit, and he cleared his throat and gave them a wry smile. They were gathered round the kitchen table, his two eldest children and Ben, drinking tea and talking through Jem's progress, and Lucy reached out a hand and squeezed his shoulder. 'Sorry,' he muttered, patting her hand. 'It got to me. But he says he's still mad with me. He thinks I don't want to be his father.'

'Do you?' Jack asked. 'Because I could understand if you didn't. I was appalled when India died and I was told Freddie was mine—talk about hurled in at the deep end. It really wasn't easy, but you've got to give it a go, Dad, because— well, he's the best thing that's ever happened to me, him and Alison and our growing family. But it was Freddie that turned me around, and he's given me so much.'

'I'm sure you're the best thing that's ever happened to him, as well. And I do want to be his father. I just hope I can do him justice.'

'Of course you can! It's not about being perfect, it's about being there,' Lucy told him. 'And listening. You could maybe do a bit more of that. But we were never short of love, and that's what he needs most of all. To know you love him.'

'I do.' He swallowed and tried to smile. 'He hugged me. When I said goodbye. He's never hugged me before.'

Lucy tutted again, and got up and came round and snuggled onto his lap. 'You soft old thing,' she said kindly, and he laughed and tapped her on the bottom.

'Less of the old,' he told her, and hugged her back, then frowned and looked down at her slightly rounded abdomen. 'Are you pregnant again?'

She blushed. 'Um—I might be.'

'I think you might. Congratulations. I take it this is planned?'

Ben's lips twitched. 'Sort of. She caught me in a weak moment. I think it's a ploy to be on permanent maternity leave.'

Nick laughed again. 'Come on, let me up. I have to go and see your little brother.'

Jem was tired—exhausted, really, after a busy day with two lots of visitors and all the upset of the previous day—and he was still getting used to being out in an open ward with six-bed bays, rather than his own quiet little side room, so Kate and Nick didn't stay late, and were home by quarter to eight.

Home, he thought, turning into the drive, and wondered how, in just a little over forty-eight hours, it could possibly feel like home.

Because Kate was there.

There was no other possible reason, and he ushered her in, poured her a glass of wine while she let the dog out and fussed over him, then scrubbed the new potatoes while she sat and sipped the wine and watched the last pink streaks of the sunset fade over the sea.

'Anything I can do?' she asked him, feeling guilty for sitting there, but he just smiled at her and carried on scraping and scrubbing.

'No. You stay there and enjoy being waited on. You heard the doctor—I have to spoil you.'

She chuckled. 'If you insist. So how was Lucy?'

'Ah, Lucy. Pregnant again.'

Kate smiled indulgently. 'Have you only just realised?' she said.

He rolled his eyes. 'Of course, you're a midwife. You notice these things.'

'That's right,' she said smugly. 'So, what are you feeding me for supper?' she asked, and he grinned.

'Sea bass, courtesy of Toby Penhaligan.'

'Sea bass? Really? Are you going to make the house smell of fish?' she queried, and he laughed.

'I shouldn't think so, the extractor fan's like a jet engine, I'll be surprised if it doesn't suck the fish out of the pan. I tell you what, while I do this, why don't you go and have a shower?'

'Do you mind?'

'Not at all. Consider it all part of your pampering,' he said, and his eyes raked slowly over her and he smiled. 'You could even wear something pretty.'

Pretty? Her heart thudded, and she felt a sudden flutter of nerves. He was looking at her as if...

Oh, lord. She wasn't ready for this. Last night she had been, but tonight, just like that, without the benefit of cuddling up to him and getting in the mood, she felt a shiver of ice slide down her spine. Nick wasn't coy, and he wouldn't be a shy lover. He'd want the lights on and access to every part of her, and she wasn't sure she could do this. Not now, and maybe not ever.

'I'll see what I've got. It might just be jumper and jeans,' she said, and headed for her bedroom, panic clawing at her throat.

He put the potatoes in the pan and glanced at his watch. She might be half an hour in the shower and then getting ready, so he had time to light the fire to give it time to warm up the room.

He brought some wood in, and while he was laying the fire, he heard a noise coming from the area of her bedroom.

'Kate?'

He walked down the corridor towards her room, and heard the shower running, and then a muffled sob.

He rested his head against the door. Not again. He couldn't do this again.

So he went into her room and stood by the window, staring out into the courtyard and listening in agony as she wept just feet away from him. There was nothing he could do—nothing he would let himself do—but wait until the crying stopped, and a minute later she turned off the water, then he heard the door open and she walked into the room, closing the door and then dropping her towel.

And then she saw him, and gasped, scrabbling for the towel, her eyes red-rimmed and wild with some unfathomable emotion.

He reached for her, shocked at the ravaged look on her face, the pain in her eyes, desperate to comfort her, but she wouldn't let him.

'Nick, no,' she said, pushing him away and trying to turn her back to him, the towel twisted somehow round her now. 'Please!'

'Don't be silly, I've seen you cry umpteen times in the last few days,' he said gently, his hands cupping her shoulders, but she shook her head.

'No—it's not that. Please, Nick, just go—'

She broke off, the smothered sobs returning, and he felt swamped by her pain, the light slowly dawning as he realised belatedly why she'd turned away.

'Oh, my love, my darling girl, come here,' he said tenderly, turning her back into his arms and folding her against his chest once more, his hands stroking her back rhythmically through the damp towel. 'After all we've been through, do you really think a few scars are going to make any difference to me?'

'They make a difference to me,' she sobbed, pushing him away again, but he wouldn't let her go this time, he couldn't, because the pain and fear for her, suppressed for nearly a year now, were rising up and choking him, and he cradled her tenderly against his heart and rocked her. Rocked them both.

'I thought you were going to die,' he said unevenly. 'I thought I was going to lose you, lose everything that kept me sane. You're my best friend, Kate, the one person who really understands me; the only thing that's kept me going is working with you, having you there near me, even if you weren't with me. I prayed so hard that you'd make it, even if you ended up with Rob—that didn't matter, just so long as you were alive, just so long as I knew you were somewhere in the world. Why the hell should I care about a scar?'

'Oh, Nick,' she whispered tearfully, and, resting her head against his shoulder, she slid her arms round him and held him. 'I'm sorry. I didn't even think about how you might have felt, just that you hadn't been there for me, but nobody was there for you. I'm so, so sorry.'

She breathed deeply, then looked at him again. 'It's just— Nobody's seen it, and when you said wear something pretty, I felt ridiculously shy all of a sudden, and I thought, what if it turned you off?'

'Kate!' he chided softly, gutted that she thought so little of him. 'How shallow do you think I am?'

'I don't. It's how shallow I am.'

He gave a ragged sigh and cradled her head against his shoulder. 'Can we start again? Wear something that makes you feel good. Something that makes you feel all woman, because you are, Kate. You're a beautiful woman, and I want to show you that, but only when you're ready. There's no pressure. I don't care if it takes months. Years. I want you, and I'll wait for you.'

She sucked in a breath and took a little step back. 'I'll see what I can find. Why don't you go and start cooking?'

CHAPTER TEN

'ANYTHING I can do?'

He lifted his head and smiled at her, but he didn't comment on her clothes, and she felt perversely irritated. 'You could top and tail the mangetout, if you're bored. And you look lovely, by the way. Beautiful.'

The irritation dissolved in an instant, replaced by a rush of heat and affection for this complicated and loveable man. He brought her the packet of peas, a pan and a small knife, dropped a tender, lingering kiss on her lips, and she sat at the table with a silly smile and trimmed the peas and sipped another glass of wine while he put the fish on to cook and prodded the potatoes. Music was playing in the background, something soft and smoky and sensual, and between that and the wine and the last streaks of the sunset fading into the night, it was the perfect romantic setting.

All she needed was her son back home, safe and sound, and her happiness would be complete. Once she'd found the courage to make love to Nick, at least.

Did he feel the same way about it? She glanced across at him, and saw he was humming softly as he worked. He looked happy enough. It was lovely to be able to sit there and enjoy all of the house without moving, she thought, and told herself it could be permanent, that they could stay there and make it their home.

'Right, let's have those peas. How's your wine?'

'It's fine. I don't need any more. I'm still on the occasional anti-inflammatory and I don't like to mix drugs and alcohol.'

'I thought that was what the modern youth did.'

'It is. I'm not the modern youth.'

'I'm thankful for that.'

They shared a smile, and then with a shake of his head, as if he was collecting himself, he turned back to his cooking and the moment was gone.

'That was gorgeous, Nick. Thank you.'

'My pleasure. It was worth being grilled by Toby Penhaligan to get those sea bass. They were gorgeous.'

'Did he give you a very hard time?'

Nick shrugged. 'The jungle drums are obviously working, but I suppose we should expect that. I think we need to present a united front, for Jem's sake, and if the gossip gets too much—well, who knows what the future might hold?'

His words hung in the air, and Kate met his eyes and saw a hope in them that must surely be reflected in her own. She wanted him. She wanted to be with him, to spend her life with him, and their son did, too.

And to do that, she had to find the courage to do what she had to do next.

'Nick? Will you do something for me?'

'Sure. What is it?'

'Will you make love to me?'

He froze, his glass suspended above the table, and after what seemed like for ever he set it back down very, very carefully and uncurled his fingers from the stem.

'Are you sure?' he asked hoarsely.

'Yes. Yes, I'm sure, but I'm scared.'

'Oh, Kate…'

He stood up and came round to her side, taking her hands

in his. 'You don't have to be scared. This is me. Why on earth are you scared?'

'Because—I just am. It's been a long time, Nick. And—well, I don't look the same.'

'You know what I feel about that,' he said.

'But it's not only about what you feel, it's about what I feel, and I feel—I know it's stupid, I know it's irrational, I've seen lots of women who've had breast surgery, but they weren't me. This is me, my body, and that makes it different. And illogical,' she explained, and he frowned slightly and squeezed her hand.

'I can understand that, but, Kate, I could have lost you, but I didn't. You're here with me, now, and that, at the end, is the only thing that matters. That you're alive and well.'

'And then there's the competition,' she went on, ignoring him. 'I'm not Annabel,' she said, pointing out the obvious. 'Or any one of the other glamorous women you've been seen with.'

He sighed and shifted to the chair beside her, lifting her hand and pressing it to his cheek. 'I know you're not Annabel,' he said gently. 'You don't have to live up to her, Kate. I loved her, just not the way I've always loved you. You were always my soul mate. You were the one I should have been with all this time. She was a lovely girl, and she turned into a kind, sensitive and generous woman; as a mother, I couldn't fault her. As a wife, she was perfect. We were good friends in many ways, but there was no great passion there, no desperate yearning. And as for the other women—there's only really been one since Annabel, and she has no expectations. I've seen her from time to time. Her name's Louise. We've had dinner, gone to the cinema.'

'Made love?'

'I'm not a monk, Kate. Neither am I promiscuous. The others have just been passing distractions, but I haven't slept with them. And I'm not going to beat you up about Rob.'

'What makes you think I slept with him?'

He shook his head and gave a wry smile. 'I saw you. I came to see you, last summer. I wanted to talk to you, and I pulled up outside. And Rob was kissing you, in the kitchen, right in front of the window. And then you walked away, and a light came on upstairs, and you shut the bedroom curtains. It wasn't rocket science, Kate.'

She felt sick. 'Nick, you weren't meant to see that.'

'Of course not. But you're adults, so why not? After all, we weren't going anywhere, were we, at the time, and he's a good guy. So—why not? It's what people do. I know that. And I can understand it, but it's all very well in theory, but in practice, I realised I was jealous.'

'Because even though you didn't want me, you didn't want anyone else to?'

'But I did want you. I just didn't know how to ask. I went to see Louise, after I drove away that night. I thought—what was sauce for the goose, I suppose. But, well, let's just say I think I was a bit of a disappointment to her. I couldn't get you out of my head, couldn't stop seeing you kissing him, and I didn't want to be with her. I didn't want to be with anyone if I couldn't be with you, and obviously I couldn't. So I went home, picked up a bottle of Scotch from the kitchen, walked down to the beach and drank half of it. I haven't seen her since.'

'So who was the woman at Ben and Lucy's barbecue last summer?' she asked.

'An old friend from London. She's divorced, she was down here on holiday, and she was lonely.'

Kate smiled indulgently. 'I think she was probably more than lonely, the way she was looking at you.'

He shrugged. 'I'm a good-looking guy—what can I say?' he murmured, and she laughed, as he'd meant her to. But then his smile faded, and he lifted his hand and touched her cheek. 'She was nothing, Kate. Nothing happened with her,

I promise. I can't dismiss Annabel, she was my wife, the mother of three of my children, a very important person in our lives, and I loved her. But there truly has been no one else who matters at all, no one who's ever claimed my heart or made me want to behave like an irrational teenager or a romantic fool. No one else who's been such a good friend to me no matter how badly I've behaved. No one else that I've loved the way I love you. The way I've always loved you.'

'Oh, Nick. What happened to us?' she asked softly, and he stood up slowly and drew her to her feet.

'I don't know. I just know that now we seem to have a chance, and I want to take that chance with you, Kate. Let me try again,' he murmured softly. 'I know I don't deserve it, but give me a chance to prove that I can be a good husband and father. We're stuck with each other for good now, anyway, as Jem's parents—why not do it properly? There's so much at stake here now—so much that's infinitely precious that I really don't think I can bear to lose.'

Her mouth dropped open slightly, and she stared at him in confusion. 'Are you—? Did I imagine it, or did you just ask me to marry you?'

He felt emotion choke him, and swallowed. 'I'm not sure. I think I might have done, but not just because of Jem. I can be a father to him whatever, if I get the chance, and that's down to him. And if he hates me, if he wants me out of his life…'

'He doesn't. He won't.'

'Then give me a chance, Kate. Let's wind back the clock and start again, only as adults with hopefully a bit more judgement and common sense and compassion. See if we can make it work this time.'

She studied him doubtfully. 'Do you think we can do that?'

'I think we can try.'

'Maybe.'

'Is that a maybe maybe, or a definite maybe?' he asked, sure his smile didn't reach his eyes because her answer was so important to him.

'I think that's a definite maybe,' she said, her smile slow, and he felt the tension drain out of him. And then ratchet up again another gear. He lifted his hand and grazed his knuckles gently against her cheek.

'I want to make love to you,' he murmured, 'but I want you to be sure that you're ready for this, because if you're going to change your mind, I'd rather you did it now.'

She gave a quiet sigh. 'The only thing that would change my mind is Jem, and he seems to love you. He's always been very fond of you, and now, knowing you're his father just seems to be strengthening that bond. So, no, I'm not going to change my mind, Nick. But I am still scared.'

He drew her into his arms and cradled her against his heart. 'Don't be scared, my love. I'll take care of you. I'll always take care of you.'

He let her go, then took her hand and led her slowly and carefully up the stairs to his room, closing the door behind them just in case Bruno decided to follow them, but he was lying on a rug chasing rabbits in his sleep, and she didn't think he'd worry.

'Do you want the lights off?' he asked, and she swallowed.

She had to do this. She had to be brave enough to show herself to him, to open up all her physical and emotional scars to him and trust him to heal them. But the lights...

'How about the bathroom light? We could leave the door open,' he suggested, and she nodded, ridiculously nervous now.

He turned back the bed, stripped off his clothes down to his boxers—jersey boxers that fitted snugly over his firm, muscular buttocks and thighs and did heart-stopping things in other areas—and then held out his hand to her.

She went to his side, and he stared down at her, his eyes sombre. 'Are you sure, Kate?' he said softly. 'We've had years to talk this up in our heads, and I don't want to disappoint you.'

'You won't disappoint me.' She knew he wouldn't. She didn't know how, she just knew. She went up on tiptoe and brushed her lips against his, then dropped back onto her heels and waited.

He unbuttoned the silky blouse she'd put on, the sheer fabric sliding against her skin as he loosened it and slipped it over her shoulders. He laid it carefully on the chair, then his fingers found the zip on her trousers and slid it down, the faint noise loud in the breathless silence. The button was next, and then they joined the blouse on the chair and he stood back and looked at her, standing there in her underwear.

'You're still a really beautiful woman, Kate,' he said softly. 'Come here. I need you.'

He held out his hand, and she put hers in it and went into his arms, closing the gap between them slowly, so that when their bodies touched, it was like coming home.

She rested her head on his shoulder, and he slid his arms round her waist and held her gently against his body, so she could feel the beating of his heart, the rise and fall of his chest as he breathed, the warmth of his skin, and as she lifted her head, his came down and his lips found hers, meshing and melding in a gentle dance that was filled with promise.

She knew he wanted her. She also knew he'd wait for her, give her time for her fears to fade, and it gave her the confidence to step back out of his arms and take off the last of her clothes, so she was standing in front of him naked.

And then she waited.

Her trust was unbearably touching.

He felt his eyes fill with tears, and because he knew she wanted him to, he made himself look down, to study the scar on her left breast, the fine line that ran round underneath it in the crease, the hollow left by the surgery that had saved her life. The skin was a little discoloured from the radiotherapy, but that would fade with time. And it was very neat. The doctor in him admired the surgery. The man wanted her, more than he'd ever wanted any other woman in his life, and if it killed him, he was going to do her justice now.

Her courage humbled him, and he gave her an unsteady smile. 'I feel a little overdressed,' he said gruffly, and skimmed off his boxers, tossing them aside and standing in front of her, wondering how he measured up to Rob and hating himself for caring about something so trivial. Well, at least she could see that he wasn't in the least put off by her appearance. In fact, if she kept him waiting much longer...

'Nick?'

He met her eyes.

'Make love to me.'

He lifted her carefully onto the bed, tutting at the faint bruising on her right foot, touching his lips gently to the little stain. He could imagine her feet trapped in the footwell, knew that if the fuel tank had blown, she would have died.

Don't think about that, he told himself, and moved up, skimming past her thighs, not allowing himself to linger till he reached her waist, then trailing his tongue slowly around her navel, dipping into it, teasing her till she trembled.

Then he moved higher, his hand cupping her left breast, pressing a gentle, healing kiss to the scar. She shuddered a little, and he moved on, his lips sipping and tasting the other breast, reluctant to miss a single inch of her. She moaned and arched up, her body image issues forgotten now, need taking over, the need that had haunted them both for so very many years. The purely sensual need that their one tragic night had never addressed.

He moved up until his face was level with hers, and kissed her as he'd always wanted to kiss her, long and slow and deep—heavy, drugging kisses that cranked up the heat and made his body burn for her.

And hers for him. She plucked at him, her fingers restless, her breathing light and rapid, almost hyperventilating. 'Nick, please…now,' she begged, and doing what he'd failed to do before, taking the time to protect her, he moved over her and thrust slowly, lingeringly home.

She gasped, her body bucking beneath his, and he locked his mouth to hers, plundering it as he drove into her again and again and again, until at last he could hold it no more and he let himself go, joining her in the long freefall into ecstasy.

The next few days were blissful.

The weather was gorgeous, and when they weren't in the hospital visiting Jem, they were at the barn, sitting under a little ornamental tree in the courtyard garden with the dog at their feet and drinking coffee or sipping wine, and every now and then he'd cook them something wonderful.

And his hidden talent for waiting on her was turning into an art form. He ran errands for her, spoiled her rotten, massaged her neck when it ached and then, when she was boneless and utterly relaxed, he'd make love to her.

They were slow, lazy days, days in which they all recovered from what had been a gruelling ordeal, and gradually they relaxed into a quiet, orderly routine.

He went back to work in the mornings, coming home to cook them lunch before driving to the hospital to visit Jem. He'd settled really well in the new ward, made friends, watched the ducklings grow and gradually, bit by bit, he was getting back on his feet.

Jess Carmichael had been to see him, and he was less angry with his parents, more accepting now that there had been valid reasons why his parentage had been kept from him. 'She's a wonderful person,' Kate said. 'I don't know how I would have coped last year without her. She's a miracle.'

She wasn't the only miracle. Lucy had formed a wonderfully close attachment to Jem, and on a day when Nick was there alone because he'd treated Kate to a pamper break, she brought the children in to see him.

'Hey, you've got the monsters,' Jem said with a grin, and Lucy chuckled.

'Annabel, say hello to Uncle Jem,' she said, letting go of her daughter's hand, and his eyes widened.

'Wow—I really am an uncle, aren't I? That's weird—awesome! Hi, Annabel.'

'We bringed you grapes,' Annabel said, handing him the bag shyly.

'That's because Grandad ate the last lot,' Lucy pointed out with a firm look at her father, and he rolled his eyes.

'Naughty G'andad!' Annabel said, and stared at them longingly.

Jem gave her some, and she settled down on the floor by the window and ate the grapes and counted the ducklings, while Lucy hung onto the baby and tried to keep him out of mischief.

'I can't believe he's a year old,' she said.

'I can't believe I'm a grandfather,' Nick said drily.

Lucy grinned. 'Oh, I can. Look at the grey hairs, Dad! But I can't believe Annabel's nearly two and a half. It seems like five minutes. Joshy, no! You can't have the grapes.'

'Gape!' he yelled, his little fist working, and lunged for them, slipping out of Lucy's grasp and cracking his head on the edge of the clipboard hanging on the end of the bed.

'Oh, I don't believe it!' Lucy wailed, lifting him up and hugging him while Nick looked at the little gash on the screaming toddler's temple.

'He'll live, but it needs gluing,' Nick said, pressing a clean tissue to the cut and holding it there.

'Oh, well, at least it's into the hairline,' she said with a sigh. 'Come on, Annabel, we're going to have to take him to see Daddy. Joshy's got a little cut.'

'Leave her here, she'll be fine with me,' Nick said, and she smiled gratefully and hurried along the corridor and out of the ward, Josh's screams fading as she took him further away.

'Joshy's screaming,' Annabel said matter-of-factly. 'He always screams.'

'He's a little boy. They get in trouble a lot, but he'll be fine,' Nick said with a reassuring smile, and sat down on the floor with his granddaughter and watched the ducklings.

'Oh, Megan, brilliant—are you busy?'

She wasn't, but she didn't want to hang around in A and E any longer than she had to. She'd managed to avoid Josh O'Hara so far, but she could hardly refuse to help Ben Carter. She stepped into the cubicle and smiled at the woman. Lucy. She'd seen her on Paeds, visiting Jem, and knew she was Ben's wife. 'Well—no, not really. What's the matter?'

'This is our son,' he said. 'He's managed to cut his head, and we could do with a hand to hold onto him while I glue it, but he's like an eel and the nurses are all busy.'

'I can do eels,' she said, conjuring up a smile, and she took him from Lucy, steeling herself against the warm, sturdy little body writhing against her.

'Shh, shh,' his mother said, holding his hands and kissing them and blowing raspberries on them, and Megan sat down and held the child's head firmly against her shoulder while Ben glued the little laceration.

'Did you make that kid scream loud enough?' a lazy, sexy voice asked as he finished, and Megan felt her blood run hot and cold.

Ben lifted his head and laughed. 'Yes, thank you for your concern. This is my son—Josh, say hello to mini-Josh. We even gave him your name, so don't be too rude about him. I take it you've met Megan Phillips, our paeds registrar?'

Met her? Oh, yes, he'd met her. And seeing her there, comforting the wriggling, unhappy baby, sent a shaft of pain right through him, stealing his breath away.

Megan looked up at him, a desperate pleading in her eyes, but she needn't have bothered. He was in no hurry to have the past dragged out for public consumption.

'We met the other day up on Paeds,' he said, being deliberately noncommittal, and to his relief his pager went off and he was able to walk away.

Away from Megan and the child, but not his memories...

Nick got back to the barn to find Kate there, home after her spa day relaxed, sleepy and looking utterly irresistible.

So he didn't even try. 'Good day?' he asked, snuggling up to her on the sofa, and she turned into his arms and kissed him.

'Lovely. I've been spoiled to bits. Thank you.'

'My pleasure.' He nuzzled her neck. 'You smell nice. Do you smell nice all over?'

'I don't know. You probably ought to check.'

She did, he discovered, although he got blissfully distracted and forgot what he was supposed to be looking for, and it was almost an hour later before he remembered about little Josh's accident.

He told Kate, lying lazily beside her on the big bed with the view of the sea in the distance and wondering when he was going to wake up and find it was all a dream.

'Poor little mite. You ought to ring and find out how he is.' She trailed her hand over his chest and propped herself up, looking down at him with a slightly bemused smile.

'What?'

'I find it really hard to believe I'm sleeping with a grandfather,' she teased, and he closed his eyes and groaned as she slid her hand down his ribs and kept going.

'I was a very early starter,' he reminded her, and caught her hand. 'Stop. I have to phone Lucy.'

'Mmm. You do. And then we need to go to the hospital. I haven't seen Jem all day, and I miss him.'

She handed him his mobile, and he rang Lucy.

'So how's the little hooligan?' he asked, and she chuckled.

'OK. He's running around as if nothing's happened. There's something funny going on with Josh O'Hara and Megan Phillips, though,' she told him. 'Ben doesn't remember him ever talking about a Megan, but she was helping with holding him and Josh came in and Ben introduced them, and there was a definite atmosphere. He said he'd met her on Paeds, but I'm sure there was more to it. Something in his eyes.'

'Don't go there, Lucy,' he warned. 'Lots of people have a past. Sometimes it's best left where it belongs. Just remember Pandora's box.'

'Oh, don't worry, I'm not going to say anything, but at least Ben's alerted so he can keep an ear open in case of trouble. You never know when Josh might need a friend.'

'You're a good girl,' he told her with quiet pride. 'You've got your mother's kindness. Give the kids a hug from me, and we'll see you tomorrow.'

Kate met his eyes. 'What was that about?' she asked as he put the phone down.

'Nothing, really. They think Josh and Megan might have a past, and not a happy one, judging by the sound of it.'

She frowned. 'Do you know, I was thinking the other day she looked sad and a little lost. Poor girl. Poor both of them, whatever it is.'

She glanced at her watch. 'Come on, Grandad. We need to get a move on.'

'You realise if you marry me they'll be calling you Grannie,' he said slyly, and her eyes widened.

'Well, that's a good reason not to,' she said, but he just laughed and got out of bed, hauling her up into his arms and kissing her soundly.

'Coming in the shower with me?' he asked, and she chuckled.

'Now, there's an offer I can't refuse,' she said.

They took Bruno in to see Jem the next day, after arranging access to the courtyard off the ward with the help and permission of the ward sister and Sid Evans, the ancient and very co-operative handyman, who was only too happy to let them into the garden through the locked outer gate.

Jem was delighted to see him, and Bruno, far from being over-excitable and boisterous, sniffed him cautiously, licked his hand and, when he leant forwards and brought it in range, his face, and then sat beside him, his head on his knee, gazing adoringly at him and moving not a muscle.

'Do you think Bruno realises he's not well?' Kate murmured to Nick.

'I have no idea, but if you told me that, I'd believe it. He's much livelier with me than he is with you, so maybe he knows I'm stronger. He knows I can take it, so he jumps all over me.'

'Yes, and you shouldn't let him! And am I imagining it or did I see dog hair on the sofa yesterday?'

He looked guilty, and she laughed and told him off.

'He's not allowed on the furniture! Especially when it's not ours!'

'He just wanted a cuddle,' Nick said, revealing more of the sentimental side of him she'd hardly known existed.

But there was lots about him she hadn't known. She'd expected him to be a skilful lover, for instance, but he was far more than that, he was patient, humorous and teasing and then, when the chips were down, shockingly passionate. She discovered highs she hadn't known existed, and she just hoped she'd never have to discover the lows to balance them.

Or maybe they'd already had their lows. Maybe now it was time for their highs, their time served, and this was their time.

She hoped so, because to walk away from this was going to be far harder than walking away from him before, and she'd thought that would break her.

But Jem wasn't home yet, and that was the acid test, whether he'd accept Nick being part of their lives, whether he'd accept his authority, learn to take his say-so without question instead of debating every issue to death. And Nick might have to learn to compromise, not something that was second nature to him.

Jem came 'home' three days later, to the barn, and Bruno was overjoyed.

He followed him everywhere, sat beside him, and had to be dragged off to go for walks. Long, energetic walks along the cliffs that helped Nick work off some of the unforeseen frustration. Because since Jem had been home, there had been no long, lazy love-making, no romantic dinners, no casual touches, random kisses in the kitchen, unscheduled hugs that had gone on to become something much, much more.

And he was climbing the walls.

Not that he was any stranger to sexual frustration, but having her so close, wanting her so much, needing her for so very, very long and finally having her there—it was eating him alive.

So he walked the dog, and he went to work to try and forget about her, and every time he came home she'd look up and smile, and the need would slam through him and he'd be back to square one.

But Jem was flourishing, growing stronger every day, and with the help of Lauren, the physio, he was doing strengthening exercises that helped to keep his body balanced. Kate was still not working, but she was driving Jem here, there and everywhere, loving her new car, and she brought him down to the surgery to see Lauren three times a week, and sometimes, if they were lucky, they could catch a few minutes alone together.

But even though that time alone was short, Nick had no complaints. The crooked little slab pot Jem had made her on the day of his accident always sat in pride of place in the middle of the dining table, and today she was arranging yellow tulips in it, a troubled look on her face, and he left the cooking and went and hugged her.

'He's all right,' he murmured, knowing the pot served as a reminder of how close she'd come to losing him.

'I know.' And she turned in his arms and kissed him, then rested her head against his shoulder for a moment before easing away. Just in case Jem came in. Just in case he saw them and it upset him.

They were very wary about that. Jem had forgiven his mother, her reasons for not telling him the truth had been understandable, but Nick's initial reluctance to accept Jem as his son had left deep scars, and although he called him Dad and seemed to love him, there was still a certain wariness.

But Nick couldn't wait any more—couldn't go on like this, living in the barn and playing happy families and hiding his head in the sand. Jem was now strong enough to go up steps, and soon would be able to climb the stairs. Which meant if necessary they could go home to their house, and he could go home to his, and life could carry on as it had been, with a few adjustments.

It would be down to Jem to make that decision, and it was time to ask him to make it.

So when he got home from work that afternoon, he went

and found him. It wasn't hard. He just patted the dog when he came to greet him, and then followed him when he ran off again.

They were in the garden, sitting in the courtyard under a tree, Kate reading a book, Jem doing a maths puzzle—in a book, this time, the games console having been returned to Lucy—and he looked up and grinned. 'Hi, Dad,' he said, and carried on.

'Oh, you're back early! I'll go and put the kettle on,' Kate said with a welcoming smile, getting to her feet and squeezing his hand in passing. 'In fact, I need to ring Chloe. Want to keep Jem company?'

'Sure.' It was, after all, why he was there, and this just made it easier. He smiled reassuringly, and she smiled back and went in, and he sat down beside his son and turned towards him, his arm along the back of the bench.

'Jeremiah, can we talk?'

He put the puzzle book down and looked at Nick warily. 'Why do I always get the feeling that when you call me Jeremiah I'm in trouble?' he asked, and Nick chuckled.

'You're not in trouble, son. Far from it. I want to ask you something—well, several things, really. First of all, and probably most important, are you happy?'

'What, here?'

'Here, with me here, with us as a family—all of it, really.'

'Oh. Well—yeah. The house is great, but I know it's only for now, but us—yeah, it's good. You're a bit stuffy sometimes, and you tell me what to do, but I guess that's just being a dad, and I want a dad, so it's cool.'

Hurdle one, he thought with a sigh of relief. 'What about your mother? Do you think she's happy?'

'Oh, yeah. She's much smilier. She's like she used to be, before she was ill, but more than that, too. Like she's really happy, all the time.'

'And do you think that's anything to do with me?' he asked tentatively, and Jem nodded.

'I guess. She watches you sometimes, and gets a soppy look on her face, a bit like when she looks at Bruno, but sort of more. And I think she likes it that we're all together.'

Nick felt a huge weight lift off his chest, but a sudden attack of nerves took him by surprise and he rubbed his hand over his leg, surreptitiously wiping his palm, flexing the fingers of the other hand.

'Um—there's something else, too. It's sort of a tradition that when a man wants to marry a woman, he asks her father for permission, so he has his blessing first. And your mum hasn't got a father, and her mother lives a long way away, and I was thinking, you're the man in her life, really. So I was wondering, if I wanted to ask your mother to marry me, would you be happy with that?'

Jem stared at him. 'You want to marry Mum?'

He nodded, and Jem frowned thoughtfully. 'So we'll live together always? Like a proper family?'

He nodded. 'If that's what you want, and what your mum wants. But it won't make any difference to you and me, really, because I love you, and you'll always be very precious to me. And I want to be a part of your life, whatever happens, so don't think that if I don't marry your mother, you won't see me whenever you want to, because you will. But we don't want to make you unhappy. We've done enough of that, for one reason or another, and we want to do the right thing now, which for me means spending as much time with you as you feel you'd like, and being with your mother if I can, because I love her, and I always have. I just couldn't be with her before. But if you have a problem with that, then we can talk about it, maybe find another way that I can spend time with her. It's up to you, really.'

'Wow. So if I say yes, we can all be together? For ever? Like a real family?'

He opened his mouth to say yes, but couldn't speak, so he just nodded, and Jem grinned even wider.

'Excellent! Wow, that would be epic! But no yucky stuff when I'm around,' he added firmly, and Nick had to stifle a smile.

Actually, no, he didn't. He grinned back, and said, 'Absolutely no yucky stuff at all. No PDAs whatsoever.'

Jem frowned in confusion. 'They're funny diary things, aren't they? Like phones and stuff all in one?'

'That's personal digital assistants. This PDA means public displays of affection.'

'Oh. Right. That's OK, then. No PDAs.'

'Except at the wedding. I'll be expected to kiss her at the wedding.'

His son's eyes widened. 'Wow—are you going to have a real wedding?'

'I don't know. I haven't asked her yet—not properly.'

'Are you going to go down on one knee? 'Cos she might like that. It was on a film, and she went all pink and blew her nose.'

'I haven't got that far,' he said laughing, 'but I'll bear it in mind.'

'And she'll want a ring.'

'And a house. Yours isn't big enough, mine's—well, it's in a very busy place, and there isn't much garden for the dog. But—how would you feel about living here? If we could buy it?'

His eyes grew even wider. 'Here? For ever?'

He nodded, and to his surprise Jem's eyes filled. 'Mum would love that,' he said unsteadily. 'And so would the dog.'

'And you?'

'And me,' he said, and Nick forgot everything about PDAs and yucky stuff, and, putting his arms round his son, he hugged him firmly to his chest.

'That's settled, then,' he said, releasing him, and cleared his throat. 'I'd better ask her.'

'I'll go and tell her you want to talk to her,' Jem said, getting up and limping hurriedly towards the house.

'Hey, Jem, I wasn't going to do it now—'

He turned. 'What? You want to wait? Why?'

Why, indeed. He smiled. 'OK. Tell her I'd like to speak to her. I'll be down the garden.'

He walked slowly down across the lawn to the fence, and leant on the top rail staring out over the sea in the distance, twisting a blade of grass into a little circle around his finger and plaiting the ends in.

'Nick? What's going on? Jem said you want me.'

He turned and smiled, and held out his hands, taking hers and drawing her closer. 'Clever boy. I do.'

She blushed slightly and laughed. 'Don't be silly. What did you want?'

'You. In my life. For ever.' He glanced towards the house, and saw Jem standing outlined in the window, the dog at his side. He'd had his orders. With a wry smile, he went down on one knee in front of her, looked up into her slightly shocked, welling eyes and, his son forgotten, he said, 'Kate, I love you. I've always loved you, through everything. You've been the one constant in my life, the rock that's always been there. I need you, but more than that, I need you to need me, to want me, to smile every time you see me, to open your arms to me because you want to hold me, to make me feel whole again. I don't want you unless you want to be with me. This isn't for Jem. He's another thing altogether, and I'll always be part of his life. This is about us, you and me, and how we feel.

'I know I'm not much of a catch—and you probably never thought when you fell in love with me that I'd be a grandfather when I got round to doing this—but will you do me the honour of sharing the rest of your life with me? Will you marry me, Kate?'

'Oh, Nick,' she said, biting her lip and pressing her fingers to her lips as the tears cascaded down her cheeks. 'Oh, my darling, of course I'll marry you! I've waited years for you—I'd given up hope. Oh, Nick, of course I'll marry you,' she said again, so he took her hand and slipped the little twisted circle of grass onto her ring finger.

'This is just for now, because Jem said you should have a ring, but we'll go and get you a proper one,' he said, and as he got to his feet and she fell sobbing into his arms, he turned his head and gave Jem a thumbs-up.

There was a cheer from the house, and she lifted her head and looked up at him. 'What are you doing?'

'He's watching us.'

She turned and looked at him, and held out her arms, and he limped down the path to them, meeting them at the edge of the lawn, and their arms wrapped around each other, the three of them together, laughing and crying and holding on, because finally—finally!—it was all going to be all right…

EPILOGUE

HE GAVE Kate away, their son, so proud, so serious, walking her down the aisle of the crowded church and standing straight and tall beside her, and, when the time came, he placed her hand in his father's with the greatest solemnity and then gave him the biggest grin she'd ever seen.

And Nick grinned back, and winked at him, and then they turned back to Jeff Saunders and made their vows, long overdue but so very heartfelt, and when Jeff said, 'You may kiss the bride,' she saw Nick wink at their son as he bent his head to kiss her, and a great cheer went up from the congregation.

Family, friends, patients—there wasn't a soul there who wasn't cheering this long overdue couple on their way, and Kate felt her eyes fill as Nick touched his lips to hers and sealed their vows with a tender, lingering kiss.

While the choir sang, they signed the register, Jack and Lucy their witnesses, and then turned and walked back down the aisle between all the people who'd come to see them do what should have been done so many years ago.

Her mother was there, mopping her eyes and smiling, and Nick's children, of course—Lucy, Kate's very pregnant matron of honour, with Ben and their children; Jack, his best man, with his growing family and of course Jem, fully recovered and fizzing with excitement and pride at his role in the proceedings.

Nick's niece Charlotte was there with her husband James, and Jess Carmichael, the counsellor who'd helped them all so much, with her 'plus one'. And of course the practice was closed, their on-call covered by an agency because everyone was there with an assortment of babies and children.

Showered with love and good wishes, they walked down between the pews, packed so tightly that Health and Safety would have had a fit, dozens more standing outside or crowded into the doorway, listening over a PA link, and as they came out into the glorious September sunshine, everyone cheered and showered them with rose petals.

Cameras were clicking, everyone was hugging them, and Kate thought she'd never been kissed by so many people in her life. All sorts of people. Friends, family, colleagues, but others, patients, neighbours, people she'd known all her life, people who'd taken this little broken family to their hearts and made them whole again with their kindness and acceptance.

Nick stopped and looked around. 'Thank you so much for coming. I'm sorry we can't fit everybody for the reception,' he said, 'but if you go up to the Smugglers' and see Tony, there's a drink there for all of you on the house.'

That raised a cheer, and in a blizzard of rose petals Nick and Kate walked down the path, through the lychgate and to the waiting car.

'You're coming with us,' Kate heard Lucy say to Jem, and they entered the car alone, Jem standing with his sister and brothers. The chauffeur handed them glasses of champagne, and as they linked arms and drank and the cameras were popping, the car pulled slowly away.

'All right?' Nick said softly, and Kate smiled back at him.

'Very all right,' she said, and kissed him again.

* * *

'Good party?'

'Fantastic party. It's a good party house.'

He chuckled and slid his arms round her from behind, nuzzling her neck. 'No doubt we'll regret that when he's seventeen,' he said wryly, and she laughed.

'We'll get over it.' She turned in his arms, lifting her face up and kissing him softly in the moonlight. 'I want to be alone with you. It's been utterly fabulous, but I just want them to go now. Is that really selfish of me?'

He laughed quietly. 'No, not at all. I feel just the same. I love them all to bits, but I want them to go now.'

'So how do we get rid of them all?'

'We don't, Jack does. I've bribed him. We're having the kids for them next weekend when they go away. And when the coach turns into a pumpkin, he's kicking them all out. He said we should have gone away, but why would we, when we live here, in this beautiful place? We've waited all our lives for this. I don't want to run away from it.'

'Nor do I, but I wish they would.'

There was a quiet cough, and she looked up to see Jack standing a few feet away, an indulgent smile on his face. 'You need to come for the last dance, and say goodbye,' he told them, and so they went into the marquee on the lawn, swirling round the dance floor one last time before they saw their guests off, closed the front door behind them and turned.

'It's a mess!' Kate wailed, but Nick just scooped her up in his arms and carried her up the stairs.

'It's fine,' he said firmly. 'We're going to Ben and Lucy's for lunch tomorrow with Jack and Alison and all the children, and the catering team's coming back to sort it. You don't have to do a thing. And besides, you're busy.'

'I am?'

'Oh, yes.'

She gave a slow smile.

'I do love it when you're masterful, Dr T.,' she said, and kissed him...

ST PIRAN'S:
RESCUING PREGNANT
CINDERELLA

CAROL MARINELLI

CHAPTER ONE

'I'M READY to come back to St Piran's.'

No words filled the silence, there was no quick response to her statement, so Izzy ploughed on, determined to make a good impression with Jess, the hospital counsellor. 'I'm really looking forward to being back at work.' Izzy's voice was upbeat. 'I know that a few people have suggested that I wait till the baby is born, I mean, given that I can only work for a couple of months, but I really think that this is the right thing for me.'

Still Jess said nothing, still Izzy argued to the silence. 'I'm ready to move on with my life. I've put the house on the market….' She felt as if she were at an interview, effectively she *was* at an interview. After the terrible events of four months ago, Ben Carter, the senior consultant in A and E, had told her to take all the time she needed before she came back to the unit where she worked as an emergency registrar.

It would have been far easier to not come back, and at nearly twenty-eight weeks pregnant she'd had every reason to put it off, but Izzy had finally taken the plunge, and instead of ringing Ben to tell him her decision, she had dropped by unannounced. But to her surprise, instead of welcoming her back with open arms, Ben had gently but firmly informed her that it would be *preferable* if she see one of the hospital counsellors.

'I'm fine!' Izzy had said. 'I don't need to see a counsellor.'

'You are seeing someone, though?' Ben had correctly interpreted the beat of silence.

'I was.' Izzy had swallowed. 'But I'm fine now.'

'Good!' Ben had clipped. 'Then you won't have a problem speaking with someone else.'

'Ben!' Izzy had hardly been able to contain her fury. 'It's been four months! You know me—'

'Izzy!' Ben had interrupted, refusing to be manipulated. 'I worked with you daily, I've been to your home, I got on well with Henry and yet I had no idea what you were going through, so, no, I'm not convinced I do know you or that you'd come to me if you had a problem.'

Izzy had sat with pursed lips. Ben could be so incredibly kind yet so incredibly tough too—he would let nothing jeopardise the safety of his patients or his staff and he was also completely honest and open, so open it actually hurt to hear it sometimes. 'I've spoken with my senior colleagues…'

'You've discussed me?'

'Of course,' Ben had replied. 'And we all agree that coming back to A and E after all you've been through is going to be tough, that we need to look out for you, and rather than us asking every five minutes if you're okay, which I know will drive you crazy, I'm going to insist that you see someone. I can page Jess Carmichael—she's good, all very informal, you can go for a walk, have a coffee…'

'I'm not sitting in the canteen, chatting about my life!' Izzy had bristled. 'I'll see her in her office.'

'Fine,' Ben had responded, and then his voice had softened. 'We want what's best for you Izzy.'

So here she was, on a Friday lunchtime, just before her first shift back, *again* sitting in a counsellor's office, telling the same thing to Jess that she had to Ben, to her mother, to her friends, that she was fine.

Fine!

'It's often suggested,' Jess said, when Izzy had told her that her house was on the market, 'that people wait twelve months after a bereavement before making any major life changes.'

'I'm twenty-eight weeks pregnant!' Izzy gave a tight smile. 'I'd suggest that change is coming whether I'm ready or not. Look…' She relented a touch because Jess was nothing other than nice. 'I don't want to bring the baby home to that house—there are just too many memories. I really want a new home by the time the baby comes.'

'I can understand that,' Jess said. 'Have you people to help you with moving?'

'Plenty,' Izzy said, 'Now I just need someone to make a half-decent offer on the house.'

'How will you feel—' Jess had a lovely soft Scottish accent, but her direct words hit a very raw spot '—when a domestic abuse case comes into the department?'

Izzy paused for a moment to show she was giving the question due thought then gave her carefully prepared answer, because she'd known this would be asked. 'The same as I'll feel if a pregnant woman comes into the department or a widow—I'll have empathy for them, but I'm certainly not going to be relating everything to myself.'

'How can you not? Izzy, you've been through the most awful experience,' Jess said and even her lilting voice couldn't soften the brutal facts. 'You tried to end a violent, abusive relationship to protect the child you are carrying, and your husband beat you and in his temper drove off and was killed. It's natural to feel—'

'You have no idea how I feel,' Izzy interrupted, doing her best to keep her voice even, a trip down memory lane was the last thing she needed today. 'I don't want the "poor Izzy" line and I don't want your absolution and for you to tell me that none of this was my fault.'

'I'm not trying to.'

'I've dealt with it,' Izzy said firmly. 'Yes, it was awful, yes, it's going to be hard facing everyone, but I'm ready for it. I'm ready to resume my life.'

Only Jess didn't seem so sure, Izzy could tell. She had made such an effort for this day—she was immaculately dressed in a grey shift dress with black leggings and black ballet pumps, her blonde short hair, teased into shape, and large silver earrings adding a sparkle to her complexion. She had been hoping to look every inch a modern professional woman, who just happened to be pregnant. She would not let Jess, let anyone, see behind the wall she had built around herself—it was the only way she knew to survive.

Jess gave her some coping strategies, practised deep

breathing with her, told her to reach out a bit more to friends and Izzy ran a hand through her gamine-cut blonde hair that had once been long and lush but which she'd cut in a fit of anger. Just when Izzy thought the session was over, Jess spoke again.

'Izzy, nothing can dictate what comes into Emergency, that's the nature of the job.' Jess paused for a moment before continuing. 'No matter what is going on in your life, no matter how difficult your world is right now, you have to be absolutely ready to face whatever comes through the doors. If you feel that you'd rather—'

'Are you going to recommend that I be sent to Outpatients?' Izzy challenged, her grey eyes glittering with tears that so desperately needed to be shed but had, for so long, been held back. 'Or perhaps I can do a couple of months doing staff immunisations—'

'Izzy—' Jess broke in but Izzy would not be silenced.

'I'm a good doctor. I would never compromise my patients' safety. If I didn't feel ready to face A and E, I wouldn't have come back.' She gave an incredulous laugh. 'Everyone seems to be waiting for me to fall apart.' She picked up her bag and headed for the door. 'Well, I'm sorry to disappoint you all, but I refuse to.'

Izzy was a good doctor, of that Jess had no doubt.

As she wrote her notes, she was confident, more than confident, that Izzy would do the right thing by her patients, that she was more than capable to be working in Emergency. But at what cost to herself? Jess thought, resting back in her chair and closing her eyes for a moment.

Jess wanted to send a memo to the universe to insist only gentle, easy patients graced Izzy's path for a little while.

Only life wasn't like.

Jess clicked on her pen and finished writing up her notes, worried for her client and wishing more progress had been made.

Izzy Bailey, while still fighting the most enormous private battle, was stepping straight back into the front line.

CHAPTER TWO

'OBSTETRIC Team to Emergency.'

Izzy heard the chimes as she tossed her coffee and sandwich wrapper in the bin and did a little dance at the sliding door that refused to acknowledge her, no matter how many times she swiped her card. An impatient nurse behind her took over, swiping her own card, and Izzy tailgated her in.

They'd start her in Section B.

Of that she was sure.

Writing up tetanus shots and suturing, examining ankles and wrists... Despite her assured words to Jess earlier, Izzy was actually hoping for a gentle start back and was quietly confident that Ben would have arranged for one.

'Obstetric team to Emergency.'

The chimes sounded again, but Izzy wasn't fazed. It was a fairly familiar call—frenzied fathers-to-be often lost their way and ended up bringing their wives to Emergency rather than Maternity.

Izzy glanced at her watch.

In ten minutes she'd be starting her first shift...

Walking through another set of sliding doors, which this time opened without the use of her card, Izzy found herself in the inner sanctum of the emergency unit.

She'd timed it well, Izzy thought to herself.

By the time she'd put her bag in her locker, it would be almost time to start, which meant that she could bypass the staffroom, the small talk...

'Izzy!' Beth, an RN she'd worked with over the years, was racing past. 'Cubicle four... Everyone's tied up... She just presented...'

Except Jess *had* been right.

There would be no gentle easing in, Izzy fast realised as Les, the porter, relieved her of her bag. Beth brought her up to speed as best she could in short rapid sentences as they sped across the unit.

'About twenty-three weeks pregnant, though she's vague on dates,' the rapid handover went on. 'She won't make it to Maternity, I've put out a call...'

'Who's seen her?' Izzy asked as she squirted some alcohol rub on her hands.

'You,' came Beth's response

Oh, yes!

She'd forgotten just how unforgiving Emergency could be at times. Just then she saw Ben, wrapping a plastic apron around himself, and Izzy was quite sure he'd take over and usher her off to Section B.

'Have you got this?' Ben said instead, calling over his shoulder as he sped off to Resus.

'Sure!'

'Her name's Nicola,' Beth said as Izzy took one, very quick, deep breath and stepped in.

'Hi, there Nicola. I'm Izzy Bailey, the emergency registrar.' Izzy wasn't sure who looked more petrified, the student nurse who'd been left with the patient while Beth had dashed for a delivery pack or the mother-to-be who brought Izzy up to date with her rapid progress even before Izzy had time to ask more questions—it was Nicola who pulled back the sheet.

'It's coming.'

'Okay.' Izzy pulled on some gloves as Beth opened the delivery pack, Nicola was in no state to be sped across the floor to Resus. 'Let Resus know to expect the baby,' Izzy said. 'Tell them to get a cot ready.' She took a steadying breath. 'Emergency-page the paediatric team.'

'Vivienne!' Beth instructed the student nurse to carry out Izzy's instructions, and Vivienne sped off.

'There's going to be a lot of overhead chimes,' Izzy explained to Nicola, 'but that's just so we can get the staff we need down here quickly for your baby.'

The membrane was intact, Izzy could see it bulging, and she used those few seconds to question her patient a little more, but there were no straightforward answers.

'I only found out last week. I've got a seven-month-old, I'm breastfeeding…'

'Have you had an ultrasound?' Izzy asked.

'She's just come from there,' Beth said for Nicola, but, as was so often the case in Emergency, a neat list of answers rarely arrived with the patient. They would have to be answered later, because this baby was ready to be born.

He slipped into the world a few seconds later, just as

a breathless midwife arrived from Maternity and the overhead speaker chimed its request for the paediatric team to come to Emergency. He was still wrapped in the membrane that should have embraced him for many months more and Izzy parted it, using balloon suction to clear his airway. He was pale and stunned, but stirring into life as Izzy cut the cord. Though outwardly calm, her heart was hammering, because difficult decisions lay ahead for this tiny little man.

'You have a son,' Izzy said, wrapping him up and holding him up briefly for Nicola to see. Though seconds counted in the race for his life, Izzy made one of the many rapid decisions her job entailed and brought the baby up to the mother's head, letting her have a brief glimpse of him. Nicola kissed his little cheek, telling him that she loved him, but those few brief seconds were all there was time for.

Beth had already raced over to Resus, and Izzy left Nicola in the safe hands of the midwife and student nurse as she walked quickly over to Resus holding the infant. A man, dressed in black jeans and a T-shirt, joined her. Walking alongside her, he spoke with a heavy accent.

'What do we know?'

'Mum's dates are hazy,' Izzy said, and though he had no ID on him, there was an air of authority to him that told her this was no nosey relative. 'About twenty-three weeks.'

'Mierda!' Izzy more than understood his curse—she was thinking the same—this tiny baby hovered right on the edge of viability. At this stage of pregnancy every

day *in utero* mattered, but now he was in their hands and they could only give the tiny baby their best care and attention.

'Diego.' Beth looked up from the warming cot she was rapidly preparing. 'That was quick.' The chimes had only just stopped summoning the staff, but he answered in that rich accent, and Izzy realised he was Spanish.

'I was just passing on my way for a late shift.' He had taken the baby from Izzy and was already getting to work, skilfully suctioning the airway as Izzy placed red dots on the baby's tiny chest. 'I heard the call and I figured you could use me.'

They certainly could!

His large hands were rubbing the baby, trying to stimulate it, and Izzy was incredibly grateful he was there. His dark hair was wet so he must have stepped straight out of the shower before coming to work. He had gone completely overboard on the cologne, the musky scent of him way too heavy for a hospital setting. Still, she was very glad he was there. As an emergency doctor, Izzy was used to dealing with crises, but such a premature baby required very specific skills and was terrifying to handle—Diego was clearly used to it and it showed.

'Diego's the neonatal…' Beth paused. 'What *is* your title, Diego?'

'They are still deciding! Sorry…' Dark brown eyes met Izzy's and amidst controlled chaos he squeezed in a smile. 'I should have introduced myself. I'm Nurse Manager on the neonatal unit.'

'I guessed you weren't a passing relative,' Izzy said, but he wasn't listening, his concentration back on the baby. He was breathing, but his chest was working hard, bubbles at his nose and lips, and his nostrils were flaring as he struggled to drag in oxygen.

'We need his history,' Diego said as he proceeded to bag the baby, helping him to breathe. He was skilled and deft and even though the team was just starting to arrive he already had this particular scene under control. 'You're late.' Diego managed dry humour as the anaesthetist rushed in along with the on-call obstetrician and then Izzy's colleague and friend Megan.

Her fragile looks defied her status. Megan was a paediatric registrar and was the jewel in the paediatric team—fighting for her charges' lives, completely devoted to her profession. Her gentle demeanour defied her steely determination when a life hung in the balance.

Megan would, Izzy knew, give the baby every benefit of every doubt.

'Ring NICU.' This was Diego, giving orders, even though it wasn't his domain. They urgently needed more equipment. Even the tiniest ET tube was proving too big for this babe and feeling just a touch superfluous as Megan and Diego worked on, it was Izzy who made the call to the neonatal intensive care unit, holding the phone to Diego's ear as he rapidly delivered his orders.

Though Megan's long brown hair was tied back, the run from the children's ward had caused a lock to come loose and she gave a soft curse as she tried to concentrate on getting an umbilical line into the baby.

'Here,' Izzy said, and sorted out her friend's hair.

'*About* twenty-three weeks, Megan.' Diego said it as

a warning as the baby's heart rate dipped ominously low, but his warning was vital.

'We don't know anything for sure!' Megan words were almost chanted as she shot a warning at Diego. 'I'll do a proper maturation assessment once he's more stable. Izzy, can you start compressions while I get this line in?'

Diego was pulling up the minuscule drug dosages; the anaesthetist taking over in helping the tiny baby to breathe. The baby was so small Izzy compressed the chest rapidly with two fingers, hearing the rapid rhythm on the monitor.

'Nice work.' Megan was always encouraging. The umbilical line in, she took the drugs from Diego and shot them into the little body as Izzy carried on with compressions for another full minute.

'Let's see what we've got.' Megan put a hand up to halt Izzy and the babe's heart rate was up now close to a hundred. There were more staff arriving and a large incubator had arrived from the neonatal unit along with more specialised equipment, but until the baby was more stable it wouldn't be moved up to the first-floor NICU. 'We're going to be here for a while.' Megan gave Izzy a grim smile. 'Sorry to take up all your space.'

'Go right ahead,' Izzy said.

'How are things?' an unfamiliar face came in. 'Ben asked me check in—I'm Josh, A and E consultant.' She'd heard there was a new consultant, that he was Irish and women everywhere were swooning, but no one was swooning here! Izzy couldn't really explain it, but suddenly the mood in the room changed. Izzy wondered if perhaps if Josh's popularity had plummeted, because there was certainly a chill in the air.

'It's all under control.' It was Izzy who broke the strange silence. 'Though the babe might be here for a while.'

'How many weeks?' Josh's voice was gruff, his navy eyes narrowing as he looked down at the tiny infant.

'We're not sure yet,' Megan responded. 'Mum was in Ultrasound when she went into labour.'

'We need to find out.' Josh's was the voice of reason. Before there were any more heroics, some vital facts needed to be established. 'Do you want me to speak with Mum?'

'I'll be the one who speaks with the mother.' Megan's voice was pure ice. 'But right now I'm a bit tied up.'

'There's a full resuscitation taking place in my department on a baby that may not be viable—we need to find out what the mother wants.'

Megan looked up and Izzy was shocked at the blaze of challenge in them. 'It's not like it was eight years ago. We don't wrap them in a blanket now and say we can't do anything for them.'

'I'll tell you what!' A thick Spanish accent waded into the tense debate and abruptly resolved it. 'While you two sort out your own agenda, why don't you…' he looked over at Izzy '…go and speak with the mother? You have already met her, after all. See if you can clarify the dates a bit better—let her know just how ill the baby is and find out if someone can pull up her ultrasound images.'

'Sure!'

She was more than grateful for Diego's presence, and not just for the baby—Izzy hadn't known what was happening in there. She'd never seen Megan like that! Her response had been a blatant snub to Josh's offer to speak with the mother, but Izzy didn't have time to dwell on it—instead she had a most difficult conversation in front of her.

'I don't know...' Nicola sobbed as Izzy gently questioned her. 'My periods are so irregular and it's my fourth baby, I was breast feeding...'

'The doctors will go through your scans and assess your baby and try to get the closest date we can,' Izzy said gently, 'but I have to tell you that things aren't looking very good for your son.' Izzy suddenly felt guilty talking about this to the mother when she was pregnant herself, and was incredibly grateful when Diego came into the cubicle. He gave her a thin smile and, because he would be more than used to this type of conversation, Izzy allowed him to take over.

'Another one of my staff is in with your baby,' he said, having introduced himself to the mother, and did what Megan had insisted Josh didn't. Izzy felt the sting of tears in her eyes as very skilfully, very gently Diego talked Nicola through all that had happened, all that was now taking place and all that could lie ahead if her baby were to survive.

'Right now,' Diego said, 'we are doing everything we can to save your baby, but he is in a very fragile state. Nicola. Do you understand what I said to you about the risks, about the health problems your baby might face if he does survive?'

'Do everything you can.'

'We will,' Diego said. 'Megan, the paediatrician, will come in and speak at more length with you, but right now she needs to be in with your son.' He was very kind, but also very firm. 'We're going to be moving him up to the NICU shortly, but why don't I get you a wheelchair and we can take you in to see him before we head off?'

To Izzy it was too soon, Resus was still a hive of activity, but she also knew that Diego was right, that maybe Nicola needed to see for herself the lengths to which they were going to save the baby and also that, realistically, this might be Nicola's only chance to see her son alive.

She didn't get to hold him, but Diego did ask for a camera and took some pictures of Nicola next to her son, and some close-up shots of the baby. And then it was time for him to be moved.

'Nice work,' he said to Izzy as his team moved off with its precious cargo, Diego choosing to stay behind. 'Thank you for everything, and sorry to leave so much mess. I'm going to have a quick run-through of your equipment, if that's okay. There are a few things you ought to order.'

'That would be great,' Izzy said. 'And thank you. You've been marvellous!'

'Marvellous!' He repeated the word as if were the first time he'd heard it and grinned, his teeth were so white, so perfect. If the rest of him hadn't been so divine, she'd have sworn they were capped. 'You were *marvellous* too!' Then his eyes narrowed in closer assessment.

'You're new?' Diego checked, because even though he was rarely in Emergency he was quite sure that he'd have noticed her around the hospital.

'No. I've worked here for ages. I've been on…' She didn't really know what to say so she settled for a very simple version. 'Extended leave.' She gave him a wide smile. 'You're the one who's new.'

'How do you know that?' He raised the most perfectly shaped eyebrow, and if eyes could smile, his were. 'I might have been here for years. Perhaps I did my training here…' He was teasing her, with a question she was less prepared to deal with than a premature birth. 'Why do you think I'm new?'

Because I'd have noticed you.

That was the answer and they both knew it.

Now there was no baby, now there was no emergency to deal with, now it was just the two of them, Izzy, for the first time in, well, the longest time, looked at a man.

Not saw.

Looked.

And as she did so, the strangest thing happened—the four months of endless chatter in her head was silenced. For a delicious moment the fear abated and all she was was a woman.

A woman whose eyes lingered for a fraction too long on a beautiful man.

His hair had dried now and she noticed it was long enough to be sexy and short enough to scrape in as smart. He was a smudge unshaven, but Izzy guessed that even if he met a razor each morning, that shadow would be back in time for lunch. Even in jeans and a T-shirt, even without the olive skin and deep accent, there was a dash of the European about him—his black jeans just a touch tighter, his T-shirt from no high street store that Izzy frequented. He was professional and he was well groomed, but there was a breath of danger about him, a dizzy, musky air that brought Izzy back to a woman she had once known.

'Well,' he said when the silence had gone on too long, 'it's nice to stand here *chatting*, but I have to get back.'

'Of course.'

'A porter took my bag. Do you know where I can find him?'

'Your bag?' Izzy blinked, because it was the sort of thing she would say, but rather than work that one out, she went and called the porter over the Tannoy.

'Come up and see him later,' Diego suggested.

'I will,' Izzy said, consoling herself that he would have extended that invitation to any doctor, that the invitation wasn't actually for her, that it had nothing to do with him.

Except Diego corrected her racing thoughts.

'I'm on till ten.'

What on earth was that?

She'd never been on a horse, yet she felt as if she'd just been galloping at breakneck speed along the beach. Izzy headed for the staffroom, in need of a cool drink of water before she tackled the next patient, wanting to get her scrambled brain into some sort of order after the adrenaline rush of earlier.

A premature delivery would do that to anyone, Izzy told herself as she grabbed a cup. Except, as a large lazy bubble in the water cooler rose and popped to the surface, she felt as if she were seeing her insides spluttering into life after the longest sleep.

She couldn't have been flirting.

She was in no position to be flirting.

Except, Izzy knew, she had been.

They had been.

The lone figure in the staffroom caught her by surprise and Izzy had begun to back out when she saw who it was. Josh was sitting there, head in hands, his face grey, and Izzy was quite sure she was intruding.

'Don't go on my account,' Josh said. 'I was just heading back. How is she?' he asked.

'Upset,' Izzy admitted. 'I think she was only just getting used to the idea of being pregnant, but...' Her voice trailed off, Josh nodded and stood up and walked out, but before that, even as she spoke, realisation dawned.

Josh hadn't been enquiring how the mother was.

Instead he'd been asking about Megan.

CHAPTER THREE

'Are you sure you don't want me to stay and help clear the board?' Izzy checked as the clock edged towards ten.

'Go home and get some well-earned rest,' Ben said. 'You haven't had the easiest start back.'

'And I thought you'd break me in gently.'

'Not my style,' Ben said. 'You did great, Izzy. Mind you, you look like you've been dragged through a hedge!'

The power dressing had lasted till about three p.m. when she had changed into more familiar scrubs, her mascara was smudged beneath her eyes and her mouth devoid of lipstick.

It had been Chest Pain Central for the rest of the shift and apart from two minutes on the loo, Izzy had not sat down.

'One day,' Izzy said, 'I'm going to manage to stay in my own clothes for an entire shift. I am!' she insisted as Josh joined them. She'd had a good shift. Josh had been lovely—as sharp as a tack, he had been a pleasure to work with, his strong Irish brogue already familiar to Izzy.

'It will never happen!' Josh said. 'I thought the same—that maybe when I made consultant… I had some nice suits made, didn't I, Ben?'

They had been friends for years, Izzy had found out, had both worked together in London, and as Izzy grinned and wished them both goodnight she was glad now about her decision to return to work.

It *was* good to be back.

The patients didn't care about the doctor's personal life, didn't know the old Izzy, they just accepted her. Any doubts she might have had about the wisdom of coming back at such a fragile time emotionally had soon faded as she had immersed herself in the busy hub of Emergency, stretching her brain instead of being stuck in that awful loop of wandering around her home, thinking.

It was only now, as she stepped out of her professional role, that the smile faded.

She didn't want to go home.

She stared out past the ambulance bay to the staff car park and she felt a bubble of panic. She could call Security to escort her, of course. Given what had happened, who would blame her for not wanting to walk though the car park alone.

It wasn't even dark. It was one of those lovely summer nights in St Piran when the sky never became fully black.

It wasn't just the car park she was afraid of, though,

she decided as she turned and headed up the corridor to the stairwell.

She just wasn't ready to go home.

Her fingers hovered over the NICU intercom, wondering what exactly she was doing. Usually she wouldn't have thought twice about this. The old Izzy had often popped up to the wards to check on cases she had seen in Emergency, but her pregnant status made it seem more personal somehow and it wasn't just the baby she had delivered that had drawn her there tonight. Still, despite more than a passing thought about him now as she neared his territory, it wasn't just Diego pulling her there either—it was after ten, the late staff would long since have gone.

There was a very private answer she was seeking tonight.

It *was* more personal because she was pregnant, Izzy admitted to herself. She wasn't just here to see how the baby was doing, rather to see her reaction to it, to see if the little scrap she had delivered that morning might somehow evoke in her some feeling for the babe she was carrying.

She was being ridiculous, Izzy told herself, as if a trip to the NICU would put her mind at ease.

Turning on her heel, Izzy decided against visiting.

She'd ring the NICU tomorrow and find out how he was doing.

'Hey!' Having made up her mind and turned go, Izzy jumped slightly as the doors opened and she was greeted by the sound of Diego's voice.

Even before she turned and saw him, even though it

was just one syllable he'd uttered, she knew that it was him and she felt her cheeks colour up, wondering what reason she could give as to why she was there.

'You're here to see your delivery?' He wasn't really looking at her; instead he was turning on his phone and checking the messages that pinged in.

'If that's okay...' She was incredibly nervous around him, flustered even, her words coming out too fast as she offered too much of an explanation. 'I often chase up interesting cases. I know it's a bit late, so I decided to ring tomorrow...'

'Day and night are much the same in there,' he said. 'It won't be a problem.'

'I'll just ring tomorrow. I'm sure they're busy'

She'd changed her mind before she'd seen him, yet Diego wouldn't hear it.

'One moment,' he said. 'I'll take you in. Let me just answer this.'

She didn't want him to take her in.

She glanced at the ID badge he now had around her neck.

Diego Ramirez was so not what she needed now.

Still, he was too engrossed in his phone to read her body language, Izzy thought. His *bag* was a large brown leather satchel, which he wore over his shoulder, and on *anyone* else it would have looked, well, stupid, but it just set him aside from the others.

God, what was it about him?

Diego didn't need to look at Izzy to read her. He could *feel* her tense energy, knew she was nervous, and he knew enough to know that a pregnant woman who had delivered a prem baby would, perhaps, have a few questions or need a little reassurance.

Any of his staff could provide that, Diego said to himself as he checked his message from Sally.

The term 'girlfriend' for Sally, would be stretching it, but she *was* gorgeous and she was sitting outside his flat in a car right this minute, texting to see when he'd be home.

He loved women.

He loved curves on women.

He loved confident women

He loved lots of uninhibited, straightforward sex— and it was right there waiting at his door.

Busy at work—txt u tomoz x

Not regretfully enough he hit 'send', but he did wonder what on earth he was doing. Why, instead of heading for home, he was swiping his ID card to gain entry into the area and walking this slinky-malinky long-legs, who was as jumpy as a cat, through his unit?

'Wash your hands,' Diego prompted, following his own instructions and soaping up his hands and rather large forearms for an inordinate amount of time. 'It is a strict rule here,' he explained, 'and one I enforce, no matter the urgency. And,' he chided as Izzy turned off the handle with her elbow, 'I also ask that staff take an extra moment more than is deemed necessary.'

Oh.

Chastised and not liking it a bit, Izzy turned the tap on again and recommenced the rather long ritual.

'I do know how to wash my hands.'

He didn't answer.

'I don't have to be told.'

He turned and looked at her rigid profile.

'Yes, Doctor, you do.' He turned off the tap and pulled out a wad of paper towels. 'Doctors are the worst culprits.'

She rolled her eyes and he just laughed.

'By the way,' Diego said. 'I'm not.'

It was Izzy who didn't answer now, just pursed her lips a touch as she dried her own hands, refusing to give him the satisfaction of asking what the hell he was talking about. Instead she followed him through NICU, past the endless incubators, most with their own staff member working quietly on the occupant.

It was incredibly noisy—Izzy remembered that from her paediatric rotation, but she'd been such a confident young thing then, curious more than nervous. Now it seemed that every bleep, every noise made her jump.

'Here he is. Toby is his name.' Diego looked down into the incubator then spoke with the nurse who was looking after the infant Izzy had, just that afternoon, delivered. Yet when he glanced over at the rather brittle doctor he found himself momentarily distracted, watching Izzy frown down at the tiny infant, then watching as her huge eyes darted around the large ward, then back to the baby.

'He's doing well,' Diego explained, 'though it is minute by minute at the moment—he's extremely premature, but Megan has done a thorough maturation assessment and thinks he's more like twenty-four weeks.'

'That's good news,' Izzy said, only Diego didn't look particularly convinced. 'Well, it's good that she delivered in hospital,' Izzy said, 'even if she was in the wrong department.' She stared at the baby and as she felt her own kicking she willed herself, begged herself to feel something, this surge of connection to her own babe that she knew she should feel.

'Do you get attached?' Izzy asked, and Diego shook his head.

'Too dangerous here. It's the parents who get to me if anything.'

She'd seen enough. The baby was tiny and fragile and she hoped and prayed he would be okay, but the bells weren't ringing for her, the clouds weren't parting. There was no sudden flood of emotion, other than she suddenly felt like crying, but only because of her lack of feeling for her own baby she carried. 'Well, thank you very much.' She gave a tight smile. 'As I said, I just thought I'd pop in on my way home.'

'I'll walk with you,' Diego offered.

'There no need.' Izzy said, but he ignored her and fell into step beside her. She really wished he wouldn't, she just wanted out of the stifling place, away from the machines and equipment, away from babies, away from the endless guilt…

'How far along are you?'

'Sorry?'

'How many weeks pregnant?'

She was momentarily sideswiped by his boldness and also glad for the normality of his question. It was the question everyone *hadn't* asked today—the bump that everyone, bar Jess, seemed to studiously avoid mentioning.

'Twenty-eight weeks,' Izzy said. 'Well, almost,' she continued, but she had lost her audience. Diego had stopped walking and she turned her head to where he stood.

'Here.'

Izzy frowned.

'Over here.' Diego beckoned her over and after a slight hesitation she followed him, coming to a stop at an incubator where a tiny baby lay. Tiny, but comparatively much larger than the little boy she had delivered that afternoon. 'This little one is almost twenty-nine weeks, aren't you, *bebé*?' Diego crooned, then pumped some alcohol rub into his hands. 'You're awake…'

'I thought you said you didn't get attached!' Izzy grinned and so too did the nurse looking after the little girl.

'If that's Diego detached,' joked the nurse, as Diego stroked her little cheek and chatted on in Spanish, 'then we're all dying to see him in love.'

'She's *exceptionally* cute,' Diego said. 'She was a twenty-four-weeker too, though girls are tougher than boys. She's a real fighter…' His voice seemed to fade out then, though Izzy was sort of aware that he was still talking, except she didn't really have room in her head to process anything else other than the baby she was looking at.

This was what was inside her now.

This was what had bought her up to the NICU tonight—a need for some sort of connection to the baby growing inside her. And Diego had led her to it.

Her little eyes were open, her hands stretching, her face scrunching up, her legs kicking, and Izzy watched, transfixed, as the nurse fed her, holding up a syringe of milk and letting gravity work as the syringe emptied through the tube into the infant's stomach as Diego gave her a teat to suck on so she would equate the full feeling with suckling.

'She's perfect,' Izzy said.

'She's doing well,' Diego said. 'We're all really pleased with her.' He glanced at Izzy. 'I imagine it's hard to take in.'

'Very,' Izzy admitted.

'Come on,' he said, when she had stood and looked for a moment or two longer. 'You should be home and resting after they day you've had.' They walked together more easily now, Izzy stopping at the vending machine and trying to choose between chocolate and chocolate.

'You'll spoil your dinner.'

'This is dinner!' Izzy said, and then grimaced, remembering who she was talking to. 'I mean, I'll have something sensible when I get home...'

He just laughed.

'Don't beat yourself up over a bar of chocolate!' Diego said. 'You need lots of calories now, to fatten that baby up.' He could see the effort it took for her just to sustain that smile. 'And you need to relax; they pick up on things.'

'I do relax.'

'Good.'

He fished in his satchel and pulled out a brown bag. 'Here, Brianna forgot to take them.'

'What are they?' For a moment she thought they were sweets. 'Tomatoes?'

'Cherry tomatoes.'

'Miniature cherry tomatoes,' Izzy said peering into the bag. 'Mini-miniature cherry tomatoes.'

'Keep them in the bag and the green ones will redden. I grow them,' Diego said, then corrected himself. 'I grew them.' He frowned. 'Grow or grew? Sometimes I choose the wrong word.'

They were outside now, heading for the car park..

Izzy thought for a moment and it was so nice to think about something so mundane. 'Grow *or* grew. You grow them and you grew these.'

'Thank you, teacher!'

He was rewarded by her first genuine smile and she looked at him again. 'So what's this about your job title?' Izzy remembered a conversation from Resus.

'The powers that be are revising our titles and job descriptions. Two meetings, eight memos and guess what they came up with?' He nudged her as they walked. 'Guess.'

'I can't.'

'Modern Matron!' She could hear someone laughing and realised with a jolt it was her. Not a false laugh but a real laugh, and then he made her laugh some more. 'I said, "Not without a dress!" And I promise I will wear one; if that is the title they give me. Can you imagine when my family rings me at work.' He glanced at her.

'Surgeons, all of them. I'm the *oveja negra*, the black sheep.'

'I like black sheep,' Izzy said, and then wished she hadn't, except it had honestly just slipped out.

They were at her car now and instead of saying goodnight, Izzy lingered. He was sexy and gorgeous but he was also wise and kind and, despite herself, somehow she trusted him, trusted him with more than she had trusted anyone in a very long time.

'You said that babies can pick up on things...' Izzy swallowed. 'Do you believe that?'

'It's proven,' Diego said.

'So if you're stressed or not happy...'

'They know.'

'And if you're not sure...' She wanted him to jump in, but he didn't, he just continued to lean on her car. She should just get in it. Surely she should just drive off rather than admit what she didn't dare to. 'I mean, do you think they could know if you don't...?' She couldn't say it, but Diego did.

'If you don't want them?'

'Shh!' Izzy scolded, appalled at his choice of words.

'Why?' There was a lazy smile on his face that was absolutely out of place with the seriousness of her admission. 'It can't understand your words—they're not *that* clever.'

'Even so!' She was annoyed now, but he just carried on smiling. 'You don't say things like that.'

'Not to an over-protective mum!'

Oh!

She'd never thought of it like that, never thought that her refusal to voice her thoughts, her refusal to even let herself properly *think* them might, in fact, show that she did have feelings for the life inside.

It was her darkest fear.

Of the many things that kept her brain racing through sleepless nights, this was the one that she dreaded exploring most—that her feelings for her baby's father might somehow translate to her baby.

That love might not grow.

'You're not the only woman to be unsure she's ready,' Diego said. 'And lots of mothers-to-be are stressed and unhappy, but I'm sure you're not stressed and unhappy *all* the time.' His smile faded when she didn't agree and they stood for a quiet moment.

'What if I am?'

He was silent for a while, unsure why a woman so beautiful, so vibrant, so competent would be so unhappy, but it wasn't his business and for a dangerous moment Diego wished it was. So instead he smiled. 'You can fake it.'

'Fake it?'

'Fake it!' Diego nodded, that gorgeous smile in full flood now. 'As I said, they're not *that* clever. Twice a day, fake happiness, say all the things you think you should be saying, dance around the house, go for a walk on the beach, swim. I do each morning, whether I feel like it or not.'

He so didn't get it, but, then, how could he?

'Thanks for the suggestions.' She gave him her best bright smile and pulled out her keys.

'Goodnight, then.'

'Where are you parked?'

'I'm not. I live over there.' He pointed in the direction of the beach. 'I walk to work.'

'You didn't have to escort me.'

'I enjoyed it,' he said. 'Anyway, you shouldn't be walking through car parks on your own at night.'

He really didn't get it, Izzy realised.

He was possibly the only person in the hospital who didn't know her past, or he'd never have said what he just had.

She turned on the engine and as she slid into reverse he knocked on her car window and, irritated now, she wound it down.

'Sing in the shower!' He said. 'Twice a day.'

'Sure' Izzy rolled her eyes. Like *that* was going to help.

'And by the way ,' he said as she was about to close her window, 'I'm not!'

Izzy pulled on her handbrake and let the engine idle and she looked at those lips and those eyes and that smile and she realised exactly why she was annoyed—was she flirting?

Did twenty-eight weeks pregnant, struggling mentally to just survive, recently widowed women ever even begin to think about flirting?

No.

Because had she thought about it she would never have wound down that window some more.

'Not what?' Izzy asked the question she had refused to ask earlier, her cheeks just a little pink.

'I'm not a frustrated doctor,' Diego said, 'as many of your peers seem to think every male nurse is.'

'Glad to hear it,' Izzy said, and took off the hand-brake, the car moving slowly beside him.

'And I'm not the other cliché either!' he called, and her cheeks were on fire, yet for the first time in the longest time she was grinning. Not forcing a smile, no, she was, from ear to ear, grinning.

No, there was absolutely no chance that Diego Ramirez was gay!

'I'd already worked that out!' Izzy called as she pushed up her window. 'Night, Diego!'

'It went well, Mum!' Izzy buttered some toast as she spoke to her mother and added some ginger marmalade. 'Though it was strange being back *after*...' Izzy stopped, because her mother didn't like talking about *before*, so instead she chatted some more, told her mum about Toby, but her mum didn't take the lead and made no mention of Izzy's pregnancy.

'So you had a good day?' her mother checked as Izzy idly opened the brown paper bag and took out a handful of tiny tomatoes. They tasted fantastic, little squirts of summer popping on her tongue, helping Izzy to inject some enthusiasm into her voice.

'Marvellous,' Izzy said, smiling at the choice of word and remembering Diego's smile.

It was actually a relief to hang up.

She was so damn tired of putting others at ease.

So *exhausted* wearing the many different Izzy masks...

Doctor Izzy.

To add to Daughter Izzy.

Domestic Abuse Victim Izzy.

Grieving Izzy.

Mother-to-be Izzy.

Coping Izzy.

She juggled each ball, accepted another as it was tossed in, and sometimes, *sometimes* she'd like to drop the lot, except she knew she wouldn't.

Couldn't.

She could remember her mother's horror when she had for a moment dropped the coping pretence and chopped off her hair. Izzy could still see the pain in her mother's eyes and simply wouldn't put her through it any more.

Oh, but she wanted to, Izzy thought, running her bath and undressing, catching sight of herself in the mirror, her blonde hair way-too-short, her figure too thin for such a pregnant woman.

How she'd love to ring her mum back—ask her to come over, to *take* over.

Except she knew she couldn't.

Wouldn't.

Since that night, there had been a huge wedge between them and Izzy truly didn't know how to fix it. She just hoped that one day it would be fixed, that maybe when the baby came things would improve. Except her mother could hardly bring herself to talk about the impending arrival.

Damn Henry Bailey!

Whoosh!

The anger that Jess had told her was completely normal, was a 'good sign', in fact, came rushing in then and, yes, she should do as Jess said perhaps, and write pages and pages in her journal, or shout, or cry, or read the passage in her self-help book on anger.

Except she was too tired for Henry tonight.

Too fed up to deal with her so-called healthy anger.

Too bone weary to shout or cry.

She wanted a night off!

So she lit six candles instead, the relaxing ones apparently, and lay there and waited for them to work, except they didn't.

She *had* to relax.

It was important for the baby!

Oh, and it would be so easy to cry now, but instead she sat up and pulled the plug out, and then she had another idea, or rather she decided to try out Diego's idea.

She'd fake it.

Cramming the plug back in the hole, she topped up with hot water and feeling stupid, feeling beyond stupid, she lay back as the hot water poured over her toes and she sang the happiest song she could think of.

A stupid happy song.

And then another.

Then she sang a love song, at the top of her voice at midnight, in her smart townhouse.

And she was used to the neighbours banging on the walls during one of her and Henry's fights, so it didn't really faze her when they did just that. Instead she sang louder.

Izzy just lay there in the bath, faking being happy, till her baby was kicking and she was grinning—and even if, for now, she had to fake it, thanks to a male nurse who wasn't a frustrated doctor and certainly wasn't the other cliché, by the time her fingers and toes were all shrivelled up, Izzy wasn't actually sure if she was faking it.

For a second there, if she didn't analyse it too much, if she just said it as it was…

Well, she could have almost passed as happy!

CHAPTER FOUR

DIEGO was not in the best of moods.

Not that anyone would really know.

Though laid back in character, he was always firm in the running of his unit. His babies came first and though friendly and open in communication, he kept a slight distance from his staff that was almost indefinable.

Oh, he chatted. They knew he loved to swim in the Cornish sea, that he came from an affluent long line of doctors in Madrid, they even knew that he was somewhat estranged from his family due to his career choice, for Diego would roll his eyes if any of them rang him at work. His staff knew too about his rather pacy love life—the dark-eyed, good-looking Spaniard was never short of a date but, much to many a St Piran's female staff member's disgust, he never dated anyone from work.

No, the stunning women who occasionally dropped in, waiting for him to finish his shift, or called him on the phone, had nothing to do with hospitals—not public ones anyway. Their hospital stays tended to be in private clinics for little *procedures* to enhance their already polished looks.

There was just this certain aloofness to Diego—an independent thinker, he never engaged in gossip or mixed his private life with his work.

So no one knew that, despite his zealous attention to detail with his precious charges that day, there was a part of Diego that was unusually distracted.

Cross with himself even.

Okay, his relations with women veered more towards sexual than emotional, and if his moral code appeared loose to some, it actually came with strict guidelines—it was always exclusive. And, a man of honour, he knew it was wrong to suddenly be taking his lunches in the canteen instead of on the ward and looking out for that fragile beauty who was clearly taken.

Wrong, so very wrong to have been thinking of her late, *very late*, into the night.

But why *was* she so stressed and unhappy?

If she were his partner, he'd make damn sure…

Diego blew out a breath, blocked that line of thought and carried on typing up the complicated handover sheet, filling in the updates on his charges, now that Rita the ward clerk had updated the admissions and discharges and changes of cots. It was Monday and there was always a lot to be updated. It was a job he loathed, but he did it quicker and more accurately than anyone else and it was a good way of keeping current with all the patients, even if he couldn't be hands on with them all. So Diego spent a long time on the sheet—speaking with each staff member in turn, checking up on each baby in his care. The NICU handover sheet was a lesson in excellence.

'I'm still trying to chase up some details for Baby Geller,' Rita informed him as Diego typed in the three-days-old latest treatment regime. 'Maternity hasn't sent over forms.'

'He came via Emergency.' Diego didn't look up. 'After you left on Friday.'

'That's right—the emergency obstetric page that went out.' Rita went through his paperwork. 'Do you know the delivering doctor? I need to go to Maternity and get some forms then I can send it all down and he can fill it in.'

'She.' Diego tried to keep his deep voice nonchalant. 'Izzy Bailey, and I think I've got some of the forms in my office. I can take them down.'

'Is she back?' Rita sounded shocked. 'After all that's happened you'd think she'd have stayed off till after the baby. Mind you, the insurance aren't paying up, I've heard. They're dragging their feet, saying it might be suicide—as if! No doubt the poor thing *has* to work.'

Diego hated gossip and Rita was an expert in it. Nearing retirement, she had been there for ever and made everyone's business her own. Rita's latest favourite topic was Megan the paediatrician, who she watched like a hawk, or Brianna Flannigan, the most private of nurses, but today Rita clearly had another interest. Normally Diego would have carried on working or told her to be quiet, but curiosity had the better of him and, not proud of himself, Diego prolonged the unsavoury conversation.

'Suicide?' Diego turned around. 'Are you talking about Izzy's husband?'

'Henry Bailey!' Rita nodded. 'It wasn't suicide, of course; he just drove off in a blind rage. She'd left him, but he turned up at work, waited for her in the car park…' She flushed a little, perhaps aware that she was being terribly indiscreet and that Diego was normally the one to halt her. 'I'm not speaking out of turn; it was all over the newspapers and all over the CCTV, though of course it would have been before you arrived in St Piran's.'

No, it wasn't his proudest morning, because once the handover sheet was complete, Diego headed for his office and closed the door. Feeling as if he was prying but wanting to know all the same, it didn't take long to find out everything Rita had told him and more. Oh, he would never abuse his position and look up personal information, but it was there for everyone, splashed all over the internet, and as he read it he felt his stomach churn in unease for all she had been through.

Pregnant, trying to leave an abusive marriage, real estate agent Henry Bailey had beaten his wife in the darkened hospital car park. Rita was right, the whole, shocking incident had been captured on CCTV and images of footage and the details were spelt out in the press.

He felt sick.

Reading it, he felt physically sick and also strangely proud.

Her first day back.

Mierda! He cursed himself as he remembered his

throw-away comment about the car park. He replayed the conversation they had had over and over and wished he could start with her again.

His door knocked and he quickly clicked away from the page he was viewing, before calling whoever it was to come in, but he felt a rare blush on his cheeks as the woman herself stood before him. Diego actually felt as if he'd been caught snooping as Izzy let herself in, a wide smile on her face, and he wondered how on earth she managed it.

She had leggings on again and a bright red dress with bright red lipstick and, Diego noticed, bright red cheeks as he just continued to stare up at her.

'You need me to sign off on the delivery?' It was Izzy who broke the silence; Diego was momentarily lost for words. 'Your ward clerk just rang…'

'We would have sent them down to you.'

'Oh!' Izzy blushed a shade darker as she lied just a little. 'I thought it sounded urgent.'

'I should have some forms…' He was unusually flustered as he rummaged through his desk. 'Or I'll ring Maternity. Here…' Diego found them and was pathetically grateful when the door knocked and one of his team stood there. with a screaming baby with a familiar request.

'Would you mind?'

'Not at all.' He washed his hands, *thoroughly*, then took the screaming baby and plonked it face down on his forearm, its little head at his elbow, and he rocked it easily as he spoke.

'Genevieve!' he introduced. 'Goes home this week, please God! I do not envy her parents.'

Well, Genevieve looked as if she'd happily stay with Diego for ever! The tears had stopped and she was already almost asleep as he bounced away.

'If you want to get started on the forms I'll just go and get the details you'll need.' He paused at the door. 'I was just about to get a drink…'

'Not for me, thanks,' Izzy said, and then changed her mind. 'Actually, water would be great.'

'Would you mind…?' It was his turn to say it and he gestured to the baby. Izzy went to put out her hands and then laughed.

'Joking!' she said, then went over to his sink and *thoroughly* washed hers. 'Am I clean enough for you?'

Oh, God, there was an answer there!

And they just both stood there, looking a bit stunned.

Izzy flaming red, Diego biting down on his tongue rather than tell her he'd prefer her dirty.

And thank God for Miss Genevieve or he might just have kissed her face off!

Diego got them both water.

Well, he couldn't do much with two polystyrene cups and tap water but he did go to the ice dispenser and then had a little chat with himself in his head as he walked back to his office.

What the hell was wrong with him?

He hardly knew her, she was pregnant, and she obviously had *major* issues.

Why was he acting like a twelve-year-old walking

past the underwear department in a department store? Nervous, jumpy, embarrassed, hell, he couldn't actually fancy her, and even if he did, normally that didn't pose a problem—he fancied loads of women.

This, though, felt different.

Maybe he felt sorry for her? Diego wondered as he balanced a file under his arm and two cups in one big hand and opened his office door.

But, no, he'd been thinking about her long before Rita had told him what had happened.

Then she looked up from the form she was filling in and smiled, and Diego was tempted to turn round and walk out.

He more than fancied her.

Not liked, not felt sorry for, no. As he washed his hands and took Genevieve from her and sat down behind his desk it wasn't sympathy that was causing this rather awkward reaction.

Diego was used to women.

Beautiful women.

Ordinary women.

Postnatal women.

Pregnant women were regular visitors to his unit—often he walked a mum-to-be around his unit, telling her what to expect once her baby was born.

He was more than used to women, yet not one, not one single one, had ever had this effect on him.

'How is Toby doing?' Izzy looked up from the forms and Diego made a wobbly gesture with one hand.

'Can I have a peek?' Izzy signed off her name and then reached for her water. 'I'm done.'

'Sure,' Diego said. 'I'll put this one down and take you over—we've moved him.'

Genevieve was sleeping now, and Izzy walked with him to the nursery. It was a far more relaxed atmosphere there.

There were about eight babies, all in clear cribs and dressed in their own clothes, the parents more relaxed and, Izzy noticed, everyone had a smile when Diego walked in and put Genevieve back in her cot.

He was certainly popular, Izzy thought as they head back out to the busy main floor of NICU.

'You need to—'

'Wash my hands,' Izzy interrupted, 'I know.'

'Actually…' Diego gave a small wince. 'Your perfume is very strong. Perhaps you could…'

'I'm not wearing perfume,' Izzy said as she soaped up her hands, 'and you're hardly one to talk, I can smell your cologne from here!'

'I don't wear cologne for work.'

'Oh.' Izzy glanced over. 'Then what…?' She didn't finish, she just turned back to the taps and concentrated really hard on rinsing off the soap.

She could smell him.

If she breathed in now she could taste him—she'd even commented to Megan on his cologne, but Megan had said… Izzy swallowed as she recalled the flip conversation. Megan hadn't even noticed it…

She could smell him and Diego could smell her and they'd just told each other so.

There was no witty comeback from that.

It was the *most* awkward five minutes of her life.

Okay, not *the most* awkward—the last few months had brought many of them. Rather it was the most pleasantly cringe-making, confusingly awkward five minutes of her life.

She peered at Baby Geller and asked after his mother, Nicola. She tried to remember that breathing was a normal bodily function as the nurse who was looking after the babe asked Diego to hold him for a moment while she changed the bedding. The sight of the tiny baby nestled in his strong arms, resting against his broad chest, was just such a contrast between tenderness and masculinity that it had Izzy almost dizzy with the blizzard of emotions it evoked.

'I'd better get back.' Her mouth felt as if was made of rubber—even a simple sentence was difficult.

She managed a smile and then she turned and walked briskly out of the department. Only once she was safely out did she lean against the wall and close her eyes, breathing as if she'd run up the emergency exit steps. Shocked almost because never in her wildest dreams had she considered this, even ventured the possibility that she might be attracted to someone.

She was so raw, so scared, so just dealing with functioning, let alone coping, that men weren't even on a distant horizon yet.

And yet...

She'd never been so strongly attracted to someone.

Never.

Even in the early days with Henry, before he'd shown his true colours, she hadn't felt like this. Oh, she had loved him, had been so deeply in love she'd been sure of it—only it had felt nothing like this attraction.

An attraction that was animal almost.

She *could* smell the delicious fragrance of him.

Right now, on her skin in her hair, she leant against the wall and dragged in the air, and still his fragrance lingered in her nostrils.

'Izzy!' Her eyes opened to the concerned voice of Jess. 'Are you okay?'

'I'm fine!' She smiled. 'I was just in NICU, and it's so hot in there…' God, she felt like she'd been caught smoking by the headmistress, as if Jess could see the little plumes of smoke coming from behind her back. She tried to carry on as if her world hadn't just upended itself. Jess would hardly be thrilled to hear what was going through her patient's mind now.

It was impossible that it was even going through her mind now.

There wasn't room in her life, in her heart, in her head for even one single extra emotion, let alone six feet two of made-in-Spain testosterone.

'How are you finding it?' Jess asked as they walked in step back to the emergency department, and then Jess gave a kind smile, 'I'm just making conversation…'

'I know.' Izzy grinned and forced herself back to a safer conversation than the one she was having with herself. 'Actually, it's been really nice. It's good having something else to think about.'

Only she wasn't just talking about work.

CHAPTER FIVE

'THE nurses are all tied up and I've got to dash over to the children's ward,' Megan said into the phone. 'I'll ask Izzy.'

'Ask Izzy what?'

She'd been back a full week now.

It was late.

She was tired.

And the patient she was dealing with wasn't exactly helping Izzy's mood.

'I've got a patient on NICU,' Megan explained. 'A new admission. His mum's bipolar and Diego wants some sedation for her. The baby was an emergency transfer so there's no local GP and her medications are all at home. She's getting really agitated, and really it sounds as if she just needs a good night's sleep and then her husband can bring in her meds in the morning. Diego wants her seen straight away, though. Is there any chance? I'd do it but I've *got* to go up to the ward.'

'You'll have to speak to Josh or one of the nurses,' Izzy was unusually terse. 'I'm about to suture someone and then I'm going home.'

She was aware of the rise of Megan's eyebrow. Normally Izzy was accommodating, but Diego's name seemed to be popping up in her day all too often—and her thoughts were turning to him too, rather more than Izzy was comfortable with.

Still it wasn't just a sexy neonatal nurse that had caused Izzy's terse reaction. Just as Jess had predicted, there would be patients that would touch a very raw nerve with Izzy, and even though she had assured Jess she would have no trouble dealing with them, Evelyn Harris *had* hit a nerve.

In her early forties she had presented having tripped over the cat and cut her head on the edge of the coffee table. Vivienne, the student nurse, had had a quiet word with Izzy before she had examined her, telling her that she had noticed some other bruises on her arms when she had checked her blood pressure and, sure enough when Izzy had *checked* the blood pressure again, she had seen the new fingertip bruises, but had chosen not to comment.

'You're going to need a few stitches!' Izzy had said instead. 'How's the cat?'

The relief in the room at Izzy's small joke had been palpable, Evelyn had laughed and John Harris had said the cat would be in the naughty corner, or some other light-hearted thing, and Izzy had smiled back.

Had let him think, as he no doubt did, that she was stupid.

'Vivienne?' Izzy called out to a student nurse. 'Could you set up the minor theatre?' She smiled at

Mrs Harris. 'I'll take you over and I'll be in with you in a moment.'

'I'll stay with you,' Mr Harris reassured his wife, and then explained why to Dumb Doctor Izzy. 'She doesn't like needles.'

'Sorry!' Izzy breezed. 'We can only have the patient.' She gave a very nice smile. 'We shan't be long, at least I hope not. You're my last patient for the night...' She chatted away, not letting the husband get a word in, acted dizzy and vague and rushed, as if getting home was the only thing on her mind, telling them both to take a seat outside minor ops. Then she headed for the annexe, checked who the on-call social worker was for the night and was just considering her options when Megan had asked the favour. With her emotions already bubbling to the surface, the thought of seeing Diego was the last thing she needed.

There was something about him that got under her skin, though in a nice way, and Izzy, right now, just wasn't comfortable with nice.

Wasn't used to nice.

And was nowhere near ready for it either.

As Izzy came into the minor theatre, Vivienne was just bringing Evelyn through and Mr Harris's voice came through the open door as his wife stepped inside.

'I'm right outside, darling,' he said, only Izzy could hear his clear warning.

'Lie down here, Evelyn,' Izzy said, then headed over to the small bench in the corner and turned on the radio. 'Let's have some music to distract you.' She washed her hands and pulled on some gloves and then gently gave the wound a clean before injecting in some local anaesthetic. 'I'm fine on my own, Vivienne,' Izzy said. 'It's pretty busy out there.'

'I'm to cut for you,' came the response, but Izzy could cut her own stitches and wanted to be alone with Evelyn, except Vivienne wouldn't budge. 'Beth told me to get into Theatre as much as I could.'

'Could you get me some 3-0 catgut?' Izzy said, knowing they had run out but checking the wound as if that was the thread she needed. 'There's none here, but I think there should be some in the store cupboard.'

'There isn't any,' Vivienne said. 'I did the stock order with Beth this afternoon.'

Vivienne needed a crash course on taking a hint, but Izzy didn't have time right now. Evelyn only needed a couple of stitches and Mr Harris would no doubt start to get impatient soon, so Izzy dragged the stool over with her foot and given the time constraints realised she would have to be more direct than she would normally choose.

'Evelyn,' Izzy said, 'is there anything you want to tell me?'

'Nothing.'

'I know,' Izzy said gently. 'I know that you didn't just trip…' She watched her patient's nervous lick of her dry lips, her eyes anxiously dart to the theatre door. 'He can't hear,' Izzy said. 'That's why I put the radio on. You can talk to me.'

'Can you just do your job and suture me?' Evelyn bristled. 'I tripped! Okay?'

'There's a bruise on the opposite cheek, finger marks on your arms. I can sort out help...'

'Really?' The single word was so loaded with sarcasm, just so scornful and filled with dark energy that Izzy let out a breath before she spoke next.

'I can ring the social worker. There are shelters...'

'I've a seventeen-year-old son.' Evelyn's lip curled in bitter response. 'The shelters won't let me bring him with me. Did you know that?' she challenged, and Izzy shook her head.

'So what do you suggest, Doctor? That I leave him with him?'

'No, of course not, but if I get someone to speak with you, they could go through your options. I can speak to the police. You don't have to go back tonight.'

'You're not helping, Doctor,' Evelyn said. 'In fact, you could very well be making my life a whole lot worse.'

The stitches took no time, and Izzy knew that dragging it out and keeping Evelyn's husband waiting would only make things worse for her patient, but as Vivienne snipped the last thread Izzy had one more go.

'Is there anyone you can talk to? A friend perhaps...'

'You really don't get it, do you?'

Except Izzy did.

'I don't have *friends*! At least, none of my choosing.'

Evelyn struck a dignified pose as she swung her legs down from the gurney and Izzy recognised the glare in her eyes only too well, because she had shot out that look many times before if anyone had dared so much as to assume that her life was less than perfect.

'Do I need to sign anything?' Evelyn asked.

'No.' Izzy shook her head. 'If you…' She looked at Evelyn and her voice trailed off. Evelyn's decision to stay wasn't going to change, not till her son's future was taken care of. Izzy just hoped to God she'd survive that year. 'When was your last tetanus?'

'I had one…' Evelyn swung her bag over her shoulder '…six weeks ago.'

I'll bet she did, Izzy thought as she stood there, clearing the trolley. She could see her hands shaking as she disposed of the sharps and as Evelyn left Theatre, Izzy had to bite on her lip as the young nurse's disbelieving voice filled the still room.

'Straight back to him…' Her voice was incredulous. 'Why doesn't she just lea—' And then Vivienne's voice abruptly halted as perhaps she remembered who she was talking to and what had had happened the night Izzy had tried to *just* leave.

'She has her reasons,' Izzy said. 'And, frankly, if that's your attitude, she's hardly likely to share them with you.'

'I'm sorry, Izzy.'

And she could have left it there, but Izzy chose not to. Vivienne was thinking of a career in Emergency and, well, it was time she faced a few home truths.

'You're a nurse,' Izzy said, and her voice wobbled with long-held emotion, 'not the bloody jury. Remember that when you're dealing with patients in Emergency.'

Her shift was nearly over and all she wanted was out,

so she left the messy trolley and was tempted to just go to the lockers and get out of there. She was angry and close to tears and there was Evelyn walking out of the department, her husband's arm around her. Then he stopped and fished his phone from his jacket and took a call, and Evelyn patiently waited then she turned and for a second. For just a teeny second their eyes locked and and it was the secret handshake, the password, the club, and Evelyn's expression changed as she realised her doctor was a fully paid up member...

'Mrs Harris...' Izzy scribbled down her mobile number on a head injury information chart and walked briskly over. 'Sorry.' Izzy gave a busy shrug. 'I forgot to give you this. Here's your head injury instructions, have a read through...'

'Thank you.'

'And watch out for that cat!' Izzy added, then gave a vague smile at Evelyn and one to her husband before they walked off into the night. Izzy's heart was thumping, not sure what she had just done and not sure what she would even do if Evelyn did call.

She just wanted to do something.

'Izzy!'

That Spanish voice was too nice for her mood right now.

'Can I ask a favour?' Diego gave her a smile as he poked his head out of a cubicle, but she didn't return it.

'I'm about to go off duty.'

'I was off duty forty minutes ago and I'm back on in the morning.' Diego wasn't quite so nice now. One of his mums was about to tip into trouble, the mother of one his precious babies no less. He had spent two hours dealing with red tape, trying to get hold of her GP to fax a prescription, to no avail, or to get a doctor on NICU to see Maria, but of course she wasn't actually a patient at the hospital.

Yet!

Maria was growing more agitated by the minute and no one seemed to give a damn. 'I have a woman who gave birth four days ago, following twenty-four hours of labour. Her child has multiple anomalies, she has hardly slept since her baby was born and she and her husband have driven one hundred miles today as there was no room for them in the helicopter.' Oh, he told her, even if it was Izzy, he told her, even as she opened her mouth to say that she'd see the patient, still he told her, because Diego knew Izzy was far better than that. 'Now she can't settle and is doing her best not to go into meltdown. Can I get a doctor to prescribe me some sedation?'

'I'm sorry, okay?' Izzy's apology was instant and genuine—she had never been one to dash off at the end of her shift, but Evelyn had unsettled her, not to mention Diego. She was having great trouble keeping her mask from slipping, but it wasn't the patients' fault. 'Of course I'll see her.'

Maria was agitated and pacing and the very last thing she needed was endless questions and an examination, and Izzy could see that. Diego had given her a good brief and on gentle questioning Izzy found out what medications the patient was on.

'If I could just get some sleep,' Maria pleaded, and Izzy nodded.

'I'll be back in just a moment.'

She was and so too was a nurse from the neonatal unit to relieve Diego.

'Take two tablets now,' Izzy said, and gave the hand-over nurse the rest of the bottle. 'She can have two more at two a.m., but don't wake her if she's resting. Will someone be able to check her?'

'Absolutely,' Diego said. 'Maria's staying in the parents' wing, but I'll get my staff to pop in and see her through the night.'

'I'm sure,' Izzy said to her patient, 'that once you've had a decent rest you'll be feeling a lot better. I'm on in the morning,' Izzy added, writing some notes. 'If Maria doesn't settle,' Izzy added to the nurse, 'she'll need to come back down to us.'

It was straightforward and simple and as the nurse took Maria back up to the ward, Diego thanked her.

'I'm sorry if I came on strong.'

'Not at all,' Izzy said. 'She needed to be seen. It's just been a…' She stopped talking; he didn't need to hear about her difficult shift, so she gave him a brief smile and walked on.

Except Diego was going off duty too.

'How's faking it going?' Had he fallen into step beside her that morning, or even an hour ago, Izzy would have managed a laugh and a witty retort, but even a smile seemed like hard work right now, so she just hitched her bag up higher and walked more briskly through the sliding doors and into the ambulance forecourt. But Diego's legs were longer than hers, and he kept up easily.

'Izzy, I was wondering….'

'Do you mind?' She put up her hand to stop him talking, gave an incredulous shake of her head. What was it with people today that they couldn't take a hint if she stood there and semaphored them? 'I just want…' Oh, God, she was going to cry.

Not here.

Not now.

She hadn't yet cried.

Oh, there had been *some* tears, but Izzy had been too scared to really cry, to break down, because if she did, maybe she wouldn't stop.

Scared that if she showed her agony to others they would run when they saw the real her, and scared to do it alone because it was so big, this black, ever-moving shape that had no clear edges, that grew and shrank and transformed.

But she couldn't outrun that black cloud tonight.

She was trying not to cry, trying to breathe and trying to walk away from him to get to her car, as she had tried to that awful night.

No, there was no getting away from it.

Her hands were shaking so much she dropped her keys and it took all her strength not to sink to her knees and break down right there. Instead she got into the car, sat gripping the wheel, holding it in and begging it to pass, but it held her a moment longer, pinning her down. She sat in her car and she was tired, so tired and angry and ashamed and sad…

Sad.

Sad was bigger than angry, bigger than tired, bigger than her.

It was in every cell and it multiplied. It was the membrane of every cell and the nucleus within, it spread and it grew and it consumed and she couldn't escape it any longer. As she doubled over she could feel her baby kick inside and it was so far from the dream, so removed from anything she had envisaged when she had walked down that aisle, that the only word was sad.

She didn't even jump when the passenger door opened and Diego slid into the passenger seat.

'Can't you just leave me alone?'

Diego thought about it for a moment then gave an honest answer. 'It would seem not.'

'You know, don't you?' Izzy said, because everyone else did and so he surely must.

'A little,' Diego admitted. 'I didn't at first, but that morning, when you came to my office, I'd just found out.'

'I thought you were a bit awkward.'

Maybe for a second, Diego thought, but he'd been awkward for another reason that morning, but now wasn't really the time to tell her.

'I've done something stupid…' Izzy said. 'Just then, when you asked me to see Maria.' He sat patiently, waiting for her to explain. 'I had a woman, I think her husband beats her—actually, I don't think, I know. She wouldn't let me help her. I can see now that I rushed in, but I didn't want her to go home to him. I knew what he'd be like when they got home, you could just tell he was annoyed that she was even at the hospital, even though he'd put her there. Anyway, she wouldn't let me get a social worker or the police....' She turned and saw the flash of worry on his face. 'I didn't confront him or anything, he's none the wiser that I know.'

'You can't help her if she doesn't want it.'

'I gave her my phone number.' Izzy waited for his reaction, waited for him to tell her not to get involved, that she had been foolish, but instead he thought for a long moment before commenting.

'I think,' he said slowly, 'that your phone number would be a very nice thing to have.' She blinked. 'And I'm not flirting,' Diego said, and she actually gave a small smile. 'Other times I flirt, but not then. Did *you* talk to anyone?'

'No,' Izzy admitted. 'Megan, we're friends,' she explained, 'asked me what was wrong once, and I remember then that I nearly told her. God—' regret wrapped her words '—I wish I had. I was on my way to my mum's when it happened—I was going to tell her. Henry and I had had a massive row that morning. I knew I was pregnant, that I had to get out of the marriage. I told him I was leaving, I still wasn't sure how, but I came to work, scraped through the shift and afterwards I was going to land on my parents' doorstep...' she gave a shrug '...or Megan's. All I knew was that I wasn't going home.'

'What if someone had given you a phone number?' Diego asked. 'If you had known that that person knew what it was like...'

'I'd have rung them,' Izzy said. 'Not straight away

perhaps.' Then she nodded, confirmed to herself that she hadn't done a stupid thing. 'What do I say if she rings?'

'What would you have wanted someone to say to you?'

'I don't know,' Izzy admitted. 'Just to listen…'

She'd answered her own question and Izzy leant back on the seat and closed her eyes for a moment, actually glad that he had got into the car, glad that he hadn't left her alone, glad that he was there.

And she didn't want to think about it any more so instead she turned to him.

'I forgive you.'

'*Cómo?*' Diego frowned. 'Forgive me for what?'

'Having a satchel.' She watched as a smile spread across his face and she smiled too. 'I never thought I could,' Izzy said, seriously joking, 'but I do.'

'Leave my satchel alone,' Diego said, and he saw something then, her humour, a glimpse of the real Izzy that would soon be unearthed, because she would come out of this, Diego was sure of that. She would grow and she would rise and she would become more of the woman he was glimpsing now.

He knew.

And he knew if he stayed another minute he'd kiss her.

'I'd better go,' Diego said, because he really thought he'd better.

'I'll drive you.'

'No, because then I would have to ask you in.'

'Would that be so bad?' Izzy asked, because it felt as

if he was kissing her, she could see his mouth and almost taste it on hers. Sitting in the car, she didn't want him to get out and she didn't want to drive on. She wanted to stay in this moment, but Diego was moving them along.

'If you come in, I might not want you to leave…' It was big and it was unexpected and the last thing either had planned for, yet, ready or not, it was happening. 'We need to think.'

He climbed out of her car and Izzy sat there. Without him beside her logic seeped in.

It was way too soon.

It was impossibly way too soon.

And yet, had he chosen to, he could have kissed her.

CHAPTER SIX

QUÉ diablos estás haciendo?

As Diego pushed through the waves, over and over he asked himself what on earth he was doing.

On leaving Izzy, he'd gone home to find Sally in the car outside his flat, with a bottle of wine and a dazzling smile, but instead of asking her in, he'd sent her on her way. The words 'It's been good, but…' had hung in the air, as had the sound of her tears, but it had been the only outcome to their relationship, Diego had realised as he'd let himself into his flat.

It *had* been good.

Sencillo, Diego's favourite word—straightforward, uncomplicated. Sally had been all those things and everything Diego had thought he wanted in a relationship. Only his life had suddenly become a touch more complicated.

He needed to think and he couldn't do that with Sally. Wouldn't do that to Sally and also he needed to be very sure himself.

Walking out of the water towards the beach, he wasn't sure if he was even pleased that Izzy had taken his advice, for there she was, walking along the beach, her face flushing when she saw him.

'I thought you were on an early…'

'I'm on a management day, so I don't have to be in till nine,' Diego explained, then he teased, 'Why? Were you trying to avoid me?'

'Of course not!' Izzy lied.

'It's good to see you out.'

'It's good to be out,' Izzy admitted. 'I used to walk on the beach each morning. I don't know why I stopped.'

'You've had a lot to deal with.'

Which she had, but Izzy hadn't walked since her marriage, another little thing she'd given up in an attempt to please Henry, but she didn't say anything.

'Do you want company?'

And she looked into dark eyes that were squinting against the morning sun, his black hair dripping, unshaven, wet, and his toned body, way smoother than a name like Ramirez suggested, and she didn't know what she wanted because, here was the thing, she'd spent the whole night in turmoil, telling herself she was being ridiculous, that it was impossible, that she should be sorting out herself instead of getting involved with someone.

She didn't actually have to tell herself. The books said the same too, even Jess.

But here, on the beach, when she should be thinking alone, it was his company her heart required. Here in the lovely fresh start of morning it just seemed natural for them to talk.

They walked along the beach, admiring the rugged

Cornish coastline. Despite the warmth of summer, the wind was up, making the beach the coolest place as the breeze skimmed off the ocean and stung her cheeks, and it was a relief to talk about him.

'This beach is one of the reasons I choose to settle in St Piran. I love the beach.'

'What about Madrid? Do you miss it?'

'The nearest beach is Valencia. Over a hundred miles away…' Perhaps he realised he was being evasive. 'Sometimes I miss it. I have been away two years now…' She glanced at him when his voice trailed off.

'Go on.'

'My family and I were rowing—we did not part on good terms,' Diego admitted. 'We get on a bit better now. I talk to my mother often on the telephone, but for a while there was no contact.'

He left it there, for now. But there was something about the ocean. It was so vast and endless that it made honesty easier, problems mere specks, which was perhaps why they found themselves there so often over the next few days. They would walk and talk and try to put on hold the chemistry between them and instead work on their history. They sat in the shallows, just enough for the cool water to wash around their ankles and up their calves, and they talked. It was absolutely, for Izzy, the best part of her day and she hoped Diego felt the same.

'I told you it was expected that I would study medicine? It did not go down well when I chose to study nursing instead. Padre said it was women's work…'

'Not any more.'

'He ridiculed it, my brothers too. I also studied *parte-ro*, I'm a midwife too,' Diego explained. 'My mother said she understood, but she would prefer I study medicine to keep my father happy.' He gave a wry smile. 'That was the rule growing up and it is still the rule now—keeping him happy. Getting good grades, melting into the background, anything to keep him happy. I wish she had the guts to leave him.' He looked over at Izzy. 'I admire you for leaving.'

'I didn't have children,' Izzy said. 'And it was still a hard decision. Don't judge her for staying, Diego. What made you want to do nursing?'

'My elder sister had a baby when I was eighteen. He was very premature and my sister was ill afterwards. I used to sit with him and I watched the nurses. They were so skilled, so much more hands on than the doctors, and I knew it was what I wanted to do. Fernando was very sick—I was there night and day for ten days. My sister had a hysterectomy and was very sick too…' There was a long silence. 'She was at another hospital so she didn't get over to see him—she was too ill.' Diego suddenly grimaced. 'I shouldn't be telling you this…'

'I'm not that precious.' Izzy squeezed his hand.

'He died at ten days old. It was tough. In those ten days I really did love him and even now sometimes my sister asks for details about him and I am glad that I can give them to her.'

'What sort of details?'

'He loved to have his feet stroked and he loved to be sing to.' He gave a slight frown and Izzy just sat silent rather than correct his grammar. 'My sister had always sung to him while she was pregnant and I taped her singing and played the songs.'

'It must be hard,' Izzy said. 'Your work must bring it all back…'

'No.' His response surprised her. 'It has certainly made me a better nurse. I know, as much as I can know, how helpless and scared the parents feel. How you constantly watch the monitors and become an armchair expert, but never, not even once, have I come close to the feelings I had for Fernando with a patient. I suppose I detach, of course there are stories and babies that touch you more than others, but you could not do this job and care so deeply at that level.'

And she looked at him and couldn't see how his parents could be anything but proud. She had seen his work at first hand, the way his colleagues and all the parents respected him. There had been an almost audible sigh of relief that Diego had been around when Toby had been born and she told him that.

'There is a managerial position at my father's hospital—I am thinking of applying for it. Of course, it has not gone down well. He says it would be an embarrassment to the Ramirez name if I take it.'

They were only just getting to know each other, but still her breath caught at the impossibility of it all, of anything happening between them, and she tried to keep the needy note from her voice when she asked a question.

'Why would you go back?' Izzy asked, 'After all that, if they don't respect what you do…'

'I respect what I do now,' Diego said. 'That is the difference. I would like to go back and be proud.'

He would go back.

They were sitting in the sand at the water's edge. Izzy's shorts were soaking, the water rushing in then dragging back out, as if taking all the debris of the past away. But the tide returned and bought with it fresh problems and Izzy told herself to slow down, to not even think about it, that his decisions didn't affect her. They were friends, that was all—they hadn't so much as kissed.

Except Diego discounted that theory before it had even properly formed.

She could feel his face near her cheek and knew if she turned her head their lips would meet.

It was six a.m. and the clearest her head would be all day, but she turned to him, to the sweet, confusing relief of his mouth. He tasted like a blast of morning, with the promise of night. It was a kiss that was tender on the outside—a mesh of lips, a slow, measured greeting, but there was raw promise beneath the surface, his tongue sliding in, offering a heady taste of more, and Izzy wanted more. She liked the press of him, the weight of him that pressed her body back to the sand. There was the tranquillity of escape she found as his kiss deepened and his hand moved naturally, sliding around her waist to caress her, and then even before Diego paused, Izzy's lips were still.

She rested her head on his shoulder a moment to steady herself, the weight of her baby between them.

'I think...' Izzy pulled her head up and made

herself look at him '…we should pretend that just didn't happen.'

'It did, though,' Diego pointed out.

'Well, it can't again,' Izzy said, and she hoisted herself to standing. 'Let's just keep it as friends,' Izzy insisted, because that was surely all they could be for now, except her lips were tender from the claim of his kiss as she tried to talk about *other* things, and as they walked back her hand bunched in a fist so she didn't reach out and take his.

They were back at her car, his apartment just a short walk away, and how he wanted to take her up there, to peel off her wet clothes and call in sick, spend the day getting to know her in the way he so badly wanted to.

And friends could kiss goodbye on the cheek, except they had passed that now and any contact between them was dangerous.

He faced her, but that only made him want to kiss her again so Diego looked down and saw the swell of her stomach, her belly button just starting to protrude, and his hand ached to capture it, only his mind wasn't so sure.

'We have a lot to think about,' Diego said, 'or maybe it's better not to think about it, just…' He looked up at her and his face was honest and it scared her, but somehow it made her smile as he offered her a very grown-up slant on words said in playgrounds the world over. 'I don't want to be your friend any more.'

CHAPTER SEVEN

'YOU'RE expected to go, Diego!' Rita was adamant. 'You can't not go to the Penhally Ball.'

They'd been having this conversation all morning. Rita had found out that he wasn't going and it seemed every time he passed her work station, she thought of another reason why he must go.

He'd just come from a family meeting with the parents of Toby Geller, which had been difficult at best, and, really, the last thing Diego cared about was if he was *expected* to attend some charity ball that was being held on Saturday.

'You're going, aren't you, Megan?' Rita looked up and Diego rolled his eyes as Megan gave a thin smile.

'It is expected,' Megan agreed, but from her resigned voice it was clear she wasn't looking forward to it.

'All the units send their senior staff,' Rita said, still talking as she answered the phone.

'Spare me,' Diego said. 'Is it awful?'

'No.' Megan shook her head. 'It's actually a great night…'

'So why the long face?' He was friends with Megan.

Well, not 'ring each other up every night and why don't we go for coffee type friends', but certainly they were friendly and Diego couldn't help but notice she was unusually low.

'Just one of those days!' Megan said, which given they had just been in with Toby's parents, could have explained it, except Megan hadn't been her usual self lately. Diego suddenly wondered if it had anything to do with the rumours that were flying around the hospital about Izzy and himself.

Diego hadn't realised just how many people he knew. And Izzy too.

It seemed that everywhere they went, be it a walk on the beach or to a café near his flat, they would bump into someone from work. But it wasn't just the rumour mill causing problems. Izzy was almost nine weeks from her due date now, and despite them both trying to be nothing more than just friends, that kiss had unleashed the attraction between them. It was so palpable, so present, it was killing Diego not to whisk her away from the home she was selling and bring her back to his flat, feed her, nurture her and make love to her. Except in a few weeks' time, Izzy would be a mother, which meant there would be a baby, and that was something way down on his list.

So far down, he hadn't actually thought whether one day he might want one of his own—let alone someone else's.

But he wanted her.

'It's a lovely night.' Rita just wouldn't let up; she was off the phone and back to one of her favourite subjects—prying about Megan. 'All the money raised goes to the Penhally Rape Crisis Centre. Will you be taking anyone, Doctor?'

Ah, but Megan was always one step ahead. 'You heard the man.' Megan flashed Rita a smile that was false. 'He doesn't want to go.'

'Oh!'

Diego couldn't help but grin as a Rita's eyes momentarily widened as she wondered if she'd stumbled on the news of year, but then she remembered the latest information from her sources. She turned back to the computer and resumed typing. Attempting nonchalance, she tested the seemingly gentle waters. 'It's good to support these things.' Rita tap tapped away, 'Look what happened to our own lovely Izzy. I'd have thought you, Diego, more than anyone, would…' And she stopped, just stopped in mid-sentence, because even if she wasn't looking at him, even if Diego hadn't spoken, the atmosphere was so tense, she just knew he wasn't smiling now. 'We should all do our bit,' Rita attempted, typing faster now, hoping she'd rectified it, and hoping Diego hadn't understood what she had implied.

She was wrong on both counts.

'Me? More? Than? Anyone?' Diego's voice was pure ice as he challenged her—each word separate, each word a question, and Diego looked at Megan, who shook her head in disbelief at Rita's insensitivity. 'What do you mean by that, Rita?'

Still she typed on. 'Well, you're a nice young man, I thought you of all people…' Her face was pink and she licked her lips before carrying on. 'Well, that you'd support such a thing.'

'Do you know why I hate gossip, Megan?' Diego looked at his friend.

'Why?' Megan answered.

'Because the fools that spread it get it wrong. Because the fools that spread it are so miserable in their own lives they have to find that part in others…' Rita stood up.

'I have to get on.' She picked up some papers, *any* papers, and walked off, but Diego's voice chased her.

'Because though they insist their lives are perfect, gossiping about others ensures that for that moment no one is gossiping about them.'

Rita spun on her heel. 'You can't stop people talking.'

'Ah, but you can,' Diego said, and pointedly turned to Megan, ignoring Rita completely. 'Before you go, I've got two in the nursery that need their drug charts re-written and Genevieve is ready to go home. Her mum wants to thank you.'

It was a relief to talk about work.

For Megan to fill in the drug charts and then to head to the nursery where Genevieve was wearing a hot pink all-in-one with a hot pink hat, and a car seat was waiting to finally, against all the odds, take her home. Diego smiled as Megan picked up the little lady and gave her a cuddle, and he could see the tears in her eyes too because, unlike Diego, Megan did get attached. She gave her heart and soul to her patients, took it personally when a battle was lost. Diego wasn't sure it was a healthy thing for her to do, but today was a good day and those, Diego suddenly realised, were the ones Megan struggled with most.

'We can't thank you enough.' Genevieve's mum was effusive in her gratitude. 'It's because of you that we get to take her home.'

Yes, today was a good day.

'Good job,' Diego said before he headed back to his charges. 'For a while there I didn't think we'd get to this day with Genevieve. You never gave in, though.'

'I never would,' Megan said, and then she paused and her voice was more pensive than jubilant. 'Be careful, Diego.'

He knew exactly what they were talking about.

'We're just friends,' he said, but he could hear the protest in his heart and Megan could hear it in his voice.

'She's fragile…'

'She's getting stronger,' Diego countered, because he would not label Izzy, because he could feel in his soul all she was going to be.

'Just, please,' Megan said, and it was the most she would say to him, 'handle with care.'

'You're looking well.' Gus smiled as he called Izzy into his surgery.

He was a wonderful GP. He read through her charts and checked her blood pressure, even though the midwife had done the same and told Izzy it was fine.

'How is it?'

'Perfect,' Gus said. 'How have you been feeling?'

'Very well,' Izzy said, and it was the truth. For the first time in her pregnancy it wasn't Henry and the nightmare of her past that consumed her, it was something far nicer.

There had been no repeat of that kiss, but there was an energy and promise in her days now and Izzy knew it was just a matter of time.

'You're eating well?' Gus checked, and though his face never flickered, Izzy was a doctor too and could hear the slight probing nature of his question. Often her antenatal visits seemed more like a friendly catch-up, but today Gus was going through her notes, double-checking everything.

'I'm eating really well.' Which was true. In the very dark weeks after Henry's death, even though eating had been the last thing on her mind, Izzy had made herself eat, for the baby's sake. She had even gone as far as to set a reminder on her mobile, forcing down smoothies or even just a piece of toast. But since she'd been back at work, and of course since she'd met Diego, her appetite had returned—for food, for life. She was laughing, she was happy, she was eating—except her weight, Gus said, was down.

It seemed ironic that when she was eating the most, when she was happiest, she hadn't put on any weight. Gus asked her to lie on the examination bed, and though he was always thorough, today his examination took a little longer than usual.

'You're a bit small,' Gus said, and Izzy lay there staring at the ceiling, because if Gus said she was a bit small, then she *was* small. He ran a Doppler over her stomach and listened for a couple of moments to the baby's heartbeat, which was strong and regular. 'How's the baby's movement?'

'There's lots,' Izzy said, trying to keep her voice light and even.

'That's good.' He was very calm, very unruffled and he helped her sit up and then she joined him at his desk.

'Are you worried?' Izzy asked.

'Not unduly,' Gus said. 'Izzy, you've had unbelievable stress throughout this pregnancy—but you're thirty-one weeks now and this is the time that the baby starts to put on weight, so we really do need to keep a slightly closer eye on you. I was going to schedule an ultrasound for a couple of weeks, but let's bring that forward.' He glanced at his watch. It was six on Friday evening. 'Let's get this done early next week and then…' She was due to start coming to fortnightly visits now, but Gus was nothing if not thorough. 'Let's get the scan and I'll see you again next week.'

'You know that I'm working?' Izzy felt incredibly guilty, but Gus moved to reassure her.

'Lots of my mums work right up till their due date, Izzy. You're doing nothing wrong—for now. I just want you to try and reduce your stress and really make sure you're eating well. You need some extra calories. I'd suggest you add a protein shake to your breakfast.'

'I'm supposed to be going to the Penhally Ball tomorrow…'

Out of the blue Diego had suggested they go together—face the gossip and just get it over and done with, and what better way than at the Penhally Ball, when everyone would be there. They had, Diego had pointed out, absolutely nothing to be ashamed of. To the world they were friends and friends went out! Except Izzy still cared what others might think and almost hoped Gus would shake his head and tell her that the weekend might be better spent resting on the couch with her feet up, thus give her a reason not to go, but Gus seemed delighted. 'That's good—I'm glad you're starting to go out.'

'Shouldn't I be resting?'

'Izzy, I'm not prescribing bed rest—I want you to relax and a social life is a part of that. I just want to keep a closer eye on you.'

'The thing is...' She was testing the water, just dipping in her toe. She respected Gus, and his reaction mattered. 'Things have been awful, but for the last few weeks, for the first time since I've been pregnant, I haven't had any stress or, rather, much less, and I have been eating better...'

'Well, whatever it is you're doing, keep it up,' Gus said, and Izzy gave a small swallow.

'I'm going to the ball with a friend, Diego.'

'Ramirez.' Izzy frowned as Gus said his surname.

'You know him?'

'There aren't too many Diegos around here. The neonatal nurse?'

And she waited for his shock-horror reaction, for him to tell her she should be concentrating on the baby now, not out dancing with male *friends*, but instead Gus smiled.

'He seems a nice man.'

When Izzy just sat there Gus smiled. 'You deserve nice, Izzy.'

She still didn't know it.

CHAPTER EIGHT

SHE'D cancel.

Izzy could hardly hear the hairdresser's comments as she sat with a black cape around her shoulders, pretending to look as a mirror was flashed behind her head.

'It looks fantastic!'

Well, she would say that, Izzy thought to herself. The hairdresser was hardly going to say, 'It looks awful and what on earth were you thinking, taking a pair of scissors to your locks, you stupid tart?' But as the mirror hovered behind her Izzy actually did look, and for once she agreed with the woman who wielded the scissors.

Okay, maybe fantastic was stretching things a touch, but it had been three months and three trips to this chair since that moment of self-loathing and finally, finally, she didn't look like a five-year-old who had taken the kitchen scissors to the bathroom. The last of her home-made crop had been harvested, the once jagged spikes now softened, shades of blonde and caramel moving when her head did, which it did as Izzy craned her neck for a proper look.

'I've hardly taken anything off at the front or sides,

just softened it a touch, but I've taken a fair bit off the back…'

Izzy could have kissed her but instead she left a massive tip, booked in for six weeks' time, skipped out to her car and somehow made it home without incident, despite the constant peeks in the rear-view mirror at her very new 'side fringe'.

And then she remembered.

She was cancelling.

So why was she running a bath and getting undressed?

A tepid bath so it didn't fluff up her hair.

She couldn't do it, couldn't go, just couldn't face it.

So instead of climbing in to the water she wrapped herself in a towel and padded out to the living room.

She had every reason to cancel, Izzy told herself as she picked up the telephone, except there was a voice-mail message. It wasn't Diego stuck at work, as she had rather hoped, but the real estate agent with a pathetic offer. 'It's a good offer, you should seriously consider it,' played the message. Henry had been a real estate agent and had practically said those words in his sleep so she deleted it and got back to fretting about Diego. The fact that she was pregnant and had worked all morning, the fact that she wasn't ready for the inevitable stares if she walked into the Penhally Ball with a dashing Spaniard on her arm when she should be home…

Doing what? Izzy asked herself.

Grieving, feeling wretched…

Her introspection was halted by the doorbell. No doubt the postman had been while she was out and it was her neighbour with another box of self-help or baby books that she had ordered on the internet during one of her glum times—a book that at the time she had convinced herself would be the one to show her, tell her, inform her how the hell she was supposed to be feeling...

'Diego?'

It was only five p.m. and he shouldn't be there, the ball didn't start till seven.

There was no reason for him to be there now and, worse, she was only wearing a towel.

'I thought I'd come early.' He leant in the doorway and smiled, and either the baby did a big flip or her stomach curled in on itself. He was in evening wear, except he hadn't shaved, and he looked ravishing, so ravishing she wanted to do just that—ravish him, drop the towel she was clinging to, right here at the front door. 'To save you that phone call.'

'What phone call?' Izzy lowered her head a touch as she let him in, wishing there had been a warning sign on the kitchen scissors to inform her that it would be a full twelve to eighteen months before she could again hide her facial expressions with her hair if she chose to lop it all off. A fringe simply wouldn't suffice. Her whole body was on fire, every pulse leaping at the sight of him.

'The one where you tell me your back is aching, or you're tired or that it was lovely of me to ask, but...'

'I was just about to make it,' Izzy admitted.

'Why?'

'Because it's too soon.'

'For what?'

'For me to be out, for me to be…' She blanched at the unsaid word.

'Happy?' Diego offered. 'Living?'

Neither was quite right. Izzy didn't correct him at first, she just clung to her towel, not to keep him from her but to keep her from him, and she stared at a man who had brought nothing but joy into her life. She wanted more of the same.

'For me to be seeing someone,' Izzy corrected. 'Which I think I am.'

'You are,' he confirmed, and crossed the room. It was a relief to be kissed, to kiss him, to be kissed some more, to kiss back. He was less than subtle, he was devouring her, and any vision that their next kiss would be gentle and tender was far removed from delicious reality. Diego had waited long for another kiss and he was claiming it now, pressing her against the wall as she rejoiced in him, her towel falling. He kicked it away and all she wanted was more, more, more.

He tasted as he had that morning but decisiveness made it better. He smelt as he always had, just more concentrated now, and this close to Diego, this into Diego, she forgot to be scared and hold back.

Izzy just forgot.

She could have climbed up the wall and slid onto him he felt so delicious, but just as her senses faded to oblivion, Diego resurrected one of his.

'Is that a bath?'

Now, this bit she didn't get.

Sense *should* have prevailed.

In her mad dash to turn off the taps, okay, yes it was okay that he followed, but then, *then* she should have shown him the door, should have closed it on him and had a few moments' pause, except she let him help her into the bath and then she remembered to be practical. 'Diego, we can't.'

'I know.' He took off his jacket, hung it on the doorhandle and then sat on the edge and looked at her, and she couldn't believe how normal it felt.

'We can't,' he confirmed, because of the baby she carried. 'How far along are you again?' He grinned and then rolled his eyes as he did the mental arithmetic, because this thing between them had already been going on for a couple of weeks!

'Poor Diego.' Why was she laughing? Lying in the bath and laughing like she was happy. And the fact that she was made her suddenly serious.

'How can this work—ever?' Izzy asked, because surely it was impossible. 'You're going back to Spain.'

'Nope.' He shook his head. 'I didn't apply.'

'There'll be other jobs though. One day you will go back.' And he couldn't argue with that, so instead she watched as he rolled up his sleeves and two tanned olive hands took a lilac bar of soap and worked it. She could see the bubbles between his fingers, see the moist, slippery sheen of his hands, and her body quivered and begged for them to be on her. As his hands met her shoulders her mind stopped looking for reasons to halt this and her brain stopped begging for logic and all she did was feel—feel his strong fingers on her tense shoulders, feel the knots of tight muscles spasm in momentary protest as this large Spaniard had the nerve to tell them to let go. For months, no, maybe a year, or had it been longer, those muscles had been knotted with the serious job of holding her head up high and now they were being told to let go, to give in, that they could relax, regroup and get ready for the next mountain Izzy was certain that she would surely have to climb. But Diego's hands worked on and convinced her shoulders, if not her mind, to do as the master skilfully commanded, and let go.

Her fringe almost met the water with the relief.

Like popping a balloon she just gave in, just groaned as her tension seeped into the water and then steamed out into the room.

She just couldn't let go for long, though.

'I can't get my hair wet!' She flailed at all his hands were offering, she just couldn't relax and enjoy it in long stages. 'How can this work, Diego?' she asked again.

'*Sencillo*,' Diego said, 'It doesn't have to be complicated. Why not just for now? Why not for as long as we make each other happy?'

'Because in nine weeks I'll be diving into postnatal depression and I won't be making anyone happy!'

She wanted guarantees.

Wanted a little piece of paper stamped with *I won't hurt you* to be handed to her now, except she'd had that once, Izzy realised as she lay there, a big piece of paper called a wedding certificate, and it hadn't counted for a thing.

Before Diego had come along living had been like essential surgery without analgesia.

Why would she deny herself the balm of relief?

And there was a wobble of guilt there, but for him. 'What if I'm using you!' God, she had never been so honest, and certainly not with a man. All her relationships had been Izzy pleasing others, Izzy saying the right thing, and now here she was, ten minutes into a new one and saying the wrong thing, saying truthfully what was on her mind. 'What if I'm using you to get through this?'

And he thought about it for a moment, he actually did, and then he came to his decision.

'Use away!'

'What if I'm avoiding my pain by…?'

'Shut up.' He grinned and leaned over and kissed her a nice lazy kiss. Then he kissed her shoulder and along the slippery wet lines of her neck.

Oh, Diego loved women. He loved curves on women and two of Izzy's were floating on the water, just bobbing there, and his hands moved to her shoulders, because it seemed more polite. But then his hands just moved to where they wanted to be and he caressed them, caressed her. His big, dark hands cupped and soaped her very white, rather large, to Izzy rather ugly breasts, but maybe they weren't so ugly, because from the trip in his breathing and the bob of his tongue on his dark lips, she had the feeling that one tug of his tie and he'd be in the water with her, and there would be two empty seats at the Penhally Charity Ball.

'We can't,' she said again and it was the feeblest of protests, because the stubble of his chin was scratching her breast now, his tongue on her nipple and her fingers in his hair.

'You can,' Diego said, as his hand slid beneath the water.

She never fully forgot about the hell of the past months and years. No matter how good, how happy, how busy she was, no matter what conversation she was holding, it never completely left her mind, but as his hand slid beneath the water and Izzy could feel his fingers at the top of her thighs, ever-present thoughts started to fade. She could feel his hot mouth on her cool shoulder and always, always, always she had thought of pleasing *him*, not Diego, but *him*, and the mute button hit and there was nothing to think of but this, nothing to relish but Diego's tender explorations as she wriggled in his palm.

Her cynical voice gave one last call for order. After all, she didn't come with instructions, and he must do this an awful lot, because his fingers read her so well, but she was kissing his neck and above his white collar, coiling her wet fingers in his dark hair as a heavenly regular pressure beat beneath the water. And suddenly she didn't care if he did this a lot, he was doing it to her, right now, and he could go on doing it for ever, it was so divine. He stroked her back to life, cajoled her hibernating clitoris from its dreamless sleep, and it stretched and peeked out and Izzy was sure this feeling must end, that she'd shift or he'd pause and that the magic would stop, and she didn't want it to.

She couldn't lean back because she didn't want to.

She couldn't reach for the sides of the bath because then she couldn't hold him.

She held his shirt-clad back with wet arms and

muffled her face in his neck and beneath the cologne that he was wearing tonight was the true scent of him, the one that every cell in her body had flared for on sight and burnt now with direct contact.

Let go, his fingers insisted. *Let go*, the stubble of his chin told her eyelids as she pressed her face into him. She could hear the lap, lap, lap of the water and the patience yet relentlessness of him and she did as his fingers told her, she didn't know what she said and she didn't know what she did—she just let go. She was almost climbing out of the bath and into his arms, but he held her down and it was so much better than being just friends. And as she opened her eyes he closed his; as he struggled to get through the next nine seconds, Izzy was wondering how they'd get through the next nine weeks. She wanted more of him.

'We're going to be late.' He was trying to sound normal.

Really, really late, because Izzy now had to sort out her hair and do her make-up *and* show him where the ironing board was so he could iron his shirt dry.

But it was more than worth it.

CHAPTER NINE

She had known heads would turn and they did, but what Izzy hadn't expected were the smiles that followed the arches of the eyebrows as they walked in together.

Real smiles, because how could they not?

Izzy had been through so very much and her friends and colleagues had been worried about her, had not known how to react in the face of such raw pain and grief, but tonight she was glowing and it wasn't just from the pregnancy.

'Don't you dare say you're just friends, because I won't believe you.' Megan came over as Diego went to the bar. 'Friends,' Megan said, 'are able to go two minutes without eye contact,' she pointed out as she caught Izzy and Diego share a lingering look from across the room. 'Friends don't light up a room with their energy when they walk in. Friends don't cause every head to turn. Friends, my foot…' Megan laughed.

'Okay, 'Izzy said, and though it was all a bit like a runaway train, she felt exhilarated as she rode it, smiled as she said it: 'We're more than friends.'

'Happy?' Megan checked.

'Very.'

'Then I'm happy for you,' Megan said. Izzy was sure she would have loved to have said more, but sometimes good friends didn't. Sometimes good friends had to let you make your own success or mistakes and be there for you whatever the outcome. Megan confirmed that with her next words.

'I'm always here.'

'I know that.'

'So how did you manage the night off? I thought you were on.'

'No.' Izzy shook her head, 'I told you, I'm only doing days till the baby's born. I thought you were on call?'

'Richard didn't want to come to the ball, so he's covering for me,' Megan said. 'So who's holding the fort in A and E tonight?'

'Mitch,' Izzy said.

'He's only a resident.'

'Oh, Ben is on call, said he might pop in if he can get away....' And her voice trailed off, because Izzy realised then that Megan hadn't actually been enquiring about her roster, she had been fishing to find out the whereabouts of someone else. And as Megan stood and kissed Izzy on the cheek and headed off into the throng of people, Izzy found a corner of an unexpected jigsaw.

She could see Megan, her usually pale cheeks, suddenly flushed and pink, desperately trying to focus on a conversation, but her green eyes kept flicking over to Josh. It was as if there were an invisible thread between them, a thread that tightened. She watched as

Josh worked the room, each greeting, each two-minute conversation seemed to be dragging him on a human Mexican wave towards Megan. The pull was so strong, Izzy could have sworn she could have reached out and grabbed it.

And then it snapped.

Izzy watched as a blonde woman walked over, all smiles, and kissed Josh possessively on the lips. Izzy saw the wedding band glint on her finger and as Megan's face turned away, Izzy knew Megan had just seen it too.

'Excuse me...' All the colour had drained out of Megan's face and she walked quickly to the ladies. Izzy looked over at Josh who was concentrating on something his wife was saying, but then he caught her eye and Izzy couldn't read his expression, but something told her it was a plea to help.

'Here...' Diego was back with the drinks and it was Izzy's turn to excuse herself, but by the time she got to the ladies Megan was on her way out.

'Hey?' Izzy smiled. 'Are you okay?'

'I'm great!' Megan gave a dazzling smile. 'It's always a good night.'

'Megan?' Izzy caught her friend's arm, but Megan shook it off.

'I must get back out there.'

Oh, she wanted to know what was going on, to help, to fix, to share, only it was clear all Megan wanted to do was to get through this night.

'Sit with us,' Izzy suggested. 'I thought we would be with the emergency guys and girls or NICU, but we left the booking too late and we're with the maternity mob. Come and keep us company.' It was the best she could do for Megan right now and when Megan jumped at the suggestion, Izzy knew she had been right.

There was something going on with Megan and Josh.

Or, Izzy pondered, there had been.

It was actually a good night—the food was wonderful, the company great. Diego was clearly a hit with the maternity team as well, but as the table was cleared and the dancing commenced Izzy was uncomfortable all of a sudden in the hard chair. Stretching her spine, she shifted her weight and she was glad to stretch her legs when Diego asked her to dance.

It was such bliss to be in his arms.

To smell him, to be held by him.

She wished the music would last for ever—that somehow she could freeze this moment of time, where there was no past to run from and no future that could change things. She wished she could dance and dance, just hold this moment and forever feel his breath on her neck and his warm hands on her back, to feel the bulge of her pregnant stomach pressed to his and to remember…

She was dizzy almost remembering a couple of hours earlier.

'Glad you came?' Diego asked.

'Very,' Izzy said, and then pulled back and smiled. 'And more than a little surprised that I did.'

Every day he saw another side to her.

Diego was far from stupid. Of course he had questioned the wisdom of getting involved with someone at such a vulnerable time—fatherhood was not on his agenda. After a lifetime of rules and the stuffy confines of his family, he had sworn it would be years before anyone or anything pinned him down. He was devoted to his work and everything else was just a pleasure, but now, holding her in his arms, life was starting to look a little different.

'Hey.' He'd sensed her distraction. 'What are you watching?'

'What's going on,' she asked, 'with Megan and Josh?'

Diego rolled his eyes. 'Not you too? Rita, my ward clerk, is obsessed with them.'

'Megan's been different lately,' Izzy insisted. 'Surely you've noticed?'

'I've had my mind on other things,' he said, pulling her in a little tighter. 'There's nothing going on,' Diego said assuredly, and glanced at the subjects of their conversation. 'They're not even talking to each other.'

Which was such a male thing to say, but Megan was right, Izzy thought, watching Josh's eyes scan the room as he danced with his wife, watched them locate and capture and hold their target, almost in apology, until Megan tore hers away.

Friends don't share looks like that.

But in that moment all thoughts of Josh and Megan faded, all thoughts of Diego and romance too, because the back pain she had felt while sitting returned, spreading out from her spine like two large hands, stretching around to her stomach and squeezing. It wasn't a pain as such, she'd been having Braxton-Hicks' contractions, but this felt different, tighter. This didn't take her breath, neither did it stop her swaying in the darkness with Diego, but she was more than aware of it and then it was gone and she tried to forget that it had happened. only Diego had been aware of it too.

He had felt her stomach, which was pressed into his, tighten.

He didn't want to be one of those paranoid people. She was just dancing on so he did too, but he was almost more aware of her body than his own. He could feel the slight shift and knew that even though she danced on and held him, her mind was no longer there.

'You okay?'

'Great,' she murmured, hoping and praying that she was. The music played on and Diego suggested that they sit this next one out. Izzy was about to agree, only suddenly the walk back to their table seemed rather long. The music tipped into the next ballad and Izzy leant on him as the next small wave hit, only this time it did make her catch her breath and Diego could pretend no more.

'Izzy?' She heard the question in his voice.

'I don't know,' she admitted. 'Can you get me outside?' she said, still leaning on him, waiting for it to pass. 'In a moment.'

Their exit was discreet. He had a hand round her waist and they didn't stop to get her bag, and as the cool night air hit, Izzy wondered if she was overreacting because now she felt completely normal.

'Izzy.' Discreet as their exit had been, Gus must have

noticed because he joined them outside, just as another contraction hit.

'They're not strong,' Izzy said as Gus placed a skilled hand on her abdomen.

'How far apart?' Gus asked, and it was Diego who answered.

'Six, maybe seven minutes.'

'Okay.' Gus wasted no time. 'Let's get you over to the hospital and we can pop you on a monitor. I'll bring the Jeep around.'

'Should we call an ambulance?' Diego asked, but Gus shook his head.

'We'll be quicker in my Jeep and if we have to pull over, I've got everything we need.'

'I'm not having it,' Izzy insisted, only neither Diego nor Gus was convinced.

It was a thirty-minute drive from Penhally. Diego felt a wave of unease as Izzy's hand gripped his tighter and she blew out a long breath. He remembered his time on Maternity and often so often it was a false alarm, the midwives could tell. Izzy kept insisting she was fine, that the contractions weren't that bad, but he could feel her fingers digging into his palms at closer intervals, could see Gus glancing in the rear-view mirror when Izzy held her breath every now and then, and the slight acceleration as Gus drove faster.

His mind was racing, awful scenarios playing out, but Izzy could never have guessed. He stayed strong and supportive beside her, held her increasingly tightening fingers as Gus rang through and warned the hospital of their arrival. A staff member was waiting with a wheelchair as they pulled up at the maternity section.

'It's too soon,' Izzy said as he helped her out of the Jeep.

'You're in the right place,' Diego said, only he could feel his heart hammering in his chest, feel the adrenaline coursing through him as she was whisked off and all he could do was give her details as best as he could to a new night receptionist.

'You're the father?' ahe asked, and his lips tightened as he shook his head, and he felt the relegation.

'I'm a friend,' Diego said. 'Her...' But he didn't know what to follow it up with. It had been just a few short weeks, and he wasn't in the least surprised when he was asked to take a seat in a bland waiting room

He waited, unsure what to do, what his role was—if he even had a role here.

Going over and over the night, stunned at how quickly everything had changed. One minute they had been dancing, laughing—now they were at the hospital.

The logical side of his brain told him that thirty-one weeks' gestation was okay. Over and over he tried to console himself, tried to picture his reaction if he knew a woman was labouring and he was preparing a cot to receive the baby. Yet there was nothing logical about the panic that gripped him when he thought of Izzy's baby being born at thirty-one weeks. Every complication, every possibility played over and over. It was way too soon, and even if everything did go well, Izzy would be in for a hellish ride when she surely didn't deserve it.

They could stop the labour, though. Diego swung

between hope and despair. She'd only just started to have contractions…

'Diego.' Gus came in and shook his hand.

'How is she?'

'Scared,' Gus said, and gave him a brief rundown of his findings. 'We've given her steroids to mature the baby's lungs and we're trying to stop the labour or at least slow down the process to give the medication time to take effect.'

'Oh, God…' Guilt washed over him, a guilt he knew was senseless, but guilt all the same. However, Gus was one step ahead of him.

'Nothing Izzy or you did contributed to this, Diego. I've spoken with Izzy at length, this was going to happen. In fact…' he gave Diego a grim smile '…an ultrasound and cord study have just been done. Her placenta is small and the cord very thin. This baby really will do better on the outside, though we'd all like to buy another week or two. I knew the baby was small for dates. Izzy was going to have an ultrasound early next week, but from what I've just seen Izzy's baby really will do better by being born.'

'She's been eating well, taking care of herself.'

'She suffered trauma both physically and emotionally early on in the pregnancy,' Gus said. 'Let's just get her through tonight, but guilt isn't going to help anyone.'

Diego knew that. He'd had the same conversation with more parents than he could remember—the endless search for answers, for reasons, when sometimes Mother Nature worked to her own agenda.

'Does she want to see me?'

Gus nodded. 'She doesn't want to call her family just yet.'

When he saw her, Diego remembered the day he had first met her when she had come to the neonatal ward. Wary, guarded, she sat on the bed, looking almost angry, but he knew she was just scared.

'It's going to be okay,' Diego said, and took her hand, but she pulled it away.

'You don't know that.'

She sat there and she had all her make-up on, her hair immaculate, except she was in a hospital gown with a drip and a monitor strapped to her stomach, and Diego wondered if she did actually want him there at all.

She did.

But how could she ask him to be there for her?

She was scared for her baby, yet she resented it almost.

Nine weeks.

They'd had nine weeks left of being just a couple, which was not long by anyone's standards. Nine weeks to get to know each other properly, to enjoy each other, and now even that nine weeks was being denied to them.

How could she admit how much she wanted him to stay—yet how could she land all this on him?

'I think you should go.'

'Izzy.' Diego kept his voice steady. 'Whatever helps you now is fine by me. I can call your family. I can stay with you, or I can wait outside, or if you would prefer that I leave…'

He wanted to leave, Izzy decided, or he wouldn't have said it. The medication they had given her to slow down the labour made her brain work slower, made her thought process muddy.

'I don't know...' Her teeth were chattering, her admission honest. Gus was back, talking to a midwife and Richard Brooke, the paediatric consultant, who had just entered the room. They were all looking at the printout from the monitor and Izzy wanted five minutes alone with Diego, five minutes to try and work out whether or not he wanted to be there, but she wasn't going to get five minutes with her thoughts for a long while.

'Izzy.' She knew that voice and so did Diego, knew that brusque, professional note so well, because they had both used it themselves when they bore bad tidings. 'The baby is struggling; its heartbeat is irregular...'

'It needs time to let the medication take effect.' Izzy's fuzzy logic didn't work on Gus. He just stood over her, next to Diego, both in suits and looking sombre, and she felt as if she were lying in a coffin. 'We want to do a Caesarean, your baby needs to be born.'

Already the room was filling with more staff. She felt the jerk as the brakes were kicked off the bed, the clang as portable oxygen was lifted onto the bed and even in her drugged state she knew this wasn't your standard Caesarean section, this was an emergency Caesarean.

'Is there time...?' She didn't even bother to finish her sentence. Izzy could hear the deceleration in her baby's heartbeat, and knew there wouldn't be time for an epidural, that she would require a general anaesthetic, and it was the scariest, out-of-control feeling. 'Can you be there, Diego?' Her eyes swung from Diego to Gus. 'Can Diego be in there?'

For a general anaesthetic, partners or relatives weren't allowed to come into the theatre, but the NICU team were regularly in Theatre and after just the briefest pause Richard agreed, but with clarification. 'Just for Izzy.'

'Sure,' Diego agreed, and at that moment he'd have agreed to anything, because the thought of being sent to another waiting room, *knowing* all that could go wrong, was unbearable, but as he helped speed the bed the short distance to Theatre, Diego also knew that if there was a problem with the babe, he wanted to be the one dealing with it. This was no time for arrogance neither was it time for feigned modesty—quite simply Diego knew he was the best.

The theatre sister gave Diego a slightly wide-eyed look as she registered he was holding hands with her emergency admission, whom she recognised too.

'Diego's here with Izzy,' the midwife explained. 'Richard has okayed him to go in.'

'Then you'll need to go and get changed,' came the practical response. 'You can say goodbye to her here.'

And that was it.

Diego knew when he saw her again, she would be under anaesthetic.

Izzy knew it too.

'I'm glad you're here…' She was trying not to cry and her face was smothered with the oxygen mask. 'You'll make sure…'

'Everything is going to be fine.' His voice came out

gruffer than he was used to hearing it. He was trying to reassure her, but Diego felt it sounded as if he was telling her off. 'Better than fine,' he said again. His voice still didn't soften, but there wasn't time to correct it. 'Thirty-one-weekers do well.'

'Thirty-two's better.'

'I'll be there,' Diego said. 'And it *is* going to be okay.'

He couldn't give her a kiss, because they were already moving her away.

He turned to Gus, who as her GP would also have to wait outside the operating theatre, and exchanged a look with the worried man. 'Go and get changed, Diego,' Gus said, and his words shocked Diego into action. He changed his clothes in a moment, then put on a hat and made his way through to Theatre.

'Diego!' Hugh, the paediatric anaesthetist greeted him from behind a yellow mask. 'Extremely bradycardic, ready for full resus.'

'Diego's here with the mother.' Brianna was there too, ready to receive the baby, and her unusually pointed tone was clearly telling her colleague to shut the hell up.

The surgeon on duty that night had already started the incision, and Diego knew the man in question was brilliant at getting a baby out urgently when required, but for Diego the world was in slow motion, the theatre clock hand surely sticking as it moved past each second marker.

'Breech.' The surgeon was calling for more traction. Diego could see the two spindly legs the surgeon held in one hand and for the first time in Theatre he felt nausea, understood now why relatives were kept out and almost wished he had been, because suddenly he appreciated how fathers-to-be must feel.

Except he wasn't the father, Diego told himself as the baby's limp body was manoeuvred out and the head delivered.

This baby wasn't his to love, Diego reminded himself as an extremely floppy baby was dashed across to the resuscitation cot.

He *never* wanted to feel like this again.

He never wanted to stand so helpless, just an observer. It would, for Diego, have been easier to work on her himself, yet he was in no state to.

He could feel his fingertips press into her palms with impatience as Hugh called twice for a drug, and though the team was fantastic, their calm professionalism riled him. Richard was fantastic, but Diego would have preferred Megan. Megan pounced on tiny details faster than anyone Diego had seen.

'She's still bradycardic,' Diego said, when surely they should have commenced massage now.

'Out.' Brianna mouthed the word and jerked her head to the theatre doors, but he hesitated.

'Diego!' Brianna said his name, and Diego stiffened in realisation—this wasn't his call, only it felt like it.

Brianna's brown eyes lifted again to his when Diego would have preferred them to stay on the baby, and he knew he was getting in the way, acting more like a father than a professional, so he left before he was formally asked to.

CHAPTER TEN

'THAT's it, Izzy…' She could hear a male voice she didn't recognise. 'Stay on your back.'

She was under blankets and wanted to roll onto her side, except she couldn't seem to move.

'You're doing fine,' came the unfamiliar voice. 'Stay nice and still.'

'Izzy, it's all okay.'

There was a voice she knew. Strong and deep and accented, and she knew it was Diego, she just didn't know why, and then she opened her eyes and saw his and she remembered.

'You've got a daughter.' His face was inches away. 'She's okay, she's being looked after.'

And then it was fog, followed by pain, followed by drugs, so many drugs she struggled to focus when Diego came back in the afternoon with pictures of her baby.

'She looks like you,' Diego said, but all Izzy could see were tubes.

'Are you working today?'

Diego shook his head. 'No. I just came in to see you.' And he sat down in the chair by her bed and Izzy went to sleep. He flicked through the photos and tried very hard to only see tubes, because this felt uncomfortably familiar, this felt a little like it had with Fernando and he just couldn't go there again.

He certainly wasn't ready to go there again.

There was a very good reason that a normal pregnancy lasted forty weeks, Diego reflected, putting the photos on her locker and heading for home—and it wasn't just for the baby. The parents needed every week of that time to prepare themselves emotionally for the change to their lives.

He wasn't even a parent.

It was Tuesday night and a vicious UTI later before anything resembling normal thought process occurred and a midwife helped her into a chair and along with her mother wheeled her down to the NICU, where, of course, any new mum would want to be if her baby was.

'We take mums down at night all the time,' the midwife explained, when Izzy said the next day would be fine. 'It's no problem.'

Except, privately, frankly, Izzy would have preferred to sleep.

Izzy knew she was a likely candidate for postnatal depression.

As a doctor she was well versed in the subject and the midwives had also gently warned her and given her leaflets to read. Gus too had talked to her—about her difficult labour, the fact she had been separated from her daughter and her difficult past. He'd told her he was there if she needed to talk and he had been open and upfront and told her not to hesitate to reach out sooner rather than later, as had Jess.

She sat in a wheelchair at the entrance to NICU, at the very spot where she had first flirted with Diego, where the first thawing of her heart had taken place, and it seemed a lifetime ago, not a few short weeks.

And, just as she had felt that day, Izzy was tempted to ask the midwife to turn the chair around, more nervous at meeting her baby than she could ever let on. Diego was on a stint of night duty and she was nervous of him seeing her in her new role too, because his knowing eyes wouldn't miss anything. What if she couldn't summon whatever feelings and emotions it was that new mums summoned?

'I bet you can't wait!' Izzy's mum said as the midwife pressed the intercom and informed the voice on the end of their arrival. Then the doors buzzed and she was let in. Diego came straight over and gave her a very nice smile and they made some introductions. 'Perhaps you could show Izzy's mother the coffee room.' Diego was firm on this as he would be with any of his mothers. If Izzy had stepped in and said she'd prefer her mum to come, then of course it would have happened, but Izzy stayed quiet, very glad of a chance to meet her daughter alone.

'I already know where the coffee room is,' Gwen said, 'and I've already seen the baby.'

'Izzy hasn't.' Diego was straight down the line. 'We can't re-create the delivery room but we try—she needs time alone to greet her baby.'

Which told her.

'You know the rules.' He treated Izzy professionally and she was very glad of it. They went through the hand-washing ritual and he spoke to her as they did so.

'Brianna is looking after her tonight,' Diego said. 'Do you know her?'

'I don't think so.'

'She's great—she was there at the delivery. I'll take you over.'

Nicola, Toby's mother, was there and gave Izzy a sympathetic smile as she was wheeled past, which Izzy returned too late, because she was already there at her baby's cot.

Brianna greeted her, but Izzy was hardly listening. Instead she stared into the cot and there she was—her baby. And months of fear and wondering all hushed for a moment as she saw her, her little red scrunched-up face and huge dark blue eyes that stared right into Izzy's.

Over the last three days Diego had bought her plenty of photos, told her how well she was doing and how beautiful she was, but seeing her in the flesh she was better than beautiful, she was hers.

'We're just giving her a little oxygen,' Brianna explained as Diego was called away. 'Which we will be for a couple more weeks, I'd expect…' She opened the porthole and Izzy needed no invitation. She held her daughter's hand, marvelling that such a tiny hand instinctively curled around her index finger, and Izzy knew there and then that she was in love.

'She looks better than I thought…' Izzy couldn't actually believe just how well she looked. Her mum had been crying when she'd returned the first day from visiting her granddaughter and Richard, the consultant paediatrician, had told her that her baby had got off to a rocky start.

'She struggled for the first forty-eight hours, which we were expecting,' Brianna said calmly, 'but she picked up well.'

Diego had said the same, but she'd been worried he'd just been reassuring her, but now she was here, now she could see her, all Izzy could feel was relief and this overwhelming surge charging through her veins that she figured felt a lot like love.

'Now, would you like to hold her?' Brianna said to Izzy's surprise. 'She's due for a feed, but she needs it soon, so would you like to give her a cuddle first?'

She very much would.

Brianna brought over a large chair and Izzy sat, exhausted, then got a new surge of energy.

'Open up your pyjama top,' Brianna said

'It's popping open all the time...' Izzy said, staring down at her newly massive breasts that strained the buttons.

'Your skin will keep her warm and it's good for both of you.'

She hadn't expected so much so soon. Her dreams had been filled with tiny floppy babies like ugly skinned rabbits, yet her baby was prettier and healthier than her photos had shown. Brianna was calm and confident and then there she was, wearing just a nappy and hat and resting on her chest, a blanket being wrapped around them both, skin on skin, and Izzy at that moment knew...

She knew, as far as anyone could possibly know, that the doom and gloom and the shadow of PND was not going to darken her door.

She could feel her baby on her skin and it was almost, Izzy was sure, as if all the darkness just fell away from her now, as pure love flooded in.

A white, pure love that was tangible, that was real. All the fears, the doubts, the dark, dark dread faded, because she had never been sure, really, truly sure that love *could* win, that love would come, that it would happen.

But it just did.

Diego witnessed it too.

He had seen many moments like this one, both in NICU and in the delivery room, and it was more something he ticked off his list than felt moved by—especially in NICU, where bonding was more difficult to achieve. Only it wasn't a list with Izzy, because it did move him, so much so that he came over and smiled down as he watched.

It crossed so many lines, because he didn't want to feel it, and also, as Gwen came over, Diego realised he had sent her own mother away.

Yet he was here.

'She's a Ross all over, isn't she?' Gwen said, and Diego saw Izzy's jaw clench as her mother stamped her territory on her granddaughter and told her how it would be. 'There's nothing of him in her.'

Of course, Henry's parents begged to differ when they came two days later to visit.

They had been in France, trying to have a break, after the most traumatic of months, and had cut their holiday short to come in and visit what was left of their son.

It was an agonising visit. Emotions frayed, Henry's mother teary, his father trying to control things, telling Izzy their rights, blaming her at every turn till she could see clearly where Henry had got it from! And, that evening, as soon as they left, Izzy sat on the bed with her fingers pressed into her eyes, trying to hold it together, wondering if now tears would come.

'Bad timing?' Izzy jumped as heard footsteps and saw Josh, the new consultant, at her door. 'I'll come by another time.'

'I'm fine.' Izzy forced a smile. 'Come in.'

'You're sure?' he checked, and Izzy nodded.

'I'm sorry to mess up the roster.'

'That's the last thing you should be worrying about,' Josh replied, just as any boss would in the circumstances, and it was going to be an awkward visit, Izzy knew that. A guy like Josh didn't really belong in the maternity ward with teary women. 'Ben's on leave, but he rang and told me you'd be stressing about details like that, and could I come up and tell you that you're not to worry about a thing and that if there's anything we can do for you, you're to ask.

'Is there anything,' Josh pushed, 'that we can do for you now?'

'I'm being very well looked after. I'm fine, really, it's just been a difficult evening.' She waited for a thin line from Josh about the baby blues, or something like that, but he just looked at her for a long time before he spoke.

'I'm quite sure this is all very difficult for you,' Josh said.

And he was just so disarmingly nice that Izzy found herself admitting a little more. 'Henry's parents just stopped by. They've gone to see the baby.'

'Henry's your late husband?' Josh checked, and Izzy nodded.

'I'm sure you've heard all the gossip.'

'I don't listen to gossip,' Josh said, 'though Ben did bring me up to date on what happened before you came back to work, just so that I would know to look out for you. You know Ben's not into gossip either, but he felt I should know—not all of it, I'm sure, but he told me enough that I can see you'd be having a tough time of it.'

His directness surprised her. Instead of sitting stiffly in the chair and making painful small talk, he came over and sat on the bed, took her hand and gave it a squeeze and a bit of that Irish charm, and Izzy could see why he was such a wonderful doctor.

'Henry's parents blame me,' Izzy admitted. 'They thought our marriage was perfect, they think I'm making it all up.'

'They probably want to believe that you're making it all up,' Josh said wisely.

'They were in tears just before, saying what a wonderful father Henry would have been, how a baby would have changed things, would have saved our marriage, if only I hadn't asked him to leave. They don't know what went on behind closed doors.'

'They need to believe that you're lying,' Josh said. 'But you know the truth.'

'A baby wouldn't have changed things.' With his gentle guidance Izzy's voice was finally adamant. 'Babies don't fix a damaged marriage. That was why I had to leave. I can't even begin to imagine us together as parents. A baby should come from love…'

'Do you want me to call Diego for you?' Josh said, but Izzy shook her head.

'He's already been to visit,' Izzy said. 'He's on a night shift tonight. I can't ring him for every little thing.'

'Yes,' a voice said from the doorway, 'you can.' There stood Diego, but only for a moment, and she dropped Josh's hand as he walked over.

'I'll leave you to it.' Josh smiled and stood up. 'Now, remember, if there's anything we can do, you just pick up that phone. Even if it's just a decent coffee, you've got a whole team behind you twenty-four seven. Just let us know.'

Izzy thanked him, but she sat there blushing as he left and waited till the door was closed.

'Nothing was happening.' Izzy was awash with guilt. 'I was just upset, so he held my hand—'

'Izzy!' Diego interrupted. 'I'm glad Josh was here, I'm glad you had someone to hold your hand.'

Yet she still felt more explanation was needed. 'Henry would have had a fit if he'd—'

'Izzy! I'm not Henry—I don't care how many times I have to say it—I'm nothing like him.'

And he wasn't.

She leant on his broad chest and heard the regular beat of his heart, felt the safe wall of his chest and the wrap of his arms, and if she didn't love her so, it would be so easy to resent her baby—because nine weeks of just them would have been so very nice.

'I'd better go.' Reluctantly he stood up. 'I'll drop by in the morning and let you know what sort of night she had.'

'Tilia,' Izzy said.

'Tilia,' Diego repeated, and a smile spread over his face. 'I like it. What does it mean?'

'It's actually a tree...' Izzy's eyes never left his face, because somehow his reaction was important. 'I'm only telling you this—my mum would freak and I can't have a proper conversation with Henry's parents. It's a lime tree. Henry proposed under this gorgeous old lime tree...' Still he just looked. 'We were happy then.'

'I think it's wonderful,' Diego said. 'And one day, Izzy, you'll be able to talk about him to Tilia, and tell her about those good times.' He gave her a kiss and headed for work, and Izzy lay back on the pillow and even though he'd said everything right, she still couldn't settle.

She looked at new photos of herself holding Tilia and she didn't see the drips or tubes, she just saw her baby.

And there in one photo was a side view of Diego.

The three of them together, except he wasn't kneeling down with his arms around her.

She couldn't imagine these past weeks without him.

Yet she was too scared to indulge in a glimpse of a future with him.

She kept waiting for the axe to fall—sure, quite sure that something this good could never last.

A midwife took her drip down and turned off the lights but the room was still bright thanks to the full moon bathing St Piran's, and while Izzy couldn't get to sleep, Diego on the other hand would have loved to because between visiting Izzy and working he still hadn't caught up from Tilia's rapid arrival.

It was a busy night that kept him at the nurses' station rather than the shop floor, where Diego preferred to be.

And, worse, from the computer he could hear her crying.

He glanced up and Brianna was checking a drug with another nurse working at the next cot, and Diego could hear Tilia crying. Brianna must have asked the other nurse for an opinion on something, because they were reading through the obs sheet. It was *normal* for babies to cry—he barely even heard it, so why did he stand up and head over?

'Brianna.' He jerked his head to Tilia's cot and he wished he hadn't, knew he was doing something he never would have done previously. If a baby was crying it was breathing was the mantra when matters where pressing. But Brianna didn't seem worried at his snap. Actually, she was more discreet than anyone he had ever met, but he could have sworn he saw her lips suppress a smile.

And as for Josh, well, as tired as he might be, bed was the last thing he wanted.

He'd visited Izzy when really he hadn't had to. Ben had actually asked for him to drop in over the next couple of days, but Josh had convinced himself that it was his duty to go after his shift.

Then, having visited her, he had hung around till someone had made some joke about him not having a home to go to, so eventually he'd headed there, but had stopped at the garage first.

As he pulled up at the smart gated community and the gates opened, Josh checked his pager and knew in his heart of hearts he was hoping against hope for something urgent to call him in.

God, had it really come to this, sitting in his driveway, steeling himself to go inside?

Izzy's words rang in his ears.

'A baby wouldn't have changed things... Babies don't fix a damaged marriage... I can't even begin to imagine us together as parents... A baby should come from love...'

There *had* been love between him and Rebecca.

A different sort of love, though, not the intense, dangerous love he had once briefly known. That had been a love so consuming that it had bulldozed everything in its path. He closed his eyes and leant back on the headrest and for the first time in years he fully let himself visit that time.

Felt the grief and the agony, but it was too painful to recall so instead he dwelt on the consequences of raw

love—a love that ruined lives and could destroy plans, a
love that had threatened his rapid ascent in his career.

His and Rebecca's love had been different—safer
certainly.

She wanted a successful doctor—*that* he could
provide.

They had been good for each other, had wanted the
same, at least for a while.

Josh could see her shadow behind the blinds, see
her earrings, her jewellery, the skimpy outlines of her
nightdress that left nothing to the imagination, and knew
what Rebecca wanted from him tonight.

And he also knew that it wasn't about him.

'At least I'll have something to show for four years of
marriage…' He recalled the harsh words of their latest
row and then watched as she poured herself a drink
from the decanter. He felt a stab of sympathy as he
realised that Rebecca needed a bit of Dutch courage to
go through with tonight.

Maybe he should get a vasectomy without her knowing, but what sort of coward, or husband, did that? Josh
reeled at his own thought.

So he checked his pocket for his purchase from the
garage, because he couldn't face her tears from another rejection. They hadn't slept together in weeks, not
since…

Josh slammed that door in his mind closed, simply
refused to go there, and tried very hard not to cloud the
issue. In truth his and Rebecca's marriage had been
well into injury time long before they had come to St
Piran.

He went to pocket the condoms, to have them conveniently to hand, because no doubt Rebecca would ensure they never made it up the stairs and he knew for a fact she'd stopped taking the Pill.

'What the hell am I doing?' he groaned.

Yes, it would be so much easier to go in and make love.

Easier in the short term perhaps to give her the baby Rebecca said she wanted.

But since when had Josh chosen the easy path?

He tossed the condoms back into the glove box, a guarantee of sorts that he wouldn't give in and take the easy way out.

There was a conversation that needed to take place and, no matter how painful, it really was time.

They owed each other that at least.

Taking a breath, he walked up the neat path of his low-maintenance garden, waved to his neighbours, who were sipping wine on their little balcony and watching the world go by.

'Beautiful night, Josh.'

'It's grand, isn't it?' Josh agreed, and turned the key and stepped inside.

To the world, to his neighbours, the dashing doctor was coming home after a hellishly long day to his wonderful smart home and into the loving arms of his beautiful trophy wife.

It *was* a beautiful night.

The moon was big and round and it just accentuated the chaos as Evelyn Harris surveyed the ruin of her kitchen, plates smashed and broken, her ribs bruised and tender, the taste of blood in her mouth. She heard her husband snoring upstairs in bed.

She picked up the phone and not for the first time wondered about calling Izzy—but would the doctor even remember her? Surely it was too late to ring at this hour, and her son had an exam in the morning and she had lunch with John's boss's wife to get through, so she put down the phone and chose to sleep on the plush leather sofa.

Izzy was right.

Nobody *did* know what went on behind closed doors.

CHAPTER ELEVEN

'SHE's a tough little one.'

Like her mother, Diego thought.

Tilia, though small for dates and premature, was also incredibly active and strong. She had only required a short time on CPAP and was doing well on oxygen.

It really was a case of better out than in—now she could gain weight and as was often the case with babies who had been deprived nutrition *in utero*, Tilia's forehead often creased in concern as if she was constantly worried as to where her next meal was coming from.

'She wants her mum.' Brianna could not get Tilia to settle. 'I might ring Maternity and see if Izzy's still awake, she might get a nice cuddle. Then I'm going to have my coffee break. Could you watch mine for a moment while I call?'

They often rang Maternity, especially when babies were active and if there was a nurse who could bring the mother over—well, the middle of the night was a nice time to sit in rocking chair and bond a little. But when Diego had left Izzy she had been drained and exhausted and she could really use a full night's sleep—not that he was going to say that to Brianna. The gossip was already flying around the hospital since their appearance at the ball—had a certain little lady not put in such an early appearance, they might have been old news now, but given the turn of events and that Diego had been in the labour ward and was up twice day visiting on Maternity, he felt as if all eyes were on them. The scrutiny was just too fierce and strong at such a fragile time.

He was actually more than glad to be on nights, away from Rita's probing, and he had deliberately allocated Brianna to care for Tilia.

Brianna was one of the most private people Diego had met. She said nothing about her private life. She was there to work and work she did, loving and caring for her charges—gossip the last thing she was interested in.

'They've given Izzy a sleeping tablet,' Brianna said when she came back. 'Never mind, little lady, I'll give you a cuddle.'

'You go and have your break,' Diego said. 'I'll sort her.'

He didn't want to be doing this.

Or had he engineered it?

Diego didn't want to examine his feelings. Brianna was long overdue her coffee break, it was as simple as that. So he washed his hands in his usual thorough manner, put on a gown and then unclipped the sides of the incubator.

Often, so very often he did this—soothed a restless baby, or took over care while one of his team took their break.

And tonight it would be far safer to remember that.

He would sit and get this baby settled and perhaps chat with another nurse as he did so, or watch the ward from a chair.

He sat and expertly held Tilia, spoke as he always did to his charges—joking that he would teach her a little Spanish.

Which he did.

Then Chris, another of the nurses on duty that night, came over and asked him to run his eyes over a drug.

Which he did.

And then he felt something he hadn't in more than a decade.

Something he had tried never to feel since Fernando.

He adored his babies, but they weren't *his* to love.

He had loved Fernando, had held him three times in his little life, and it had never come close since.

But holding Tilia, it came close.

Dangerously close.

She wasn't a patient and she wasn't his new girl-friend's baby.

She was Tilia.

Izzy's baby.

But more than that.

He smelt that unmistakable baby smell that surrounded him each day but which he never noticed, he looked into huge eyes that were the same shape as her mother's and she had the same shape mouth. Even her nostrils were the same.

And there, sitting with all the hissing and bleeping

and noise that was a busy neonatal unit, Diego, felt a stab of dread.

That he might lose her too.

He looked over to where Toby's mother had come in, restless and unable to sleep, for just one more check on her son, and he knew how she felt—how many times in the night at eighteen he had woken with a sudden shock of fright and rushed to check on Fernando, asking the nurses to check and check again, petrified that they had missed something, but it wasn't that fear that gripped him as he held Tilia.

'You're going to be fine,' Diego said to Tilia in Spanish. 'You're going to be clever and grow healthy and strong…'

Only would he be around to see it?

'And your mother's getting stronger each day too,' Diego went on. 'Just watch her grow too.'

He wanted that for Izzy. He vowed as he sat there, holding her baby while she could not, that he would help Izzy grow, would do everything to encourage her, even if that meant that she grew away from him.

How could he let himself fall in love with this little babe when who knew what her mother might want days, weeks or months from now? When who knew what he might want?

Diego ran a finger down her little cheek.

But how could he not?

Staying in the parents' wing had been the right choice.

It was a precious time, one where she caught up on

all she had missed out on, one where there was nothing to focus on other than her baby.

Always Diego was friendly, professional, calm, except for the visits before or after her shift, when he was friendly and calm but he dropped the professional for tender, but there was never any pressure, no demands for her time. Now, as Tilia hit four weeks, the world outside was starting to creep back in and for the first time since her daughter's birth, Izzy truly assessed the situation, wondering, fearing that it was as she had suspected—that her daughter's birth had changed everything for them, that his lack of demands meant a lack of passion.

A soft rap at her door at six-thirty a.m. didn't wake her. She'd been up and fed Tilia and had had her shower, and often Diego popped in at this time if he was on an early shift, bearing two cups of decent coffee and, this morning, two croissants.

'She went the whole night without oxygen.' Izzy beamed.

'We'll be asking her to leave if she carries on like this!' Diego joked, and though Izzy smiled and they chatted easily, when he left a familiar flutter took place in her stomach. Tilia was doing well, really well, and though at first the doctors had warned it could be several weeks before her discharge, just four short weeks on Tilia was defying everyone—putting on weight, managing the occasional bottle, and now a whole night without oxygen and no de-sats. Discharge day would be coming soon, Izzy knew, but if Tilia was ready, Izzy wasn't so sure she was.

Diego was working the floor today. Once a week he left his office and insisted on doing the job he adored. From nine a.m. he was working in Theatre with a multiple birth and a baby with a cardiac defect scheduled for delivery. The unit was expecting a lot of new arrivals, and it fell to him to tell the mother of a thriving thirty-five-weeker that her room would be needed in a couple of days.

He'd stretched it to the limit, of course.

Not just because it was Izzy, not just that she was a doctor at this hospital, but with all she had been through, he would have done his best for any woman in that situation—though he waited till he was working to tell her.

'She won't take it.' Izzy was in the nursery, feeding her daughter, jiggling the teat in Tilia's slack mouth. 'She took the last one really well...'

He tickled her little feet and held his hand over Izzy's and pushed the teat in a bit more firmly, tried to stimulate the baby to suck, but Tilia was having none of it, her little eyelids flickering as she drifted deeper into sleep. Izzy actually laughed as she gave in.

'She's not going to take it.' There was no panic in her voice, Diego noted. Izzy was a pretty amazing mum. Often with doctors or nurses they were more anxious than most new parents and even though he'd expected that from Izzy, she'd surprised him. She revelled in her new motherhood role and was far more relaxed than most.

'They're like teenagers,' Diego said, 'party all night, and sleep all day. That last feed would have exhausted her.'

Chris, one of the nurses, came over and saw the full

bottle, and because Tilia was so small and needed her calories, she suggested they tube-feed her, and Izzy went to stand to help.

'Actually, Chris, I need a word with Izzy.'

'Sure.' Chris took Tilia and Izzy sat, frowning just a little, worried what was to come because Diego, when at work, never brought his problems to the shop floor.

'Is she okay?' Her first thought was something had been said on the ward round that morning and he was about to give her bad news.

'She's wonderful,' Diego assured her. 'So wonderful, in fact, that I need your room for some parents we are getting whose baby will not be doing so well.'

'Oh.'

'I know it seems pretty empty over in the parents' wing at the moment, but I'm getting some transfers from other hospitals today, and I have some mothers in Maternity now needing accommodation too. You don't need to leave today…'

'But it would help?'

'It would,' Diego admitted. Normally they gave more notice, but Izzy had been told last week that if the room was needed, given her close proximity to the hospital and Tilia's improving status, she was top of the list to leave if required. Izzy had been happy with that. Well, till the inevitable happened.

How could she tell Diego that she didn't want to go home?

More than that, she had never wanted to bring her baby back to the home she had shared with Henry.

'Izzy!' Rita was at the nursery door. 'You've got visitors. Mr and Mrs Bailey, Tilia's grandparents…'

He saw her lips tense and then stretch out into a smile and he'd have given anything not to be on duty now, to just be here with her as she faced all this, but Diego knew it would surly only make things worse. So instead he stood, smiled as he would at any other relatives and said to Izzy, 'I'll leave you to it.' Just as he would to any of the mums—except he knew so much more.

'Could I have a word, Doctor?' Mr. Bailey followed him out.

'I'm not a doctor; I'm the nurse unit manager. Is there anything I can help you with?'

Up shot the eyebrows, just as Diego expected. 'I'd prefer to speak to a doctor,' Mr Bailey said. 'You see, we're not getting enough information from Izzy. She just says that Tilia is doing well and as her grandparents we have a right to know more.'

'Tilia *is* doing well,' Diego said. 'We're very pleased with her progress.'

'I'm not sure if you're aware of the circumstances. Our beloved son passed away and Izzy is doing her level best to keep us out of the picture. Tilia's extremely precious to us and we will not be shut out.'

And at that moment all Diego felt was tired for Izzy.

'I'd really prefer to speak with a doctor.'

Which suited Diego fine. 'I'll just check with Izzy and then I can page—'

'Why would you check with her? I've already told you that she's doing her level best to keep us misinformed. I know she seems quite pleasant, but she's a manipulative—'

'Mr Bailey.' Diego halted him—oh, there were many things, so many things he would have loved to have said, but he was far better than that. 'I will first speak to Tilia's mother. Let's see what she says and then we can take it from there.'

Of course she said yes.

Diego looked over when Richard agreed to speak to them and could see Izzy sitting by Tilia, looking bemused and bewildered, and if he'd done his level best to keep work and his private life separate, right now he didn't care.

'They don't trust me to tell them everything!' Izzy blew her fringe upwards. 'They're annoyed I waited two days to ring them after she was born…'

'They're just scared you'll keep them from seeing her.'

'Well, they're going the right way about it!' Izzy shot back, but Diego shook his head.

'Don't go there, Izzy.'

'I won't!' Izzy said, but she was exasperated. 'They've been in every day, I've dressed her in the outfits they've bought, I text them a photo of her each night. What more do they want?'

'Time,' Diego said. 'And so do we.' He glanced over to make sure no one was in earshot 'Do you want to come to my place tonight?' He saw her swallow. 'I'm closer to the hospital. If it makes the transition easier…'

'Just for tonight,' Izzy said, because she didn't want

to foist herself on him, but she couldn't stand to be alone at the house on her first night away from Tilia.

'Sure.'

He got called away then, and Izzy sat there awash with relief, grateful for the reprieve, until it dawned on her.

She was staying the night with Diego.

How the hell could she have overlooked that?

CHAPTER TWELVE

SHE felt incredibly gauche, knocking at his door that evening. 'Where did you disappear to?' he asked as he let her in. 'I wasn't sure if you were coming.'

'I got a taxi and took my stuff home,' Izzy said airily, because she certainly wasn't going to admit she'd spent the afternoon in the bathroom—trying and failing to whip her postnatal body into suitable shape for Diego's eyes. 'By the time I got back for her evening feed, your shift had ended.'

'You've got hospital colour!' Diego smiled as she stood in the lounge. 'I never noticed it on the ward but now you are here in the real world, I can see it.'

There was a distinct lack of mirrors in Diego's flat, so Izzy would just have to take his word for it, but she was quite sure he was right. Apart from an occasional walk around the hospital grounds, a few very brief trips home and one trip out with Megan, she'd been living under fluorescent lighting and breathing hospital air, and no doubt her skin had that sallow tinge that patients often had when they were discharged after a long stay.

'Have a seat out on the balcony,' Diego suggested. 'Get some sun. I'll join you in a minute.'

It *was* good to sit in the evening sun. Izzy could feel it warming her cheeks and she drank in the delicious view—the moored boats and a few making their way back in. There was no place nicer than St Piran on a rosy summer evening, made nicer when Diego pressed a nice cold glass of champagne in her hand.

'One of the joys of bottle-feeding!' Diego said, because Izzy's milk supply had died out two weeks in.

And then he was back to his kitchen and Izzy could only sit and smile.

He was such a delicious mix.

So male, so sexy, yet there was this side to him that could address, without a hint of a blush or a bat of an eyelid, things that most men knew little about.

'How does it feel to be free?' Diego called from the kitchen as she picked a couple of tomatoes out of the pots that lined his balcony.

'Strange,' Izzy called, but he was already back. 'I keep waiting for my little pager to go off to let me know she needs feeding. I feel guilty, actually.'

'It's good to have a break before you bring her home.'

'Most new mums don't get it.'

'Most new mums have those extra weeks to prepare,' Diego said, arranging some roasted Camembert cheese and breadsticks on the table, which Izzy fell on, scooping up the sticky warm goo with a large piece of bread.

'I've been craving this,' Izzy said. 'How did you know?'

'Tonight, you get everything that has been forbidden to you in pregnancy, well, almost everything. Some things can wait!' Diego said, as Izzy's toes curled in her sandals. His grin was lazy and slow and she hated how he never blushed, hated that her cheeks were surely scarlet. God, she'd forgotten how they sizzled, Izzy thought as he headed back to prepare dinner.

There *were* so many sides to Diego and recently she'd been grateful for the professional side to him and for the care he had shown off duty too, but she was in his territory now, not pregnant, not a patient, not a parent on the unit. Tonight she was just Izzy, whoever Izzy was.

And that night she started to remember.

'You can cook!' Izzy exclaimed as he brought a feast out to her—shellfish, mussels, oysters, prawns and cream cheese wrapped in roast peppers, and all the stuff she'd craved in the last few weeks of her pregnancy.

'Not really. You could train a monkey to cook seafood.' Diego shrugged. 'And the antipasto is from our favourite café…'

She didn't know if it was the champagne or the company, but talking to Diego was always easy so she figured it was the latter. They talked, and as the sky turned to navy they laughed and they talked, and more and more she came back.

Not even Izzy Bailey, but a younger Izzy, an Izzy Ross, who she had stifled and buried and forgotten.

Izzy Ross, who teased and joked and did things like lean back in her seat and put her feet up on his thighs, Izzy Ross, who expected a foot rub and Diego obliged.

But it was Izzy Bailey who was convinced things were all about to change.

'So, what did the real estate agent say?'

'That it's a good offer!' Izzy poked out her tongue. 'It's not, of course, but it's better than the last one, though they want a quick settlement.'

'Which is what you wanted?'

'When I was pregnant and hoping to find somewhere before she was born.' She looked at him. 'In a few days she'll be home,' Izzy said, 'and as well as having a baby home, I'm going to have to pack up a house and find a new one, and I'm going to have to find a babysitter just so we can *date*.' Her voice wobbled. 'We haven't even slept together and we're talking nappies and babysitters...'

He had the audacity to laugh.

'It's not funny, Diego.'

'You're making problems where there are none. Sex is hardly going to be a problem.'

God, he was so relaxed and assured about it, like it was a given it was going to be marvellous.

The icing on the cake.

'Come on.' He stood up.

'Where are we going?'

'The movies and then there's a nice wine bar, they do music till late...'

'I don't want to go to the movies!' Izzy couldn't believe Mr Sensitive could get it so wrong. 'And if you think I've got the energy to be sitting in a wine bar...'

'I thought you wanted us to date!'

'Ha, ha.'

'Izzy, you need time with your baby and that's the priority. I'll slot in, and if it's an issue that we haven't slept together yet, well, we both know it's going to be great.'

'You don't know that.'

'Oh, I do.' Diego grinned. 'I'm looking forward to getting rid of your hang-ups.'

'Can you get rid of them tonight?'

And suddenly he didn't look so assured.

'It's too soon…'

'No,' Izzy said slowly. 'No heavy lifting, no strenuous exercise…'

'Do you want me, Izzy?' He was always direct and now never more so. 'Or do you just want it over?'

'I don't know,' Izzy admitted, and there should have been a big horn to denote she was giving the wrong answer, but she was incapable of dishonesty with him—or rather she didn't want to go down that route, saying the right thing just to keep *him* happy. She wanted the truth with Diego even if it wasn't what he wanted to hear.

'What are you scared of?'

'That I'll disappoint you,' she admitted. 'Because on so many levels I disappointed him.' She snapped her mouth closed. Diego had made it very clear that he didn't compare to Henry, which he didn't, but… She looked over to where he stood, tried to choose words that could explain her insecurities, but there were none that could do them justice. 'Things weren't great in that depart-ment,' she settled for, but Diego's frown just deepened.

'I know I was pregnant and so there must have been a relationship…' She swallowed. 'His parents take it as proof that our marriage was healthy, that…' She couldn't explain further and thankfully she didn't have to because Diego spoke.

'It would be nice,' Diego said slowly, 'if babies were only conceived in love…' There was silence that she didn't break as he thought for a moment. 'If there was some sort of…' Again he paused, trying to find the English for a word he hadn't used in his time in the country 'Cósmico, contraception.' It was Izzy who then frowned and she gave a small smile.

'Cosmic.'

'Cosmic contraception,' Diego continued, 'where no experimenting teenagers, no rape victims, no women in a terrible relationship who just go along with it to keep the peace…' His strange logic soothed some of the jagged parts of her mind. She liked his vision and it made her smile. 'Here's a happy couple,' Diego continued, 'said the sperm to the egg. You know it doesn't work like that.'

'People think…'

'People are stupid, then.' Diego would not let her go there, would not let her care what others thought. 'People choose to be ignorant rather than face unpleasant truths. You know what your marriage was like and you don't have to live it again, explaining details to me, to justify why you're pregnant. But I will say this.' For the first time his voice bordered on angry. 'If he expected a great sex life, if he was disappointed by your lack of enthusiasm in that department after the way he treated you, then he was the most stupid of them all.'

And he was so convincing that she was almost… convinced.

Almost.

But still the cloud of doubt hung over her and Diego could see it.

It had never been his intention to sleep with her tonight.

For her to stay was a hope, but sex—hell, wasn't that supposed to be the last thing on her mind?

Wasn't it too soon?

And he liked straightforward, only this was anything but.

But he looked over to where she sat, not in the least offended that she wanted it over with, another thing to tick off her list as she moved on with her life. And again it wasn't a time for arrogance or feigned modesty. He knew he was good, knew he could make her happy—and wasn't happy part of their deal?

'I'll sleep with you on one condition.'

Why did he always make her smile?

'That you never fake it for me.'

'Or you.'

'Er, Izzy,' he said, and that made her blush and give an embarrassed laugh.

'I mean, don't pretend afterwards that it's okay, just so you don't upset me.'

Diego rolled his eyes, but he was smiling now too. 'The talking doesn't stop when we get to the bedroom. I can do both!'

And he knew then that they could talk about it for ever, but words could only reassure so far. This was so not what he had imagined for tonight. There was something almost clinical about it and yet Diego had so much confidence in her, in them, in all they were going to be, that if this was a hurdle for her, perhaps it was better to jump it.

He pulled her onto his lap, but his kisses weren't working. He could feel her trying, feel her doing her very best to relax, but he wouldn't put her through it. He pulled back his lips, looked into her eyes and feigned a martyred sigh 'Shall we just get this over with?'

She almost wept with relief.

'Please.'

'Ring the hospital.'

Which took away her little excuse to suddenly stop later. Diego was onto her, she realised.

So she rang and, no, Tilia didn't need her to come in.

Oh, God, what was she doing?

She felt as if she was walking into Theatre for surgery as he took her hand and they headed for the bedroom. Izzy half expected him to tell her to get undressed and pop on a gown and that he'd be back in five minutes.

Couldn't it happen more seamlessly?

Couldn't they just have had a kiss on the balcony and somehow ended up naked on his massive bed without the awkward bit in the middle? But that hadn't worked and Izzy realised she would have been faking it because she would know where it would lead, to this, the bit she was dreading, the part that was holding her back from moving on.

God, it was a room built for nothing but a bed. Izzy gulped.

Massive windows, floorboards and one very large, very low bed and not much else, bar a table that doubled as a washing basket.

'Where are your things?' Izzy would rather deal with basics than the bed.

'What things?'

'Alarm clock, books…' Her hands flailed. 'A mirror, a wardrobe…'

'Here's the wardrobe.'

Okay, there it was, hidden in the wall, but apart from that…

'Curtains?' Izzy begged.

'It looks out to the ocean,' Diego said, and to her horror he was stripping off. 'And I don't need an alarm clock—I wake at five.' He was unbuckling his belt, his top already off, stripping off like a professional and chatting about nothing as Izzy stood, champagne in hand, wishing she'd never started this.

'Five?'

'It's hell.' He pushed his denim jeans down past thick thighs as he explained his plight to a distracted audience. 'Even when the clocks change my brain knows and I wake up.'

Oh, God.

He wasn't *erect* erect, but he was erect enough that it was pointing at her—this conversation going on as this thing waggled and danced and she did her best not to look at it, tried to worry about windows and passing ships, but he was completely naked now.

'Are you always this uninhibited?'

'I've been undressing for bed for many years now,' Diego said, and then his voice was serious. 'Let's just start as we mean to go on.'

But would he want to go on afterwards?

'I've changed my mind,' Izzy said, in the hope of delaying the inevitable, so sure was she that when he found out just how hopeless she was, he wouldn't want her or, worse, would feel stuck with her.

'Why don't we just sleep together?' Diego suggested. 'Given it will probably be our one interrupted night for the foreseeable future.'

And though she wanted to turn and flee, he was right, Izzy realised, because as hellish as this was for her, next time there might be more than passing ships to worry about. There might be a baby in the room too!

'I forgot my phone…'

'Your phone?' Izzy said to his departing back, and as he spoke about staff ringing some nights if there was a problem, and he'd rather that… Izzy took the moment to get out of her clothes and under the sheet before he returned.

Just as Diego had expected her to do.

He didn't need his phone, of course.

And he was, in fact, nervous.

Just not for the same reasons as Izzy.

Diego liked sex.

Correction.

Diego *loved* sex.

And he liked relationships too, but short-term ones.
There was nothing short term about Izzy.

As he climbed into bed and turned and faced her,
it was the sense of responsibility that unnerved him a
touch.

Not just the obvious, not just Izzy and her baby, but
a self-imposed responsibility towards Izzy, because in
every area of her life she was getting it together, managing it herself, but for this part to be right she needed
another, and she had trusted herself to him.

'Better?' Diego asked, and, yes, it was.

Much, much better, not because she was in the dark
and under a sheet, just better because she was, for the
first time, lying next to him and he was so solid and
bulky and just him.

'In a few short weeks,' Diego said into the darkness,
'you'll be ripping your clothes off in the middle of the
day and we'll be on the kitchen floor!'

'Your confidence is inspiring.'

'Oh, you will!' Diego said. 'Remember the bath?'

How could she forget?

'That just sort of happened.'

Izzy lived on her nerves.

Diego lived on instinct.

Instinct that told him his parents were wrong, that
he'd do better by not following their chosen course for
him.

Instinct that had told him over and over again that, despite neat numbers on a chart, a baby was struggling.

And instinct was all very well, but it got in the way
sometimes.

Like now, when he knew he should be closing his eyes and trying to sleep, to let her come to him, a little problem arose.

Or rather quite a big problem that crept along the side of her thigh, nudging her like a puppy that wanted to be stroked.

'*Perdón*!' Diego said, and he would have moved away but he heard her sort of laugh and he wasn't a saint. She was right there next to him and naked and warm and he'd had to go and remind them both of that bath.

Yes, it was instinct that drove his lips to her neck, the hand that wasn't under her roaming her body a little and then, for Izzy, instinct overrode nerves.

His lips were soft but firm at the same time, kissing her, breathing onto her skin. Diego, a man who had only ever given, now wanting badly, and from his deep murmurs of approval as his hands slid to her breasts it was her that he wanted.

And she wanted a little more of him too.

She turned and faced him, so she could kiss him properly, not the nervous kiss about where this might lead she had endured on the balcony, but a bolder kiss, knowing where this might lead, in the bedroom.

He tasted of him, his tongue cool and lazy and then suddenly insistent and then back to lazy. He drove her wild with his mouth, because her body was at its own bidding now. Her thighs parted a little and captured him as they kissed, he could feel himself hard but smooth between the tender skin of her thighs, and she wanted him higher, her legs parting, only Diego wasn't rushing.

'I know where you were this afternoon…' His hand

was there, exploring where she had shaved. 'Next time I'll do it.' And she felt this bubble of moisture at the very thought as his fingers slipped in and it felt divine.

'Condoms!' Izzy said, common sense prevailing, even if the last thing she wanted was him getting up and heading for the bathroom.

But this was Diego.

He sort of stretched over her and she felt his arm rummage in the dark beneath the bed and come up with the goods.

Oh, God, he was so male, so… She flailed for a word…basic.

It was the only one she could think of and it didn't really suit, but it was the best she could do.

And then he rolled off her and lay on his back and Izzy came up with another word.

Raw.

He didn't slip it on discreetly as he kissed her. No, he lay back and she watched, she actually propped up on her elbow and watched, this shiver inside as he gave himself two slow strokes, two long, slow strokes that had Izzy licking her lips and feeling suddenly contrary. This was something she had wanted over and done with, something she still wanted over and done with, except she was balling her fist not to reach out and touch him.

So she did.

Like warm silk he slid down her palm, the pulse of him beneath her fingers, and she did it again and it felt so nice that she did it again, till his hand closed around hers and halted her.

'Aren't I doing it right?' said her old fears, and for a moment there was no reply.

'Izzy.' He paused again. 'Any more right and we won't need the condom.'

And then she got her seamless kiss, because that was what he did, he rolled over and kissed her, his tongue, his breath filling her mouth and his body over her and then the nudge of him between her legs.

And she was scared, but she wanted him.

Like hating flying and preparing for take-off, wanting just to get there, except there's a slight delay in departure and cabin crew are bringing round drinks and you taste your first Singapore sling.

Oh, my!

He was slow and tender and, yes, she was ready, and it had little to do with nerves that he had to squeeze inside. Izzy screwed her eyes closed, told herself to breathe as her body stretched to greet him, the slow fill of him more than she could accommodate, except slowly she did.

And then she breathed out as he slid out, right to the tip and she braced herself for him to fill her again, which he did.

And then again and each time she had to remember to breathe.

His elbows held most of his weight, his rough chin was on her cheek and his breath tickled at her ear, and suddenly Izzy remembered where she was and it wasn't happening so easily. She knew she should be a touch more enthusiastic, but she was a mother now and surely sensible, so she made the right noises and lifted her hips and would have settled for his pleasure, except Diego had other ideas.

He smothered her feigned gasps with his mouth and offered her more weight, wrapping his arms around her, kissing her, not harder but deeper, and she remembered his demand that she not fake it. So she lay there and let herself just feel him—lay there as he kissed her eyes and then her cheeks and then she felt the shift in him, the kissing stopping, his heavier weight and the ragged breathing in her ear, and she forgot where she was again, forgot about rather a lot of things, just the delicious feel of him, and the scratch of his jaw and the stirrings of the orgasm he had given her before. Then she found that she *was* making noises now, but of her body's own accord, and as he bucked deep inside her, she did something she would never have envisaged from this night.

'Not yet.'

She was too deep into herself to wonder at the transition to voicing her wants, her real wants, but Diego recognised it and it gave a surge of pleasure that almost tipped him over. He would have waited for this for ever, yet now was struggling to wait another minute, but for Izzy he did.

He could feel her pleasure and it was his.

Both locked in a dance that moved faster than them.

'Not yet!' She was in another place and he could hear her calling and he chased her, he was holding back and driving harder, he could hear her moans, feel the surge in her that was akin to panic, but he knew her body too, could feel her body tight around him, feel her trip and he just knew.

Knew she needed all of him before she could give that bit more.

Her words were futile, Izzy realised, because Diego was moving at a different speed now, reaching for the finish line with a surge of energy that had her breathless.

She could hear her name, feel the unbridled passion and just the sheer strength of him as he thrust inside her. And she stopped trying then, stopped trying to chase or catch him, she just felt the moment.

Felt him over her, in her and his arms behind her, she could hear her name, taste his skin, and then it was his name she heard her voice calling, his name said in a tone she didn't recognise, then a shout of surprise as she let go.

Her thighs were shaking and her hips pushing up against his, her hands digging into his back, and deep inside she trembled as Diego pulsed into her.

And most delicious of all, it didn't matter that she was a teeny bit late for the party, she was there, she had made it, her late entrance dazzling, because he got to feel every beat of it as he delivered those last emptying strokes and instinct had served him well.

As he felt her crash and burn beneath him, as he tried to get his head out of white light and back to the dark, he knew he had just met the real Izzy.

'Tell me again,' Diego said, when he could get the words out, 'what exactly your hang-ups are.'

CHAPTER THIRTEEN

'SHE's fine!' a night nurse greeted her as Izzy dashed in at seven a.m.

She'd given Diego a fifteen-minute head start so they didn't arrive together and it seemed to take ages for the intercom to answer when she buzzed, because the staff were all in handover.

Izzy felt guilty with pleasure and was sure there must be a penance to pay for having such a wonderful night, except Tilia was fine—completely adorable and wide awake. Chris, her nurse for the day, informed Izzy when she came out of handover that Tilia might even be ready for her first bath.

Izzy was glad to have Chris beside her, encouraging her.

Tilia seemed so small and slippery and she wouldn't stop crying.

'I thought they liked their bath,' Izzy said.

'Just rock her a little.'

Which Izzy did, and Tilia's cries softened.

Her tufts of hair were shampooed and by the time Izzy had dried and dressed her, it was all sticking up and Izzy thought her heart would burst as she sat in the rocking chair and held her.

'How soon do you think?' Izzy asked the perpetual question.

'When she's taking all her feeds and just a bit bigger,' Chris said. 'She's doing so well. I know you're impatient to get her home, but she still needs top-ups and a little one like this…' She took an exhausted Tilia from Izzy and popped her in her cot then put the saturation probe on her, checked her obs and popped a little hat on. 'Even a bath wears them out. Why don't you go down to the canteen and get some breakfast?' Chris suggested, rightly guessing that Izzy hadn't eaten.

'Good idea,' Izzy agreed. 'I'll go and see if Nicola wants to come down with me.'

'Actually,' Chris said gently, 'maybe it's best if you leave Nicola for now.'

'Oh!' Izzy waited for more information, only she wasn't a doctor on duty here and there was no information forthcoming. 'I'll be at the canteen, then,' Izzy said. 'I've got my pager.'

She walked through the unit, her eyes drawn to Toby's cot. There was Nicola and her husband, and Diego was sitting with them. His face was more serious than she had ever seen it and Izzy felt sick as Megan came into the unit and instead of waving to Izzy just gave a very brief nod and headed over to them.

It was the longest morning.

Tilia awoke at eleven but wouldn't take her bottle and Izzy came close to crying, except she shook her head when Chris passed her a box of tissues.

'You are allowed to cry.'

But it seemed so petty. Tilia was thriving, okay, a little slower than Izzy would like, but she was getting bigger and stronger every day and, anyway, Izzy knew, there was a lot more to cry over than that—and now just wasn't the time to.

'Hey, where's Chris?' Diego gave her a tired smile as he came in later to get an update.

'Two minutes,' Chris called from the sinks, where she was helping another mum with a bath.

'How are you?' Diego asked.

'Good.'

'Tilia?'

'Misbehaving—she won't take her feeds.'

'She had a bath, though,' Diego said, but she could tell he was distracted and who could blame him?

'How's Toby?'

'He's not good,' Diego said. 'I know you helped deliver him.' He was walking a fine line. 'We can talk another time.'

'Sure.'

'Two more minutes!' Chris called again.

'I'm going to be working late tonight.' His voice was low. 'I can give you a key if you want…'

'I might go home tonight,' Izzy said, hoping he wouldn't take up her offer of an out. 'I'm really tired and you're working…'

Except he took it. 'Sure.'

And then Chris was walking over, ready to bring Diego up to date with her charges, and Izzy didn't see him again apart from the back of his shoulders for the rest of the day.

And that night, when she sat at home, she told herself she was being ridiculous—he was working late, he had every reason to be sombre, and she had been the one to say she'd prefer to go home, but, just as a mother could often pin-point the moment their child became sick long before the doctors were concerned even when the child itself said it was well, Izzy could sense change.

Even as she tried to leave the past where it belonged, she could sense a shift, could sense a black cloud forming, and it had hovered over Diego today.

'Neonatal Unit—Diego speaking.'

'It's me.' Izzy hadn't really expected him to answer the phone. It was edging towards ten p.m., which meant he had done a double shift. 'I was just ringing to check up on Tilia.'

'She's had a good night so far, I think,' Diego said. 'I'll just have a word with the nurse who's looking after her.' And she sat there and held her breath as he did what all the nursing staff did when a mother rang at night to check on their baby. She could even hear his voice in the background and Izzy held her breath as he came to the phone. 'She's settled and she's taken her bottle. You can relax, she's having a good night.'

'Thank you.'

He said goodnight, he was lovely and kind, but he was Nurse Unit Manager and that was all.

Something had changed.

Izzy just knew it.

The phone rang again and Izzy pounced on it, sure

it was Diego, only it wasn't, and she frowned at the vaguely familiar voice. 'I'm sorry to trouble you. It's just that you gave me your number. You're the only one who seemed to understand it's not as simple as just leaving…'

'Evelyn?'

'I can't go on like this.'

'Evelyn.' Izzy kept her voice calmer than she felt. 'Where are you now?'

'I'm at home. He's at the pub…' Even if she wanted to dwell on Diego or Tilia, or to just go to bed, Izzy pushed it aside and listened. So badly she wanted to tell Evelyn to get out, to just pack her bags and go, but Izzy remembered how she had rushed it last time, knew that it was good Evelyn was taking this small step, so, instead of jumping in and fixing, Izzy bit her tongue and just listened, learning fast that sometimes it was the best you could do.

'Are you okay?' Izzy was quite sure Megan wasn't. She had come and sat with her in the canteen and Izzy could tell she'd been crying, but, then, so had a lot of people.

Toby had passed away last night and both Diego and Megan, Izzy had heard from another mother, had stayed till the end.

'I've been better,' Megan admitted. 'All I put that baby through and the parents too—and for what?'

'Don't,' Izzy said, because they'd had these conversations before. Megan set impossible standards for herself, wanted to save each and every baby, and took it right to her heart when nature chose otherwise. 'Look at Genevieve!' Izzy said.

'I know.' Megan blew out a breath. 'This really got to me, though, and Diego—he doesn't normally get upset, but I guess finding out his dad's so sick…' Her voice trailed off, realising she was being indiscreet. 'I shouldn't have said that.'

'I'm not going to tell him.' Izzy felt her throat tighten. It was such a tightrope—they were all friends, all colleagues, all different things to each other. 'What's wrong with him?'

Megan screwed her eyes closed. 'Izzy, please don't.'

'Just because I've had a baby it doesn't mean my brain's softened. Nobody would tell me anything about Toby, forgetting the fact I delivered him, and now I'm not supposed to be told Diego's father's sick. I knew there was something wrong last night.'

'He probably doesn't want to worry you.'

'Well, I am worried,' Izzy said. 'Is it bad?'

Reluctantly Megan nodded but no more information was forthcoming and Izzy sat quietly for a moment with her thoughts. 'I've had an offer on the house,' Izzy said, 'but they want a quick settlement. Thirty days.'

'Ouch!' Megan said. 'Will you be able to find somewhere?'

'Probably.'

'What about your mum's?' Megan managed a smile at Izzy's reaction. 'Okay, bad idea.'

'I think I should be concentrating on Tilia, not trying to find somewhere to live.'

'There's always Diego's,' Megan teased, adding when

she saw Izzy close her eyes, 'I was joking—I know it's way too soon to even be thinking—'

'But I do,' Izzy admitted, and Megan's eyes widened.

'You hardly know each other.'

'I know that.' Izzy nodded. 'I can't stand being in the house, but I think it's best for now…' She was trying to be practical, logical, sensible. 'I don't want to force any decisions on us.' She looked at her friend. 'I'm trying to hold onto my heart here. I'm trying to just be in the now with him, but practically the day I met him I was knocked sideways. I felt it, this connection, this chemistry.' She looked at Megan, who was frowning. 'Sounds crazy, doesn't it?'

'No.' Megan swallowed and then her voice was urgent. 'Don't sell your house.' Megan, who normally was happy to sit and just listen, was practically hopping in her seat to give advice. 'Izzy, Diego's lovely and everything…' She was struggling to give the right advice, tempted to tell Izzy to turn tail and run because she'd felt that way once too and look where it had left her. Love had swept in for Megan and left a trail of devastation that all these years on she was still struggling to come to terms with—pain so real that she still woke some nights in tears, still lived with the consequences and would till the day she left the earth. 'Be careful, Izzy,' Megan said, even if wasn't the advice Izzy wanted. 'Maybe you should have some time on your own. At least, don't rush into anything with Diego—you've got Tilia to think of. Diego's father's sick, he could just up and go to Spain…' And then Megan stopped herself, saw Izzy's stunned expression and realised she had been too harsh, realised perhaps she was talking more about herself than her friend.

'Izzy, don't listen to me,' Megan begged. 'Who am I to give advice? I haven't been in a relationship in ages, I'm married to my career.' Megan swallowed. 'And I don't have a child. I'm the last person to tell you what you should be doing. Maybe speak to Jess...' She was close to tears and feeling wretched. The last thing Megan had wanted to do was project her own bitterness onto Izzy, especially at such a vulnerable time, but the last few weeks had been hell for Megan—sheer hell. Since Josh had come to work at St Piran's she was struggling to even think straight. 'Maybe you should talk to Jess,' Megan said again as her pager went off, summoning her to the children's ward. She gave her friend's hand a squeeze. 'You'll make the right choice.' She turned to leave, but there he was, right there in front of her.

'Megan...' Josh said. 'Did you get my message?'

She went to walk on, but Josh was insistent.

'Megan, we need to talk—there are things we need to discuss.' He caught her wrist and Megan looked at his hand around hers, their first physical contact in years, and she couldn't stand it because it was there, the chemistry, the reaction, her skin leaping at the memory of him, and it terrified her—it truly terrified her. She shook him off.

'There's nothing to discuss,' Megan said.

'There's plenty,' Josh insisted, and she felt herself waver, because there *was* so much to discuss but, worse, she knew that he felt her waver, knew they were still in sync. 'Not here,' Josh said, because heads in the corridor were turning.

Megan grappled for control of her mind, held onto the pain he had caused as if it were a liferaft, because if she forgot for a moment she would sink back into his charm.

And she remembered more, enough for a sneer to curl her lips.

Then she let herself remember just a little bit more, enough to force harsh words from her lips.

'Where, then, Josh?' Megan spat. 'Where should we meet?' She watched as he ran a tongue over his lips, knew then he hadn't thought this out, perhaps hadn't expected her to agree. 'There's a nice restaurant on the foreshore,' she sneered. 'Oh, but we might be seen!' she jeered. 'How about Penhally, or is that too close? Maybe you could pop over to mine…' She was blind with rage now, shaking just to stop herself from shouting. 'You're married, Josh, so, no, we can't meet. You're a married man.' If she said it again, maybe if she said it enough times, she would come to accept it. 'Which means there is absolutely nothing to discuss.'

And she remembered some more then, not all of it, because that would be too cruel to herself, but Megan remembered just enough of what she had been through to make the only sensible choice—to turn on her heel and walk quickly away.

She wasn't upset that he hadn't told her about his father.

In truth, Izzy knew he hadn't had a chance. Her dad

had been over the last two nights trying to get the spare room ready for Tilia, who had, after twelve hours of not taking a drop from the bottle, awoken from her slumber and had taken her feeds like a dream. Now on the eve of her discharge, they were scrambling to find two minutes alone.

She was sitting in the nursery, feeding Tilia her bottle, Brianna was on her break and Diego was doing Tilia's obs.

'Do you want me to come over tonight?' Diego offered. 'Help you get everything ready for tomorrow?'

'My mum's coming,' Izzy said, but right now she didn't care about her mother's reaction. 'I could cancel, tell her why perhaps…about us.'

'I think…' she sensed his reluctance '…you should wait till Tilia is no longer a patient.'

He was right, of course he was right, but though there were a million and one reasons they hadn't had any time together, Megan's words had hit home. Izzy was sure, quite sure, that Diego was pulling back—he looked terrible. Well, still absolutely gorgeous, except there were black rings under his eyes and he was more unshaven than usual and there was just this air to him that his world was heavy. And Izzy was quite sure she was a part of his problem. 'Her obs are good.' He checked Tilia's chart. 'She's put on more weight.' And then he suggested that while Tilia was sleeping she watch a video in the parents' room, but apnoea was the last thing Izzy wanted to deal with right now, she was having enough trouble remembering to breathe herself.

'I'm going to go home now.' She looked down at her

sleeping daughter, because it was easier than looking at him with tears in her eyes. She didn't want to push or question, because she didn't want to sound needy—but, hell, she felt needy.

They had made love and suddenly everything had changed.

'I'd better make sure everything's ready for the big day. I'll see you in the morning,' Izzy said, and watched him swallow. 'You can wave her off…'

'I've got a meeting tomorrow morning,' Diego said, and she couldn't mask her disappointment. She wasn't asking him to take her baby home with him, or to out them to her family, just for him to be there, even if all he could manage was professional on the day she took her daughter home, she wanted that at least.

'Can you reschedule?' She hated to nag but hated it more that he shook his head.

'I really can't.'

'There's a call for you, Diego.' Rita came over.

'Thanks.'

'The travel agent,' Rita added, and Diego wasn't sure if she'd done it deliberately, but Rita must have felt her back burning as she walked off, with the blistering look Diego gave her.

'My father,' Diego said eventually, but he could barely look her in the eyes. 'He's sick. Very sick,' he added. 'I wanted to speak to you properly—I need to go back.'

Izzy nodded and held Tilia just a little bit tighter, felt her warm weight, and it was actually Tilia who gave her strength. 'Of course you do.'

'Diego!' She could hear shouts for his attention, hear

the summons of the emergency bell, and for now the travel agent would be forgotten, but only for now. His real future was just being placed temporarily on hold.

Izzy sat there and held her baby, her world, her family, and she was sure, quite sure, that she was about to lose Diego to his.

'Thank you.' Izzy said it a hundred times or more.

To Richard, to Chris, to Rita, to all the staff that popped in to say goodbye and wish her and Tilia well, but the people that mattered most weren't there. Megan, Brianna and Diego had a 'meeting'. And though the NICU was used to babies going home, Izzy wasn't used to taking one home and wished they could have been there for this moment.

'She looks such a big girl.' Gwen was the doting grandmother now and her father carried the car seat with Tilia inside. Finally she was out of the neonatal unit and taking her baby home.

'You know I'm happy to stay over. Between your mother and I, you don't have to be on your own for a few weeks….'

Except she wanted to be alone.

Or not quite alone.

There was the one she wanted to share this moment walking towards her now, with Brianna and Megan at his side, and with a stab of realisation at her own self-ishness Izzy realised just how important their 'meeting' had been.

Diego was in a suit and he'd discarded the tie, but

Izzy knew it had been a black one. Megan was in dark grey and Brianna too.

'Hey! Looks who's going home.' Brianna snapped to happy, fussed and cooed over Tilia, and Megan gave her friend a hug, but it was more than a little awkward, almost a relief when Megan had to dash off.

Had to dash off.

Megan actually thought she might vomit.

She felt like this each and every time she had to attend one of her precious patients' funerals, but today had been worse. With Josh back in her life Megan was having enough trouble holding things together, but when even Diego had struggled through a hymn, when the one who never got too involved held the song sheet and she could see his hand shaking, this morning had been the worst of them all.

Bar one.

'Megan!' Josh caught her arm as she tried to dash past him, his face the last she needed to see now. He took in her clothes and pale cheeks, her lips so white she looked as if she might faint at any moment. 'I'm sorry…'

'Sorry?' She was close to ballistic as she shot the word out and Josh blinked.

'You've clearly just been to a funeral…'

'Perk of the job,' Megan spat. 'I get to go to lots. I get to stand there and relive it over and over.'

'Is Megan okay?' Izzy watched from a distance as her friend ran up the corridor.

'It's been a tough morning,' Diego said. 'I'll talk to

her later. You concentrate on you for now—enjoy taking Tilia home.'

'Thanks for everything,' Gwen said. 'Everyone's been marvellous.' And Izzy caught Diego's eyes and they shared a teeny private smile at her mother's choice of words.

'Thank you,' she said, and because she had hugged Brianna and Megan, she got to hug him, and then he had to go and so did Izzy, but she wished, how she wished, it was him taking them home.

CHAPTER FOURTEEN

HER parents adored Tilia.

It was, of course, a relief, but it came with a down side.

Instead of Gwen bossing and taking over and whizzing round the house doing the little jobs that were rapidly turning into big jobs, the doting grandparents sat on the sofa, cooing over their granddaughter, occasionally rising to make a drink or lunch, then it was back to admiring their granddaughter. Then when Tilia fell asleep Gwen shooed Izzy off for a sleep of her own as she headed for the door, keen to get out of the way before Henry's parents arrived, because Tilia's two sets of grandparents in the same room wasn't going to happen for a while yet.

'You're supposed to sleep when the baby does,' was Gwen's less than helpful advice.

Except Izzy couldn't.

She lay in her bed and stared at her daughter—wished her homecoming could somehow have been different, wished for so many things for her, and for herself too. Unable to settle, Izzy headed downstairs, made herself a coffee and rather listlessly flicked through her neglected post as she waited for the kettle to boil.

And it came with no ceremony no warning.

What she'd expected Izzy didn't really know. The envelope looked like any of the others from the insurance company and she just assumed there was something else they were requesting that she send. She briefly skimmed the letter, intending to read it properly later, but it wasn't a request for more information.

Instead, it was closure.

No relief washed over her. She read the letter again and stared at the cheque, and she didn't know how she felt, except it was starting to look a lot like angry. Angry at Henry for what he had done to her life, for the money that couldn't fix this, for her daughter who was without a father and for all that Izzy would have to tell her one day.

Izzy had never felt so alone.

The only person she wanted now was Diego.

Except how could she foist more of her drama on him? And, anyway, he would soon be back in Spain.

Lonely was a place she had better start to get used to.

Though she was beyond tired, when Henry's parents arrived she made them coffee and put out cake and tried small talk as Tilia slept on. In the end, Izzy gave in and brought her daughter down. She watched her mother-in-law's lips disappear when Izzy said, no, Tilia wasn't due for a feed yet and, no, she didn't need a bath.

'I'll do it,' Mrs Bailey fussed. 'You won't have to do a thing.'

'She's asleep,' Izzy pointed out, 'and a bath exhausts her.' And exhausted was all she felt when, clearly disappointed with the social skills of a tiny baby, Henry's parents left.

The house that had been so tidy looked like a bomb site; there were coffee cups and plates all over the kitchen and Izzy went to load the dishwasher but realised that she had to empty if first and right now that task seemed too big.

There were bottles to be made up, once she had sterilised them, washing to be put on—eight hours home and Izzy, who had felt so confident, who had wished for this moment, when finally she was home alone with her daughter, wanted to go back to the safety of the nursery.

She could hear Tilia waking up at completely the wrong moment, because long held-back tears were coming to the fore.

She didn't want an insurance payout, she didn't want to raise her baby alone. She wanted to have met Diego when she was who she had once been, except this was who she was now.

A mother.

Which meant even when her own heart was bleeding, she had to somehow put her grief on hold and pick up her screaming baby at the same time the phone rang and the doorbell went and she remembered that it was bin night tonight.

'She's fine,' Izzy said down the phone through gritted teeth to her mother and, holding a phone and her baby, somehow answered the front door, and there, out of his suit and in his white nursing uniform, was Diego, carrying a tray with two coffees, which he quickly put down and took from Izzy a screaming, red-faced Tilia. 'She's due for a feed,' Izzy said to Gwen. 'Babies are supposed to cry.' As she reassured her mother, Izzy glanced at Diego. She so hadn't wanted him to catch her like this. He was gorgeous amidst the chaos and started to make up bottles with his free hand far more skilfully than she could with two. The last time he had been here, her house had been spotless, ready at any given second for the real estate agent to warn her he was bringing someone round. Her intention, if Diego ever came over, had been to have Tilia asleep and the house looking fantastic. Oh, and for her to be looking pretty good too—just to show him that a baby didn't have to change things!

By the time she had hung up the phone to her mother, Diego was cooling a bottle under the tap and though pleased to see him, Izzy could hardly stand what was about to come next. She tried to make a little joke, tried to lighten the tense mood, tried to tell him in one line how she knew and understood that everything must now change.

'If you've come for torrid sex…' Izzy smiled as he came in '…you've come to the wrong house!'

'I couldn't even manage a slow one!' For the first time in days Diego grinned. 'All I want to do is sleep.'

'The perfect guy.'

She wasn't joking.

She so wasn't joking.

'I wore my uniform in case you had visitors.' He

was changing Tilia's nappy. 'I was going to say it was a house call!' He smiled down at Tilia. 'Do you think they'd have believed me?'

'I have no idea,' Izzy admitted.

'It's a good idea…' Diego seemed to ponder it for a moment. 'It's always hard when you leave NICU.'

'I would have been fine…' Izzy said, and then she paused and then she told them what she couldn't face telling her own parents yet, what she dreaded telling Henry's. 'The insurance paid.' She was so glad he didn't comment. 'The mortgage and everything,' Izzy elaborated, and Diego knew this was the very last thing she needed to deal with today. 'I just wanted to bring her home,' Izzy said. 'I just wanted one day where I can pretend it's normal for her.'

'Here.' He took the letter and folded it, threw it in the kitchen drawer as if it was a shopping list. 'Think about it later.'

But it was already there and she told Diego that and he just stood there, let her rant and rave for a while and then told her an impossible truth.

'You need to forgive him, Izzy.'

'Forgive him?' Diego was supposed to be on her side, Diego was supposed to be as angry with Henry as she was, yet he steadfastly refused to go there.

'For your daughter's sake.' Diego stood firm. 'Don't you think he'd rather be here?' Diego demanded. 'Don't you think he'd rather be here today, bringing his daughter home from the hospital, enjoying this moment? Without forgiveness you won't get peace.'

'And you know all about it, do you?'

Diego didn't answer. Instead he sat on the sofa, put his feet up on the coffee table and fed Tilia as Izzy sat there, refusing to believe it was that simple to move on.

'He's looking after her.' Diego fed Tilia her bottle. 'Maybe this is the only way he could look after you both.' He looked down at Tilia. 'You need to forgive him for this little girl's sake.' He handed her baby to her. 'You need to be able to speak to her about her father without bitterness in your voice, because you don't want her to grow up feeling it.'

'It's so hard, though.' She knew he was right, but it was *so* hard.

'Then keep working on it.' Diego was resolute. 'Fake it,' he said, 'like I told you that first day, and eventually it might even be real.'

He made it sound doable. He knelt beside her as she cradled Tilia and she couldn't imagine these past weeks without him, or rather she could and how very different they would have been!

He turned things around. His calm reason, his humour, he himself allowed rapid healing. He made her stronger, made her get there sooner, so much sooner and so much stronger that as she sat in the silence and nursed her baby, Izzy knew she could face it, could do it alone if she had to.

Thanks to Diego.

She changed Tilia, put her back into her cot and stood as she watched her daughter sleeping, and the strength of his arms around her made her able to say it.

'Your father loves you, Tilia. He's looking after you.'

And then she did what she had never done and certainly didn't want to on the day she bought her baby home. She sobbed and she cried and Tilia slept right through it, and Diego lay on the bed with her and with his help she got through another bit she had dreaded.

'You should sleep when the baby does,' Diego said, only he didn't leave her to it. Instead he took off his uniform and climbed into bed beside her. Maybe he didn't have the heart to dump her on the day her baby came home, and maybe she should just be grateful for the reprieve, but Izzy was fast realising it was better to face things and so, in the semi-dark room with his arms around her she did the next bit she was dreading and asked him about his father.

'He had a seizure. They did an MRI and he has a brain tumour—they're operating next Thursday. Izzy, I don't want to leave now, but I really feel I should go home and see him before the operation. It's just for a few days.'

'Of course you have to see him. He's your father.' And then she took a breath and made herself say it. 'Have they asked you to move home?'

There was a long silence.

'My mother asked if I could take some time and come home for a while. If he survives the surgery it will be a long rehabilitation. He won't be operating again—they expect some paralysis.' She felt the tension build in him. 'I've said I can't. The truth is, I won't. The way my father treated me, the names he called me, the taunts even now. He still goads me because I choose to nurse.' He shook his head. 'I want time with you...'

And it was the answer she wanted. It just wasn't the right one.

'You need to resolve things, Diego.'

'Flights are cheap, I can come and go. Don't worry about it, Izzy. I've been trying not to burden you with it.'

'Talk to me,' Izzy said, because she wanted more of him than he was giving.

'Okay.' He told her the truth. 'How are we supposed to get to know each other if I am in Spain? How are we supposed to make each other happy, if you are here and I am there? There's taking it slowly and then there's a place where you take it so slowly you stop.' And so then did Diego. 'We can't do this tonight. Let's not worry about it now and just try and enjoy the rest of tonight— having Tilia home…'

There was no hope of pretending a baby didn't change things because there wasn't even a crackle of sexual tension in the air. She slept like a log and actually so did Diego. And how nice it was to have her own modern matron to get up at midnight and again at four and bring her Tilia's bottle and then to put her back in her crib and to sleep again.

Diego was asleep and he rolled into Izzy, his large, warm body cradling, spooning into hers, and it was the nicest place she had ever known in her life—Tilia sleeping safely, Diego beside her, peace in her heart about Henry, summer rain rattling the windows. She had everything here in this room, only she wanted still more.

She just didn't quite know what.

Izzy found out what woke Diego at five as the most basic alarm clock stirred and she lay with him in this lovely silent place, just before waking, and Izzy closed her eyes and felt the lazy roam of his body, the natural wander of his hands before he awakened, and it wasn't sleep she wanted but him, so she pushed herself a little into him, loving the feel of a half-asleep Diego, a man following his instinctive want and her want calling him. Sex, Izzy learnt, could be peaceful and healing. She was warm and he slipped in and filled her, he was wrapped around her and deep within her, with no words needed because the air tasted of them.

She could never have imagined such peace, even as he drove in deeper, even as she throbbed in orgasm. All she wanted was peace and this every morning and the only person who could give her that was him.

'*Mierda*!' His curse woke her up an hour later, and was completely merited as it was the first time in his life he'd overslept. She drifted back to sleep as Diego dived under the shower and Izzy suddenly let out a curse of her own a few minutes later as she heard the garbage truck thumping down the street. She had to quickly find a dressing gown and race to get the bins out, then she took two coffees back to bed.

'Your razor's blunt.' He grinned as he came out of the shower and then he looked at her. 'Why is your hair wet?'

'I forgot to put the bins out last night.'

'Did you catch them?' Diego asked, and the conversation was normal and Diego looked so much better than he had last night. More than that, Izzy felt better too.

'I'll get it from everyone this morning—at least I'm only on till one,' Diego said as he hauled on his clothes.

'You'll only be a few minutes late.' Izzy grimaced as she looked at the clock, only Diego wasn't worried about the time. He drank the coffee she had made, glanced in at Tilia who was starting to stir and then went downstairs and came back with a bottle in a jug and his satchel, which looked curiously sexy over his shoulder. He mimicked nosy Rita. *'You look tired, Diego. Did you not get much sleep, Diego?* And then…' he rolled his eyes '…she'll subtly talk about the Dark Ages, when she brought her baby home from the hospital! You wait,' Diego said, and drained his coffee. 'I guarantee it.'

He didn't need to.

As he kissed her and left, Izzy lay there and tried to wrap her head around what had happened. Somehow, despite everything, last night, Tilia's first night home, *had* been wonderful, but more than that, Izzy realised, she didn't need Diego's guarantees—she was starting to find her own.

CHAPTER FIFTEEN

'THANKS for seeing me.'

She was back again, only this time she wanted to be there.

And Izzy didn't insist on the office, it was nice to just walk around the hospital grounds and not try to convince Jess everything was perfect. In fact, she rather hoped Jess would convince her that she was going out of her mind.

That she was mad, that it was absolutely ridiculous to be even considering going to Spain.

Izzy wanted logic and reason to preside, for Jess to tell her to wait twelve months, for her to tell her she was rushing in, for her to warn her to be careful.

Only when she spilled it all out, Jess didn't do that.

'I let Henry consume me,' Izzy said. 'In the end, I hardly saw my family and friends.'

'Is Diego anything like Henry?'

'No,' Izzy said. 'But as you said, people suggest you wait twelve months before making any major life decisions…'

'I offered you a theory,' Jess said, 'but as you pointed

out yourself, we don't all have the requisite twelve months to lick our wounds and heal. Life keeps coming at us, bad things, good things, wonderful things...'

'So you don't think I'm crazy to be considering going to Spain.'

'I'd think you were crazy if you were going with no consideration.' Izzy's face tightened in frustration at Jess's refusal to commit.

'Even my friends are warning me to be careful!' Izzy said, still reeling from Megan's warning. 'Megan was so...' She tried to find the right words. 'I've never seen her so upset.'

'And then she apologised,' Jess pointed out. 'Izzy, in medicine we are used to coming up with solutions.' Izzy frowned and then Jess corrected herself. 'As a doctor you are used to coming up with an answer, finding the best course of treatment, perhaps telling the patient what needs to be done. My job is different,' Jess explained. 'Of course I would love to rush in at times, but I have to ask myself, would that really help? The best I can do is allow you to explore your options—which,' she added, 'you're doing.'

'This morning,' Izzy explained, 'it was normal.' She looked at Jess. 'We could have been anywhere in the world and it wouldn't have mattered. Diego says that he doesn't want to burden me with his stuff...'

'Is it a burden?' Jess asked.

'No,' Izzy admitted. 'It's harder not knowing how he's feeling.' And Jess *was* so easy to talk to that Izzy admitted something else on her mind. 'Shouldn't I just know?' Izzy asked. 'If it's so right, what I am doing here?'

'You're looking out for you,' Jess said. 'Which shows how far you've come.' Jess gave her a smile. 'For many years, Izzy, you've had your inner voice turned off. You told yourself and others that everything was okay, when, in fact, it was far from it. Can I suggest your inner voice is coming back?'

Izzy nodded.

'You might need a little help recognising it at times, but it's there, if only you listen.'

Jess was right.

So right that there was somewhere else Izzy needed to be.

'I need to talk to Diego. I need to tell him just how much he means to me.' She stalled for a second, wondered how she could be so absolutely honest with someone if it was going to freak him out, that his girlfriend of a few weeks would drop everything and follow him to Spain with a baby in tow. 'How?'

'Maybe ring him, ask him to come over tonight.'

But she didn't mean that. 'He's at my house now,' Izzy said. 'Watching Tilia.'

'Can I ask where he thinks you are?'

'Oh, I told him I was seeing you.' Jess watched Izzy's slow reaction as her own words registered with herself. Her casual words sinking in. She had, on ringing Jess, asked Diego if he'd mind watching Tilia for an hour or so. He hadn't probed, hadn't asked why. Diego had come straight over from his half-day shift, had just accepted that this was where she wanted to be, that this was what she needed now.

'Not many people who come into my office can say that,' Jess said. 'Izzy, I think it's wonderful that you're going to talk with Diego and be honest, but can I suggest when you are telling him how you feel that you also listen? He might surprise you with what he has to say.'

'Shh!' Diego put a finger up to his lips as Izzy burst in the house. She'd practised her speech, gathering strength all the way home, and had swept into her house, ready to blurt it all out, but as she'd entered the living room Diego, lying on the sofa with Tilia on his shoulder, had halted her. 'She's nearly asleep.'

Izzy could tell from her little red face that it had been a noisy hour. There were bottles and soothers and half the contents of the nappy bag all strewn around the sofa and they sat quietly, Diego chatting low and soft in Spanish, till finally, *finally* Tilia gave in and Diego gingerly stood, taking her to her cot. Izzy had to sit, tapping her toes in nervousness, as she waited for Diego. She listened to the intercom and heard Tilia, on being laid in the cot, protest for a few minutes at being out of his arms.

Who could blame her?

'Diego.' Izzy's voice was firm when he came into the room, because if she didn't tell him now, she might never do so.

'One moment...' He flashed that lovely smile. 'I *must* eat, and make a phone call.' He picked up his phone and headed to the kitchen. 'My mother rang. I told her I would call her back as soon as I got Tilia to sleep.' He rolled his eyes, clearly not relishing the prospect.

'How is she?'

'The same,' Diego said, and he was chatting easily, slicing up bread and tomatoes as Izzy talked on.

'She wants you to come to Spain, doesn't she?'

'And as I told her, I am coming.'

She could hear him keeping his voice light, but she could see the dark smudges under his eyes, almost feel the burden he was carrying alone, and her speech went out of the window because Izzy realised it wasn't about whether she'd follow him or not—it wasn't about her, this was about Diego.

'I can understand her being upset. She knows that you need to spend some time with your father,' Izzy said. 'Not just a quick visit.'

'I have a job, I have a life here.'

'And your family is there,' Izzy said, and she watched his tongue roll in his cheek.

'Do you want pepper?' was his response, and then he changed the subject. 'I was right about Rita. All morning she spoke about bringing her daughter home from the hospital, her daughter bringing her daughter home from the hospital...' Izzy would be sneezing till next year with the amount of pepper he was shaking! 'Then she started about how the place was quiet without Tilia, how she'd love to know how she was getting on.' He looked at Izzy, a guilty smile on his face. 'Do you know what I did?'

Izzy shook her head. She didn't want to hear about

Rita, she wanted to sort out their own situation, but he did make her smile and he did make her laugh, he did make her happy, then she frowned as he continued, because in all of this he made her happy.

'She was at lunch when I left and I got a piece of A4 paper and wrote *Gone Fishing* and stuck it on her computer.'

And she could have laughed, could have just stayed happy, but Izzy was realising that wasn't quite what she wanted.

'You told me I needed to forgive Henry,' Izzy said. 'And it's the best thing I've done. You need to make peace with your father and if it means going to Spain, then that's what it means. This is something you need to sort out and I'll be okay with whatever you decide.' She took a deep breath and made herself say it. 'Whatever *we* decide.' And she was so, so wary of making demands on him, of foisting herself and her baby and all her problems onto a man who she had so recently met, so she offered a word, *we* instead of *you*, and she held that deep breath and wondered if he'd even notice.

He did.

'There's nothing to decide. We don't have to discuss it. I'm so angry with him, Izzy. Part of me doesn't even want to go for a few days, and still he goads—women's work…' He shook his head. 'You don't need this now.'

'But I do,' Izzy said. 'Because I'm a lot stronger than you think. I'm certainly stronger than I was even a few weeks ago, even since yesterday. You can tell me about things like Toby and that you've just got a call that your

father is sick and how difficult that must be for you,
how hard it was to get through Toby's funeral with your
father so ill… We chose the wrong words, Diego—that
we will last for as long as we make each other happy.
Well, that's not real life. How about we will last as long
as we make the world better for each other than it would
be without?'

'Better?'

'Better.' Izzy nodded. 'Because I'd have got through
all this and I'd have been fine, but it's been better with
you. The same way you'll get through your father's illness and whatever lies ahead…'

It was a new contract, a different agreement, and
Diego checked the small print.

'What do *you* want, Izzy?' Diego asked.

And she screwed her eyes closed and made herself
say it.

'You,' Izzy admitted. 'And I'm sorry if it's too soon
and too much and too everything, but that's how I
feel.'

'Where do *you* want to be?' She peeled her eyes open
just a little bit and he wasn't running out of the door and
collapsing under the pressure of her honest admission—
he was just standing there, smiling.

'With you,' Izzy said, and then made herself elabo-
rate. 'And if that means going to Spain, I will. As soon
as she's big enough…'

'Tilia comes first.' Diego stood firm. 'Always in
this, she must come first.' And he sounded like a father
and then she found out, he felt like a father. 'Always
people tell me that my job will get tougher when I am a

father—it annoys me, because I was there for Fernando. Always I tell them they don't know what they are talking about.' He looked right at her. 'They were right. Toby's funeral was awful, for all the reasons they are all awful, only it wasn't that my father was sick that upset me, it was how I felt about Tilia. She was a patient on my ward and I had to work, to look after her instead of be there for her...' He closed his eyes in frustration. 'Do you know what I want, Izzy?' She shook her head. 'Today, when Rita was going on, I wanted to take out my phone and show her a photo of Tilia, and I want to tell my mother when she calls and she thinks it is a baby crying at work that I am not at work—I am with my family.' She caught her breath. 'I want you and Tilia as my family.'

And good families tried to sort things out, even when the phone rang during important conversations. Diego let it continue to ring.

'Then tell her,' Izzy said.

'Tell her?' Diego checked, and Izzy nodded. 'You're sure?'

'Very,' Izzy said. 'We don't have to hide anything, we can tell people and it's up to them what they think.'

'We know,' Diego said, because they did.

It was time for the world to know the truth they had just confirmed. He pressed redial and put it on speaker and then took a deep breath as his mother answered. *'Qué pasa?'* He tipped into Spanish, chatting away to his mother, and she heard the words *bebé* and Tilia and *novia,* which Izzy knew meant girlfriend, and he occasionally rolled his eyes as his mother's voice got louder, but Diego never matched it, talking in his deep, even voice as *madre* got a little more demanding. And Izzy guessed when he used the word *prematuro* and his mother became more insistent that he was telling her it wasn't so easy—that his *familia* couldn't just pack up and come, and she stood there in wonder because he was talking to them about her, that she too was his family.

'*Te quiero.*'

He ended the most difficult call with *I love you* and when Señora Ramirez huffed, Diego grinned and said it again. '*Te quiero.*'

'*Te quiero*, Diego,' his mother admitted finally.

'Better?' Izzy asked, and after a moment he nodded. 'I said that I will be there for the operation and I have said I will come out again just as soon as I can…'

'What did she say about us?'

'That it's too fast, too soon—even though I lied.' Diego gave a bit of a sheepish grin. 'I hope you don't mind but we've been together a few months, not a few weeks.'

And then he kissed her and that made it better too.

His kiss made things better—they didn't fix, they didn't solve anything, they just made it all so much nicer.

'*Te amo*,' Diego said. 'It means I love you.'

'I thought it was *Te quiero*,' Izzy said, and she smiled because there was a lot to suddenly get used to and, oh, yes, a new language to learn too!

'*Te quiero*, what I said to my mother, does mean I love you,' Diego explained, 'but it's a different I love you. *Te amo* I save for you.' Then he kissed her again, made the world just that bit better till it was Izzy's turn to admit it.

'*Te amo.*' She spoke her first two words in Spanish to the only person who would ever hear them, to the man she had loved from the moment she had met him, to the man who, it turned out, felt the same.

And now they were a family.

EPILOGUE

You can't do it for her.

You can't change the world.

She might go back...

Diego didn't say any of those words and Izzy would love him for ever for it.

There was a trust fund for Tilia and when she was old enough and deciding her options, Izzy could tell her that her father was still supporting her.

And there was the house to fall back on as well.

A house Izzy had wanted to get rid of, a house she had hated, but now she could remember the good times there too.

And perhaps she could just sell. There were some gorgeous cottages along the coast she had considered but, as Diego had pointed out, his apartment had brilliant views and they could babyproof the balcony.

Diego was Daddy, or Papà.

They didn't ram it down anyone's throats, and certainly not to Henry's parents, but behind closed doors, when it was just they three, no one really knew that this very new couple were an established family.

And, no, Izzy couldn't change the world.

But she could help when someone wanted to change theirs.

'The washing machine jumps,' Izzy explained. 'If you put in too many towels, you'll find it halfway across the kitchen.'

'Thank you.' Evelyn stood in the hall, her face bruised and swollen, leaning on her son for support. 'We won't stay for long…'

'Stay for as long as you need,' Izzy said, and she meant it. 'Get your son through his exams, take your time…'

Many phone conversations, and a couple of sessions Izzy had arranged for Evelyn with a counsellor who specialised in these things had all helped Evelyn in her decision to take those first steps to empowerment. And on the eve of Izzy heading back to Spain, she realised why she'd chosen to keep the house.

'How long are you away for?' Evelyn asked.

'A couple of months this time around,' Izzy said. 'We're back and forth a bit. Diego's father hasn't been too well, but he's improving.' She glanced at her watch. 'I really have to go.'

And she knew, she just knew as she handed Evelyn the keys, that in six months or a year those keys would go to someone else who needed them—and Izzy wished she had a thousand keys, or a hundred thousand keys, except she didn't. She had one set and she would do her level best to use them wisely.

'How is she?' Diego asked, as Izzy climbed into the

car, and looked over at four-month-old Tilia, who was sleeping in the back.

'She's going to be fine,' Izzy said. 'She just doesn't know it yet.' She looked at Diego, his face surly as it always was as they were about to head for his home. He loved St Piran but, despite it all, he loved his family too and so, after a lot of toing and froing, they were heading for a few months in Madrid. Diego had a temporary position at his father's old hospital and Izzy, well, she wanted to practise her Spanish.

'It'll be fine.' Izzy grinned. 'Your dad's being lovely now.'

'Yes, there's nothing like a brain tumour to help you get your priorities straight in life. At least he's stopped saying I'm gay.'

That still made her laugh.

She looked at the love of her life, at a man who hadn't stuck by her—no, instead he had pushed her.

Pushed her to be the best, the happiest she could be.

To go out, to make friends, to work, to laugh, to love, to heal, and she was ticking every box.

He put a smile on her face every day and watching him scowl as Heathrow approached, and later, watching him haul the luggage off the conveyor belt when they landed in Madrid and Diego braced himself for another round of facing his demons, Izzy was more than happy to put a smile on his.

'I'd help, but I shouldn't be lifting.'

'I can manage.'

There was the stroller and another of their suitcases

whizzing past but Diego missed them and turned round, that frown on his face he got when he didn't quite get what she was saying.

'Tell him he's going to be a grandfather,' Izzy said. 'That should keep him happy.'

'A grandfather *again*,' Diego said, because at every turn, with everyone, Tilia was his, and Izzy knew a new baby wouldn't change that fact.

She knew.

'What took us so long?' Diego pulled her and Tilia into his arms, and kissed Izzy thoroughly right there in the airport, but this was Spain so no one batted an eyelid.

Six months from meeting and now two babies between them—and Izzy defied anyone to say it was way too soon.

They'd been waiting for each other all their lives.

ST PIRAN'S:
ITALIAN SURGEON,
FORBIDDEN BRIDE

MARGARET McDONAGH

CHAPTER ONE

'You need Jessica Carmichael.'

He didn't *need* anyone…not any more.

Giovanni Corezzi bit back his instant denial of the suggestion made by paediatric registrar Dr Megan Phillips. It was his first day as consultant neurosurgeon at St Piran's Hospital in Cornwall and although his primary focus was always on doing his best for his patients, he also hoped to make a good impression and to form a friendly working relationship with his new colleagues.

'Jessica Carmichael?'

He frowned, disturbed at the way the unknown woman's name flowed from his tongue. As if it were a caress. And somehow important. What nonsense was he thinking? With an impatient shake of his head, he refocused on Megan.

'Jess is a hospital counsellor. She's very knowledge-able and good with patients and their relatives,' the paediatric registrar explained with obvious admiration. 'Unfortunately we don't have extra time for everyone. Jess fills that gap.'

'I'll bear it in mind,' Gio replied, knowing the involvement of a counsellor was often helpful to his patients but reluctant to bring one in now.

'It's your decision.' Megan's disappointment and disagreement were apparent. 'I think you'd find Jess useful in Cody Rowland's case.'

Gio bit back irritation as the young registrar questioned his judgement. Instead of an instant retort, however, he considered whether he had missed anything regarding the young boy admitted to his care. Three-year-old Cody had fallen from a climbing frame two weeks previously, but had not shown any symptoms at the time. Recently he had become increasingly listless, complaining of a headache, going off his food and feeling nauseous. His frightened parents had brought him to the hospital that morning.

A and E consultant Josh O'Hara had examined Cody and called the neurology team. Busy in Theatre, Gio had sent his registrar to do an assessment. The subsequent tests, including a CT scan, had revealed the presence of a chronic subdural haematoma. As the bleed had continued and the clot had increased in size, it had caused a rise in pressure and the swelling brain to press on the skull, causing bruising and a restriction in blood flow.

Cody was now on the children's ward and awaiting surgery. Unless he carried out the operation soon, Gio feared the boy's condition would deteriorate and, if the clot and pressure continued to grow, there was a possibility of irreversible brain damage.

It was after noon and his first day was proving to be a hectic one. That morning he had undertaken three minor and routine operations—as minor and routine as any brain surgery procedures could be—and his first neurological clinic was scheduled later that afternoon.

Before that, he needed to return to the operating theatre with Cody.

'I'm sure this woman is good at her job,' he commented, 'but Cody—'

'Cody might need Jess at some point. Right now I'm thinking of his parents.'

Gio hated to admit it, but she was right. He *did* have concerns about the Rowlands and that Megan had picked up on the same signs was something he should find pleasing, not irritating.

'They aren't coping well,' he conceded with frustration. 'And their anxiety is distressing Cody. I need him to be settled for surgery—and for his parents to be calm and understand why we need to operate. I wish to press on them the urgency without further panicking them. They are listening but not hearing, you know?'

'I know,' Megan agreed. 'They're in denial...Mrs Rowland particularly.'

'Exactly so. Which is understandable. I'm not unsympathetic but I don't know how much time we have to play with.'

Megan hesitated, as if unsure of her ground. 'That's why I suggested Jess. I'm sorry to keep on about her, and I'm not questioning your skills,' she added hastily as his eyebrows snapped together. 'But I know how helpful she is in these situations. Everyone in the hospital likes Jess. She's a wonderful listener...and it isn't just the patients and their relatives who benefit. The staff frequently offload their problems on her, too. She's definitely your woman.'

Gio's frown returned in earnest, both at Megan's phraseology and the implication of her words. 'I don't know...'

Was he being too hasty? It was uncharacteristic of him not to listen to the suggestions of others, even if they were his juniors. He considered his reluctance to follow Megan's advice. Was it because he didn't want his new colleagues to think he couldn't do his job? Here he was, halfway through his first day and already needing to call in someone else to help with a case! He shook his head. What mattered was the well-being of his patients, not his own status.

Checking his watch, aware that *he* was now the one wasting precious time, he wondered how long it would take for Ms Carmichael to arrive. Once she was there, he would need to bring her up to date on the case and, as yet, he had no idea how much she understood of medical issues.

'Won't she be tied up with existing appointments?' he asked Megan. 'Cody can't afford to wait much longer.'

'Jess doesn't work like that, Mr Corezzi. She's on call and responds to whichever department or ward has need of her. It's just a matter of paging her—she usually comes right away,' the paediatric registrar explained, jotting a note on the front of Cody's file.

'Call me Gio.' He made the invitation with a distracted smile as he considered his options. He needed Cody in Theatre without further delay. If this counsellor could help facilitate that, then so be it. 'All right, Megan, please call her,' he invited, decision made, adding a word of caution. 'However, if she's not here soon, we may have to move without her.'

Megan's smile was swift. 'You won't be sorry, Gio,' she assured him, and he could only hope she was right.

'I'll ensure the operating theatre and my team are

ready. And I'll arrange for the anaesthetist to assess Cody,' he informed her. 'Everything will be in place and we can move quickly—*when* we have the Rowlands' consent.'

As Megan went to the ward office to organise the page, an inexplicable shiver of apprehension and anticipation rippled down Gio's spine. He had done the right thing for Cody. So why did he feel unsettled? And why did he have the disturbing notion that in bringing Jessica Carmichael on board he would be taking on much more than he had bargained for?

'Consultants don't spend time taking histories or chatting to patients and their relatives. That's why they have registrars and juniors,' Jess protested with a mix of wry cynicism and surprise.

Megan chuckled. 'This consultant does. He's pretty amazing, Jess, and very hands on.'

The news that Mr Corezzi remained on the ward was disturbing enough, but knowing Megan was so taken with their new consultant neurosurgeon left Jess feeling more unsettled. A sense of premonition refused to be banished. On edge, she opened her notebook and balanced it on top of the other items she carried, jotting down a few pointers as her friend gave a brief summation of Cody's case.

'Mr Corezzi…Gio…will give you more detail,' Megan added, the prospect making Jess feel more nervous.

'And Cody is three,' she mused, considering how best to help. 'I'll get Charlie.'

'Who is Charlie?'

The question came from behind her and the deep, throaty voice with its distinctive Italian accent not only identified its owner but set every nerve-ending tingling. Jess knew it was his first day there, and within moments of his arrival the overactive grapevine had been buzzing about the gorgeous new consultant. Female staff the length and breadth of the hospital had been preening themselves, eager to meet him and make an impression on him.

She had not been one of them.

Jess tensed, her knuckles whitening as her fingers tightened their grip on her files. Clutching them like a protective shield, and feeling suddenly scared in a way she didn't understand, she turned around and saw Giovanni Corezzi for the first time.

Oh, my!

For once the rumourmill had been right. The new Italian surgeon *was* something special to look at and even she, who had sworn off men a long time ago, could appreciate the view. A bit like window-shopping, she thought, smothering an inappropriate smile. You could admire the goods even though you had no intention of buying. But her inner humour vanished in the face of her body's impossible-to-ignore reaction.

She hated the breathless feeling that made it difficult to fill her lungs, the ache that knotted her stomach, the too-fast beat of her heart, and jelly-like knees that felt unable to support her. The instinctive responses were unnerving and unwanted. She had not been attracted to any man for a long time—had not expected or wished to be. Not since her life had taken an abrupt change of direction four years ago, turning her world upside down and having an irrevocable impact on her future, forcing her not only to abandon her hopes and dreams but to reinvent herself to survive. The Jess Carmichael of today was a very different person from the one then…one who could no longer indulge in many things, including uncharacteristic flights of fancy over a good-looking man, even if he did stir her blood in ways it had never been stirred before.

Trying to shrug off the disturbing feelings, she allowed herself a quick inspection of the imposing man who stood before her looking relaxed and at ease. His dark hair was short, thick and well groomed. In his early thirties, and topping six feet, he had an olive-toned complexion and the kind of chiselled jawline that would make him sought after in Hollywood or gracing the pages of fashion magazines. Not that he was fashionable at the moment, dressed as he was in hospital scrubs, suggesting he had come to the ward from the operating theatre.

The shapeless trousers and short-sleeved tunic should have been unflattering but they failed to mask the strength and lean athleticism of his body, while their colour emphasised the intense blueness of his eyes. Under straight, dark brows and fringed by long, dusky lashes, they were the shade of the rarest tanzanite. They regarded her with a wariness she shared, a suspicion that had her shifting uncomfortably, and the kind of masculine interest and sensual awareness that frightened her witless.

Aware that Megan was making the introductions, Jess struggled to pull herself together.

'Ms Carmichael.'

The throaty rumble of his voice made her pulse race and ruined her attempt at sang-froid. 'Hello, Mr Corezzi.'

Jess dragged her gaze free and focused on the leanly

muscled forearms crossed over his broad chest. As he moved, she juggled the files and assorted items she carried around the hospital, anxious to avoid shaking hands. Instead, she fished out one of her cards, careful to ensure she didn't touch him. His fingers closed around the card and she couldn't help but notice that he had nice hands. Surgeon's hands…capable, cared for and with short, well-manicured nails. There was no wedding ring and no tell-tale sign to suggest he had recently worn one. His only accessory was the watch on his left wrist with its mesh strap and midnight-blue dial.

The sound of Megan's pager made Jess jump but the distraction helped cut the growing tension.

'I'm needed in A and E,' Megan told them with evident reluctance, her cheeks pale and lines of strain around her mouth.

'Are you OK?' Jess asked, knowing her friend's reluctance stemmed from some unexplained issues she had with Josh O'Hara, the charismatic consultant who had joined St Piran's trauma team in the spring.

'I'll be fine.'

The words lacked conviction and Jess was concerned. Tall and slender, Megan appeared delicate, but although she possessed an inner strength, she had seemed more fragile than usual these last few weeks. Instinct made Jess want to give her friend a hug, but she hung back, keeping the physical distance she had maintained between herself and everyone else these last four years.

'I'm here if you need me,' she offered instead, conscious of the disturbing nearness of Giovanni Corezzi, whose presence prevented her saying more.

'Thanks.' Megan squared her shoulders, determination mixing with anxiety and inner hurt that shadowed her green eyes. 'I'll see you later. Good luck with the Rowlands. And Cody's surgery.'

Alone with Giovanni Corezzi, Jess felt a return of the tension and awareness that surged between them. Determined to focus on work, and needing to put distance between herself and the disturbing new surgeon, Jess murmured an apology and escaped to the ward office to track down Charlie.

Gio released a shaky breath as the surprising Jessica Carmichael walked away. He had no idea who Charlie was, or how he was relevant to the current problem, but he had greater things to worry about. Namely Jessica and his unaccountably disturbing reaction to her.

As the staff went about their work on the busy ward, he leaned against the wall and pressed one hand to his stomach. The moment he'd seen Jessica, it had felt as if he'd been sat on by an elephant. She was younger than he'd expected, perhaps in her late twenties. Below average height, she looked smart but casual, dressed for the August heat in a multi-coloured crinkle-cotton skirt that fell to her knees and a short-sleeved green shirt, her hospital ID clipped, like his own, to the top pocket.

Her eyes were a captivating and unusual olive green, while her hair—a gift from mother nature—was a vibrant auburn, with shades from burnished chestnut, like a conker fresh from its casing, to rich copper red. The luxuriant waves were confined in a thick plait which bobbed between her shoulder blades. He longed to see it unrestrained and to run his fingers through its glory.

When Jessica emerged from the ward office, the disturbing heaviness pressed on him once more. He straightened, shocked by the slam of attraction that shot through him. The cut of her shirt highlighted firm, full breasts, while the sway of her skirt hinted at curvy hips and thighs. He found her rounded, feminine figure so much more appealing than the reed-thin bodies many women aspired to.

Gio took an involuntary step back, disturbed by the surge of desire that threatened to overwhelm him with its unexpected intensity. This was the first time he had even *noticed* a woman for a long time. He couldn't believe it had been five years— No! He slammed his brain shut on *those* thoughts. This was neither the time nor the place. But he'd allowed a crack in the internal armour encasing the memories, the pain and his heart, and panic swelled within him. He didn't want to be attracted to anyone, yet he could not deny the strength of his reaction to Jessica or the way his body was reawakening and making new desires and needs known.

Disconcerted, he met her gaze and saw her eyes widen in shock at the unmasked emotions she read in his. She kept a safe gap between them, but she was close enough for him to see her shock turn to confusion, followed by answering knowledge and then alarm. Silence stretched and the air crackled with electricity. It was clear Jessica didn't want the attraction any more than he did, but that didn't make it go away. And, perversely, her reluctance intrigued him and made him want to learn more about her.

She stepped aside to allow a nurse pushing a wheelchair to pass, her smile transforming her pretty face and trapping the air in his lungs. Cross with himself, he was about to return to the business of Cody Rowland when she shifted the things she was carrying and he noticed the teddy-bear puppet she wore on one hand.

'Meet Charlie,' she invited, holding up the plush toy, which had marbled brown fur and a friendly, mischievous face, its mouth open as if laughing. 'He helps break the ice and explain things to young children, calming their fears.'

The husky but melodic burr of her soft Scottish accent was sensual and set his heart thudding. Feeling as flustered as a teenager with his first crush, he struggled to ignore his unwanted reaction and focus on the matter at hand.

'Very clever.' Her innovative method impressed him. He reached out and gently shook the teddy bear by the paw. 'It's nice to meet you, Charlie.'

Jessica's flustered reaction confirmed his suspicion that giving him her card had been a ruse to avoid shaking hands. Was it him, or did she dislike touching other people, too? That he was immediately attuned to her unsettled him further.

'What are the priorities with Cody?' Jessica asked, moving them onto ground which, he felt sure, made her feel more comfortable. 'Have his parents signed the consent form?'

'Not yet.' Gio ran the fingers of one hand through his hair in frustration. 'The injury occurred over two weeks ago,' he explained, unsure how much Megan had told her. 'The parents are too upset to understand that while Cody may have appeared fine at first, the situation has changed.'

'And you don't want to waste more time.'

Grateful that Jessica was on his wavelength, Gio smiled. 'Exactly so.'

'He's deteriorating more quickly?' she asked, glancing at the notes.

'What was a slow bleed building a chronic subdural haematoma could be worsening,' he outlined, sharing his concerns. 'Or something more serious could be underlying it.'

Jessica nodded, making her beautiful hair gleam. 'And the longer you wait, the more chance there is of permanent brain damage.'

'I'm afraid so.'

'His parents must be very confused.' Her expression softened with understanding. 'They may feel guilty for not realising that what seemed an innocuous incident has become something so serious.'

'There is no question of blame, although such feelings are common,' he agreed, impressed by Jessica.

Her smile was rueful. 'I come across this in a wide variety of circumstances. We need to explain things to the Rowlands without frightening them further.'

'Yes…and Megan says you're the best person to help.'

A wash of colour warmed her flawless alabaster cheeks. 'I'll do what I can, of course.'

'Thank you, Jessica.'

Again her name felt right, unsettling him and curbing his amusement at her flustered reaction. Ignoring the hum of attraction between them by concentrating on work might not be effective long term, but hopefully it would get them through this encounter.

'Do you have suggestions about the Rowlands?'

Her relief was evident and she nodded again, loosening some strands of fiery hair, which tumbled around her face. As she raised her free hand, he saw that her fingers were ring free, and that she wore a narrow silver-toned watch around her wrist. She tucked the errant curls behind her ear, drawing his attention to the attractive stud earrings she wore. Set in white metal, the olive green stones matched her eyes and he made a mental note to discover the identity of the gem that so suited her.

'We need their consent so Cody can go to Theatre without delay. Then I can spend time with them and run through everything in more detail.' Even, white teeth nibbled the sensual swell of her rosy lower lip, nearly giving him heart failure. 'Do you have a rough guestimate on how long the operation might take?' she queried, snapping his attention back to business. 'The Rowlands will ask—and I need to reorganise my schedule to support them.'

Gio was encouraged by Jessica's common-sense approach, knowledge and apparent dedication to her patients. With real hope of a resolution, he gave her all the information he could.

'Can you talk with the father while I try the mother?' she asked next, walking briskly towards Cody's room.

He would happily do anything to speed things along. 'No problem.'

Following her, he admired her gently rounded, mouth-watering curves. As she stepped into Cody's room, sunlight spilling through the window made the natural red, copper and chestnut tones of her hair glow like living flames, captivating him. And, for the briefest instant, as he stood close behind her before she shifted to give him more room, he could have sworn he caught a faint, tantalising aroma of chocolate.

Fanciful notions vanished as he observed that Cody appeared more listless than when he had checked him several minutes ago. His frightened young mother sat close to him, clinging to his hand, tears spilling down her cheeks. The father, scarcely more than a boy himself, stood to one side, pale and withdrawn, at a loss to know what to do.

Jessica glanced over her shoulder and he met her gaze. The connection between them felt electric and intense, and it took a huge effort to look away. Clearing his throat, he introduced her to the Rowlands.

As Jessica began the delicate process of winning the trust of the troubled young family, Gio released another shaky breath. He was in big trouble. He had sensed Jessica would be more than he'd bargained for. Professionally. What he could never have foreseen was the impact she would have on him personally. It was unexpected, unwanted and scary. But bubbling within, as yet unacknowledged and unexplored, was growing excitement.

Even as they worked together to see Cody and his parents through the trauma that had befallen them, Gio was aware of the simmering connection between himself and Jessica. However hard they fought it, it was not going away.

All he knew for sure was that Jessica threatened to blow the ordered and lonely world he had lived in these last five years wide apart, and that her impact on his life would not leave him unscathed.

CHAPTER TWO

SHE didn't *look* any different.

Jess peered at her reflection in the mirror above the basin in the tiny bathroom next to her office. She wasn't sure what she'd expected to see, but she *felt* different. Changed somehow. And scared. Because of Giovanni Corezzi. Thinking about him made her pulse race and raised her temperature to an uncomfortable level—one she couldn't blame on the scorching August weather.

After splashing cool water on her overheated cheeks, she buried her face in the softness of her towel. Even with her eyes closed, images of St Piran's new Italian surgeon filled her mind. Unsettled by her reaction to him, she had endeavoured to keep things on a professional footing, determined to banish the disturbing feelings he roused within her.

She hadn't wanted to like him, but it had proved impossible not to. Ignoring the inexplicable and overwhelming blaze of attraction would have been easier had he been arrogant and horrible to work with, but nothing was further from the truth. He'd been compassionate and patient. As his initial suspicion had evaporated once he had witnessed her with the Rowlands, the likelihood was that she would be called to work with him again.

What was she going to do?

Jess sighed, discarding the towel and glancing at her reflection again. Less than an hour in his company had left her shaken and anxious. Megan had been right to describe him as hands on and caring. It was something Jess admired, yet it made him even more dangerous to her.

She had to find a way to limit his impact on her. He had reawakened things long forgotten, things she would sooner remained buried. She had to fight the desire he roused in her…because nothing could come of it. *Ever.* And she was leaving herself open to heartache if, even for a moment, she allowed herself to imagine anything else.

For the last four years, since the bombshell had hit her, changing her life for ever, she had turned in on herself, keeping focused on her new career and keeping people at bay. She hadn't worked so hard to reinvent herself to allow the first man to stir her long-dormant hormones into action to undo everything she had achieved. In the unlikely event she could ever trust a man again, there was no way she could allow any kind of relationship to develop. Not beyond friendship. To do so would be too great a risk. Besides, once Giovanni learned the truth she had kept secret for so long, he wouldn't want her anyway.

Quashing disobedient feelings of disappointment and regret—and, worse, a flash of self-pity—Jess hardened her battered heart. She had to keep Giovanni Corezzi at a distance and ensure any meetings with him were kept as professional and brief as possible.

Shocked how late it was, she returned to her office. She'd had to rearrange her schedule for the Rowlands, which meant she had much to catch up on and now she would have to rush if she was not to be late for an important appointment.

Five days ago, and less than three weeks after moving into the run-down cottage she had bought near Penhally village, an unseasonal storm had caused serious damage. Today the insurance company's assessor was carrying out an inspection, after which Jess hoped permission would be given for the repairs. The sooner the better... before anyone discovered the unconventional lengths she was going to to keep a roof over her head.

Smothering her guilt, she took care of a few urgent tasks before shutting down her computer. She just had time to dash across the grounds to see hospital handyman Sid Evans and collect the precious cargo he was watching for her.

'Hello, Jess, love,' the kindly man greeted her as she hurried through his open workshop door. 'Everything is ready for you.'

'Thanks, Sid.'

'Here we are, all present and correct,' he told her in his lilting Welsh accent as he handed her a basket.

'I'm sorry to rush, Sid. Thanks for your help.'

'No worries.' He smiled, but Jess could see the sadness that lurked in his eyes. Following the recent death of Winnie, Sid's beloved wife of forty years, Jess had taken time to visit with him. 'And I'm the one who's grateful. You've been wonderful, love, letting me talk about my Winnie. I'll not forget it.'

'It's been my privilege,' she replied, a lump in her throat.

Jess hurried back to the psychology unit, glad everyone had left for the day, allowing her to sneak the basket into her odd little annexe at the back of the building. Dubbed the 'cubby hole', it had been assigned to her as the only spare room available, but she couldn't have been more pleased. Apart from the office and next-door bathroom, it had an adjoining anteroom and a basic kitchen. Away from the main offices, it gave her privacy, which suited her just fine. Especially with circumstances as they were...circumstances no one else knew about and which brought another surge of guilt.

Setting down the basket, Jess checked the contents then picked up her bag and keys. The sooner she went home, the sooner she could return to St Piran's. Hopefully she would be too busy in the coming hours to think about Giovanni Corezzi.

Opening her office door, she hurried out, only to collide with something solid and warm and smelling divinely of clean male with a hint of citrus and musk. Her 'Oh' of surprise was muffled against a broad chest as she lost her balance.

'Easy there,' Giovanni's voice soothed.

His hands steadied her, closing on her bare arms above the elbows. She felt the impact of his touch in every particle of her being, the brush of his fingers on sensitive skin making her tingle. She felt as if she'd been branded. A bolt of awareness and long-suppressed need blazed through her, scaring her.

The urge to lean into him and savour the moment was very strong. It seemed for ever since she had been touched and held, even in a platonic way. Not that there was anything *platonic* about the way Giovanni made her feel! But that knowledge acted like a bucket of icy water. Panic gripped her, both at the physical contact and her overwhelming reaction to this man. The need to break the spell overrode everything else and she struggled free, her desperation causing her to push away from him with more force than she had intended.

'What are you doing here?' she challenged brusquely.

Intense blue eyes regarded her with curiosity. 'Forgive me, I didn't know this part of the hospital was out of bounds.' His tone was gently teasing, but a blush stained her cheeks in acknowledgement of her uncharacteristic rudeness.

'It's not, of course, Mr Corezzi, but—' Jess broke off. Everything about him threw her into confusion.

'Please, call me Gio. I came to update you on Cody,' he explained, his throaty voice and sexy accent sending a shiver down her spine. 'And to thank you for your help.'

Her breath locked in her lungs as he rewarded her with a full-wattage smile. 'I was just doing my job.'

'I also wish to discuss another patient soon to be admitted whom I feel will benefit from your involvement,' he continued.

'That's fine. But is it urgent? I'm in a hurry.'

Although she had softened her tone, his dark eyebrows drew together in a frown. 'It's not urgent, but I hoped you'd have a minute...'

'I'm afraid I don't.' Jess cursed her stiltedness. She seemed unable to behave normally around him. 'I'm sorry, I have to rush home. I'll talk with you later.'

Eager to make her escape without him seeing inside her office and discovering the secret she had kept hidden so far, Jess fumbled behind her for the handle and pulled the door closed with a determined snap. She turned round, removing herself from his inspection, locked her office and pocketed the key. Then, carefully skirting him, she walked briskly to the main entrance, conscious of him following her.

'Jessica…'

The way he said her name tied her insides into knots. It wasn't just his voice or pronunciation but that he alone used her full name and made it sound like a caress. Thankful she had a genuine excuse to escape, she opened the front door and stepped aside for him to exit ahead of her.

'I have to run,' she said, concerned at his reluctance to leave.

A muscle pulsed along the masculine line of his jaw, indicating his dissatisfaction. When he stepped outside, allowing her to do the same, the door swinging closed and the lock clicking into place, Jess released the breath she hadn't realised she'd been holding.

He looked down at her, a brooding expression on his far-too-handsome face. 'Later.'

It was more demand than question and it filled Jess with alarm…and a dangerous sense of excited anticipation that was the most scary of all.

'Later,' she allowed reluctantly.

As she hurried towards her car, she sensed him watching her. So much for her earlier resolution. He was going to be more difficult to avoid than she'd anticipated. And this second encounter had confirmed what a risk he posed to the carefully constructed world she had manufactured for herself. Now a sexy Italian neurosurgeon had bulldozed his way into her life and was in danger of unravelling everything she had worked so hard for.

* * *

Heavy-hearted at the way his first day at St Piran's was ending, Gio washed, disposed of his scrubs and dressed in the jeans and short-sleeved shirt he had pulled on after arriving home. He'd not long left the hospital after making a final check of his patients when the emergency call had come for him to return.

A multidisciplinary team had assembled in Theatre, but despite their best efforts their nineteen-year-old casualty had succumbed to severe chest trauma and brain damage after an alcohol-induced accident.

Gio sighed at the waste of a life. Pain stabbed inside him as his thoughts strayed to another young life that had been cut cruelly short and he closed his eyes, determined to control his emotions and push the destructive memories away. Instead, he found himself thinking of Jessica Carmichael.

His impulsive visit to her office in the psychology unit—situated in one of the buildings adjacent to the main hospital and abutting the consultants' car park—had not gone to plan. He usually got on well with people. *'You could sell sand in the desert, Cori!'* Remembering the teasing words brought both amusement and an ache to his heart. Friendliness, politeness and a touch of flattery soothed troubled waters, but it wasn't working with Jessica, who remained tense and reserved.

Their unsatisfactory encounter had disappointed and confused him. He lived for his job, trying each day to make up for the failings that had haunted him for the last five years. Which was why his immediate and intense response to Jessica had shocked him. She had affected him on a deeply personal level. And he didn't *do* personal. Not any more. His reaction—and the attraction he wished he could deny—left him disconcerted and off balance.

When she had rushed out of her office and cannoned into him, instinct had taken over and he'd caught her as she'd stumbled. He'd felt the incredible softness of her skin under his fingers, the press of her femininely curved body against him, and he'd breathed in the teasing aroma of chocolate that lingered on her hair and skin. His attraction and body's response to her had been instant and undeniable.

But it was Jessica's reactions that had left him puzzled and unsettled. Her alarm had been real, and he had not imagined the panic in her beautiful green eyes as she'd wrenched herself free. For some reason Jessica didn't like to touch or be touched and he was determined to find out what lay behind it. There were several possibilities and each one caused him concern.

Gio stepped out of the surgeons' wash room, unsure what to do next. Why had Jessica been so dismissive of him and in such a rush to leave? He was positive she had felt the same bolt of awareness that had slammed into him when they'd first met. And that it had scared her. So could it be, he wondered, heading to the paediatric intensive care unit to check on Cody, that Jessica's cool professionalism and anxiety were flight responses? Was she trying to ignore the feelings and make them go away? If so, he could tell her it didn't work.

Using his swipe card, he let himself into PICU. Aside from the noise of the various monitoring machines and ventilators, the unit was quiet and dimly lit. He nodded to the charge nurse on duty and made his way to the bay that held Cody's bed. As he approached, he heard voices, one of which was Jessica's. He halted, surprised. What was she doing back here at this time of night? Curious, he listened before making his presence known.

'And when I think what could have happened,' Elsa Rowland commented, fear and guilt lacing her voice.

'You mustn't blame yourself, Elsa,' he heard Jessica respond softly, the gentle burr of her Scottish accent so attractive to him. 'A chronic subdural haematoma builds gradually. It can be weeks, even months, before the symptoms show. You did the right thing bringing Cody to A and E as soon as you realised something was wrong.'

'Thank you.' The woman's relief was tangible. 'I know Mr Corezzi explained it all to us but I didn't take anything in. And someone told me he's new. The thought of Cody's head being cut open is frightening.'

'Of course it is. But you can trust Mr Corezzi. He might be new to St Piran's but he's a very skilled and highly respected consultant neurosurgeon and he's come to us from London with a tremendous reputation,' Jessica explained to the anxious woman, her glowing endorsement of him taking Gio by surprise.

'Cody looks so still and small. Are you sure everything is all right?' the tearful mother asked, and although Gio wanted to reassure her, he was keen to hear what Jessica would say.

'He's doing very well,' she replied, her tone conveying sympathy and authority. 'It's standard procedure for him to be in Intensive Care following the operation.'

Gio was impressed. He was also intrigued by the depth of Jessica's knowledge. She seemed too assured and informed for someone with no medical training.

'Ally's gone to get something to eat. The nurses want

us to go home, but I can't bear to be away from Cody,' Elsa fretted.

'There's a cot in a room nearby for parents to use, and I'd advise you both to get what sleep you can there. But after tonight it would be best to get back into a normal routine. You and Ally need to keep strong so you are fit and ready to take Cody home,' Jessica urged, her common-sense approach pleasing him. 'I'll see you again tomorrow, but you can ring me if you need anything.'

There was a pause in the conversation and Gio waited a moment before making a sound and entering the bay. Elsa Rowland gave him a weary smile as he greeted her, but his attention immediately strayed to Jessica. She tensed, her gaze skittering to his and away again, a delicate flush of colour staining her cheeks.

As he checked Cody, who was sleeping peacefully, and looked over his chart, Gio was attuned to Jessica. What was she doing back at the hospital? Had she misled him when she'd said she was leaving for the day? He hoped to find answers as soon as Cody's father returned and, after a few pleasantries, Gio was able to escort Jessica out.

'I was surprised to see you,' he told her once they had left the unit and were in no danger of being overheard. 'I thought you had left for the day.'

Once more a tinge of colour warmed her smooth cheeks. 'I had to rush home to meet the insurance company's assessor. I said I'd be back,' she added defensively, refusing to meet his gaze.

She *had* said that but he'd assumed she had meant the next day. Apparently unsure what to do with her hands now that she was no longer carrying the assorted paraphernalia he'd seen her with before, she pushed them into her skirt pockets.

'What about you? Why are you still here?'

Her questions cut across the electrically charged atmosphere that hummed between them.

'I was called in after a young woman was knocked down by a coach.' He gave her a brief summary of the events and the unsuccessful struggle in the operating theatre. 'Her injuries were too severe…there was nothing we could do.'

Jessica's expression softened, understanding and sympathy visible in her olive-green eyes, and in her voice when she spoke. 'What a rotten end to your first day.'

'It could have finished on a better note,' Gio admitted with a rueful shrug, running the fingers of one hand through his hair.

Leaning back against the wall, Jessica met his gaze, and he witnessed her first real smile for him. *Dio*, but she was beautiful! The heavy weight settled back on his chest, making it difficult to breathe, and he felt each rapid thud of his heart.

'If it's not too late and you still want to talk about your patient…' Jessica's words trailed off and she bit her lip, looking hesitant and unsure.

'That would be good, thank you.' He'd take any opportunity to spend time with this elusive and most puzzling woman. 'Shall we go to the canteen? I've not eaten and the now congealed ready meal waiting in my microwave holds no appeal.'

Gio thought she was going to refuse and he found himself holding his breath as he waited for her answer. That it meant so much to him and he wanted so badly to be in her company should have worried him—*would* have worried him even one day ago. But in the short hours since he had met Jessica he felt changed somehow. Where this inexplicable but intense attraction was heading he had no idea, but he was keen to find out.

'All right.'

However reluctantly given, her agreement cheered him, and as he walked by her side down the deserted hospital corridor he felt as if he was setting out on one of the most important journeys of his life…with no map to help guide him and no clue as to the final destination.

CHAPTER THREE

'THAT wretched woman!'

Jess looked up in surprise as Brianna Flannigan, a nursing sister from the neonatal intensive care and special care baby units, banged a plate down on the canteen table and sat down, joining Megan and herself.

'What woman?' Jess and Megan asked in unison, concerned that the gentle, dedicated and softly spoken Brianna was so upset.

'Rita.'

Rita was the ward clerk in NICU/SCBU and renowned for nosing into other people's business, making her opinions, and often her disapproval, known. Few people took notice of her, but none wanted to fall under her spotlight. Both Brianna and Megan had suffered when Rita had picked on them in the past, and news she was hassling Brianna again brought out Jess's protective instincts.

'I'm sorry.' She sent her friend a sympathetic smile. 'What brought this on?'

Brianna idly pushed her salad around the plate. 'Now Diego and Izzy are no longer occupying Rita, she's refocused on me,' Brianna explained, frustration and displeasure in her lilting Irish voice.

'Tell her to mind her own business…that's what I do,' Megan riposted, stirring a sugar into her mug of tea. 'Not that it stops her. She's started making comments about me again, too.'

Jess knew Rita wasn't easily diverted once she set her mind on something. She suppressed a shiver. The idea of anyone probing into her past and her secrets was too awful to contemplate.

'She's always been nosy and judgemental. I thought she'd given up on me, but now she's asking where I came from and what I did before I joined St Piran's,' Brianna continued.

Jess recognised the dark shadows in her friend's brown eyes and couldn't help but wonder what had put them there.

'She'll never change,' Megan predicted. 'If she's not prying into someone's business, she's having a go about single mothers…or teenage ones. And don't get her started on her daughter.'

'What's wrong with her daughter?' Jess queried with a frown.

Megan dunked a biscuit in her tea. 'Nothing. That's the point. Marina's been happily married for twenty years and has several children—I've treated some of them for the usual childhood accidents and illnesses. They're a great family. Noisy and loving. Maybe that's what bugs Rita. She claims Marina married beneath her and shouldn't have had such a big family,' Megan finished, brushing crumbs from her lip.

'It's true she picks on Marina,' Brianna agreed. 'She finds fault with her grandchildren, too.'

The talk made Jess even more grateful that she had managed to avoid Rita's attention and speculation.

Megan and Brianna were the closest she had to friends, yet they knew no more about her than she did about them, even after the years they had known each other. Which was probably why they got along so well. The mutual trust was there and they guarded each other's privacy, sharing an unspoken agreement not to ask personal questions, yet they could turn to one another should they need to, knowing their confidence would be respected.

'Rita's also asking questions about Gio Corezzi,' Brianna added, snapping Jess from her thoughts.

'Why would she start on him?' she asked, fighting a blush at the mention of Gio's name. 'She hasn't even met him, has she?'

Brianna nodded. 'She met him this morning. We all did. We have a baby with hydrocephalus—along with several other problems, the poor mite—and Richard Brooke called Gio up to the unit for advice,' the caring Irish woman explained, referring to the consultant who headed NICU.

'What sort of questions is Rita asking?' Jess queried, striving for casual indifference.

'She wants to know why someone who was such a wow in London would chose to "*bury himself*" in Cornwall,' Brianna told them, spearing some food with her fork. 'She saw Gio in the consultants' car park with James Alexander, chatting about cars—apparently they own the same model Aston Martin, but in different colours, so Rita's sure Gio's loaded.'

'For goodness' sake,' Megan responded, with the same disgust Jess was feeling.

'Rita asked Gio if his wife would be joining him here.' Brianna paused, and Jess steeled herself for what her friend would reveal next. 'Gio said, "Unfortunately not," and you could see the speculation in Rita's eyes until Gio added, after a deliberate pause, "She's *dead*." It was just awful. I felt terrible for him. He looked so sad. Even Rita was embarrassed, and that's saying something.'

As Brianna and Megan discussed Rita-avoidance tactics, Jess sat back and battled her emotions. Her heart squeezed with pain at the news of Gio's loss. Concerned for him, she also felt guilty for the unstoppable flicker of relief that he wasn't already taken. Not that *she* had any future with him. Or with anyone. But she couldn't help wondering what had happened…or question why he hadn't told her himself. Not that it was her business. She respected his privacy. And she hadn't told him *her* secrets.

Discovering how protective and possessive she felt of Gio was disconcerting. She knew the answer to some of Rita's questions, but she would never divulge them. Not even to Brianna and Megan. Not because they might gossip, they wouldn't, but for much more complicated reasons. She didn't want to admit to her friends, or to herself, how much she enjoyed and looked forward to Gio's company.

After Gio had returned to the hospital on the evening of his first day and had found her in PICU with the Rowlands, they had spent well over an hour in the canteen together. She'd had little time to wonder if he'd overheard any of her conversation with Cody's mother because she'd been pole-axed by the charge of electricity and blaze of sensual awareness that hit her every time she saw him. He'd looked gorgeous in jeans and a blue shirt, the shadow of stubble darkening his masculine jaw making him seem rakish and dangerous.

The canteen had been far less crowded than it was now, Jess acknowledged, shifting her chair in to allow a group of nurses to pass and access a nearby table. Gio had chosen a full meal, while she'd opted for a small bottle of mineral water and a packet of sandwiches… out of habit selecting things in disposable packaging. She hadn't budgeted for an extra snack, but as she'd not eaten anything but a banana and an apple since breakfast, she'd been hungry.

Having sunk everything she'd had into buying her cottage, she was counting every penny. The storm damage had been an unforeseen disaster but the insurance company was going to cover repairs for her roof despite the policy only being a month old. Having overstretched herself on the property, she was having to be frugal with everything else, not that she had hinted at the sorry state of her finances to Gio—or anyone else.

'Have you always worked here?' Gio had asked, turning their conversation that first night away from his patients and to work in general as he'd tucked into his dessert.

'No. I joined St Piran's when I was in the final year of my training,' she'd explained to him, amazed he'd found room for apple pie and cream after the large portion of lasagne that had preceded it. 'They asked me to stay on once I'd qualified.'

What she hadn't told him had been the extent of her relief that she'd not needed to move on again, something she had done several times since the life-changing bombshell had brought things crashing down around her. She'd carved out a niche for herself in St Piran, fulfilling a role that patients, relatives and staff all appreciated and which allowed her some welcome autonomy.

'You don't see patients in your office?' Gio had queried.

'Very rarely—although I have done so if circumstances required it,' she replied, thinking of Izzy, the young A and E doctor who, then six months pregnant, had wanted to return to work after taking leave following the traumatic time she had experienced.

It hadn't been easy, for Izzy or herself, but things had worked out well. Now Izzy had a beautiful baby girl and an amazing new man in her life in the shape of attractive Spaniard Diego, who had been a charge nurse in NICU/SCBU, and Jess wished them all the happiness in the world.

'My role is more immediate,' she had gone on to tell Gio. 'I give emergency help to those who need it, be that on the wards, in A and E, or elsewhere in the hospital.'

'Like the Rowlands.' Gio's smile had nearly stopped her heart.

'Y-yes.' Flustered, she'd tried to get a grip. 'There can be a wide variety of situations…parents making difficult decisions about treatment for their child, or a young man who has crashed his motorbike and, overnight, has gone from being fit and active to waking up in hospital to the news he'll never walk again. Or it could be an older person who's had a stroke and is unable to return to their home. Or a relative in A and E trying to come to terms with a sudden bereavement.'

Something dark and painful had flashed in Gio's intense blue eyes, alerting Jess to the possibility there had been some traumatic event in his past. She hadn't pried, and Gio had declined to refer to it, but she had wondered about his background.

'So you see people through those first stages?' he'd asked next, pushing his empty dish aside and reclaiming her attention.

'That's right. Sometimes people need a shoulder to cry on and a friend in their corner. Others need greater help and back-up. I can liaise with other departments and with agencies outside the hospital that can offer care, advice and support, like social services, or relatives who have expectations that the patient may not want,' she'd explained, finding him easy to talk to. 'My job is to support them and their rights, and to help them achieve the best solution to whatever problem they're facing. If they need ongoing counselling once they leave hospital, they are assigned to one of my colleagues through Outpatients, or to an outside support organisation.'

Gio had shaken his head. 'I hadn't realised the full extent of what you do for people. It's very impressive... *you're* very impressive. I can see why everyone here respects you so much.'

The admiration in his eyes and praise in his sexy voice had warmed her right through and brought an uncharacteristic sting of tears to her eyes. 'It's hardly brain surgery,' she'd quipped to mask her embarrassment.

Gio's husky chuckle of appreciation had tightened the knot of awareness low in her tummy, and a sudden wave of longing had stolen her breath and made her realise how alone she had been these last four years. She enjoyed a friendship with Megan and Brianna, but it didn't extended beyond work and could never fill the cold and lonely void that had grown inside her since her life had turned upside down.

'Your first day's been hectic and hasn't ended in the best of ways, but how have you found St Piran's?' Jess had asked, anxious to move the conversation away from herself.

'I would rather not have returned to Theatre for that poor girl tonight,' he'd admitted, and she had seen the lines of tiredness around his eyes. 'But I've enjoyed today and it's good to be in near the beginning of a new unit for the hospital. It was one of the reasons I took the job. I was impressed with Gordon Ainsworth, the senior neurological consultant, the state-of-the-art equipment and the plans to increase the neurosurgical services here. Being able to help shape those services and build my own team appealed to me. Of course, many people cannot understand why I would leave London to come here.'

'It's none of their business, is it? If it's what you want, that's all that matters,' she'd told him, his surprised expression suggesting her matter-of-fact support had been in short supply.

'Thank you.' His slow, intimate smile had threatened to unravel her completely. 'St Piran's offered me new challenges and fresh opportunities, as well as the chance of more rapid career progression.'

It had made sense to her. 'Better to be a big fish in a small pond?'

Again the smile with its devastating effect on her. 'But it's much more than that…more than what I might gain for myself.' He'd leaned forward and folded his arms on the table, a pout of consideration shaping his sexy mouth. 'I commit a fair bit of time and money to a charitable trust that not only funds research, equipment for hospitals in various countries and support for patients and their families with brain tumours and other neuro-logical conditions. We also bring children in desperate need of specialist treatment to the UK.'

She hadn't been surprised to learn of this side to him. She'd seen the kind of doctor he was. Instinct had told her how important the charity work was to him, and she'd suspected there was far more to it than he had told her…reasons why the trust was so close to his heart.

'That's fantastic. And it must be so rewarding.'

'It is. That St Piran's is interested and has given per-mission for me to continue to bring over a number of children each year, donating the hospital facilities free of charge, was a huge factor in my decision to come here.'

Jess had been fascinated as he'd talked more about the work he'd done with the trust. Her heart had swelled with pride as she'd thought about his selflessness and determination to use his skills to help others.

'He is *very* handsome, isn't he?'

Brianna's comment impinged on Jess's consciousness and she blinked, looking up and following her friend's gaze in time to see Gio carrying a tray across the can-teen and sitting at a table with Ben Carter and James Alexander. Her pulse raced at the sight of him and she had to beat back a dart of jealousy at Brianna's evident appreciation of Gio's looks.

The man in question turned his head and met her gaze. For several moments it was as if there was no one else in the canteen—the myriad conversations going on all around her faded to a background hum and every-thing was a blur but Gio himself. A shiver ran down her spine and a very real sense of fear clutched at her.

Less than a week and already this man had breached her defences and become all too important to her.

What was she going to do? If she allowed the friendship to develop, she knew things would end in heartbreak. Despite knowing that, and despite a desperate need to preserve all she had achieved these last four years, she wasn't sure she could give Gio up.

A sudden clatter and burst of laughter from across the room caught the attention of everyone in the canteen and snapped Gio's gaze away from Jessica. He glanced round in time to see three junior doctors trying to contain the mess from a can of fizzy drink as the liquid spewed from the top in a bubbly fountain, soaking everything and everyone within range.

'The Three Stooges,' Ben commented wryly.

James chuckled. 'Were we ever that young and foolish and confident?'

'Probably!' Ben allowed.

Gio tried not to dwell on the past. His memories were mixed, all the happy ones overshadowed by the bad ones and the blackest time of his life. Ben and James, fellow consultants with whom he had struck up an immediate rapport, began detailing the merits of the three rowdy young doctors, but Gio's attention was inexorably drawn back to Jessica. The now familiar awareness surged through him, tightening his gut and making it difficult to breathe.

Jessica was sitting with two other women. Megan Phillips, the paediatric registrar with whom he worked frequently. And Brianna Flannigan, a kind and dedicated nursing sister in NICU/PICU, whom he'd met for the first time that morning. On the surface, the three women shared many similarities and yet they were distinctly different. And it was only Jessica who made his pulse race and caused his heart, which he had believed to be in permanent cold storage, to flutter with long-forgotten excitement.

They had sat in this very canteen and talked for a long time that first night, yet he'd discovered precious little about her. He, on the other hand, had revealed far more than he'd intended.

Her understanding and support about his move to Cornwall had warmed him. Many people had appreciated his need to leave Italy for New York five years ago. Some had comprehended his decision to leave New York, and the team of the neurosurgeon who had taught him so much, to move to London. But very few had grasped why he had chosen St Piran's over the other options that had been open to him—options that would have meant more money and working at bigger hospitals.

Those things hadn't interested him, which had not surprised Jessica. St Piran's offered the opportunity of advancing to head of department within a decade, Gordon Ainsworth grooming him to take over when he retired, but it had been the administration's support of his charity work that had swayed his decision.

He'd told Jessica about the trust but *not* why it was so important to him. Not yet. That he was thinking of doing so showed how far she had burrowed under his skin. Even as warning bells rang in his head, suggesting he was getting too close too quickly, he couldn't stop himself craving her company and wanting to know more about her.

They'd seen each other often during the week, working together with a couple of new patients and a rapidly improving Cody Rowland. Their friendship grew tighter all the time but Jessica remained nervous. She'd relax for a time then something would cause her to raise her defensive wall again. Her working hours puzzled him, and the extent of her medical knowledge continued to intrigue him.

The little she had revealed about herself centred around her work at St Piran's. Listening to her describe her role, and witnessing her way with people—including the use of Charlie, the teddy-bear hand puppet, to interact with frightened children—had left him full of admiration for her devotion and skill.

'Much of my work involves supporting people who face life changes and difficult decisions caused by illness or accident. It's a huge shock to the system,' she'd told him and, for a moment her eyes had revealed such intense pain that it had taken his breath away.

He'd wanted to comfort and hug her, but he'd resisted the instinctive urge, aware of Jessica's aversion to touching and being touched…one of her mysteries he hoped to unravel. But the incident had left him in little doubt that she'd experienced some similar trauma. As had he, he allowed, with his own dart of inner pain.

'Patients and relatives often try to be strong for each other,' Jessica had continued with perceptive insight, 'when often they need to admit that they're scared and have a bloody good cry.' She'd sent him a sweet, sad smile that had ripped at his already shredded heart. 'I'm merely a vehicle, a sounding board, someone outside their normal lives on whom they can offload all the emotion.'

What toll did that take on her? Gio wondered

with concern. And who was there for her? They were questions to which he still had no answers.

Without conscious decision or prior arrangement, they'd met each evening in the canteen, lingering over something to eat, discussing work, finding all manner of common interests in books, music and politics, both of them steering clear of anything too personal.

He'd learned very quickly to tread carefully, watching for the triggers that caused her withdrawal. He liked her, enjoyed her company and was comfortable with her but also alive, aroused and challenged, feeling things he'd not experienced in the five long years since his world had come crashing down around him.

Taking things slowly was a necessity. For both of them. But every day he became more deeply involved. So much so that having to say goodnight to her and return alone to his rented house was becoming increasingly difficult.

'Oh, to be that young and free from responsibility.'

Edged with bitterness, the words were voiced by Josh O'Hara and pulled Gio from his reverie. The Irishman took the final empty chair and set his plate down on the table. Gio regarded the other man, wondering what had sparked his reaction.

'Something wrong, Josh?' Ben asked, a frown on his face.

'Bad day.' He pushed his food aside untouched. 'I've just had to DOA an eighteen-year-old…I was going to say *man*, but he was scarcely more than a boy with his whole life ahead of him.'

Gio sympathised, recalling how he'd felt a few days ago when the young woman had died in Theatre from multiple injuries. 'What happened?'

'He was an apprentice mechanic at a local garage, driving the work van and following another mechanic who was returning a customer's car after service,' Josh explained, emotion in his accented voice as he told the story. 'Some bozo going home from a liquid lunch at the golf club and driving far too fast ploughed into the van. The boy wasn't wearing his seat belt, the van had no air-bags, and he went through the windscreen. He had horrible head and facial injuries—apparently he'd been a good-looking boy, not that I could tell—and a broken neck.'

Gio exchanged glances with Ben and James, both of whom were listening with equal solemnity and empathy. 'And the drunk driver?' Ben queried, voicing the question in all their minds.

'Yeah, well, there's the rub. There's no justice in this world.' Josh gave a humourless laugh. 'The boy's colleague, who witnessed the crash, is in shock. The drunk driver hasn't got a scratch on him. The police have arrested him and I hope they throw the book at him, but whatever sentence he gets won't be enough to make up for that young life, will it?'

'No,' Gio murmured with feeling.

As his three companions discussed the case, Gio struggled to contain memories of another injustice and senseless loss of life, one he had been unable to prevent and which had plunged him into the darkest despair he had ever known. A darkness he had believed he would never escape. His gaze returned to Jessica, who, in just a few days, had brought flickerings of light and hope back into his life.

A shaft of sunshine from the window beside her made the vibrancy of her rich auburn hair gleam like pure flame. Brianna also had auburn hair but hers was a much lighter shade, lacking the coppery chestnut richness of Jessica's. Megan, whose hair was darker, was the tallest of the three, slender and fragile-looking. Brianna, an inch or two shorter, was lithe and athletic, while Jessica was shorter still and more rounded, her shapely feminine curves so appealing to him. She looked up and, as their gazes clashed once more, she sent him a tiny smile.

'From the Three Stooges to the Three Enigmas,' Ben remarked, his gaze following Gio's to Jessica's table, just as the rowdy young doctors left the canteen.

Fearing his new friend would detect his interest in Jessica, Gio dragged his gaze away and pretended not to know what Ben meant. 'Sorry?'

'Brianna, Jess and Megan,' Ben enlightened him. 'St Piran's Three Enigmas.'

'It's interesting that the three of them gravitated to each other,' James said, as he looked across at them.

Ben shrugged. 'I'm not surprised. They have so much in common. All three are intensely private and have somehow managed to elude the gossip-mongers. And all three have also ignored the attention showered on them by the majority of the single—and some not-so-single—men in the hospital. I don't think anyone knows anything more about them, or their lives outside work, than they did the day each of them began working here,' Ben finished.

'How long *has* Megan been here?' Josh asked, his apparent nonchalance only surface deep, Gio was sure.

'It must be, what…seven years? Maybe eight,' Ben pondered, and Gio noticed the set of Josh's jaw and the way he flinched, as if the time was somehow important.

Gio glanced over to Jessica's table again, his gaze resting a moment on Megan. He was just about to smile at her when he realised that she wasn't looking at him but at Josh. Pale faced and seemingly upset, Megan turned away.

Across from him Josh looked strained and affected by the silent exchange. There was a story there, Gio realised, but it was none of his business. He had enough to concern him settling into a new job, a new town, and dealing with the sudden and unexpected resurgence of his libido.

As the four of them prepared to return to their respective departments, their break over, Gio noticed activity at Jessica's table, too. She was standing up and reaching for her pager, a frown on her face as she read the message.

He wondered what had happened and who needed her now. Like a schoolboy with his first crush, he hoped he would meet up with Jessica later, craving the moments at the end of the day when he had her to himself, at least for a while.

She was becoming ever more important to him and he was both scared and excited to discover what was going to happen.

CHAPTER FOUR

As HER pager sounded, Jess rose to her feet, frowning as she read the call for her to attend A and E urgently.

'I have to go,' she explained as her friends said good-bye. 'I'll see you later.'

Jess squeezed her way between the tables, wishing she was as slender as Megan and Brianna. Before she left the canteen, she couldn't resist looking back at Gio. Her gaze clashed with his, delaying her, her footsteps slowing as if ruled by an inbuilt reluctance to leave him.

Gio waved, drawing Ben's attention as the men stood up from their table. Ben smiled at her, and she blushed, hoping he would think she was including all of them, and not that she had any special interest in Gio, as she sketched a wave in return and hurried out of the canteen.

As she made her way to A and E, her thoughts remained with Gio. Beyond the dangerous attraction, she enjoyed his company, admired him, professionally and personally, and felt good with him. If she had any sense, she'd guard her heart and keep her distance, but she feared it was already too late. She'd begun to slide down the slippery slope by foolishly convincing herself it was

OK to be friends with him…provided they both knew friendship was all it could be.

She knew Gio was curious and wanted to know more about her, but he'd been circumspect so far and she was grateful. Meeting in the canteen each evening challenged her resolve but his comments on how he hated returning to the empty house he was renting had touched a chord within her. She knew all about the loneliness found between the walls of somewhere that didn't feel like home. One more of the many things they had in common.

Arriving in A and E, Jess set thoughts of Gio aside. Ellen, a senior staff nurse in the department, greeted her and outlined the reason for the call.

'The girl came in very distressed, asking after a young man killed in a road accident,' the middle-aged woman explained, shaking her head. 'She's terribly young, Jess, but she insists she's the girlfriend. Unfortunately we're rushed off our feet and as she's not physically injured or ill, we don't have time to spend with her, but we didn't want her to leave in such a state.'

'I understand. Has she been told anything?' Jess asked, her heart going out to the unknown girl.

Ellen sighed again. 'I'm afraid one of the inexperienced clerks told her the boyfriend, a lad named Colin Maddern, had died.'

'Oh, hell.'

'Exactly.' The nurse's displeasure matched her own. 'The girl wants Colin's things. He had no one but her. And there are photographs of her in his jacket, so she's genuine. I've checked with the police and they don't need anything, so I'll arrange to have the jacket and the possessions we salvaged brought to her.' Ellen nodded in the direction of the closed door to one of the quiet rooms used for relatives. 'She's in there. She wants to see him, but…'

'You don't think it's a good idea,' Jess finished for her.

'No, I don't. The poor boy wasn't wearing a seat belt and there was no air-bag fitted. He was hit at speed, went through the windscreen and was killed. A broken neck. And his face is a mess.'

Jess struggled to keep her emotions from showing. 'And the other driver?'

'Returning home drunk after lunch at the golf club. The police have arrested him. Needless to say he's not even bruised. Josh had to deal with both of them and he's furious. It's so unfair,' Ellen finished, mirroring Jess's own sentiments and explaining the grim expression on Josh's face when he'd arrived in the canteen.

'Do we know the girl's name?' Jess queried, jotting a few notes on her pad.

'No. Other than asking for Colin—and his things— she's not said anything. She broke down after she learnt of his death.'

'Thanks, Ellen.' She would not have relished the task of delivering the news, but Jess wished the girl had learned the truth in a more gentle and caring way. 'I'll see what I can do.'

The woman smiled. 'If anyone can help her, love, it's you.'

Jess hoped so. After Ellen had gone, she drew in a breath, hoping to find the right things to say in an impossible situation. Tapping on the door, she opened it and stepped inside. A junior nurse sat awkwardly near the sobbing girl, and jumped to her feet, clearly glad to leave.

Once they were alone, Jess pulled a chair closer and sat opposite the plump form huddled on the two-seater sofa. With her face buried in her hands, a curtain of straight, corn-coloured blonde hair swung forward, hiding her face from view. A cooling cup of tea remained untouched on the table beside her.

'Hello. I'm Jess Carmichael. I've come to see if there's anything I can help you with.' Jess waited for some kind of response or acknowledgement of her presence. 'I'm very sorry to hear about the accident.'

Slowly the girl looked up, her hands dropping away from her face and falling to her lap. Jess barely managed to smother a shocked gasp as she discovered how terribly young she was...no more than sixteen. Grey eyes were awash with tears, leaving no doubt at the depth of her devastation.

'They won't let me see him,' she murmured. 'Is it because I'm not officially family?'

Jess hesitated, unsure how to explain without causing further upset. 'It's a difficult decision. I'd urge you to think carefully, because once it's done, it can't be undone. They advised you against seeing Colin because of the nature of his injuries,' she continued, deciding it was important to tell the truth, even as the words caused the girl to flinch. 'Wouldn't you rather your last memory of him was a good one? What would he want for you?'

'Colin wouldn't want me to do it,' she admitted, a frown creasing her brow.

'There's no hurry to make a decision, so have a think about it.'

'OK.'

Jess hoped she would decide not to see him. 'Is there someone I can call for you? Your parents, maybe?'

'No!' The denial was instant and accompanied by a vigorous shake of her head. 'I can't.' Taking a tissue from the box on the table, she blew her nose. 'No one knows about Colin and me.'

Jess let it go for now, not wanting to pressure the girl or distress her further, hoping instead to build rapport and a level of trust that would enable her to help if she could.

'Can you tell me your name?'

The girl fiddled nervously with the chain around her neck, suddenly clutching it before tucking it inside her blouse and doing up the top button, as if to hide it. Before Jess could consider the odd behaviour, the girl shifted nervously, her gaze darting around the room.

'Marcia Johns,' she finally offered, barely above a whisper.

'Thank you, Marcia.' Jess smiled, accepting the name, even though she was unsure at this point whether or not it was genuine. 'Would you like to talk about Colin?'

A firm nod greeted the suggestion, and although tears shimmered in her eyes, a wobbly smile curved her mouth, revealing how pretty she could be. 'Yes, please. Is that OK?'

'Of course. I'd like to hear about him. When did you meet?'

'Over a year ago when I started my summer job,' she explained. 'Colin worked nearby. He was three years older than me, and never in a million years did I imagine him noticing *me*. Tall and handsome, with dark hair and blue eyes and a gorgeous smile, he was the one all the girls wanted. I'm shy and overweight and always fade into the background,' Marcia continued, revealing low self-esteem. She shook her head, as if in wonder, and gave a little laugh. 'When Colin began spending time with me, I couldn't believe it! There were all these thin, pretty girls chasing after him but he kept saying it was me he wanted, that he saw the real me inside. That I was kind and smart and funny, and he loved me the way I was.'

What a lovely young man, Jess thought, seeing how Marcia lit up talking about him. And what a terrible tragedy that his life had been cut so short. Sensing Marcia's need to talk, she encouraged her to continue.

'We were going to get married when I finished school and got a full-time job,' she said, toying with the friendship ring that encircled the middle finger of her right hand, no doubt a gift from him, Jess thought. 'His father died when he was twelve, and his mother when he was sixteen, so Colin had to look out for himself. He was much more responsible and steady than the boys I knew at school. There was never much money, but that didn't matter. We spent all our time together, walking on the beach, having picnics, watching DVDs or listening to music at his flat, talking for hours. Talking about everything. For the first time I felt as if someone really knew me and understood me.'

'Don't you feel that at home?' Jess probed, hoping to find out more about Marcia's background.

'Not really.' She gave a casual shrug, but it obviously mattered to her. 'We're a big family. My parents are busy working and caring for us all, and my brothers and sisters are all outgoing and active, and so much more attractive than I am. They all have the family colouring. I got the eyes but my hair is dead straight and mousy blonde. I'm interested in books and music, not sports. I don't understand them and they don't understand me. I know they love me,' she added, wiping away the twin tears that tracked down her rounded cheeks. 'They just don't *see* me. Everything is so hectic and noisy. I don't think they notice whether I'm there or not.'

'But Colin noticed.'

'Yes. Yes, he did.'

Jess understood how special and important the young man must have made Marcia feel, boosting her confidence and setting her free from the shadow of her vibrant family. Marcia might be very young, but she had a sensible head on her shoulders and for her, her relationship with Colin had been a close and genuine one.

Marcia pulled her shoulder bag on to her lap and rummaged inside for a moment before producing a couple of photos and handing them across.

'Thanks.'

Jess looked down at the first picture, seeing a very handsome young man dressed in jeans and a black leather jacket, wavy black hair brushing over the collar. The blue eyes were startling, full of intelligence, humour and kindness, his smile adding to the impression of warmth and friendliness. The second picture, of Marcia and Colin together, banished any lingering doubt about the full extent of this young girl's relationship with Colin. No one seeing the two young people together could question their feelings. Their happiness and love shone out, and the expression of devotion on Colin's face as he looked at a laughing Marcia brought a lump to Jess's throat.

'They're lovely. Thank you for showing me,' she murmured, handing the pictures back.

Marcia looked at them for several moments before tucking them carefully back in her bag. She sobbed, pressing a hand to her mouth, despair in her eyes.

'What am I going to do?' Rocking back and forth, tears flowed in earnest once more. 'Colin was my whole life. I love him so much. And I need him. He can't be gone. He *can't*. It isn't fair. Oh, God… Why? *Why* has this happened? What's the point in anything if Colin isn't with me?'

As she tried to comfort the girl, Jess wished she had answers to explain the cruel and senseless loss of a life. Fresh anger built within her at the driver who had thoughtlessly climbed behind the wheel of his car, his selfish actions shattering two young lives. He should be made to see Colin's lifeless, damaged body, and witness the terrible grief Marcia was suffering. What words could she possibly offer the girl that didn't sound trite?

A knock at the door announced the arrival of Ellen and provided a welcome distraction. 'May I come in?'

As Marcia nodded and mopped her tears, Jess met the kindly nurse's gaze, seeing the sympathy and sorrow in her eyes.

'I have Colin's things for you, love,' Ellen said, setting a black leather jacket on the seat beside Marcia, the same jacket Colin had worn in the photos.

Marcia drew the jacket into her arms, closing her eyes and burying her face in the wear-worn leather. 'I saved up for ages to buy this for his birthday. It smells of him,' she whispered, clutching the familiar garment more tightly to her and rubbing one cheek against it.

A lump in her throat, Jess exchanged a glance with Ellen. Maybe having Colin's jacket would bring Marcia some comfort and familiarity in the difficult times ahead.

'Here are the photographs and the other things Colin had with him,' Ellen said, holding over a large padded envelope.

Refusing to let go of the jacket, Marcia took the envelope with her free hand. 'Thank you, it means a lot. And thanks for being so kind to me.'

'You're welcome, my love.' Suppressed emotion made Ellen's voice huskier than normal. 'I'm so sorry.'

After Ellen had left them alone once more, Jess allowed Marcia some quiet time. While she waited, she took a page from her notebook and jotted down some information for the girl to take away with her.

'I don't like to think of you going home alone, Marcia. You've had a horrible shock. Are you sure I can't call your parents? Or I could arrange for someone here to take you home,' Jess suggested, willing to drive her there herself, but Marcia was withdrawing and shaking her head.

'No. No, I don't want that.' She took another tissue and mopped her eyes. 'Thank you. I'll be all right.'

Jess didn't believe it for a moment, but she couldn't force her and she didn't want to break the tentative trust between them. All she could do was encourage Marcia to keep in touch.

'You can contact me here at any time, Marcia,' she told her, adding another telephone number to the list. 'I've also given the details for the Samaritans. If you need to talk to anyone in confidence, day or night, you can call them. I volunteer once a week, usually on Friday evenings, but you can talk freely to anyone.'

'OK.'

Jess was relieved as Marcia took the sheet of paper, looked it over, and then tucked it into her bag, suggesting she might actually use it and not toss it into the first litter bin she came across.

'I'd really like to know how you are. And if there's anything I can do...' She let the words trail off, not wanting to nag.

The sound of her pager intruded. Smothering her frustration, Jess checked the display before glancing around the room and discovering there was no telephone.

'I've taken up too much of your time,' Marcia murmured, beginning to gather her things together.

'No, no, it's fine, honestly.' Jess smiled and told a white lie. 'I'm not in a hurry. I just have to reply to this. If you don't mind waiting, I'll just pop into the next door room to use the phone. I'll be back in a jiffy.'

Jess found a phone and made the call. She doubted she'd been gone more than a minute, but by the time she returned, Marcia had gone.

'Damn it!'

Upset, she rushed down the corridor and back into the busy casualty department, asking a couple of nurses and the clerks at the desk if they had seen Marcia come though, but no one had noticed her. Not even the security guard by the main doors. It brought back Marcia's own words...she faded into the background and no one saw her.

Cursing the appalling timing of the interruption, Jess went outside, hoping to catch a glimpse of Marcia, but it was hopeless. The sense of disappointment was huge. She couldn't bear to think of Marcia alone with her grief, unable and unwilling to seek the comfort of a family who loved her but seldom had time for her.

An image of Marcia and Colin before the tragedy, so happy and in love, fixed itself in her mind. Why did awful things happen? She could make no sense of the cruelty that had befallen two lovely young people. She swallowed, blinking back tears.

'Jessica, are you all right?'

Gio's voice behind her had her spinning round in surprise. 'What are you doing here?'

'I was in A and E and saw you run outside.' The expression in his blue eyes, so warm and intimate, robbed her of breath and held her captive as he raised a hand and with exquisite gentleness removed a salty bead of moisture suspended from her lashes, his fingers brushing her cheek. His voice turned even huskier. 'I was worried about you.'

Everything in her screamed at her to lean into his touch, craving what she had denied herself for so long, but reality intruded, the instinct for self-preservation ingrained. She jerked back, feeling the colour staining her cheeks as Gio regarded her in silence, speculation, concern and a frightening resolve in his eyes.

'Tell me what's wrong,' he invited as they headed back to the hospital.

Sighing, Jess gave him a brief summary of what had happened, unable to prevent her emotion from showing. 'It was just awful.'

'I'm sorry.' He shook his head, murmuring what sounded like a curse in Italian. 'Josh was talking about the accident in the canteen.'

Back in the room where she had spoken with Marcia, Gio remained with her, increasing her sense of awareness. 'I feel as if I failed her,' she admitted.

'Of course you didn't,' he chided gently.

'I don't know.' With another sigh, she gathered up her things. 'I'm even more sure now that Marcia Johns is not her real name.'

'Definitely not.'

The edge of amusement in Gio's voice had her head snapping up. There was nothing remotely funny about the situation. But before she could remonstrate with him, he shook his head and pointed to something behind her. She turned round, noticing for the first time the information posters on one wall of the room.

The 'infomercials' were sponsored by well-known drug companies and 'Marcia' had been clever enough, despite her distress, to cobble together a false name on the spur of the moment, using parts of two words from the company name emblazoned in large letters on one of the posters. Jess cursed herself for having been so thoroughly duped. She was also disappointed that the girl had felt the need to deceive her.

'She had her reasons, and I'm sure they were personal to her and nothing to do with you.'

Jess knew Gio's words were offered by way of consolation, but they did little to ease her upset and concern. 'Marcia' would remain in her thoughts and she would worry about her unless and until she had any further news of her. She could only hope that at some point the girl would use one of the contact numbers she had given her and get in touch.

'I know how much you care,' Gio said now, scarily attuned to her thoughts. 'You would not be so good at your job if you didn't, but you cannot carry the burden of everyone's problems on your shoulders, Jessica.' He stood in front of her, tipping her chin up with one finger until her gaze met his. 'Who is there for you?'

She felt branded by the contact and once more she stepped back to break it, resisting the urge to press her free hand to the spot that still tingled from the soft touch of his fingertip. This was ridiculous! She needed to give herself a stern talking to. Squaring her shoulders, she headed for the door.

'I'm fine,' she told him, injecting as much firmness into her voice as possible.

'You are here at all hours, taking on the burden of everyone else's problems,' he continued, refusing to let it go. 'Who listens to yours?'

Frightened that his perceptiveness and caring were chipping away at the defences that had protected her these last four years, she laughed off his question and repeated the words she used as a mantra to convince others…and herself. 'I'm fine!'

He took her by surprise—again—politely opening the door for her and following her out. So grateful was she that he had let the subject drop, she was not adequately on her guard.

'Where are you going now?' he asked.

'Hmm…' Jess frowned, trying to remember what had been on her agenda before the call had come in for her to attend A and E.

'If you have a few minutes to stop off at my office, I have some things to discuss with you.'

Although she would sooner have parted company there and then so she had time to re-erect her barriers against him, she was relieved he had focused back on work matters. Cursing her weakness and the voice in her head that tormented her about her vulnerability to this man, Jess found herself assenting to his request.

'All right.'

'Thank you.'

His smile of satisfaction made her uneasy. What had she agreed to? And why did she feel he'd set her up and she'd fallen for it—as she feared she had for him—hook, line and sinker?

CHAPTER FIVE

'COME this way.'

Jess found herself ushered into Gio's office, his hand at the small of her back sending a charge of electricity zinging through her. He had a disturbing habit of touching her. As he closed the door, Jess took the opportunity to put some much-needed distance between them. The room was by no means small but, confined in it with Gio, it seemed claustrophobic and she felt an urgent need for the comfort of her own personal space.

'What I am about to reveal to you is strictly confidential, Ms Carmichael. You do realise that?' he asked, his expression sombre...but for a tell-tale glimmer of mischief in his tanzanite-blue eyes.

Jess had no idea whether he was serious, or whether he was toying with her. Why did just being in the same room with him make her feel so off kilter and peculiar? She didn't like it. What she most wanted was to escape.

'Jessica?'

She jumped, continually unnerved at the way he spoke her name, his husky, accented voice far too intimate and intoxicating. But it was the light touch of one finger on her forearm that brought her inbuilt flight response into action again as she stepped back, distracted by the way all her nerve-endings were fired into life. Startled, she met the intense blueness of his gaze, seeing the curiosity, knowledge and masculine appreciation that lurked in his eyes. She didn't want anyone interested in her or asking questions about her, least of all this man who posed a unique and definite danger.

'What's confidential?' she queried, intrigued and yet nervous.

'Apart from my secretary, no one knows about this. I'm trusting you, Jessica.'

'Yes, of course.' She agreed without hesitation. It was asked of her, in one way or another, every working day, either by a patient, relative or colleague. And very little surprised her. 'What is it?'

Gio moved to his desk and beckoned her closer. She edged forward, watching as he opened the bottom drawer of his desk, pulling it back with frustrating slowness, building her suspense as centimetre by centimetre the contents came into view.

She'd been wrong to believe he couldn't surprise her. Her eyes widened in astonishment as she found herself staring at a drawer full to the brim with…

'Chocolate!'

Gio couldn't help but laugh aloud at Jessica's stunned reaction. 'What is your poison? Plain or milk? With or without nuts?' he asked, taking a selection of bars from the drawer.

'I don't eat much chocolate.'

'But you like it,' he prompted, hearing the waver in her voice. 'You must do…given the delicious scent of your hair and your skin.'

His words brought a bloom of colour to her porcelain cheeks. But it was the longing in her eyes that betrayed her sweet tooth. And then her pink tongue-tip peeped out to moisten the sensual curve of her lips, causing his body to react in such an immediate and blatant way that he drew back in shock.

'Treat yourself,' he encouraged, thankful that she appeared unaware of his response to her and, as he waited for her to make her selection, struggled to get his mind and body back under control.

'OK.' She took a small bar of milk chocolate with a hazelnut praline centre. 'Thank you.'

'Good choice,' he murmured as she moved away.

Taking a bar of dark chocolate with almond for himself, he put the rest away and closed the drawer. Sitting down, he opened his chocolate, his gaze remaining on Jessica as she inspected the expensive high-class packaging, noting the moment realisation dawned.

'*Cioccolato Corezzi?*' She looked up, stunning green eyes wide with interest. '*You* make this chocolate?'

'My family do. My paternal grandfather began the company over fifty years ago, and Papá and Mamma have grown it from a small specialist business with one shop in Turin into what it is today—one of Italy's most famous hand-made chocolate houses.'

'You're understandably proud of them.' She smiled, snapping off a square and popping it into her mouth, nearly killing him as those mesmerising eyes closed and a blissful look transformed her face as she savoured the flavours he knew would be bursting on her tongue. 'Oh, this is *amazing*!'

'Thank you.' Her opinion was important to him and her enthusiasm made him feel warm inside.

Snapping off another square, she laughed. 'No, thank *you*!' she insisted, before popping the chocolate into her mouth to savour the taste as before.

It was the first time he'd heard her laugh. It was a warm, throaty, infectious sound and he wanted to hear it often. Frowning, he acknowledged just how involved he was becoming.

'Did you never want to follow in your parents' footsteps?' she queried after a moment, perching on the edge of his desk, stretching her skirt across the pleasing curve of womanly thighs.

'No,' he answered, his voice rough. Clearing his throat, he sat forward. 'It was never an option, and my parents knew it wouldn't have suited me. Besides, I would have eaten all the profits!'

Taking a bite of his chocolate, he enjoyed another of her throaty chuckles.

'You must have lorry loads of it delivered, judging by your drawer!'

Having her relax enough to tease him was an unexpected pleasure, as was listening to the softness of her accent. He wondered how she had come to be in Cornwall, so far from home, but he refrained from asking…for now.

'Now you know my secret,' he said, keeping his tone light and teasing. 'It's only fair you tell me one of yours, no?'

The change in her was immediate and, while he regretted her withdrawal and the loss of their rapport, he was intrigued by her reaction and eager to find out its cause. Her whole body tensed, as if she was closing in on herself. Sliding off the desk, she turned away, but not before he had seen the hurt and loneliness she worked hard to hide. Stepping across to the window, her shoulders lifted as she breathed in a slow, deep breath. Finally, she turned round, popping the last piece of chocolate in her mouth and scrunching up the wrapper.

'I'm not very interesting, and I don't really have any secrets,' she told him with a manufactured smile, not meeting his gaze.

Oh, but she most certainly did. He knew it. And he was determined to uncover them and understand what she was anxious to hide. Behind the façade she presented to the world, the real Jessica was far from fine.

'I ought to be going,' she announced, picking up the collection of items she had with her all the time in the hospital.

'What *do* you carry around in there?' he asked with a mix of interest and amusement.

Her voice sounded strained now, all traces of the fun Jessica reined in and back behind her protective wall. 'I have my notebook and diary,' she began, looking down at the pile in her arms.

Gio listened as she told him about the information sheets, details of various diseases and injuries and their treatments, names and contacts for self-help groups and a welter of other things people might need. Her mobile phone, like her pager, was either attached to her waistband or in her pocket, depending on the clothes she was wearing. He suspected Jessica used the things she carried as a barrier, a shield between herself and others. He wanted to know why. The list of questions he had about her continued to grow.

Disappointment speared inside him as Jessica moved towards the door. 'Thanks for the chocolate.'

'Any time. I'll tell my secretary you have free access

to my secret drawer.' He smiled, drinking in his fill of her while he could. 'See you later. And try not to worry about your girl.'

'I'll try. Bye.'

The door closed softly behind her. At once the room felt different…and he felt lonely without the vibrancy of her presence. *Dio.* A week ago, if anyone had told him he'd be attracted to another woman, he would have believed it impossible. But Jessica had shaken him to his foundations—and out of the darkness that had enveloped his life for the last five years.

'Megan, are you all right?'

'Yes.' It was a lie, but she managed a smile for Jess. 'I'm sorry, I was miles away.'

Her friend sent her an understanding smile. 'Josh?'

'Yes,' Megan repeated, a deep sigh escaping.

It had been a huge shock to discover that Josh had joined the St Piran's trauma team back in the spring. Megan had assumed he was still in London. Wished he *was* still in London. Working with him when she was on call to A and E from Paediatrics was difficult and she had found it harder still since little Toby's funeral.

'He wants to talk,' Megan confided, her recent confrontation with Josh in the canteen still fresh in her mind. Why did he want to rake over the past? Did he think she didn't live with it every day of her life?

'Would talking to Josh be such a bad thing?'

Megan's stomach churned in response to Jess's softly voiced question. Her friend knew there was past history with Josh, but Megan hadn't divulged any details. She had never told anyone what had happened. She felt too guilty, too confused, too stupid, too hurt.

'What's the point?' Bitterness laced her voice but she was unable to soften it. 'It's over. Done. What good would be served stirring it up eight years on?'

'Perhaps *you* need to talk as much as Josh thinks *he* does,' Jess suggested, confusing her more.

Megan frowned. 'What do you mean?'

'It's clearly still causing you heartache. Things are unresolved in your own mind.' Jess paused a moment, her dark green gaze direct. 'Forget Josh and his reasons for wanting to talk. Think about yourself. Do *you* have questions that need answering before you can put things behind you once and for all?'

Too many to count, Megan allowed silently, one hand unconsciously moving to press against the flatness of her belly, a wave of pain rolling through her at all that was lost—all that Josh had taken from her. The thought of facing him after eight years was too scary to contemplate.

'Maybe, but—' Megan broke off, uncertain and indecisive.

'But?' Jess probed gently.

'Seeing him again hurts so much and has brought back so many difficult memories.' She bit her lip, ashamed that she had been so foolish over Josh—and that part of her remained drawn to him, despite everything that had happened. 'I'm so angry with him, Jess. And with myself. Yes, there are things I want to know, but I'm not sure I can cope with what he has to say.'

'Only you can decide if finding out what you need to know will help you find peace with the past.'

Megan nodded. Her friend's words made sense. She just wasn't sure what to do. The fact that Josh now had a picture-perfect wife, aside from causing her added pain and distress, complicated things even more. Although the body language she had witnessed between him and his beautiful wife, Rebecca, suggested that things might not be right in Josh's marriage, he *was* married, so having contact with him beyond the professional was inappropriate.

'It scares me, Jess.'

Her words whispered from her as she faced the awful truth—underneath the pain, anger and betrayal, a spark of the elemental chemistry still burned. She was as vulnerable to him as she had always been.

'Emotions are complicated and the dividing line between love and hate can be wafer thin.' Jess's pager sounded and she glanced at it, a faint blush colouring her cheeks. 'Sorry, Megan, I have to go.'

'Problems?'

Jess shook her head. 'It's time for the neurosurgery case meeting. Gordon Ainsworth and, um, Gio, asked me to attend,' she explained, gathering up her things. Pausing, she smiled. 'Think things over. If you need to talk, you know it will remain confidential between us.'

'Thanks, Jess.'

'Take care, Megan. And good luck.'

Megan watched the other woman walk away, her vibrant auburn hair restrained in a plait. Recalling her friend's blush, and thinking about the electric atmosphere she had noticed whenever Jess and Gio were together, she wondered if something was brewing there. It would be wonderful to see Jess happy. She was so private, and always seemed so alone. Megan shook her head, realising how alike they were. She respected Jess, and trusted her, and she knew how lucky she was to have her to talk to.

Unfortunately, her friend couldn't tell her what to do. No one could. Decisions about Josh, and whether to face the past, were hers alone.

Gio stepped into the warmth of the August evening. Dusk was falling, and he glanced up at the darkening sky, expelling a sigh. He'd been called in earlier that Saturday evening after Josh O'Hara's concern had grown about a man who had collapsed while on an outing to the beach with his wife. Further tests, including CT and MRI scans, had revealed that the man had a tumour growing in his brain, affecting his optic nerve and sensory centre. Surgery was scheduled for Monday.

The man and his wife would benefit from Jessica's input. He'd speak with her on Monday. Which was nearly thirty-six hours away and too long to wait, especially as he hadn't seen her since the previous afternoon, when she had attended what would become a regular Friday meeting for the neurological unit. Her presence had been beneficial to the team—but distracting for him on a personal level. He shook his head. Until a few days ago he hadn't *had* a personal level.

Confused that his life had turned upside down, he walked towards the almost deserted consultants' car park. The previous night had been the first when they'd not met up for an end-of-the-day chat. Jessica had been unable to come because she volunteered for the Samaritans and spent several hours there each Friday evening. He wasn't surprised. Once more she was devoting her time to other people's problems. Was it a way of avoiding her own?

In the car, he leaned back and rested his head, reflecting on how long and lonely the weekend was becoming without Jessica. He swore softly to himself. What a sorry state he was in. Part of him rebelled. He didn't want any new woman in his life. Or so he had thought until Jessica. Now he couldn't stop thinking about her or wanting to be with her. He wanted to learn her secrets and encourage the real Jessica out from behind her defensive wall. Was he the only one to notice the loneliness and hurt that lurked in the depths of her beautiful green eyes?

Starting the engine, he reversed out of his parking space, his gaze straying to the psychology building.

'What the hell?'

He braked, letting the powerful engine idle as he observed the light that shone from Jessica's office window. The rest of the building was in darkness. Had she forgotten to switch off the light the day before? He saw a flicker of movement inside and cursed. Jessica was here? *Now?* Returning his car to its parking space, he switched off the engine, climbed out and locked the door.

As he walked towards the building he reflected on Jessica's odd behaviour and her reluctance to let him see inside her office. He'd brushed it off as a quirk, but her furtiveness made him certain that something more was going on and he couldn't let this go.

Frowning, he remembered when he'd visited her office. She'd rushed home to meet her insurance company's assessor and he'd forgotten to ask why. Was something seriously wrong?

The outer door of the psychology building was locked, but his swipe card and ID code gained him access. Relocking the door, he made his way through the darkened foyer and down the corridor to Jessica's room. It was uncharacteristic for him to be impolite but, not wanting to give her time to shut the door in his face, he checked to see if it was unlocked. It was. He gave a sharp rap and swung the door open, astonished at the scene that greeted him.

Jessica, bare-footed and dressed in a pair of cotton shorts and a sleeveless tank top, which emphasised her voluptuous curves and set his pulse racing, was sitting cross-legged on a blow-up mattress on the floor. A pillow and a few items of bed linen were folded at one end. For the first time, he saw her hair in all its heart-stopping glory as it fell around her shoulders, the curtain of copper-red and burnished chestnut curls enveloping her in a halo of fire.

But she was not alone. Her companions held him transfixed and momentarily speechless. Two small, playful kittens frolicked around her, Tabby balls of fluff on stubby legs and paws that looked too big for them. His gaze returned to Jessica. The smile had frozen on her face and panic was setting in.

Determined to discover what was going on, but not wanting to alarm her, he closed the door and crossed to her before she had time to get up. He dropped to his knees, sitting back on his heels, smiling as the kittens investigated him, sharp claws digging into his thighs as they used him as a climbing frame.

Gently, he slid a palm under each warm, rounded little body, lifting them close for a better view, seeing the similarities and differences in what were clearly siblings' faces. He loved animals, and would have surrounded himself with them, but Sofia had been allergic to several kinds of animals, making pets impossible.

Thinking of his beloved wife, taken from him so devastatingly five years before, brought the familiar pain and he closed his eyes, rubbing his face against the two fluffy animals, feeling the dual purrs vibrating against his hands.

Gio opened his eyes and focused on Jessica, who sat little more than a foot away, shocked to silence, a whole mixture of emotions chasing themselves across her expressive green eyes. Turning the kittens so they were facing her, he held them against his chest, enjoying their softness and the feel of their heartbeats.

'What are their names?'

His question apparently threw her because she stared at him for several moments as if expecting him to launch into an interrogation. She bit her lip, diverting his attention to the tempting swell of her mouth. As she sucked in a breath, his gaze rose to clash with hers once more.

'Th-that's Dickens,' she finally informed him, her voice unsteady and her hand shaking as she pointed to the kitten in his left hand, which had a dark face, pink nose and round green eyes, not unlike her own in colour.

'And this one?' he asked of the kitten in his right hand, which had slanting, almond-shaped eyes in a darker shade than its sibling's.

'Kipling.'

She looked lost and alone so he handed Dickens to her, and she clutched him close as if needing the comfort.

'They are favourite authors of yours?'

Jessica nodded, her curls swaying like dancing flames. 'Partly. But also for their characters. They're very mischievous and inquisitive. With him,' she continued, pointing to the kitten cradled in his hands, 'I kept thinking he's just so naughty, just so cute, just so everything, and so I thought of Kipling and his *Just So* stories.' She was still tense, but a smile tugged her mouth as she looked at the kitten she held. 'This one was into everything and I was always asking what the dickens he was up to. The names stuck.'

'How long have you had them?'

'About six weeks. Their mother was an unknown feral stray who had a litter in the barn on a farm near my cottage,' she told him, relaxing a little. 'Flora, who lives there, and who is a nurse at the doctors' surgery in Penhally, isn't sure what happened to the mother, but the kittens were abandoned and Flora took care of them. She couldn't keep them all and was looking for homes for the others. I took these two.'

'What happens to them during the day?' he asked, intrigued how she had organised things.

'They stay with Sid Evans—he's the hospital handyman.' Gio nodded, confirming he knew of the man. 'He lost his wife recently and I've spent some time chatting to him,' Jessica continued, although he was unsurprised to learn of her kindness. 'He was very down and told me he wasn't allowed pets at his flat. So I asked the hospital management if he could have the kittens in his work room during the day and they said yes.' A warm smile curved her mouth. 'Sid loves having them.'

'I'm sure he does.' He admired her even more for her thoughtfulness. He also suspected that Jessica had set things up so that Sid felt valued, believing he was doing her a good turn. He was sure the hospital management didn't know where the kittens spent the night. 'How long have you been camping here?'

His question, getting to the core of the issue, had her tensing up again and she ducked her head, her hair falling forward, hiding her face.

'Talk to me,' he encouraged softly. With one finger beneath her chin, he urged her to look up again. 'What's going on, Jessica?'

Very conscious of Gio's touch, Jess trembled. The pad of one finger, that was all, and yet her whole body felt alive, charged and vitally aware of him. It was so long since she'd been touched…at least before this week when Gio had done so several times, stirring up desires she'd managed to banish for the last four years. But she had to quash the yearnings Gio had reawakened because he—like everyone else—was out of bounds. Steeling herself, she drew back enough to break the physical connection, concerned how much she missed the contact.

In shock from Gio's sudden arrival, fear built now that one of her secrets, albeit the least monumental and important of them, had been discovered. She didn't want to tell him anything but how could she bluff her way out? Even if she could excuse the kittens, the damning evidence of the makeshift bed was impossible to explain away.

'Jessica?'

'I, um, recently moved into my cottage,' she began shakily, unsure how much to tell him. 'The storm ten days ago destroyed the roof, causing water damage and the electricity being shut off. I tried to stay there anyway…'

'*Dio!* With no power and no roof?' he exclaimed, muttering something uncomplimentary in Italian.

Jess lowered her gaze. 'It was only one night. I was

concerned for the kittens,' she explained, failing to add that not only had it been miserable with no electricity or hot water but that she'd been spooked in the isolated cottage with no security.

'So you've been staying here since then?'

'Yes,' she admitted with reluctance.

She couldn't help but be mesmerised by the way Gio continued to stroke Dickens, his fingers sinking into the soft fur. The kitten was enjoying it if his purrs were anything to go by. It made her think dangerous and never-to-be-allowed things...like how it would feel to have Gio's fingers caress *her* body from top to toe. She had no doubt she'd be purring, too.

Looking down lest he read anything in her eyes, Jess struggled to push her wayward thoughts away because no matter how much she may crave his touch, it wasn't going to happen.

'Why here, though?' Gio's voice reclaimed her attention. 'Why not stay at a hotel...or with friends?'

She fudged an answer, mumbling about the need to keep the kittens with her and everywhere being fully booked at the height of the season, because no way was she going to tell him the truth about the sorry state of her finances or that she didn't *have* any friends. Not the kind she could stay with, anyway. To explain either would involve the impossible—revealing what she could never reveal...*why*.

Why she had crashed and burned so badly...

Why her life had changed so drastically and irrevocably four years ago...

And why she was now counting the cost in so many ways, not just financially but professionally—hence her change of career and re-training in her mid-twenties to become a counsellor—and socially—keeping people at a distance and denying herself the closeness, emotional or physical, she had once enjoyed as a normal part of life. Nothing about her life these last four years had been normal. But she'd succeeded, she was coping…or had been until Gio had arrived, bringing home all she had lost and making her yearn for things she could never have again.

'It's only for a short while.' She crossed her fingers, hoping that was true. 'The insurance company have agreed to the repairs and the builders are starting work next week. As soon as possible, I'll move back in.'

'You can't stay here and live like this until then, Jessica,' he protested, clearly upset about the situation.

'It's not so bad,' she countered, trying for a carefree smile. 'I don't have any choice.'

'Of course you do.'

His words and the determined tone of his voice made her nervous. 'What do you mean?'

'As of now, you're moving in with me.'

CHAPTER SIX

UNOBSERVED, Gio leaned against the doorjamb and watched as Jessica carried out some graceful Tai Chi movements. She was dressed in a loose T-shirt, shorts that left shapely legs bare from mid-thigh down, and a pair of trainers, her vibrant curls restrained in a ponytail. He never tired of looking at her. Taking a sip of his coffee, he waited for her to finish her routine.

It was the August bank holiday weekend and they both had two days off. Jessica had been in his house for two weeks. She'd protested, but there had never been any question in his mind about where she should stay. He couldn't let her camp in her office. She'd wanted to pay rent, he'd said no, but they'd compromised and she made a contribution towards food and supplies.

She'd also set rules. No touching. And nothing more than a platonic friendship. He'd agreed. Sort of. Temporarily. If setting them and keeping things on a friendly footing was what Jessica needed to begin with, he would play along. For now. That she'd felt the need to make rules at all proved she felt the same electric awareness he did.

He was using the time to gain Jessica's trust and continuing to get her used to his touch. He stopped the moment she withdrew or showed signs of disquiet. As the days went by, it was taking her longer to step away. He had yet to discover why she struggled so hard to deny the attraction.

Having coaxed her and the kittens home that Saturday night, the next day they had driven to her cottage. He'd grown up bilingual thanks to his parents and his American-born maternal grandmother, but, however fluent he was in English, he swore best in Italian and he'd unconsciously reverted to his native language as he surveyed the state of Jessica's home. It had been far worse than he'd imagined.

Built of stone and sitting in an isolated spot surrounded by untended land, the large cottage was single storey. The thatched roof and rotten rafters had collapsed inwards, wrecking several rooms beneath, letting in the rain and rendering the place uninhabitable. He'd seen the promise, had visualised the picture-book traditional cottage as it would be when it was finished, but that Jessica had tried to stay in what was little more than a ruin had astounded him.

Turning round, he'd seen the pained expression on Jessica's face, and realised the effect his rant was having on her. Reverting to English, he'd gentled his tone and closed the gap between them. His nature was to touch, to hug, to comfort, and it had been difficult to stop himself from drawing her into his arms.

Slowly he'd raised one hand and cupped her cheek, marvelling at the peachy softness of her skin. 'I'm sorry. I was not shouting at you, just at the state of the place and knowing someone would sell it to you in such a perilous condition.'

Some of the tension had drained from her, and for

a second she'd leaned into his touch. He'd brushed the pad of his thumb across the little hollow between her chin and her mouth, watching as her lips had parted instinctively and her eyelids lowered in response. She hadn't actually purred like one of the kittens, but her reaction had been unmistakeable. He'd so wanted to kiss her, but the moment had ended as she'd withdrawn into herself, turning her head away to break the contact.

'If the cottage had been in better condition I couldn't have afforded it,' she'd told him. 'I knew the roof was dodgy…' She'd given a wry laugh as she'd looked at the blue sky visible between what remained of the rotten rafters. 'I didn't expect it to cave in with the first storm.'

He'd never had to worry about money, and he knew how lucky he was, never taking things for granted. The business had made his family wealthy and money cushioned many blows. Except grief. Nothing eased the pain of that, but at least he'd been in a position to fund the trust in Sofia's name and help other people. He hated to think of Jessica struggling to make ends meet, and wondered why she had apparently sunk every penny she'd had into such a run-down, if potentially lovely, cottage, with no money left over to furnish it…or why she hadn't stayed in a hotel when she'd been forced to vacate it. Why had she been so insistent on buying outright rather than taking a small mortgage or personal loan to leave her some working capital?

For now Jessica and the kittens were living with him. Having been alone for five years, he'd been nervous of her moving in but it felt scarily *right*. They fitted. As this was the first time he'd been attracted to another woman, he'd struggled with feelings of disloyalty. Something

Sofia would chastise him for, having made it clear she didn't want him to remain alone.

Living with someone revealed so much about them and unearthed little ways and habits previously unsuspected and which could be irritating out of all proportion. So far he'd not discovered anything annoying about Jessica but there were several things that intrigued and amused him. One was the collection of assorted vitamin and dietary supplements she had stacked at one end of the kitchen worktop. He had no idea what they were for or why she felt she needed them. She was fastidious about washing up any of the crockery or cutlery she used, sorting them into a neat pile separate from his.

'Do you have a hygiene fetish?' he'd asked with a chuckle that first weekend, but his humour had rapidly faded given her reaction.

'No, of course not.'

The words of denial had been accompanied by a forced, hollow laugh, but it had been the unmistakeable hurt mixed with alarm and embarrassment in her eyes that had grabbed him.

'I didn't mean to upset you,' he'd apologised softly.

'You haven't.'

It had been a lie, he knew it. Just as he knew that something about what he had said or how he had said it had stung her.

The more he observed about her, including her anxiety at touching and being touched, the more he wondered if she'd experienced a bad relationship. Had someone criticised her, controlled her or, what he most feared, hurt and abused her?

Jess pivoted on one leg, turning her body in his direction, and he stifled a laugh when she spotted him, her eyes widening in surprise as she missed her step and stumbled momentarily before regaining her balance.

'Hi,' she murmured, embarrassment now predominant in her olive green eyes.

'Morning.' He straightened as she approached him warily, always keeping that extra bit of distance. 'Are you done?'

The fingers of one hand tucked stray wisps of hair back from her face. 'Just about. Why?'

'I have something to show you. Come with me.'

'Where are we going?' Jess asked as Gio drove away from the house.

'I can't tell you.'

She frowned at his unsatisfactory response. 'Why not?'

'Because then it would not be a surprise, would it?' he reasoned with calm amusement.

With no information forthcoming, Jess rested back in the luxurious seat of the sleek sports car. She hated to admit how much of a thrill she got each time she rode in it. As Gio turned out of the drive and onto the B-road that hugged the coastline on its route to St Piran, Jess glanced across the fields to the house she had been living in for the last fortnight. How could she feel so comfortable and yet scared at the same time?

The house sat atop the cliff as if carved from the bedrock and perfectly suited its Cornish name, *Ninnes*, 'the isolated place'. At first glance it suited Gio, too— wild, remote, alone.

'It's very impressive,' she'd murmured when she had first seen inside the architect-designed property. It didn't feel like a home. Clinical, cold, unlived in, it was like a set from an interior design magazine.

'Now tell me what you really think,' Gio had invited with a smile. 'It is soulless, no? A show-house, not a home,' he added, mirroring her own thoughts. 'The agent instructed to rent a place for me must have imagined someone moving from London would like it.'

'And you don't?' she'd asked, relieved this was not what he would have chosen for himself.

'No. But it gives me time to find something I *do* want and at least I have a roof over my head in the meantime.'

A laugh had burst from her at his unintentional choice of words and the expression on his face as the reason for her reaction dawned on him…she was there because she currently did *not* have a roof over hers!

Judging by the tone of his tirade when he had seen the state of her cottage, it had been worse than he'd expected. Had the property been in better condition, it would have been way beyond her budget, even with the unexpected legacy that had allowed her to step onto the housing ladder. But she had fallen in love with the place, and its parcel of neglected land that would allow her to have more animals and grow her own produce.

That Gio had seen the potential in the cottage had pleased her, and telling him about her plans for the place had diverted him from his questions about her reasons for not taking out a mortgage or personal loan. Either would have enabled her to get on with the renovations and furnishing the house straight away, but when she had looked into funding she had been asked questions about herself that she'd no wish to answer—and which may have meant she'd have been turned down anyway. She couldn't explain that to Gio without explaining *why*. And that was impossible.

So she had succumbed to Gio's arguments and the shameful temptation of moving in with him. Dickens and Kipling were in heaven. She was halfway between heaven and hell. They'd settled into a routine, their friendship becoming closer every day. Contrarily, his agreement to her rules and conditions had brought an inner stab of disappointment, though she knew friendship was all they could ever share.

Her hormones raged in protest, and she had to fight her attraction to him. Keeping people at a safe distance had become ingrained within her these last four years, but Gio was breaching her defences. He made her want things she could no longer have, reminding her of broken dreams and abandoned hopes.

'Jessica?'

'Mmm?' She blinked as Gio's voice impinged on her consciousness. 'Sorry, did you say something?'

He chuckled. 'Several times, but you are living with goblins! That is the saying, yes?' he added as she stared at him blankly.

'Sorry?' she repeated, confused for a moment before realisation dawned. 'Oh! You mean away with the fairies! No, I was just thinking.' A flush warmed her cheeks. No way could she tell him where her thoughts had really been.

'We are here,' he said now, switching off the engine.

They were at the harbourside in St Piran, Jess discovered, scrambling out of the car before Gio could come round and offer a hand to help her. The less she touched him, the better. He took some things from the car, including a picnic basket, handing her a canvas bag with towels, spare T-shirts and some sunscreen. Apprehension unsettled her. She hadn't realised this was a day's outing.

Her gaze feasted on the sight of him dressed in deck shoes and shorts that left well-defined muscular legs bare from mid-thigh downwards. His torso was encased in a white T-shirt that emphasised the tone of his skin and hugged the contours of his athletic body. Jess bit her lip to stop a sigh of appreciation from escaping

'Have you been on a boat before?' he asked, guiding her towards a jetty along which several very expensive-looking craft were moored.

'Only a car ferry.'

His throaty laugh stole her breath. 'This isn't quite the same.'

Jess gathered that as he halted by a huge, gleaming, red-and-white speedboat. 'Oh, my.'

She gazed at the boat in awe, excitement mounting as she anticipated what it would feel like to ride in the kind of jet-powered boat she'd seen offshore racing on television. The name *Lori* was written on the side and she wondered at the significance.

'My one indulgence...apart from my car,' he told her with a touch of embarrassment.

'It's beautiful.' She smiled, imagining the thrill of speeding across the waves. 'How long have you had it?'

Relaxing, as if relieved at her reaction, he smiled the rare, special smile that reached his eyes, banishing the shadows that often lurked there and trapping the breath in her lungs. 'About eighteen months. I could not get out often when I was in London and she was moored on the south coast, but I hope to use her often here.'

Gio climbed aboard with practised ease, set down the items he was carrying and turned to help her. Jess swallowed. Adopting avoidance tactics, she gave him her bags instead of her hand.

'I can manage,' she told him, cursing the way he quirked an eyebrow and watched with amusement as she scrambled inelegantly over the side.

To her surprise, the luxury powerboat had a small but fully equipped cabin below, with a tiny kitchen, a minuscule washroom and a seating area that converted into a sleeping space for three people. They'd have to be very friendly, Jess thought. After putting the picnic items in the fridge, they went back outside and Gio collected two life-jackets from a locker.

'Are these necessary?' Jess asked as he handed one to her.

'Absolutely.' He fastened his in no time. 'I would never take risks with your safety.'

She knew that. They might not have known each other long but she trusted him implicitly. It was herself she worried about, she thought wryly as she struggled with the life-jacket, huffing with frustration as it defeated her.

'Here,' Gio chuckled, closing the gap between them. 'Let me help.'

'It's OK…'

Her protest fell on deaf ears as he took over. Did he need to touch her that much? Or so slowly and intimately? And he was far too close—so close that every breath she took was fragranced with his musky male scent, weakening her resolve and tightening the aching knot in the pit of her stomach. She couldn't stop breathing so she closed her eyes and tightened her hands into fists, praying for the exquisite torture to be over and reminding herself why she couldn't succumb to temptation. He was taking longer than necessary, surely, the brush of his fingers burning her through the fabric of her T-shirt.

'All done.'

His voice sounded huskier than usual and she opened her eyes to find herself staring directly into his. A tremor ran through her at the sensual expression he made no attempt to mask. Her body craved his touch, making it difficult for her to keep her distance, to step back now as she knew she must.

As if anticipating her retreat, he released her and moved away, but not before he dropped a kiss on the tip of her nose. Confused, Jess remained motionless for several moments. The tip of her nose felt warm and tingly…nothing to do with the late August heat and everything to do with the brush of his lips on her skin.

Why had he done that?

Why had she let him?

Panic welled within her. Maybe it would be best if she got off the boat now, before she did anything even more stupid. But while she was wrestling with indecision, considering her options, Gio effectively removed them by untying the moorings and firing the boat into life.

He settled her in the padded horseshoe-shaped seat adjacent to his, then he was manipulating the controls, inching the boat into the main harbour towards the open sea. The twin engines throbbed with leashed power, straining for freedom. Despite her uncertainties, a new burst of excitement coursed through her.

'I hate to confine your incredible hair, but you might want to tie it back—or I can lend you a baseball cap,' Gio said as the harbour entrance approached.

Taking his advice, she accepted the cap he offered, pulling her untamed curls back into a ponytail before feeding it through the slot in the back of the cap. The brim helped shade her eyes from the August sunshine.

'Hold on.'

Jess felt her heart thudding with excitement as they reached open water and gained speed, going west along the coast from St Piran. The sea was calm but the bow of the boat rose up and rode the crests and troughs. Gio opened the throttle and a whoop of joy escaped her. She felt free, truly understanding how he felt and how this blew away tensions and stresses.

'This is incredible!' She laughed, raising her voice so Gio could hear her above the noise of the engines, the whoosh of the wind and the sound of the boat hitting the water. She tilted her head back and closed her eyes, savouring the sun on her skin, the occasional salty spray and the sense of speed. 'It's amazing! I love it.'

Lying face down on a towel stretched out on the sand in the secluded cove they had discovered, Jessica stretched and sighed. 'I could get used to this.'

Gio smiled. She sounded sleepy and contented following their exhilarating morning flying across the waves. They had travelled miles, moving from the bay in which St Piran stood, through Penhally Bay and past the village of Penhally itself, with its horseshoe-shaped harbour and the rocky promontory at one end, off which,

Jessica had told him, lay the wreck of an old Spanish galleon.

They had headed part of the way back before finding their cove. After a swim, they had enjoyed their picnic lunch. As Jessica relaxed, he finished his apple, his gaze straying over her deliciously curvy figure. She had pulled her shorts on over her one-piece costume but that didn't spoil his view. Everything male in him responded to her voluptuous femininity. And her hair continued to captivate him. Freed from the cap, it seemed alive in the sunlight, the strands fanning across her shoulders like tongues of fire.

Her delight at the boat made Gio glad he'd brought her. He'd had doubts. He'd never taken anyone out with him before. Time on the boat was guarded jealously. It was his escape, his retreat, his guilty pleasure, and he'd been worried...not that Jessica wouldn't enjoy it but that having anyone with him would detract from what he gained being alone on the water. The desire for Jessica's company proved how fully she had breached his defences in the weeks since they'd met. Today he'd discovered that sharing the boat with her made the experience better than before.

'Why is your boat called *Lori*?'

Jessica's softly voiced question made him tense. She was looking at him through those sexy green eyes, and he dragged his gaze free, staring out to sea. Maybe it was time to tell her about Sofia. If he wanted Jessica to trust him and share the secrets that held her back from relationships with people, then he had to trust her, too. Which meant placing his broken heart in her hands. He cleared his throat, the emotion building before he even begun to speak.

'Lori was my wife's nickname,' he began, hit by a wave of memories. 'In Italy it is common to shorten someone's surname to use as a derivative. Sofia's maiden name was Loriani…to friends she was Lori. At school everyone called us "Lori and Cori".' A smile came unbidden. 'We used the names for each other into adulthood.'

Jessica's smile was sweet, interest and understanding in her eyes. 'That's lovely. You'd known each other a long time?'

'Since we were six.'

'Six?' she exclaimed with surprise. 'Wow!'

'Sofia's *mamma*, Ginetta, came to work for my parents,' he continued. 'She lived in, originally caring for the house—and me—while my parents worked long hours with the business. Ginetta rapidly became indispensable, and she and Sofia were soon part of the family.'

Gio paused and took a drink of water. 'Sofia and I were the same age and were friends from day one. We scarcely spent a day apart. Many people believed we'd go our separate ways with time, but it never happened. It wasn't something we planned.' He frowned, trying to find the best way to explain. 'We just never wanted anyone else, you know?' Jessica nodded and turned more towards him. 'We married at eighteen. I did my medical training and Sofia trained to be a teacher. Throughout everything we remained best friends.'

'Soul mates,' Jessica added, her voice husky.

'Yes.'

Leaning back on his elbows, enjoying the feel of the sun against his skin, he found himself telling her all kinds of stories as happy memories flowed so quickly it was difficult to catch hold of them.

'We were in no hurry to start a family of our own. Being together was all we wanted. We thought we had time...but it ran out,' he added, choking on the words.

'What happened, Gio?'

Jessica's whispered query took him back into the darkness. Voice thick, he told her of the moment they had found out that Sofia was dying.

'It is ironic, no, that Sofia should be struck down by the kind of brain tumour I now operate on often?' He heard Jessica's shocked gasp, aware that she was sitting up but too lost in his thoughts to stop now. 'Sofia's tumour was inoperable. It was virulent and resistant to treatment, claiming her quickly.'

What he didn't add aloud was how guilty he felt. And that he couldn't forgive himself for being unable to save her, tormenting himself as he relived those terrible weeks...to the signs he must have missed and failing to catch the tumour early enough to make a difference. His head knew it wasn't true, Sofia's doctors had told him time and again that it wouldn't have made a difference, but still he wondered and beat himself up over his failings.

'Gio, you're not in any way to blame.' Jessica was closer, he could feel her behind him, feel the kiss of her breath against his shoulder as she spoke, her voice gentle but firm. He heard the emotion she was keeping in check as she continued. 'It is too unspeakably cruel, for Sofia and for you.'

'I wish I had her courage. She faced death with the same warmth, bravery, humour and gentleness of spirit with which she embraced life. I was at her side every second of her brief but futile fight, and I was holding her hand when she took her final breath.'

His colleagues and the staff who had cared for her had left him alone with her. For the first time in his adult life, he had wept—for Sofia and for himself. And then he had shut down a significant part of himself, closing off his heart because it was the only way he could cope with going on alone. As he had somehow emerged from the blackest of days after her loss, he had thrown himself into his work, into making himself better, and in trying to stop others dying the way Sofia had.

'Life was nothing without her. We'd been inseparable for twenty-one years. I felt lost, cast adrift,' he admitted, the emotion catching up with him.

'Gio…'

Jessica came up onto her knees behind him and wrapped him in her arms, shocking him. Full, firm breasts pressed against his back and, as she rested her head on his shoulder, he felt her tears against his skin. As he drew in another unsteady breath, it was fragranced with the subtle aroma of her chocolate-scented shampoo and body lotion. Drawing on her comfort, he raised his hands, finding hers and linking their fingers.

'You worked so you wouldn't think,' she said, her voice throaty with emotion.

'Yes.' She understood, he suspected, because she did the same, focusing on other people's problems to escape her own.

'And the trust you told me about…'

'I set it up in Sofia's name, funding research, raising money to provide scanners and equipment for hospitals around the world and providing information and support for those struck down by neurological conditions, especially tumours.'

'Sofia would be so proud of you.'

'She would also be kicking me for not getting on with life,' he added wryly.

'But you have,' Jessica protested. 'You did what you needed to do for you and you've helped countless others through very difficult times.'

Her generosity touched him. And he savoured the closeness and physical contact, hoping Jessica would not suddenly remember her no-touching rule and take flight.

He took a deep breath, feeling calmer, telling Jessica of his discovery of the album Sofia had made of their lives, packed with photos and letters and memorabilia from childhood, through their wedding and to their last days together. He treasured it. It gave him solace, made him grateful that she'd been his life, but it also made him grieve for what would never be. Sofia was the only woman he had ever loved, the only woman with whom he had ever *made* love. In the last five years his bed had felt too big and cold and lonely, but nothing and no one had ever tempted him.

Until Jessica.

As Gio fell silent, Jess thought over all he had told her, feeling devastated for him and his wife. Many times she had wondered about the woman who had claimed Gio's heart. Sofia. She envisaged a glamorous, beautiful woman with a model-like figure. Whatever she had looked like, Sofia had been lucky to win Gio's love, devotion and loyalty. And cruelly unlucky to have been taken from him at such a young age.

Gio's fidelity and love for Sofia was in stark contrast to the thoughtlessness and infidelity shown by Duncan, Jess's ex-fiancé and the man who had changed her life for ever. Discovering Duncan had been unfaithful on too many occasions to count had been hurtful and shocking enough. Being eight weeks away from the wedding she had dreamed of for so long had made it worse. The wedding had never taken place. And the dream would now never come true for her.

There were so many things Duncan had taken from her, including her trust in people. And herself. Her life had changed beyond recognition. Her fiancé—*ex-fiancé*, she corrected with the anger and bitterness that had never left her—had seen to that.

The thought of never being close to anyone again was depressing, so she kept busy and absorbed helping others so that she had no time to think of herself. So she understood Gio's need to lose himself in work after such a heart-wrenching loss. That he blamed himself was terrible, and yet driving himself as he had meant he had given hope, care and fresh chances to his patients. Patients he tried so hard to save as he had not been able to save Sofia.

Her situation was different but the outcome had been similar. A lonely life devoting herself to caring for others. Now and again, in a weak moment, a stray thought crept in. A yearning for intimacy. Not even sex…just a need to be held and cherished. As she and Gio were holding each other now.

The reality of it was a shock. She'd acted on instinct in response to his pain, forgetting the need to keep distance between them. Now, pressed against him, her arms around his shoulders and their hands locked together, she battled the awareness and desire that were coursing through her.

How she wished she could satisfy the urge to bury her face more fully into his neck and breathe in his scent…the earthy aroma of man mixed with the subtle but arousing fragrance of his soap and warm, sun-kissed skin. It was crazy! But everything in her was drawn to him on some basic level. She couldn't give in to it. To do so would involve telling him her secrets and she couldn't do that. If she did, he would run in the opposite direction, just as everyone else in her life had done when they'd found out. She was tarnished, spoiled goods, untouchable. And she would do well to remember that when she indulged in any foolish notions about Gio.

Drawing in one last breath of his intoxicating, delicious scent, her desire for him threatening to melt her bones and turn her resolve to dust, she began to withdraw.

'I'm sorry, I shouldn't have done that,' she apologised, disconcerted when he kept hold of her hands.

'I'm not sorry.' He allowed her to place only a small distance between them before shifting so he was facing her. 'Thank you.'

Jess shook her head in confusion. 'I didn't do anything.'

'Yes, you did. You listened, you understood. You cared,' he added huskily, setting her heart thudding.

Knowing she was in big trouble, Jess sucked in a ragged breath, unable to drag her gaze free from the intensity of his. 'W-what are you looking at?' she finally asked, the electric tension increasing with every passing second.

'Your eyes.'

Jess frowned. 'What's the matter with them?'

'Nothing. They're beautiful.' He smiled, seeming closer than ever. 'This is the first time I've noticed the little specks of silver-grey in them.'

'Really?' Was that her voice sounding so breathless and confused?

'Mmm.' Blue eyes darkened as they watched her. 'I've meant to ask before…what is the gemstone in your earrings? They're the same shade as your eyes.'

Again he had thrown her and she tried to focus on his question and not on the affect of his nearness. 'Olive apatite. My grandmother had a passion for gemology and she gave them to me for my twenty-first birthday,' she told him, thinking with sadness and gratitude of the woman who had died the previous winter and whose unexpected legacy had enabled her to buy her cottage.

'They're perfect for you,' Gio told her, the approval and intimacy in his voice making her tingle all over.

Jess couldn't help but shiver as Gio ran the pad of one thumb along the sensitive hollow between her chin and her lower lip. She couldn't prevent her lips parting in response. It took a concerted effort not to sway towards him. Instead, Gio moved, oh, so slowly leaning in until warm supple lips met hers. Jess jumped. One of his hands still held hers and her fingers closed reflexively on his.

He tasted of things sinful, things long denied her but which she could know again if only she let go. Could she? Dared she? What if she did? How would she put the lid back on the box again afterwards? More than anything she wanted to forget common sense.

But she couldn't.

Gathering all the strength and willpower she could

muster, she turned her head away, breaking the spell. She heard his soft sigh, his smothered exclamation of regret and frustration, but she hardened her resolve. It was for the best, she told herself over and over again, hoping that repeating the mantra often enough would make her believe it. But the thought of telling him the truth made it easier.

The truth.

Her secret.

The one that hung over her like the sword of Damocles. Nothing could happen without him knowing—and once he knew, he would reject her anyway. Like everyone else. She valued his friendship too much to risk spoiling everything by giving in to a moment of madness, one she knew had no future to it.

'Jessica…'

'Please, Gio, don't,' she begged before he could continue. 'I can't. I'm sorry.'

His disappointment was clear, but he smiled, running one finger down her cheek. 'It's OK. I'm not giving up on you but there is no hurry. When you are ready, you will tell me…whatever it is.'

Jess had no reply to that, unable to imagine a time when she could ever reveal the truth to him.

'Friends, remember?' she said now, moving away and helping him pack their things ready to return to the boat for the journey home.

She'd told Gio to remember the rules, but she had been as guilty as him of ignoring them. With the boundaries becoming more and more blurred all the time, who most needed the instruction to behave…Gio or herself?

CHAPTER SEVEN

'MEGAN?'

Josh O'Hara looked at the fragile form of the woman who had caused much of the mental and emotional turmoil that had plagued him since he'd arrived at St Piran's and discovered her here. A blast from the past. One with which he'd never come to terms.

She turned around, her gaze scanning the A and E staffroom, and a frown formed as she realised they were alone. He felt uncertain and awkward as the silence stretched between them. They had been tiptoeing around each other for weeks now. He had questions that needed answers, but attempts to confront the past had been futile…meeting with hostility and denial.

Yet despite the dark cloud that hung over them, when Megan, as registrar on call, had come to A and E from Paediatrics, they'd worked well together and been attuned to each other. Now he had a rare window of opportunity to talk to her alone.

'Have you been in Cornwall all the time?' he asked, daring to venture onto dangerous ground.

Her gaze flicked to his and away again. 'Pretty much.'

At least she'd answered rather than walking out or telling him to back off. 'How is your grandmother?'

'She died three years ago.'

'I'm sorry.' Damn it, could he say nothing right to this woman? 'I know what she meant to you.'

Her small smile was tinged with sadness. 'I owe her everything.'

She'd told him once how her parents had been killed in a road accident when she'd been four and her grandmother had raised her. She'd not been in the best of health and Megan had been caring for her while going through medical school.

With Megan in a more conciliatory mood, he risked asking more of the questions that plagued him. 'Why here, Megan?'

'My grandmother lived in Penhally when she was young and she wanted to come home before she died. It seemed as good a place as any to be,' she finished, sounding so lost and alone that his heart ached for her.

He'd forgotten her grandmother's connection with Cornwall. Or had he? Was that why, when Rebecca had suggested leaving London, Cornwall had been the first place he had thought to go? Had he, some place deep in his subconscious, made the connection with Megan?

He remained as affected by her as he'd always been. The past would never go away. Neither could he change it. But he craved answers.

'I know you don't want to talk, and I won't ask again if that's what you choose, but I need to know, Megan—' He broke off, capturing her gaze, his heart in his mouth. 'Was the baby mine?'

He saw her shock and the pain his question caused as

she reeled back, anger replacing the hurt in her eyes. 'Of *course* it was yours. Don't judge me by *your* standards. *I* didn't sleep around.'

'Why didn't you *tell* me?' he demanded, his own hurt and anger rising with the confirmation of what he had known in his heart all along.

'How could I?' she threw back at him, her voice shaky with emotion. 'When was I meant to tell you? You refused to talk to me. And what good would it have done? What would *you* have done? You'd made it clear I meant nothing to you. You wouldn't have welcomed fatherhood...you never wanted children. Just as you rejected marriage—although *that's* changed in the last eight years.'

Pain and bitterness rang in her tone. Her accusations hurt...the more so because he recognised the truth in them. He *had* behaved badly. He'd been anti-marriage— for himself—and he'd never wanted children. Something he'd made clear to Rebecca from the first, and the reason why he was refusing her latest demands for a baby.

But he didn't want to think of Rebecca now. His thoughts were in the past. He'd had a right to know eight years ago. Hadn't he? Megan's challenge rang in his ears. What *would* he have done? He wasn't sure but it would undoubtedly have been the wrong thing. Avoidance of the truth. Running away. He'd been good at that. But knowing it *had* been his lifeless son he'd once held in his arms was devastating.

'You denied me any chance of making those decisions for myself.' The depth of his emotion shocked him and his voice was choked. 'You gave me no chance to say goodbye to my son.'

'You have a nerve. What chance did *you* give *me*

when you tossed me aside?' Tears gleamed on her lashes. 'You took my baby from me, Josh. And with him any chance of me having another child.'

'God, Megan. Those weren't my decisions.' His tone softened as her pain sliced through him. She looked more fragile than ever and he fought the urge to comfort her—something he should have done eight years ago.

Eight years...

He was plunged back to that terrible night when A and E had been in chaos following a multiple crash involving a coach of schoolchildren. He'd been a junior doctor facing something far beyond his experience as the paramedics had brought in a woman in the throes of a miscarriage and haemorrhaging terribly. Discovering it was Megan had thrown him.

'The obstetrician/gynaecologist did what was necessary to save your life. There wasn't even time to transfer you to Theatre.'

The possibility of Megan dying had been real. The surgeon had pulled the tiny baby from her body and given it to him. He'd stared at the lifeless form, too premature to survive, trying to work out dates with a brain that refused to function. A nurse had taken the baby away, and he'd been drawn back into the emergency procedure, assisting as the surgeon had made the decision to take Megan's womb.

'I asked him—*begged* him—to leave you hope for the future, but he was adamant there was no other way to stop you bleeding to death. What else could I have done?' he appealed to her, his stomach churning as he relived that awful night.

'I don't know.'

Tears ran down her cheeks and his heart, for so long

encased in a protective coating of stone, threatened to break at the depth of her sorrow and pain. He'd pushed the memories into the background, unable to deal with them. Megan had been living with them every day. He felt guilty, confused...

'What did you call him?' he asked, knowing he was tormenting them both but needing to know.

'Stephen.' Her voice was rough. 'After my father.'

'Thank you for telling me.'

They stared at each other, fighting the past, the pain, the memories—and the chemistry that, eight years on and despite all that had happened, still bubbled below the surface.

The sound of his pager announcing an incoming emergency cut through the tense silence, swiftly followed by the ring of Megan's pager, bringing their conversation to an end. Although he now had confirmation about the baby, a sense of unfinished business still remained.

Eight years ago he had known that Megan was different, had sensed she was dangerous to him. And he'd been right. The night he'd let down his guard had been the most amazing of his life. He'd told Megan things he had never told anyone else, and she had touched a place inside him in a way no other woman ever had. It had scared him. And he'd done what Megan had accused him of. He'd blanked her, keeping as far from her as possible because she'd burrowed under his skin.

If only he had been mature enough to know what he knew now. That the sort of connection he had found with Megan was rare. Not just the incredible physical passion that had overwhelmed them both but the deep mental and emotional union he'd experienced with no one but her. By the time he'd realised what he could have had and all he had thrown away, it had been too late.

He'd wobbled. Briefly. Then he'd gone on, focusing on his career and rapid advancement. Four years ago he'd met Rebecca and they'd seemed to want the same things, including no children. He'd cared about her, he'd been lonely and enjoyed having her to come home to. She'd wanted the doctor husband and the lifestyle. He'd convinced himself it was for the best, not the same as he'd had with Megan but safer.

Things had been wrong long before they'd left London. Bored, Rebecca had changed the rules, deciding she wanted a child. But as Izzy had said weeks ago when her daughter had been born, a child couldn't hold a bad marriage together and shouldn't be brought into the world for the wrong reasons. He wouldn't have a baby he didn't want with a woman he didn't love and who didn't love him.

Seeing Megan again, he saw with terrible clarity what he had thrown away, and he wished with all his heart that he had done things differently when he'd had the chance. As they walked down the corridor to the main A and E department, it occurred to him that he had still not asked Megan one of the questions that had been bugging him all along.

'Why *did* you stay the night with me, Megan?'

Her sharp intake of breath was audible, but she pushed through the swing doors into the busy department, bringing further discussion to an end. As he was directed to Resus, Megan was called to a treatment cubicle and she walked away from him without a backward glance. He had no more idea what to do about her—and his feelings for her—now than he had in the past. She was an itch under his skin that wouldn't go away, affecting him in the same unique way she had done eight years ago.

'Is there anything else I can do for you?' Jess asked, sitting beside the bed of the woman with whom she had spent a considerable amount of time over the last few days.

Faye Luxton, in her early seventies, had come in for a standard knee replacement but had suffered a severe bleed in her brain during her operation and had woken in Intensive Care to find her world turned upside down. She'd been handed over into Gio's care and, just days ago, he had needed to operate on a second bleed to remove a clot and also to put a coil around a small aneurysm that had threatened to enlarge and cause even greater problems.

Unfortunately, the damage already caused could not be reversed, although the numbness and weakness down one side of her body and her difficulty speaking were improving. Faye could still have a good quality of life, but she would no longer be able to live alone or care for herself and her animals.

With no family, Faye faced the horrible necessity of selling her much-loved home and moving into an assisted-care facility. Jess had helped support her when Social Services had come to discuss the options.

Faye had faced everything with courage, but had been distressed at times as she tried to come to terms with the drastic changes in her life. Jess had done all she could, helping Faye deal with the emotional upset.

'You've done so much.' Her speech was slow and

slurred, but clearer than it had been. 'I wouldn't have coped without you.'

'I'm sure you would. You have such a strong spirit, Faye. You've been a joy to care for and a real inspiration, too,' Jess assured her.

'I agree.'

Gio's voice sent a prickle of awareness along Jess's spine and she looked round, her gaze clashing with his as he strode through the door, his senior registrar, a couple of junior doctors and the ward's charge nurse trailing in his wake. Jess was all too conscious of Gio close beside her chair, blocking her exit, his leg and hip pressing gently against her, as he greeted Faye warmly.

'I'll step out,' Jess offered, making to rise.

'Can Jess stay?' Faye asked, looking unsettled.

Gio smiled at their patient. 'Yes, of course.'

Jess subsided back onto the chair as his hand came to rest on her shoulder. Although his attention was focused on the medical team updating him on Faye's condition, his hand lingered, and Jess felt the fire in her blood as his touch warmed her through the fabric of her shirt. His fingers gave a gentle squeeze before he released her and reached out for Faye's notes.

They were halfway through September and while they'd been on their best behaviour since their bank-holiday outing in the boat, Jess was finding it difficult to ignore the electric buzz of attraction that intensified with every passing day. But she valued their friendship too much to risk losing her head and doing anything stupid.

They'd been out on the boat twice more and she loved it. Much to her amazement, Gio had also been teaching her how to drive it. The thrill had been so huge it had even managed to take her mind off his body pressed close to hers—and the divine male scent of him—as he'd helped her work the controls.

The tragedy of his wife's death still affected her and she remained shocked at the way she had acted on instinct in response to his grief. It had scared her. With Gio it was too easy to forget the hard lessons of the last four years.

Curious, Jess had steeled herself to ask Gio more about Sofia a couple of nights ago. Gio had brought out the album Sofia had made when she'd known she was dying, creating a story of their lives in words and pictures, and Jess had choked up all over again at the incredible bond they had shared and the cruel way they had been parted.

Sofia had been a surprise. Rather than being model thin and styled to perfection, she'd been small, curvy and very much the girl next door, possessing the kind of fresh-faced natural beauty that could never be faked and that shone through because of the person she was, in her laughing dark eyes, her smile and her obvious love for Gio. And his for her.

The photos of Gio and Sofia in their teens, so much together, so right for each other and so in love, had reminded Jess of Marcia and Colin—another young couple who had been ripped apart by terrible tragedy, and one she hadn't been able to get out of her mind.

'How are you feeling, Faye?' Gio asked, sitting on the edge of the bed and taking her good hand in his.

'I'm frustrated my body won't do what I want it to. I can't even tell you properly.' Faye shook her head. 'I can't imagine life away from my home and without my animals. I'm thankful for all you've done for me, but knowing things will never be the same is difficult.'

'Of course. It's hard enough to recover from surgery without having to come to terms with such unexpected changes. Things seem overwhelming, yes?' he sympathised, stealing Jess's heart as he took a pristine handkerchief from his pocket and wiped the elderly lady's tears with gentle care.

'Yes, exactly.' Faye visibly relaxed, soothed by Gio's attention. 'I'm old and set in my ways.'

Gio gallantly protested, making her smile. 'You're doing well and we will all do everything we can to ensure you regain as much strength and capability as possible.' The air locked in Jess's lungs as his gaze flicked to her. 'Jessica is here to help make the transition as trouble-free as possible.'

'I'm so worried about my animals, but Jess is marvellous,' Faye confided to Gio. 'If other arrangements can't be made to keep them together, she's promised she'll care for them herself.'

A blush warmed Jess's cheeks as Gio looked at her, his expression unreadable.

Gio talked with Faye awhile longer before rising to his feet. His entourage exited ahead of him but he lingered, and Jess excused herself from Faye, worried about his reaction to the animal thing.

'I was going to tell you, Gio. The workmen are making good progress on the cottage, and I'll arrange to have the fences dealt with. If the animals have to be moved before I'm back home, I'll ask Flora if she has room for them until I'm ready,' she rushed to reassure him. 'I don't expect you to house them or anything. I—'

Her rushed words were silenced as Gio pressed a

finger to her lips. 'Stop apologising.' Blue eyes twinkled with amusement and something else she couldn't discern but which made her warm and tingly and a little bit scared. 'I would have been surprised had you *not* offered to step in.'

'Oh...'

He glanced each way along the corridor, his tone conspiratorial as he leaned closer to her, making her quiver with awareness as his warm breath fanned her face. 'Shall I tell you a secret?'

She nodded, unable to answer, hardly able to breathe, fighting every urge within her to touch him, hug him, kiss him.

'I was going to make the same pledge to Faye myself.'

Jess blinked, his nearness robbing her of thought. 'You were?'

'I was.'

Jess felt mesmerised, her skin aflame as he ran one finger down her cheek. The suddenness of an alarm further along the corridor had her snapping back, conscious of where they were. Disconcerted by his touch, she stepped away. There was nothing she could do to escape the non-physical connection, the electrically charged one that bound her ever more tightly to him.

Gio's hand slowly dropped to his side and she swallowed as she met his gaze. He smiled, the full-on smile that stole her breath. 'I must go,' he said, glancing at his watch. 'We'll drive out to Faye's after work to talk with her neighbour and decide what is best to be done. OK?'

'OK.'

Jess watched as he strode off to join his team. How

was she going to cope when she moved back to her own cottage with the kittens? Gio had become far too important in her life.

'Stop the car!'

Gio reacted instantly to Jessica's cry, startled when she opened the door and scrambled out before they'd come to a stop. Cursing in Italian, he parked safely at the side of the road and climbed out in time to see Jessica running along the pavement and disappearing from view around a corner. Concerned, Gio jogged after her. What was earth going on?

They were in the centre of St Piran, on the way home following their visit to Faye's smallholding. Enquiries to several rescue centres had proved futile, which left them bemused and amused to find themselves foster-parents to a motley collection of animals. There were more than Gio had anticipated. He'd wanted animals, yes, but he hadn't imagined taking on so many in one go! Jessica's enthusiasm had swayed him, though.

Now, along with Dickens and Kipling, their menagerie included a donkey, two Gloucester Old Spot pigs, three sheep of mixed heritage and several assorted chickens. Faye's neighbour would care for them in the short term until the fencing at Jessica's cottage, and the necessary movement licences, were arranged. Gio didn't want to think about Jessica moving out—he had ideas but it was too soon to discuss them—but whatever happened between Jessica and himself, he intended to share the cost and responsibility for the animals.

Rounding the corner, he saw Jessica walking back towards him, her shoulders slumped, her steps reluctant as she kept pausing and looking behind her.

'What's going on?' he asked as he joined her.

She looked up, olive-green eyes despondent. 'I saw Marcia.' Again she scanned the crowds along one of St Piran's main shopping streets.

'The girl who gave you the false name after her boy-friend died?' he asked, frowning at her nod of confirmation. 'Are you still fretting about her?'

'Yes.'

She tried to carry everyone's problems on her own shoulders. 'Jessica…'

'I saw her, Gio. She looked so alone, so lost. The girl I met was prettily plump and well groomed,' she told him, clearly upset. 'She's put on weight and hasn't been taking care of herself. Her skin was grey and her hair lank and unstyled.' Again she met his gaze, and his chest tightened at the expression in her eyes. 'I can't help but worry about her.'

'You have a special empathy with people. But you can't solve everyone's problems, *fiamma*,' he advised her, the endearment—meaning flame in Italian—slipping out without conscious thought.

'I know that, but—'

As her defensive words snapped off, Gio cupped her face. 'Marcia knows where you are. If she needs you, she'll contact you in her own time. Everyone comes to terms with grief in their own way. Believe me, I know.'

Fresh tears stung Jessica's eyes as Gio's words hit home, pain for him mingling with her anxiety for Marcia. 'I'm sorry.'

'There's nothing to apologise for.' His smile was gentle, as was his touch.

Jess bit her lip, fighting the temptation, the *need*, to step closer, to press herself against him and be hugged… held in those strong arms. 'I'm OK,' she lied, stepping back and manufacturing a smile.

'Jess!' A female voice called her name and she looked round, smiling as she saw Kate Althorp approaching. 'Hello, my love.'

'Hi, Kate, how are you? And how is Jem?' She had spent many an hour talking with the older woman, especially when her son had been badly hurt in a car accident earlier in the year.

Kate's smile was free from the shadows Jess had seen there in the past. 'Jem's made a wonderful recovery. Thank you. And we're all well.'

'I'm so glad.' She was painfully conscious of Gio beside her and, when Kate looked at him expectantly, Jess had to introduce them. 'Kate, this is Gio Corezzi. He's a neurosurgeon and joined St Piran's in August,' she explained, her gaze flicking to him and away again. 'Gio, meet Kate Althorp. She's a midwife at the surgery in Penhally.'

Jess watched as the two shook hands and exchanged pleasantries, noting how Kate glowed when faced with Gio's natural charm and humour.

'What Jess has modestly left out, Gio, is how wonderful she has been to me,' Kate told him. 'She not only helped me a year ago when I had a scary brush with breast cancer, but she was an absolute rock when my son, Jem, broke his pelvis five months ago.'

'I didn't really do anything,' Jess murmured with embarrassment.

Kate waved her protest aside. 'What nonsense! I couldn't have got through it all without you, life was so difficult,' the older woman insisted, deepening Jess's blush and her discomfort. Kate smiled up at Gio. 'Jess is one in a million.'

'Yes...I know.'

Jess opened her mouth then closed it again, unsure what to say in response to Gio's husky words.

Kate chuckled, a twinkle in her brown eyes. She glanced at her watch and sighed. 'I'm afraid I have to run. There's so little time before the wedding and I have a million things to do. You are coming, aren't you, my love? I so want you to be there, it would mean so much to me. Bring Gio,' she added with a wink.

As Kate hurried off, Jess turned to walk back towards the car, but Gio surprised her, catching her hand and leading her in the opposite direction. 'This way.'

'Where are we going?' she asked, all too conscious of the way her fingers curled naturally with his.

'You're going to need a dress for the wedding and, as Kate said, there isn't much time.' He headed in the direction of one of St Piran's classy boutiques. 'We can take care of it while we are here.'

Jessica tried to dig her heels in. No way could she afford anything from that kind of shop. 'I'm not sure if I'm going to go,' she admitted, pulling on his hand.

'Not go?' He halted, an eyebrow raised in query as he looked at her. 'Why ever not?'

She attempted a careless shrug. He'd known about the wedding—the invitation had been propped on the mantelpiece in his living room for some time—but now he'd met Kate, it was more difficult to explain. It was one thing interacting with Kate at the hospital and quite another to move things into a social context. Jess didn't do social. Telling Gio that she felt too shy and nervous to go to the wedding on her own sounded far too pathetic.

'Kate wants you to be there,' he pointed out.

'Yes, but—'

'But nothing.' Gio forestalled further protests, the smile that curved his sexy mouth doing peculiar things to her insides.

'Gio,' she protested as he started them walking again.

'I'm going to buy you a frock for the wedding, to which I shall be honoured to escort you,' he informed her, shock rendering her temporarily compliant as he guided her along and halted outside the door of the boutique.

'Gio, you can't buy me a dress!'

'Of course I can!' He tweaked the tip of her nose between finger and thumb of his free hand.

Gazing at him in confusion, her skin tingling from his touch, she swallowed, all too conscious that this man was getting far too close. The walls she had constructed for her own protection felt increasingly vulnerable. And she was scared. Scared that if she continued to allow Gio to breach her defences and become more than a platonic friend, she would end up breaking her heart all over again.

And this time she might never recover.

CHAPTER EIGHT

IT WAS wonderful to see Kate so happy. Sitting with Polly d'Azzaro and a heavily pregnant Lucy Carter, in the garden of the beautiful granite-built barn a few miles outside Penhally that was now Kate's home, Jess watched the older woman mingle with her guests. She had a broad smile on her face, her brown eyes were alight with joy, and Nick, her new husband, was never far from her side.

St Mark's, Penhally's small church, had been bursting at the seams as people had come from far and wide to attend Nick and Kate's wedding. Nick's grown-up children from his first marriage had been there to support their father and give their blessing to Kate. And Kate's eleven-year-old son Jem, who had only recently discovered that Nick was his real father, had recovered well enough from his broken pelvis to proudly walk his mother down the aisle. A lump had formed in Jess's throat as Jem had stood with his half-brothers and -sister, watching his mother marry his father, publicly acknowledging him and making them one big united family at last.

Nervous about attending the party, Jess would never have come alone. Having Gio there made her feel better.

When they'd arrived at the barn, anxiety had gripped her as she'd faced the prospect of socialising with so many people. Unconsciously she'd moved closer to Gio. A moment later her right hand had been enveloped in his left one. Far from flinching away, or reminding him of the no-touching rule, her fingers had linked with his and held on tight.

Now, several hours later, after endless chat and laughter, an informal buffet, complete with hog roast and lashings of champagne, the dancing was soon to begin. Having enjoyed things more than she'd expected to—although she'd lost count of the number of times she'd explained she and Gio were just friends—the prospect of the live band and dancing into the evening was making her tense.

Jess's gaze strayed to Gio, who was deep in conversation with Polly's husband, Luca. Both Italian and with similar tragedies in their pasts, the two men had much in common. Luca was also Jess's GP.

'Gio's very handsome,' Polly commented, following the direction of her gaze.

'Mmm.' Jess hoped her murmur of agreement sounded noncommittal, even though her heart did somersaults every time she looked at him. He was always stunning but in his suit and tie he looked like a matinée idol. 'We're just friends.'

Polly's blue eyes were filled with understanding. 'That's a shame.'

'It's for the best.' Jess's words emerged as a whisper and, however much she wanted to deny it, even she could hear the regret in her voice.

'Is it?' Polly's smile was kind. As a fellow GP at Penhally surgery, Jess knew the other woman was speaking both as a doctor and a woman. 'Are you sure, Jess?'

She nodded, glancing at Polly before her gaze was drawn inexorably back to Gio. 'Yes.' Although it was getting harder and harder to believe it.

Before Polly could say any more, Nick and Kate passed on their way indoors to prepare for the first dance. Nick looked on with an indulgent and contented smile as Kate hugged Polly, whom, Jess had discovered, was Kate's god-daughter.

'We're so glad you and Gio came, Jess, and thank you so much for your lovely gift and the beautiful words in your card,' Kate told her, linking her arm through Nick's. 'You're looking gorgeous today.'

'Thank you,' Jess murmured, taken by surprise.

She was wearing the dress Gio had insisted on buying at the boutique in St Piran. Sleeveless and deceptively simple, it fell to her knees, highlighting her curves, the shades of teal and peacock green bringing out the colour of her eyes and highlighting the rich reds in her hair, now drawn back in a ponytail. She felt guilty for giving in to temptation—and Gio's persuasion—but the instant she had put the expensive dress on, she'd fallen in love with it. The desire and appreciation in Gio's eyes when he'd seen her in it had set her blood zinging in her veins.

'Enjoy yourselves,' Nick instructed with a benevolent smile before leading Kate away.

Gio and Luca returned, bringing non-alcoholic fruit punch with them, which both she and Polly accepted gratefully. She met Gio's gaze, her stomach muscles tightening at the expression in his intense blue eyes, her hand not entirely steady as she sipped the ice-cold drink.

Jess was about to tell Gio that she'd like to leave before the dancing began when Luca's twin daughters came running towards them. She'd been shocked when she'd heard how their mother had died giving birth to them. Now four and a half, they were adorable, so alike in looks but so different in character. It was the bolder, more outgoing Toni who arrived first.

'Mummy Polly?' she asked breathlessly.

'Yes, darling?'

'Rosie wants to know if she can have more cake.'

'Does she?' Jess saw Polly's lips twitch as she saw through the ruse. 'You can tell Rosie she can have a piece if she wants one.'

Toni's eyes widened and her mouth formed a silent O as she realised what had happened and tried to work out what to do about it. Gio and Luca both chuckled. Toni glanced round at her sister and then looked pleadingly up at her father, who hid his grin by taking a drink. The little girl's anxious gaze returned to Polly.

'Would *you* like another piece of cake, too, Toni?' she queried, unable to contain her amusement.

'Yes, please!' The relief on the child's face was so funny they all laughed.

'All right,' Polly agreed. 'You can both have one more *small* piece each.'

The little girl leaned in and kissed her stepmother soundly on the cheek. 'Thank you!'

As Toni ran off to join her quieter sister, Jess experienced for the first time the pressing weight of regret that she would never know the joy of motherhood. She hadn't thought of it much before. She'd never felt a maternal yearning, neither had she and Duncan ever discussed having a family.

Now, seeing the twins, she couldn't help but wonder what Gio's children would look like...although any idea of *her* ever being with him was pure fantasy. But it hit home that this was one more thing Duncan had taken away from her.

Gio was aware of the change in Jessica but was unsure of its cause. She put on a smiling face, but a light had dimmed in her eyes. He wanted to know what had happened. Unfortunately this was neither the time nor the place to ask. He was proud of her. She'd been nervous and uncomfortable about the party, even before she had clung so tenaciously to his hand when faced with the throng of guests. But she'd gradually relaxed, especially when the d'Azzaro family had taken them under their collective wings.

He'd enjoyed himself, too. Much of that had been simply being with Jessica, but he'd also been pleased to meet Luca. Discovering that Luca's life had mirrored his own in many ways had given him much to think about, especially seeing how Luca had been able to move on to find love and happiness with Polly.

'It wasn't easy,' Luca had told him. 'For so long I lived only for my girls. I'd not even looked at anyone else after Elaine died and I never expected to love again. Then I met Polly.' His smile and tone of voice had revealed his emotion more than words. 'I'm so lucky. And grateful. Don't close your heart and mind to possibilities, Gio,' he'd advised, his dark gaze straying to where Jessica and Polly had been sitting. 'You have the chance for something special. Jess deserves the best. She's not someone to be toyed with.'

The warning had been gently given, but it was a warning nonetheless. Luca and Polly not only viewed Jessica with affection, they were also protective of her. Gio wondered what his compatriot knew but was unable to reveal because of patient confidentiality.

After the live band struck up, Nick and Kate taking the first dance, most of the guests took to the floor. Jessica, however, refused all offers. It was Luca who eventually managed to get her on her feet, and Gio was shocked by the rush of envy and possessiveness that washed over him. Luca was happily married and had no designs on Jessica, but Gio hated to see her in anyone's arms but his own.

'Would you mind dancing with me, Gio?'

Polly's request took him by surprise. 'I'd be delighted,' he agreed politely, although the only person he wanted was Jessica.

'Don't worry, it won't be for long.' Polly, a pretty blonde and tiny, smiled up at him. 'Luca's giving Jess a pep talk.'

'A pep talk?' Gio frowned. What was Luca saying to her? And why?

Polly glanced across to where her husband and Jessica were dancing. 'Be ready to take over when Luca gives the signal.'

Puzzled but intrigued, Gio did as he was bidden, eager for the moment they would swap partners and he would have Jessica in his arms at last.

'It's good to see you happy.' Luca smiled, holding Jess lightly and allowing her to determine the personal space she was comfortable with. 'Gio's a nice guy.'

'We're just friends,' Jess said for the umpteenth time. Her protest produced a teasing chuckle. 'Right!'

'We *are*.' Jess sucked in a ragged breath and tried not to keep staring at Gio. Worst of all, she struggled to banish the ridiculous jealousy that swept through her as he danced with Polly. 'I can't get involved with anyone, Luca, you know that.'

Luca's expression sobered and he steered them to a quiet corner where they wouldn't be overheard. 'I know nothing of the sort. You can have a normal relationship, Jess. I gather Gio doesn't know?'

'No.' A shiver rippled through her. 'He'd run a mile— like everyone else—if he did.' She hated the bitterness in her voice but the lessons of the last four years had been learned the hard way. 'Gio's still grieving. Even were he not, no man would want someone like me.'

'You're wrong, Jess. And you're doing Gio a big disservice,' he cautioned, his words forestalling a further protest from her. 'Give him a chance. He cares about you and knows what a wonderful woman you are. If he reacts as you fear, then he isn't worthy of you. But what if he understands? Think of all you then have to gain.'

Jess bit her lip, caught in an agony of indecision. She didn't want to lose what she already had and she didn't dare to believe she could have more.

'Don't condemn yourself to a lifetime alone. I nearly did. I was so fearful of being hurt again, but my life is so enriched thanks to Polly. Think about it,' he added, guiding her back onto the dance floor. 'It might sound like a cliché, but none of us knows what the future holds so live each day to the fullest and allow yourself to love and be loved.'

It sounded simple when Luca put it into words, but Jess knew it was anything *but* simple in reality. So distracted was she that she didn't notice Luca steering her towards Gio and Polly, but in the next moment she found herself in Gio's arms as Luca reclaimed his wife. Oh, hell! She hadn't intended dancing at all, and certainly not with Gio because of the temptation when she was near him. But she couldn't make a scene in front of everyone.

She held herself stiffly as he drew her closer, his touch, his scent, the feel of his body brushing against hers having a potent affect on her. One dance wouldn't hurt, would it? One moment out of time to enjoy being in his arms, forgetting why she had to be strong?

As she relaxed, giving up the fight, Gio drew her closer, making her even more aware of him, her body instinctively responding to his nearness. When the music ended, she sighed and made a half-hearted effort to draw away.

'Stay. Please.' The throaty warmth of his voice stripped her of any remaining willpower and common sense.

The tempo slowed and Jess found herself pressed far too intimately against him, her arms winding round him of their own volition. His fingertips brushed the bare skin between her shoulder blades, exposed by the V back of the dress, making her burn with a rush of desire. She was oblivious to everyone else, focused only on Gio, every sense heightened and attuned to him.

He bent his head, the warmth of his breath caressing her neck, the brush of his faintly stubbled jaw against her sensitive skin incredibly erotic. She'd never expected to be held again, let alone dance in public. Emotion threatened to overwhelm her and, to her horror, tears stung her eyes. She buried her face against his chest to hide them…from him and anyone else.

Revelling in this opportunity to hold Jessica properly for the first time, Gio breathed in her unique womanly scent mixed with the familiar hint of chocolate that clung to her hair and skin. Hair and skin that felt super-soft beneath his fingertips.

He was conscious of her heightened emotions, although he doubted she was aware of the way she was clinging to him. Determined not to rush or scare her, he held her, swaying to the music and waiting for her to relax, welcoming the moment she gave up whatever inner battle she was fighting and melted into him. She felt so right in his arms, her curvy body a perfect fit for his.

'Ready to go home?' he asked some considerable time later as they stepped outside to get some fresh air. He wanted her to himself, relishing these moments when he felt closer to her than ever.

She tipped her head back and looked up at the night sky. 'Yes, please.'

After saying goodbye and gathering up their belongings, they drove home in good spirits and were greeted by two sleepy kittens, who stirred long enough to be cuddled. As Jessica settled them again, he went through to the kitchen.

'Hot chocolate?' he asked, smiling at the look on her face.

'Lovely!'

'I'll make it for you the proper Italian way. None of this powdered cocoa with water in a microwave.' He gave an exaggerated shudder of disgust, making her laugh.

'And what is the proper Italian way?'

He took a large bar of *Cioccolato Corezzi's* finest dark chocolate from his stash in a kitchen drawer. 'You must begin with real chocolate. Once melted, you add a little sugar and some milk, bring it to the boil and stir. Some people make it so thick it is like a mousse and has to be eaten with a spoon,' he explained as he broke squares of chocolate and dropped them into a bowl, the satisfying snap a sign of its high quality. 'I prefer it liquid enough to drink, although I keep the teaspoon to reach the last drops!'

'It sounds sinfully delicious.'

It was Jessica who was sinfully delicious. Looking at her fired his blood and stirred his body. Waiting for the water to heat, he leaned his hip against the worktop and watched as she sat at the counter, trying to undo the barrette clasp that held her ponytail in place. Something was stuck and as she muttered to herself, making him smile, he stepped in to help.

'May I?'

Before she had the chance to refuse, he moved behind her, feeling her tense as his fingers set to work. Within moments the clip was free. Unable to resist temptation, his fingers burrowed into the fiery mass of curls that tumbled around her shoulders.

'You have beautiful hair,' he told her, hearing the roughness in his voice.

She gave a shaky laugh. 'I used to hate it.'

'No! It's amazing. Silky soft.' He leaned closer and caught the scent of her chocolatey shampoo. 'And you smell so good.'

'Gio…' Her voice sounded husky and sensual.

The sexual tension increased, electricity crackling between them. Jessica slowly slid round on the stool until she was facing him, olive-green eyes dark with awareness and unmistakeable desire.

His breath caught. 'I *have* to kiss you,' he whispered roughly.

A tremor ran through her but she didn't move away. His hands fisted in her hair as he closed the gap millimetre by millimetre, his heart thudding a rapid tattoo. Finally, their lips met. He felt heady with excitement and yet incredibly nervous as he kissed her for the first time.

They were both tentative, finding their way, learning, savouring, exploring, but the passion quickly flared out of control. Jessica's lips parted and he tilted his head, deepening the kiss. She tasted like heaven. Sweet and sensual, and so addictive. He couldn't get his fill of her. Tongues met, stroked, tempted, and he heard her soft, needy whimper as she clung to him. One hand left her hair and he wrapped his arm around her waist, drawing her into him as he stepped up between her parted thighs. She wriggled closer, pressing herself against him.

Jessica was with him, taking and giving, meeting and matching the blaze of passion that flared so intensely between them, demanding more. Gio was all too aware when instant panic set in and she began to withdraw. With a sharp cry she pulled away from him, clearly distressed.

'What is it, *fiamma?*' he asked between ragged breaths, confused and concerned as tears spilled from eyes full of torment. 'What's wrong?'

She shook her head. 'I'm sorry. So sorry. I can't do this.'

Before he could respond, she pushed away from him, slipped awkwardly off the stool and ran. He heard her footsteps on the stairs and, moments later, the sound of her bedroom door closing. What the hell had happened? Running an unsteady hand through his hair, he took a moment to gather himself together and get his body, so unused to the fiery passion that had ignited between them, back under control.

No way could he leave Jessica in such a distressed state. He wanted to know what had gone wrong, but more important was his concern for her well-being. After checking the house was secure and the kittens were settled, he finished making the hot chocolate and carried two mugs upstairs, anxious about what he might find. Taking a deep breath, he knocked on the door.

'Jessica?'

There was silence for several moments, a silence that hung so heavily around him that he could hear each beat of his heart. 'Yes?' The word was so soft that had he not been listening so intently he would not have heard her.

Cautiously, he opened the door. Dressed now in unflattering but comfortable pyjamas, Jessica was sitting in the middle of the bed, her arms wrapped around herself as she rocked slightly to and fro. She looked so lost, vulnerable and scared that his heart, which he'd thought could never feel anything again, squeezed with pain for her…and such deep affection and longing he didn't dare examine the emotions too deeply.

'May I come in?' His heart was in his mouth as he waited for her decision.

She didn't meet his gaze, but finally she nodded. He

sat on the edge of the bed, careful not to crowd her. He handed her a mug, noting that her hands were shaking as she reached for it, but she cupped it in her palms and sipped, a soft sigh escaping as she savoured the thick, chocolaty treat.

Gio followed her lead, hoping she would begin to relax. She even managed the ghost of a smile when he handed her a teaspoon so she could copy him and capture the final bits of chocolate.

'Good?' he asked, nearly having heart failure as her tongue peeped out and she licked the remains of chocolate from her lips.

'Amazing.' Her voice was still soft but sounded stronger. Popping the spoon in the empty mug, she handed it to him. 'Thank you.'

Gio set the mugs aside, feeling a growing tension now the moment had come to seek answers to some questions.

'Jessica, we need to talk.' Once more she wrapped her arms around herself, lashes lowering to hide her expression, but not before he had seen the fear in her eyes. 'I need to know. I know you guard your personal space and avoid being touched. At first I thought it was me, then I noticed it was the same with everyone. Including your clever ruse using all that stuff you carry round the hospital so you can avoid shaking hands.'

The blush that brought colour back to her too-pale cheeks was confirmation that he was right.

'My imagination is running away with itself. I'm scared to ask but…has someone hurt you in the past?' He could hardly get the words out but knew he had to. 'Were you raped or abused?'

'No.'

The denial was firm and he knew she was telling the truth. The relief was *huge*. But there was still something major and important. He knew it. She looked so alone, and the despair and hurt in her eyes tore him apart.

'May I hold you, Jessica…please?'

She raised her head and met his gaze. What she was searching for, he had no idea, but whatever it was, she apparently found it as, after the longest time, she bit her lip and nodded. The air trapped in his lungs was released in a rush of relief. He moved onto his knees and edged towards her, needing the physical contact as much as she did. When he was as close as could be, he sat back on his heels and drew her into his arms with infinite care, cradling her tense and shaking form against him.

As she gradually began to relax, she rested her head against his chest. With one hand he stroked the unrestrained glossy copper-red curls as they tumbled with abandon around her shoulders.

'Can you talk to me now?' A breath shuddered out of her in response. Her casual shrug belied the tension that poured from her and the tremble he felt ripple through her whole body. 'Jessica?'

'I don't know. I…'

The whispered words were husky with emotion and he sought to discover the cause of her hesitation and reluctance. 'What worries you, *fiamma*? Do you think I won't understand? Do you fear it will change how I think of you and feel about you?'

'I know it will,' she responded, the humourless laugh and bitter edge to her voice speaking volumes.

'Listen to me,' he instructed gently, seeking the words to reassure her. 'I don't know what experiences you've had with other people, but *nothing* you tell me will make me turn away or reject you.' Whatever route their relationship eventually took, he was unable to envisage any circumstance that would change the basic friendship and bond that had formed so quickly but so intensely between them. He dropped a kiss on the top of her head. 'Trust me. I won't let you down.'

The sincerity in Gio's voice was beyond question but Jess still hesitated. He might believe *now* that nothing would make him reject her but would he feel the same when he knew?

She recalled Luca's words. He'd advised her to give Gio a chance, pointing out that only by confiding in him would she discover the depth of his friendship and the kind of man he really was. Deep in her heart she knew. And she *so* wanted to believe. But her former friends and colleagues had turned her away and her family had disowned her.

The last few weeks with Gio had been the happiest she had known for such a long time and she was terrified that revealing the truth about herself would change for ever the nature of their friendship, maybe even end it. She didn't want to lose what she already had, but every day things were becoming more complicated because her heart and emotions were ever more entangled and it was no longer enough just to be his friend.

Those moments in the kitchen when she had allowed herself to wallow in the pleasure of being touched, followed by the most explosive and incredible kiss she had ever known, had proved that. He had breached her defences so completely and she'd been so lost in Gio and her desire for him that she'd forgotten why she shouldn't have been doing it. Reality had hit like a thunderclap and she'd run. They'd crossed the boundaries of friendship now. And in reaching for more, would she destroy what she already had?

She wouldn't know the answer unless she did as Gio asked and trusted him. Cocooned in his embrace she felt safe and protected and, for the first time in over four years, she didn't feel alone. She sucked in a deep breath, inhaling the warm musky-male scent of him that had become so familiar. And arousing. Drawing back just far enough, she looked up and met his steady, intensely blue gaze. While the arm supporting her cuddled her close, his free hand caught one of hers, raising it to his mouth and pressing a kiss to her palm before he entwined their fingers, linking them and giving her his support.

'I don't know where to start,' she admitted with a nervous laugh, feeling sick inside now the decision was made and the moment had come to share her shameful secret.

'Take your time. I'm not going anywhere,' he promised. 'Is it something that goes back to the time before you came to St Piran?'

'Yes. It started just over four years ago when I was still in Scotland,' she admitted, closing her eyes as the memories flooded back. She paused, unsure if she could continue, but Gio's support and strength gave her the courage to face what had to be faced. 'I was working in a hospital there,' she explained, ignoring for now the information about her former career. 'I was living with my fiancé, Duncan. He was my first and only proper boyfriend. I was happy. I thought I had everything I wanted, and I was busy planning the wedding, which was only eight weeks away.'

* * *

As Jessica gathered her thoughts, Gio struggled with the unreasonable jealousy that assailed him at the knowledge she had been in love and about to be married, already disliking the man she spoke of without knowing any more about him. But he hid his reaction, needing to give her all his understanding now that she had done him the honour of trusting him. He couldn't—wouldn't—let her down.

'Did Duncan work at the hospital, too?' he asked, keeping his tone neutral.

'No. He worked for a company that supplied equipment and aid for relief charities out in the field and his job took him all over the world. He was away a lot. I missed him, but I supported what he did.'

He was unsurprised by her selflessness and the sacrifices she'd no doubt made. 'It's not easy maintaining a relationship long distance.'

'No.' Another shiver ran through her and he tightened his hold, wanting to protect her from the hurt she was reliving. 'I hadn't been feeling well for a while,' she continued, and his concern for her increased. 'There was nothing specific I could put my finger on, and I put it down to the pressures of work and the excitement and lack of sleep as the wedding drew closer. Duncan had to take several trips away during those weeks and so everything fell to me. A colleague noticed how off colour I was and suggested I see a doctor. I didn't think anything of it, but because I wanted to feel right for the wedding, I made an appointment to see my GP.'

Gio felt his gut tightening with the premonition that something dark and of huge importance was about to be revealed. Looking into green eyes shadowed with fear and pain, it was the dart of shame that confused him. He raised their joined hands, pressing a kiss to her fingers.

'What happened, *fiamma*?' he prompted.

'My GP didn't think there was anything serious going on, but he organised some tests to be on the safe side. And…' She halted, her voice breaking, tears shimmering on long sooty lashes.

Gio steeled himself for whatever was to come. 'And?'

'The results came back.' A sob tore through her, ripping him to shreds. 'It t-turned out that D-Duncan hadn't been the f-faithful, loving fiancé I'd imagined,' she continued, the words stuttering through her tears. 'He'd slept with countless women during his trips abroad and thanks to him I h-have a lasting legacy. The tests, unlike Duncan, didn't lie. I…' Again she broke off, drawing in a shuddering breath, her fingers instinctively tightening on his as she raised her head, tear-washed eyes bleak. 'Gio, I was…*am*…HIV positive.'

CHAPTER NINE

'Madre del Dio.'

The words escaped on a whisper of breath when all Gio wanted to do was rage and swear at the man who had done this to Jessica. He listened as she told him how she had been diagnosed with a seroconversion illness and although it was not his branch of medicine, he knew enough to understand that this was often the first sign of illness people had after they had been infected, when the body first produced antibodies to HIV.

'I had many of the usual symptoms...a fever, aching limbs, headache and a blotchy red rash...which could have been linked to a variety of conditions,' she explained, the matter-of-fact tone of her voice belied by the shadows in her eyes. 'It was such a shock and not something I had ever anticipated.'

'Of course not. You trusted the man you were about to marry,' Gio reasoned.

She nodded, and he tightened his hold as a fresh shudder went through her. 'I must be a really bad person because I can't forgive him—not just for what he did to me but I keep thinking about the unknown number of other women out there he infected, as well, and what they might be going through. I can't even feel sorry that he was diagnosed, too,' she whispered.

'No, no, no! You are not remotely a bad person! How can you think that?' Gio swore in Italian, wishing he could let Duncan know what he thought of him. 'You are an amazing woman, Jessica. Even struggling to come to terms with what has happened to you, through no fault of your own, your thoughts are still for other people. You have the generosity of spirit to worry about the women with whom your ex-fiancé—' he stumbled over the word, choked by his anger and disgust at the man '—had been unfaithful.'

'It wasn't their fault. I've no doubt he lied to them, too.'

'And now,' he made himself ask, needing to know so much but anxious not to stress her more, 'how are you? Are you taking medication?'

'I'm OK. And I'm not taking medication yet,' she told him, and the relief was immense. 'I have regular tests to monitor my CD4 cell count, which gives an idea of the strength of my immune system. And a viral load test, which can tell how active HIV is in the body. It's only if those levels reach a certain point that medication will be necessary. It's a big step to take because once started, you can't stop. I go to London twice a year to see a specialist,' she added, surprising him.

'Why London?'

'I went there first when I left Scotland. I trust Mr Jackson. When I moved to Cornwall, he agreed to keep seeing me.' Her smile was tired but brought some life back to her eyes. 'And I have Luca and the other doctors at the Penhally surgery who take care of day-to-day things.'

Gio was relieved she had someone so good caring for her. 'Was there no one giving you support at home? What about family and friends?' he asked, taken aback by her derisive, humourless laugh. Unease curled inside him.

'I was stupidly naïve and assumed that in this day and age people would be more informed and understanding,' she began with a shiver, shifting so that she was resting against his chest. 'But they weren't. I was so shocked by the negative reactions. Some people blanked me, some were openly hostile and abusive, making a big fuss if I touched them in any way, refusing to drink from a mug or eat off a plate I might have used in the canteen. Not one so-called friend or colleague stood by me.'

As he listened to Jessica outline some of the things people had said to her and what she had put up with once her diagnosis had become known, Gio's anger rocketed. It was disgraceful that people should be so ignorant and prejudiced. And it was hardly surprising after her experiences that she'd been stripped of her confidence, her self-esteem and her trust in people.

'My family were worse.'

'What happened, *fiamma*?' he asked softly, fearing her answer.

'Shocked and upset, I went home and told them the news. My father has always been a dour, strict man with rigid opinions. He disapproved of me living with Duncan before the wedding. He said…' Her fingers tightened on his and emotion turned her voice husky as she continued. 'He said it was all I deserved for living in sin, that I had brought shame on the family, and he disowned me. He turned me out with all my belongings and told me never to contact them again. He even had me barred from visiting my grandmother, who was bedridden in a nursing home by then. She was the only one who cared. She left me the money that helped me buy my cottage, but I never had the chance to see her again before she died and tell her I loved her.'

Her words ended on a sob and the tears she had been choking back escaped. She tried to pull away from him but he drew her trembling frame more fully against him and, wrapping her protectively in his arms, he held her tight, keeping her safe as she cried out the hurt and anger. After everything Duncan had done, and the reaction of those she'd considered friends, the cruel rejection by the family meant to love and care for her must have been the ultimate betrayal and almost impossible to bear. Thinking of her alone and scared tore him apart.

He guessed she'd been bottling up the emotion for a long time and now it had been set free, like opening a dam and allowing everything backed up behind it to gush out. As he cradled her, he struggled to come to terms with the truth, the reality, the consequences...and with what her life must have been like these last four or more years.

His own eyes were moist and his heart hurt as he tried to comfort her while the storm ran its course. So many things now made sense. Her reluctance to touch and be touched, the absence of any close friendships, the lack of trust and the little habits at home like the supplements and washing her things separately. No wonder she had looked so hurt when he'd teased her about having a hygiene fetish. He smothered a groan. After all she had been through since being diagnosed, it was understandable she had developed a range of coping mechanisms.

When Jessica finally calmed, he eased back and cupped her face in his hands. Olive-green eyes were framed by tear-spiked lashes while her flawless, translucent skin was devoid of colour. Concerned for her, he dropped a light kiss on lips that still trembled.

'Don't go anywhere. I'll be back in a couple of minutes. OK?'

Her nod was weary, almost defeated. Reluctantly, he released her. He didn't want to leave her, even for a moment, but he had a few things to do. When he returned, having undressed as far as his boxer shorts, prepared his bedroom with jasmine-scented candles and turned down the bed, she was sitting motionless where he had left her, her eyes closed.

'Jessica?'

Long lashes flickered then he was staring into her eyes. She blinked, her gaze skimming over him, a flush bringing some warmth back to her pale face. Her reaction amused him, momentarily easing his concern for her.

'Hi.' He smiled as she swallowed and dragged her gaze back to his. 'Are you OK?'

She nodded, remaining silent until his next moved shocked her out of her torpor. 'Gio!' Her cry escaped as he scooped her off the bed and lifted her in his arms.

'Hold on,' he instructed.

'What are you doing?' Despite her protest, she wrapped her arms around his neck. 'Gio, I'm far too heavy.'

'Nonsense.'

He carried her from the room, only pausing long enough for her to switch out the light. Walking down the corridor, he went into his bedroom, set her gently on the bed and drew the duvet over her before walking round the other side and sliding in beside her. To his surprise and delight, she turned into his arms and burrowed into him. He stroked the glossy curls that spread across his chest, each indrawn breath fragranced with a teasing hint of her scent.

'Gio…' Her voice was soft and sleepy, and it still held the lingering legacy of the emotions that had ravaged her just a short while ago.

'Shh,' he soothed, relishing the feel of her feminine curves and the softness of her skin. 'It's very late and you've been through a lot. Sleep now. I'll keep you safe.'

It was Sunday afternoon and the closer they got to home, the more nervous Jess became. She knew what was going to happen. She wanted it. And yet she couldn't help but be as scared as she was excited. Gio, too, seemed preoccupied and edgy as the electric tension continued to build between them.

She thought back to the night before and everything that had happened after their return from the wedding and the most incredible kiss she'd ever experienced. Telling Gio how her life had been turned upside down following the HIV diagnosis had been so difficult, but he had been amazing, his supportive reaction in marked contrast to those she had encountered in the past. But now her shameful secret was out, nothing would ever be the same between them again.

Spending the night in Gio's arms had been wonderful. For the first time in a long, long while she hadn't felt alone. And she wished she could wake up with him every morning, especially if it meant experiencing the delicious caress of his hands and his lips on her bare skin.

'I want more than anything to make love to you,' he'd told her, the throaty roughness of his voice resonating along her nerve-endings. 'I have since the day I first saw you, and I've wanted you more each day since.'

'Gio,' she'd murmured in confusion, hardly daring to believe that the truth hadn't put him off. He may have held her through the night, but...

'Nothing you have told me changes anything—I only marvel more at what an incredible woman you are,' he'd continued, his words bringing a lump to her throat. 'Unfortunately, right now I have no protection.'

She had masked her disappointment. 'OK.'

'But we can improvise.' The tone of his voice and his sexy smile had sent a tremor right through her. 'We can't make love fully now but I want to bring you pleasure and show what a special and desirable woman you are.'

And bring her pleasure he had. Oh, my! A shaky little breath escaped, warmth stealing through her as her body tingled at the memory of his kisses and caresses. How delicious to wake up like that every day. But she knew it was a fantasy. She was getting too far ahead of herself.

They'd spent the day doing normal things at the house, having a late breakfast and playing with the kittens before going to see how things were progressing at her cottage. The main supporting structure had been replaced and the thatcher was well on the way to creating a beautiful new roof.

Knowing that the cottage would soon be habitable again and discovering that Gio had arranged for the fields to be cleared and the fences renewed in readiness for Faye's menagerie had brought mixed emotions. Pleasure at seeing the cottage come back to life. Surprise and gratitude at Gio's generosity. But anxiety at the knowledge she would soon have to leave his house—and him. What would happen then? Gio was adamant about sharing responsibility for the animals but how would that work? And what did it mean for them?

Next, they'd spent a couple of hours on the boat, speeding across the waves. She'd felt so close to him and, now her secret was out, she hadn't had to fight to avoid physical contact. Gio had taken every opportunity to hug and kiss her. But her nervousness had returned when they had stopped at the supermarket on the way back to the house and condoms had been added to the items in their basket.

Feeling jumpy and on edge, not at all sure what to do or say, Jess helped Gio put the shopping away and then played with Dickens and Kipling for a while before feeding them. As they curled up to sleep in a tangle of limbs, she felt even more anxious.

'I think I'll go and have a shower,' she murmured, feeling as gauche and awkward as a teenager.

Gio looked up and smiled. 'OK.'

He appeared so calm that had he not bought the condoms she would have wondered if she had dreamed everything that had happened when she had woken up that morning. And what she was anticipating would happen later. Unsettled, she went upstairs and, after undressing and tying up her wayward curls to keep her hair from getting wet, she stepped into the shower, welcoming the feel of the hot barbs on skin that still felt alive and sensitive from the caresses of Gio's hands and mouth.

Eyes closed, she tipped her head back and reached

out a hand for the chocolate-scented cleanser she loved to use, a squeal of shocked surprise escaping as, instead of encountering the plastic tube she was expecting, her fingers met male skin. Every part of her trembled as he stepped up behind her, the front of his body pressing against the back of hers, making her supremely aware of his arousal.

She heard the snap of the top on the tube she'd been reaching for and a moment later felt the touch of hands that were slick with foamy cleanser. He began at her shoulders, working slowly and sensually down her back, lingering at her rear before sweeping down her legs in long, caressing strokes that turned her knees to jelly. One arm wrapped around her waist in support, and she leaned back against him, feeling boneless and on fire as he turned his attention to the front of her.

Jess bit her lip to prevent herself crying out as he devoted time to her breasts, the exquisite torture almost too much to bear. It had been so long since she had been touched like this…and yet *never* like this because the kind of explosive passion and intense desire she shared with Gio was way beyond anything she had ever experienced before.

When she thought she would expire from the pleasure of his touch, Gio turned the cleanser over to her and allowed her the same freedom to explore and enjoy his body. She turned round on legs that felt decidedly unsteady, the blood racing through her veins as she drank in the sight of him. It was impossible not to be struck by the masculine beauty of his body, the broad shoulders and the perfectly toned muscles of his arms and torso that made her mouth water. A brush of dark hair in the middle of his chest cast a shadow on olive-toned skin, tapering to a narrow line that her gaze avidly followed down over his abdomen and navel to where it nested the potent symbol of his maleness.

She refocused on his handsome face, seeing the needy desire, which mirrored her own, in his deeply blue eyes. Feeling both shy and bold at the same time, she began her own lingering caress of his body, working the foamy, chocolate-scented suds across his skin, hearing his indrawn breath and feeling the tremor and ripple of muscle as he reacted to her touch.

With an impatient exclamation his hands closed on her upper arms, drawing her back up and into a searing kiss. She clung to him, kissing him back with equal ardour, savouring the feel of wet warm skin under her hands and the sexy, sinful taste of him in her mouth. They were both breathing heavily by the time they broke apart. Gio snapped off the water before reaching for a towel and wrapping her up in it. With evident impatience he briskly ran another towel over himself. Tossing it aside, he took her hand and led her down the corridor to his bedroom, her legs so rubbery she didn't think she could walk.

Some of her anxiety returned as she entered the room with him and saw the huge bed standing ready and waiting, the duvet turned back, the generous pillows plumped up. She knew how luxurious and incredibly sexy the gunmetal-grey sheets felt against her skin. And within moments she was experiencing them again as Gio gave her a gentle rub down with the towel before removing it and tumbling them both into bed.

Excitement and tension vied for prominence. She could feel the heat of his body even though he wasn't quite touching her. Smiling, he gently removed the pins from her hair and fanned the tresses out on the pillow.

'Do you think you are the only one who is nervous, *fiamma*?' he asked, his throaty, accented voice sounding even more sexy than usual.

Surprised, she met his gaze. 'You're nervous, too?'

Her question was met with a wry laugh. 'I listen to some of the young doctors talking in the scrub room and the canteen, discussing their conquests, and I realise what an oddity I must seem for having slept only with Sofia.'

'Then I'm odd, too, because I've only ever had one relationship before,' she told him. 'And, to me, the fact that you have never been the kind of man to sleep around is a major strength, not a weakness. You are loyal and true. And you haven't played Russian roulette with your own health or anyone else's.'

She thought of Duncan, of how he had cheated on her, and his cavalier disregard for himself, let alone her or the other women. Gio was a treasure and it was the very quality he considered an oddity that made her trust him. Had he been another Duncan, she would never be here now, on the cusp of giving herself to him in the most elemental of ways.

As if by instinct, they moved in unison to close the last of the gap between them, and the instant he touched her, the instant her lips met his, the doubts that had seemed so real for a moment dissolved into nothing. They needed no words because their bodies talked for them. Jess found she couldn't formulate a single coherent thought as Gio continued what he had begun that morning and in the shower, devoting his time and attention to her.

Every touch, every kiss, every caress of his fingers and brush of his lips and tongue built the pleasure layer by layer. She writhed against him, her body turning molten as his mouth worked down the column of her throat, setting every nerve tingling and every particle of skin on fire. He trailed down the valley between her breasts, bypassing flesh that yearned so badly for his attention and continuing down to her navel. She hadn't known she was so sensitive there but the tantalising, teasing quest of his teeth and tongue had her body arching up to meet him, seeking more.

She must have spoken the word aloud because he chuckled, the huff of warm breath against her skin a subtle and teasing caress of its own. She moaned as he finally turned his attention to her breasts, the perfect pressure of his fingers driving her crazy.

'Gio, please,' she begged, craving the touches he teasingly denied her.

Relenting, his teeth gently grazed one sensitive nipple before his tongue salved the delicious sting. Then he sent her to the stratosphere as he took the peak into the warm cavern of his mouth. When she thought she couldn't bear it a moment longer he released his prize, turned his attention to its twin and began the exquisite torment all over again.

Impatient, her eager hands traced the muscular contours of his shoulders before working down his back, urging him closer. She wanted to explore and savour him as he was doing to her, but she was so close to the edge she couldn't wait a moment longer to know the joy of being united fully with him.

He took a moment to protect them and she pleaded with him not to wait any longer as he moved to make them one. She arched up to meet him, wrapping her legs around him, gasping his name at the delicious sensations as her body welcomed his and, finally, they were one.

'Jessica…'

'Yes. Please, Gio. Don't stop.'

She had never experienced anything as magical and special as making love with Gio. It was incredible, earth-shattering and she never wanted it to end. He murmured to her in Italian as they moved together in a rhythm as old as time. She abandoned herself to him completely, as he did to her, and the mix of exquisite tenderness and fiery passion she found with him was a devastating combination.

When the inevitable moment arrived, Jess clung to him, burying her face against him, breathing in his musky scent, calling his name as they drove each other over the edge to a shattering release. As she spun out of control, she didn't care if she never came down to earth again, just so long as she was with Gio.

Gio gazed at Jessica's sleeping form, the wild fire of her hair tossed across the pillow and a couple of tell-tale little marks on her otherwise flawless, silky-smooth skin following the intensely passionate night they had shared. It had been the most incredible experience, beyond any-thing he had imagined. And it had scared him.

He wasn't sure at exactly which moment during their sensual night together it had happened, but he had sud-denly known with surety and not much surprise that he loved her. It may have happened far more speedily but, as with Sofia, they had begun as friends first and fore-most. He and Sofia had been children and their emotions had evolved slowly, whereas with Jessica the friendship and the desire had hit in tandem.

The pain of losing Sofia had nearly killed him and he'd never imagined wanting another woman again. Then he had met Jessica. He not only wanted her in every way but he liked and respected her as a person and valued the special friendship they shared. So why was he feeling so unsettled? Things had happened so fast, he had fallen so deep so quickly and he knew that if he tied himself to her and anything happened, he would never recover a second time.

Could he take the risk on Jessica's health? All he knew was that he couldn't face the prospect of burying another woman he loved. It was a possibility he couldn't ignore when making a decision that would affect both their futures.

Waking up alone had been unnerving and when she went downstairs and found Gio making coffee in the kitchen, Jess's unease increased. He greeted her with a smile, but she sensed a change in him. He was on edge, distant. And when he backed off physically, moving away when she would have stepped in for a hug, a cold chill went through her.

'What's wrong?' she asked, fear building as he failed to meet her gaze.

'Nothing. I...'

'Gio?'

He ran a hand through his hair, a characteristic sign of agitation. 'I'm just not sure what to think about this. It's all happened so quickly.'

'You regret it.' Her heart sank.

'No! Of course not. Neither of us was expecting

this. The connection was there from the first and our friendship is special and important to me,' he explained, his expression sombre, and Jess sensed a 'but' coming. 'But—' Jess allowed herself a humourless smile '—maybe we should slow things down, take some time. I'd never considered having a new relationship. I'm not sure I'm ready. Especially after what happened with Sofia.'

Everything in her screamed in protest. 'I see.'

'I need to be sure, Jessica. Not of you but of me. Losing Sofia nearly killed me and I can't go through anything like that again,' he finished, emotion heavy in his voice.

The awful thing was that she understood. She couldn't argue against his words and the chance of something happening was greater with her with the HIV hanging over her head than it was with another woman. Wrapping her arms around herself, she tried to hold everything together, to not let him see how deeply the rejection had wounded her. Because that was what it felt like. And in that moment, the truth hit home with devastating force… she loved him. In every way and with every part of her being.

Gio had said their friendship was important and apparently he considered things would go on as before, but Jess felt as if part of her was dying inside because friendship was never going to be enough now.

'I'm going to Italy at the weekend for my parents' fortieth wedding anniversary,' he reminded her, thrusting his hands into the pockets of his jeans.

Her heart breaking, Jess struggled to keep her voice as normal as possible. 'My cottage should be ready by then, so I'll move out.'

'I didn't mean that.' He frowned as if her leaving was not something he had considered.

'Living here was only meant to be temporary,' she pointed out, knowing she couldn't stay with him and not *be with* him. 'It's for the best.'

His frown deepened, confusion and disappointment mingling in his intensely blue eyes. 'If that's what you want.'

It wasn't what she wanted at all, but she didn't see how she could do anything else if what she really wanted—Gio himself—was not an option.

The next few days were like purgatory, and by the time Friday arrived, Jess was at breaking point and not at all sure how much longer she could hold on. Pretending to accept Gio's decision to return things to a platonic footing had involved the performance of her life. She hadn't been able to sleep, lying in a bed a short distance down the corridor from him, wanting more than anything to be in his arms. But it wasn't going to happen and the sooner she faced that and rebuilt her battered defences, the better it would be.

He went to Italy on the Friday and, after the loneliest night in the house without him, Jess tried to hold back the tears as she packed her things into her car and then put Dickens and Kipling into their basket for the short journey to her cottage. The kittens would miss Gio almost as much as she would, she reflected sadly. He'd been so good with them. She choked back the emotion as she recalled the way he had lain on the floor, chuckling as the two growing kittens had romped over him. And the time she'd come in late one Friday night after her session of volunteering at the Samaritans to find Gio lying asleep on the sofa, the kittens curled up on his chest in a tangle.

Feeling numb inside, she secured the house and drove away from it, wondering if it was for the last time. However much she hurt, she couldn't blame Gio. She knew how devastating Sofia's death had been and it was understandable that he was wary of embarking on another relationship, especially with someone like her. She was well at the moment, and she would do all she could to stay that way. As Luca and her specialist, Mr Jackson, frequently told her, there was no reason why she couldn't live into old age with very few problems at all. But anyone would be wary of taking on that uncertainty, especially someone who had experienced what Gio had.

No, Gio was not to blame. It was her own fault. She'd hoped for too much…had dared to dream and to believe in the impossible. Now she had to pick up the pieces because fairy-tale, happy-ever-after endings didn't happen to people like her.

'Why did you stay the night with me?'

It was one of the things Megan had most dreaded Josh ever asking and it had played over and over in her head since the day in A and E when they had done the unthinkable and faced their past.

Aside from not wanting to acknowledge the truth to herself, she certainly didn't want to tell *Josh* the answer to his question. To admit that she had been drawn to him from the first moment she had seen him and that, despite his reputation, she had yearned for him for years like some lovestruck teenager was beyond embarrassing.

Between medical school and caring for her grandmother, she'd had no time for a social life, so going to a party on New Year's Eve had been a real treat. Wearing an exquisite dress, her hair and make-up done, she'd felt like Cinderella. Only she'd been granted a bit longer before the spell had been broken…not at midnight, for her, but lunchtime the following day.

For the first time, Josh had approached her. Given his undivided attention, she'd melted like an ice cube under the noon sun. He'd made her feel special. Surprisingly, they had talked and talked, and she'd found him so much *more* than she had ever expected. He'd been funny, he'd listened as if what she'd had to say had mattered, he'd sympathised about her grandmother, and he had confided in her, too. The night had ended in the inevitable way, the sexual chemistry and tension between them impossible to resist.

Megan closed her eyes and tried to push away the painful memories. She had believed in her heart that what they had shared had been more than one night. Much more. Or she never would have gone home with Josh in the first place. They'd connected. On every level. She hadn't imagined it. And it *hadn't* just been the sex, amazing as that had been. She knew Josh had been spooked by their closeness as he'd freely admitted that he'd revealed things to her that he'd never told to anyone else. He'd told her she was different. He'd been so genuine. And she'd believed him. Had *wanted* to believe him. So badly.

They had finally, reluctantly, parted but only after Josh had made love to her one last time and had made her promise to meet him that evening. It had been noon when she had rushed home to her grandmother feeling a mix of guilt and euphoria. The hours with Josh had been the most amazing of her life and she hadn't been able to wait to see him again. So when he had stood her up, failing to meet at the agreed time and place, she had been confused and upset.

When she had finally seen him several worrying days later, he had blanked her completely, laughing with his friends, ignoring her as if their night had never happened. She'd been devastated. Even now she could remember how she had felt...used, cheap, stupid, incredibly naïve and very, very hurt.

Megan shivered in reaction as the memories of that lonely, frightening time and what had followed over the next months flowed through her. Ashamed, she had withdrawn and hidden herself away. And then she had discovered that she was pregnant. And *so* scared.

Weeks later she'd experienced a searing pain and had remembered nothing until she had woken up in hospital to learn that Josh had been part of the team who had not only taken away her baby but had performed a hysterectomy, depriving her of ever becoming a mother. She'd been devastated, the sense of loss and grief overwhelming.

Eight years on, listening to his explanation and seeing his own emotion had given her much to think about. The hurt remained, both at his rejection and at the loss of her baby. But while there was much she was still angry with him about, she no longer blamed him for the miscarriage or the lengths taken to save her life.

Despite their past and all that lay between them— including the very real presence of his wife—the chemistry remained. When they worked together in A and E, they often knew what the other was thinking or doing without the need for words.

She knew he was out of bounds. She knew what had happened the last time the chemistry had led her astray. And she couldn't forget the way Josh had rejected and betrayed her. So discovering that she was still vulnerable to him, still drawn to him and still unable to get him out of her mind, frightened her.

If she showed the slightest weakness she feared what might happen. And only heartache would lie ahead. She had learned her lesson the hard way the last time round. So why did she have the terrible feeling that history was going to repeat itself?

CHAPTER TEN

LATE on Sunday afternoon Jess walked along the surfing beach east of Penhally's harbour, lost in thought. It had been another beautiful day, but the air was cooling as the sun began its slow descent towards the horizon. Pushing her hands into the pockets of the floaty skirt that fell to her knees, Jess sighed. There was no escaping her thoughts. Thoughts that were stuck in one place and refused to budge. With Gio.

He would be back tonight and tomorrow she would see him at work. She wasn't sure how to continue pretending that nothing had happened or behave normally, accepting they could only ever be friends. *Could* she be friends when she wanted so much more? It was a question that had pounded in her head all week and she still didn't know the answer. All she did know was that she had missed him terribly and faced with a choice of never seeing him again, then, as sad and pathetic as it sounded, any part of Gio was better than no Gio at all. Even if she was dying inside. Because she had fallen in love with a man who had experienced such heartache that he couldn't take a risk on someone whose future could be as uncertain as hers.

As she neared the end of the promontory on which

the lighthouse, coastguard office and St Mark's church stood, she heard shouting and laughter, and looked up to see a couple of teenagers messing about on the rocks. She was about to turn round and retrace her steps back along the beach when the tone of the teenage voices changed and she watched in horror as one of the boys lost his footing and crashed face down amongst the rocks.

Jess ran towards the scene of the accident, as did a few other people who were further away on the beach and up on the promontory. The teenager's friend was now silent and standing motionless in shock and terror as he gazed down at his stricken comrade. Reaching the rocky outcrop, and glad she was wearing trainers, Jess began to climb.

The lower rocks were slippery, and several times she lost her own footing, resulting in umpteen cuts and bruises, but she kept going as rapidly as she could, fearing what she would find when she reached the boy. Moving towards him, she misjudged a step and fell heavily. Pain seared through her foot, leg and side, and she felt the hot stickiness of blood flowing down her calf. Ignoring it, she limped and scrambled awkwardly the rest of the way to the boy.

His injuries were worse than she'd feared. Frightened eyes stared up at her, and she struggled to mask her shock so as not to distress him further. His face had borne the brunt of his fall and, along with a lot of bleeding and considerable soft-tissue damage, she could tell that his jaw, nose and one cheekbone were all broken.

Instinct took over as she did a quick assessment. There were no other apparent injuries but that hardly mattered because there was one serious, immediate and life-threatening problem…the boy was finding it increasingly impossible to breathe.

'Has anyone called an ambulance?' she shouted to the small crowd that was gathering on the rocks above her.

'Yes,' someone called. 'ETA at least twelve minutes.'

Jess swore. They couldn't wait that long. 'I need a sharp knife—preferably a scalpel. And something like a small piece of tube, or a drinking straw. Anything narrow and hollow. He can't breathe and I have to help him,' she shouted up.

'The lighthouse and coastguard station both have full first-aid kits. I'll get one of those,' the man called down to her.

'Please hurry! There isn't much time.'

Hoping the man understood the urgency, and that the kit would contain the things she needed, Jess returned her attention to the boy and tried to talk soothingly to him as she continued her assessment. With all the blood, fragments of bone and the rapidly swelling tissues around his face, there was no way she could clear or maintain an airway. It was no surprise when he began to panic as he failed to draw oxygen into his lungs and started to lose consciousness.

It seemed an eternity before the man reappeared above her and began the dangerous climb down. His exclamation of shock when he saw the boy was understandable but Jess didn't have time to do anything but take the first-aid kit from him. She winced at the shaft of pain in her side as she dragged the heavy bag close, but she pushed her own discomfort aside and opened the kit, giving heartfelt thanks that it was an extensive and well-stocked one.

Gathering together the things she needed, she told her unknown companion what she was doing. 'I have to create an opening in his throat so he can breathe. We can't wait for the ambulance. What's your name?'

'Charlie.'

'I'm Jess. I...' She paused and sucked in a breath. 'I'm a doctor,' she told him, speaking aloud the words she had not used for four years. 'Have you got a mobile phone, Charlie?'

'Yes, right here.'

'Phone 999 and tell them we need the air ambulance, too,' she requested, knowing that if what she attempted was successful, the boy would need to get to hospital as fast as possible.

As Charlie made the call, Jess focused on the task ahead. Nervousness gripped her. Shutting out the comments from the small crowds on the rocks above her and the beach below, she steadied herself and called on all her former training. She was scared, but she'd done this a few times before. She could do it now. She had to if the boy wasn't to suffocate before the ambulance arrived. Closing her eyes, she did a quick mental run-through of the emergency procedure she had never expected to be called on to perform again.

After using an antiseptic wipe on the boy's throat, she draped some gauze around the site and then she took out the sterile, single-use blade that was in the kit. She had no local anaesthetic available, but with his consciousness level low he probably didn't need it. Unsure how aware he was, she told him what she needed to do, talking through it as much to steady herself as him.

With the fingers of one hand she felt for the correct spot on the throat and, with her other hand, made a small vertical incision through the skin. Identifying the cricothyroid membrane, she made a horizontal cut through it, careful to ensure that she didn't damage the cartilage. With no proper tracheal spreader available she had to improvise again, and she used the handle of a small knife she found in the kit, inserting it into the incision and turning it so that it created a small passage. Already there was a life-saving flow of air in and out as the boy's lungs inflated and reinflated.

'Could you cut me some strips of tape, Charlie?'

As he obliged, Jess cut a piece of plastic tube to the right length and, with great care so as not to damage any cartilage or the vocal cords, angled it and slid it into the makeshift passageway. It was a temporary measure but it would keep the boy alive and his airway open until the paramedics arrived. Taking the strips Charlie handed her, she secured the tube in place.

'Well done, Jess!' Charlie praised when she had finished, giving a thumbs-up to the crowd on the promontory and beach, who broke into spontaneous applause.

Jess sat back and let out a shaky breath. 'Thanks.'

It had only taken two or three minutes to complete the procedure and yet she felt weary and quite unsteady. Taking the boy's hand, she continued to monitor his breathing, relieved that he was awake. She gently wiped away the blood from around his eyes—brown eyes that were now open again and staring at her with a mix of relief and fright and pain.

'The ambulance will be here very soon,' she reassured him, rewarded when his fingers tightened on hers.

He was going to need an excellent maxillofacial surgeon for reconstruction, Jess reflected, her thoughts interrupted by the sound of an approaching siren, and relief flowed through her as the ambulance arrived. Charlie moved the first-aid kit out of the way, then showed the paramedics the best way down the rocks. Jess recognised both men, who greeted her by name, their surprise evident as she debriefed them and they realised the role she had played in events.

Things passed in a blur after that. Charlie left, but Jess remained where she was, answering the occasional question but mostly watching the paramedics work. It wasn't long before they were joined by the medics from the air ambulance and she had to give her debrief over again. Once the boy was stabilised, volunteers were needed to help extricate the stretcher from the difficult location, but before long he was off the rocks and on his way to St Piran's in the helicopter.

'Now, then, Jess, our heroine of the day, what about you?' Stuart asked, squatting down in front of her while Mark cleared up their things and invited the more nosy and persistent onlookers to disperse.

'Me?' Jess frowned. 'I'm fine.'

He chuckled. 'I hardly think so, love. You're pale as a ghost and your leg is a mess,' he pointed out.

'I'd forgotten all about it,' she admitted, so focused had she been on what she needed to do.

'You were a bit busy, weren't you?' His grin was infectious. 'Are you hurt anywhere else?'

'Just some cuts and bruises. I bashed my side and twisted my foot when I fell. It's nothing. I'll clean up at home,' she assured him, anxiety setting in at the prospect of either Stuart or Mark treating her.

Pulling on a fresh pair of protective gloves, Stuart sat back and looked at her. 'That's a deep cut, Jess. You've lost a fair bit of blood and it's going to need stitching. And that's without getting the other things checked out.'

Her anxiety increasing, Jess bit her lip. She wished she could dismiss her injuries and refuse treatment, but looking at her leg she could see that the wound was bad and not something she would advise anyone else to try and take care of alone. As the adrenalin that had sustained her while waiting for the ambulance wore off, her foot and her ribs were also becoming increasingly painful and she feared she might have broken at least one bone. All of which meant she was going to have to tell Stuart the truth.

Fighting back an uncharacteristic welling up of tears, she sucked in a ragged breath. 'Stuart, I...' She hesitated, frightened what would happen when he knew.

'What's wrong, Jess?' he prompted, his concern evident.

'You need to double-glove,' she told him, her voice unsteady, her lashes lowering so that she wouldn't see the expression on his face. 'I'm HIV positive.'

A few seconds of silence followed and she felt sick as she waited for the inevitable reaction to her admission. An errant tear escaped and landed on her cheek. It was Stuart's hand that reached out to wipe it away and she glanced up, wide-eyed with surprise to see nothing but understanding and compassion in the forty-year-old father-of-three's hazel eyes.

'Don't you worry, Jess, love. We'll take good care of you.'

His kindness and easy acceptance, so at odds with

her earlier experiences—apart from Gio, of course—brought a fresh welling up of emotion. As Stuart set about dressing her leg, Jess struggled to push thoughts of Gio to the back of her mind. She wished more than anything that he was there with her now. But he wasn't. She was on her own. Just as she had been these last four years.

Before she knew it, they were setting off on the thirty-minute drive from Penhally to St Piran, arriving a long time after the air ambulance had deposited their casualty. Stuart and Mark were wonderful, as was Ben Carter, into whose experienced, caring and understanding hands they delivered her.

Supportive and reassuring, Ben guarded her confidentiality and refused to make an issue of her status. By the time she had been X-rayed—thankfully there proved to be no breaks—and returned to A and E to have the deep cut on her leg stitched, her other cuts and grazes cleaned and a supportive bandage put on her swollen, painful foot, she was feeling tired and woozy. The antibiotics and pain medication she'd been given didn't help.

Dismissing the nurse who had waited with her, Ben drew up a chair, sat down and sent her a warm smile. 'I know you wanted news. The boy's name is Will. He's in Theatre and has the best of chances, thanks to you. You saved his life today, Jess. Care to tell me how you did it?' he asked, signing off her notes and closing the file.

Her defences lowered by all that had happened, not just with Will and her own injury but the deep pain of Gio's rejection and withdrawal, she found herself pouring the whole story out to Ben.

'Surgery's loss is St Piran's gain,' he told her a while later when her flow of words had ended.

'Thank you.'

'Does Gio know? Do you want me to call him?'

The two questions brought a fresh threat of tears. 'Yes, he knows,' she admitted, trying to steady her voice before she continued, forcing out the words. 'But don't call him. He's in Italy. And we're just friends.'

'Friends?' Ben raised a sceptical eyebrow.

'You heard about his wife?' she asked. When Ben nodded, she continued. 'He's not ready for a new relationship. Even if he was, it's too much for him to take on someone like me.'

'I wouldn't give up on him too quickly, Jess.'

She appreciated Ben's kindness but she had little hope left in fairy-tales. Resting her head back, feeling very tired, she sighed. 'Can I go home?'

'Not for a while, especially as you'll be on your own once you get there,' he added brushing aside her half-hearted protest.

A knock on the door curbed further conversation and senior staff nurse Ellen came in. Although she smiled, it was clear that something was bothering her and, before she closed the door, Jess heard the sound of some sort of commotion going on somewhere in the department.

'I'm sorry to interrupt,' Ellen apologised. 'Ben, we have a problem out here. Can you come?'

'Yes, of course. Rest here for a while and try not to worry about anything, Jess. I'll be back shortly to see you,' he promised, giving her hand a squeeze before pushing back the chair and rising to his feet.

'Thanks, Ben.'

'Is there anything I can get for you, love?' Ellen

asked, taking a moment to fuss with the sheet and pillows and make sure she was comfortable.

Feeling tired and washed out, Jess managed a smile. 'No, thanks. I'm fine.'

As they left the room, leaving her alone, Jess closed her eyes. It was one thing to tell her not to worry, but she was finding it impossible when her thoughts were fixed firmly on Gio. Despite thinking she could never trust a man again, in such a short time she had fallen irrevocably in love. But he couldn't feel the same about her and now, when she most needed his arms around her, he wasn't there. Ben had told her not to give up, but why would Gio want someone who was living with a condition that could change at any moment and drastically reduce her life expectancy, causing him to lose someone else?

She'd taken a huge risk, opening her heart and allowing Gio into her life, and all too briefly she'd experienced a piece of heaven before it had been ripped away from her again. She had no idea what the future held in store. After years of uncertainty, she had found a place where she felt at home and could settle. Was that now all to change because of Gio?

As much as he'd enjoyed his couple of days back home in Italy, and especially celebrating his parents' fortieth wedding anniversary, Gio continued to feel edgy and unsettled. For once it was nothing to do with returning to a place that reminded him of Sofia. His disquiet was all due to Jessica. Within hours he would be flying back to the UK and driving to the house he had shared with her in St Piran these last weeks. Knowing that she wouldn't be there made that return a dismal prospect.

'Something is troubling you, *figlio*.'

Gio looked up as his father joined him on the terrace and he gave a wry smile, unsurprised by the older man's insight. 'I'm fine, *Papà*.'

'Tell me about his woman.'

'What woman?' Gio prevaricated, shifting uncomfortably.

'You said you might be bringing a friend this weekend,' he reminded, 'but you came alone.'

'I might have meant a male friend.'

His father chuckled. 'You might. But you didn't. My guess is that you were referring to the woman who has been staying with you. The woman responsible for bringing you back to life these last weeks, bringing laughter and happiness back to your eyes.'

Gio sighed, somewhat stunned by his father's words. And by the realisation, the truth, of how much Jessica had changed him in the short time he had known her. He leaned against the railing and gazed out at the familiar Piedmont countryside. It was home—and yet now his heart felt as if it belonged elsewhere.

'Gio?'

Turning round, he pulled up a chair next to his father. 'I think I've made a big mistake, *Papà*.'

It had not been his intention to unburden himself, but now he found himself telling his father all about Jessica—and his dilemma.

'*Figlio*, you have never lacked courage. Do not start doubting yourself and your feelings now,' his father advised when he had finally run out of words.

'What do you mean?' Gio asked with a frown, running the fingers of one hand through his hair.

'Tell me,' his father asked, leaning forward and

resting his elbows on his knees, his gaze direct, 'would you have forgone the life you had with Sofia if you had known in advance that you would lose her when you did?'

A flash of anger flared within him at the question. 'Of course not!'

'That is what I thought.' His father smiled and although his tone gentled, his words lost none of their impact. 'Yet now you risk throwing away this second chance for love and happiness because you fear that you will one day lose Jessica, too.'

'*Papà...*'

His father gestured with one hand to silence him. 'Jessica is clearly a very special woman and she has become very important to you. You love her, I can see it in your eyes and hear it in your voice when you speak of her, and yet you're holding back. I know the pain and heartache you suffered when Sofia died. We all miss her. What you had together was so rare and so special. Few of us are blessed with that kind of happiness *once* in a lifetime, let alone *twice*,' the older man pointed out with a shake of his head.

In the brief pause that followed, the words sank in and Gio reflected on just how lucky he had been. He looked up as his father rested a hand on his shoulder and continued.

'We are all going to die at some time. What is important is what we do with the time we have. You have made us so proud, *figlio*, not only with your career and the work you do in Sofia's name but also because of the person you are. From all you have told me of her, your Jessica is a rare woman, and not one who would ever now trust herself to a man lightly. Yet she has trusted herself to *you*. Are you going to let her down? Are you going to let fear turn you away from love and the many years you could have together?'

The questions hit him full force, shocking him, but his father had not yet finished with him.

'Sofia would be so angry with you, Gio. She wanted you to live, to be happy, to love. Now you have found someone worthy of you, someone who has brought so much to your life. Don't throw that away, *figlio*,' he pleaded softly. 'You have our blessing, and Ginetta's, too,' he added, referring to Sofia's mother, who remained part of their family. 'You deserve new love and happiness. So does Jessica. Follow your heart...go back to the place that has become your home and show the woman who has given you so much the kind of man I know you to be.'

Hours later everything his father said still resonated in his head. It was early on Monday morning but he had given up trying to sleep. He had driven past Jessica's cottage before coming home from the airport but her car had not been there and it was clear no one was in. When he had also been unable to reach her by phone, unease had set in. Where was she?

Now he stared out of the window, seeing nothing but the darkness. There was also darkness inside himself. The house had felt cold and stark and lonely without Jessica, as he had feared it would. And so had he. All the joy and fun and warmth had left it with her departure. A departure he could blame on no one but himself.

He pressed one palm to the hollow ache in his chest. He had been so blind, so stupid. How could he have ever believed that he could live for the rest of his life in a vacuum? He hadn't been living at all, only existing. It was Jessica who had brought meaning back to his world again and had made him want to embrace life in every way.

Leaning his forehead against the coolness of the glass, he reflected on his mistakes. He had coaxed and cajoled Jessica into trusting him, caring for him, opening up to him. He'd taken what she had given him without properly considering just what it must have taken for her to trust, and exactly what that trust meant. She had shown such courage, while he had got cold feet. In doing so he had behaved as abominably as her ex-fiancé, her family and her former friends and colleagues had. How must Jessica be feeling now? *He* felt lower than low when he forced himself to consider what his withdrawal, his insistence that they could have nothing but friendship, must have done to her.

Dio!

How was he going to put things right?

Because he could see now with startling clarity that all his father had said was true. And he thought of Luca, who had been through a similar kind of loss as his own and who'd had the courage to let love back into his life again. He was a doctor, Gio chided himself. He knew that Jessica could fall ill tomorrow—but equally she could live a long and normal lifespan, keeping fit and well. Given the right care and precautions, even having a healthy child free of HIV was not the impossibility she believed it to be. Whatever she wished, he would support her all the way.

No one knew what the future held in store, just as his father and Luca had said. And facing the rest of his life alone was no longer the answer he had once thought. He could not guard himself from hurt without denying himself all the joys. And he knew now, after such a short time without Jessica, that he didn't want to waste any more time alone. Whether they had five years or fifty years, he wanted to share every moment with her. If she would forgive him and allow him a second chance.

Jessica had trusted him in the most elemental way and he had let her down. The knowledge cut him to the quick. In the face of her bravery he had been nothing but a coward. Were he to be lucky enough to win her back, he would spend the rest of their lives together proving to her that she was loved and cherished. Going downstairs, he made coffee and stepped outside into the coolness of the pre-dawn air, lost in his thoughts.

Along with the album Sofia had made of their lives had been a final letter for him. He carried it with him always, with her photo, next to his heart. He knew it word for word as she told him how much she loved him, that every moment had been worth it because they had been together, how she respected him and supported him.

'You must go on with your career, Cori, and with your life. Grieve for me, but not for too long. We have been so blessed and had so much more in twenty-two years than many people have in a whole lifetime. I know you, *amore mio*. And I beg you to move on, not to stay alone and sad for the rest of your life. I want you to be happy, fulfilled, cared for. You have so much love to give. Open your heart, Cori. For me. I will always be with you and will always love you. Look up at the night sky and the brightest star will be me smiling down on you, wishing you the best of everything and for a special woman to love you as I love you.'

His throat tight with emotion, he turned his gaze up to

the sky, finding the brightest star. He thought of Sofia's words, of her wish for him, her blessing, and realised he was letting her down by refusing to accept all life had to offer him. Had their places been reversed, he would have wanted the same for her...that she would find someone to care for her, who would make her happy. And his courageous, spirited Sofia would grieve, would never forget, but would face life with her customary bravery. Just as Jessica was doing in her own way, making a whole new life for herself after being so badly betrayed and left to cope with the devastation alone. He owed it to Sofia, to Jessica and to himself to step back into life.

He looked back at the star, opening his heart, knowing Sofia would always be there, that he would never forget and would always love her, but that there was room and a special place for Jessica, too. It was time. For a moment it seemed as if the star glowed even brighter, filling him with a sense of peace. As dawn broke, the stars fading as the sky slowly lightened, bringing a rosy glow to the magnificent Cornish coastline, Gio knew what he had to do.

CHAPTER ELEVEN

'OH, MY God.' Jess felt her whole world shattering into tiny pieces as she stared in horrified disbelief at the local newspaper. This couldn't be happening. 'How? Why?'

Ben sat solemn-faced beside her, appearing tired and drawn, as if he hadn't slept in the hours since she'd last seen him. 'I'm sorry, Jess. We tried to stop it.'

Fighting back tears and a terrible sense of doom, she re-examined the lurid headline emblazoned in large letters across the front page…

HOSPITAL HEROINE HAS HIV!

The night was a blur. She'd fallen asleep in A and E, knocked out by the medication and emotional exhaustion. 'We don't normally have staff sleeping in the department overnight but we made an exception for you,' Josh had teased her when he'd checked her over before the night shift ended.

When Ben had come back on duty, she'd discovered that the disturbance he'd been called to had been caused by Kennie Vernon, a reporter on the *St Piran Gazette*, known as 'Vermin' for his unpleasant methods and his motto of never allowing the truth to spoil a good story.

She'd met him once when he'd delved unsuccessfully into the background of a patient in her care, and he'd left an unfavourable impression. Short and stout, his greasy black hair worn in a narrow ponytail, he had a goatee beard, beady brown eyes and a shifty nature.

'One of the bystanders in Penhally overheard you telling the paramedics about the HIV and informed Kennie. The bastard ran with that angle of the story.' Ben's anger and disgust were evident. 'He came poking around A and E. I threw him out. You were sleeping, so Josh and I decided to keep you here. We didn't want you going home alone or risk you running into Kennie.'

Jess wrapped her arms around herself, unable to stop shaking. 'What am I going to do?'

'You told me about the appalling way you were treated when you were first diagnosed, but that isn't going to happen here,' he reassured her, but she lacked belief.

'Right.'

Ben took her hand. 'You'll be surprised, Jess. I'm not, because I know you are loved and respected. There may be one or two idiots, but ninety-nine percent of the hospital are supporting you. We've had endless calls sending you good wishes and they're continuing to come in.'

Jess didn't know what to say.

'We took the liberty of making some arrangements on your behalf,' he continued, and nervousness fluttered in her stomach.

'What arrangements?'

'Flora wanted to help. She said she held a spare key for your cottage in case of an emergency?' Jess nodded, trying to take everything in. 'Knowing you'd worry, she's picked up your kittens and will look after them for as long as you need.'

'Thank you,' she murmured, surprised but relieved.

'Your car remains where you left it in Penhally, so you'll need a lift to pick it up, but Megan met Flora at your cottage and collected some things you might need.'

Fresh tears pricked her eyes. For someone who seldom cried, she could have filled a swimming pool this last week. She didn't ask, but the person she most wanted to know about, and to see, was Gio. He'd be back from Italy. He might even be in the hospital, she realised, glancing at her watch, shocked by the time. What would he think? She felt sick with worry.

When Ben left, Jess gingerly slipped out of bed, thankful for the adjacent shower room that meant she didn't have to wander down the corridor in the unflattering hospital gown she was wearing. After a wash, she sat on the bed, feeling emotionally and physically battered as she wondered what to do.

'Where is she?'

Jess heard Megan's anxious question from outside and someone's voice mumble in reply. She barely had a moment to compose herself before her friend rushed in, her face pale and tears spiking her eyelashes. Without uttering a word, Megan dropped a carrier bag on the bed and wrapped her in a hug.

'You silly, silly girl,' she admonished, halfway between a laugh and a sob. 'Oh, how I wish I'd known. I can't bear to think of you going through this alone.'

Megan's acceptance and support was overwhelming. Jess began to explain, her voice shaky and whisper soft, when Brianna arrived. She looked as worried and upset

as Megan. And, like Megan, Brianna's first instinct was
to hug her.

With her friends giving the caring support she had
never expected to know, Jess told them what she had
told Gio—about Duncan, her diagnosis, the prejudice,
ignorance and discrimination she'd encountered, and
being disowned by her family. They were all crying by
the time she had finished.

'I'd have been scared witless doing an emergency cri-
cothyroidotomy,' Megan admitted when the talk moved
on to the incident on the rocks and Jess's former career.
'I'm in awe at what you did.'

Brianna hugged her again. 'We all are. You're amazing, Jess. How far through your training were you?'

'I'd qualified and had begun a trauma rotation when I
was diagnosed. I wanted to be a surgeon but was advised
to find another career.'

'That's awful,' Brianna stated.

'It is,' Megan agreed. 'But it explains why you're so
knowledgeable and able to explain things to patients
when we don't have time. Do you miss it?'

'At first I was devastated. I attended an HIV support
group and someone there suggested I think about counselling,' she told them, sharing things she'd told no one
but Gio. 'I could continue helping people but without
physical contact. I enjoy what I do and wouldn't change
it now.'

'What about Gio?' Megan asked softly.

'He wants friendship, that's all.' It didn't become any
easier with repetition. 'I understand why after he lost his
wife. And it isn't as if I have anything to offer him.'

'Stuff and nonsense!' Brianna exclaimed, her Irish
accent stronger than usual.

It hurt too much to talk about Gio so Jess changed the subject and reflected on the damage the newspaper article might have caused. The nightmare was real, the secret she had guarded was now public knowledge, and she feared the consequences. She was mulling over what to do when Ben returned.

'I'd rather you had a couple of days off and rested that leg, but sitting at home alone won't be good for you.' He frowned, deep in thought. 'We can look out for you here at the hospital. Just be sensible and don't over-stretch your side. And keep your foot up as much as possible. I've brought you some pain medication. Come and see us if you're not feeling well or you have problems with the wound.'

Jess took the tablets and smiled. 'OK. Thanks, Ben, you've been wonderful. How's Lucy?'

'About to pop!' he said, making them laugh. 'She's fed up and excited. We can't wait for the baby to arrive.'

Jess noticed Megan's and Brianna's smiles dimmed and both had pain in their eyes. She suspected her friends carried secrets and had been hurt in the past, and she wished there was something she could do to help them.

After Ben had given her a hug and final instructions, he returned to work. Megan and Brianna had to do the same but, before leaving, they arranged to meet up for lunch. Before heading to her office and what could be an uncomfortable chat with her boss, Jess changed into the clothes Megan had collected for her and went up to the ward to check on Will, anxious to know how he was. She felt nervous and unsure of the reception she would receive from colleagues and patients.

* * *

Driving to the hospital, Gio joined the queue at the traffic lights, his gaze straying to the pavement outside the newsagent's shop. His heart threatened to stop as he noted the headline on the local paper. Pasted onto a sandwich board for all to see, it shrieked out at him...

HOSPITAL HEROINE HAS HIV!

He swore furiously in Italian. There was little doubt to whom the headline referred. What the hell had been going on while he'd been in Italy? Anxious for Jessica and desperate to find out what lay behind the headline, he waited in frustration as the lights changed and the traffic moved forward then made his way as fast as he could to the hospital.

Dread clutched at him as he parked his car and hurried inside. One of the first people he saw was Ben, who gave him a brief résumé of events and then showed him the newspaper. While he felt deep concern for her well-being and fury at the thoughtless reporter, he was also full of pride at the way Jessica had saved the young man's life.

'Thank you for taking such good care of her,' he said now, shaking Ben's hand. 'Where is she?'

'She left here about five minutes ago and was going to visit Will in Intensive Care before going to her office.'

'Thanks,' he repeated.

Ben nodded, holding his gaze. 'Jess needs you, Gio,' his friend told him, and he knew he deserved the hint of chastisement that had laced the words.

'I need her, too,' he confided, earning himself a smile. 'I won't let her down again.'

Determined, he set off to find her.

* * *

'May I sit down?' Josh asked, taking advantage of the rare opportunity of finding Megan sitting alone in the canteen.

'OK.'

The agreement was grudging, but at least she *had* agreed and hadn't told him to go away. He set down his mug of coffee and pulled up a chair.

She looked at him, a small frown on her face. 'You look tired.'

'Is that a polite way of saying rough?' he teased with a wry smile, running the palm of one hand across his stubbled jaw, intrigued by the flush that brought a wash of colour to her pale cheeks.

'No, I didn't mean that.'

'I've just pulled an extra couple of night shifts and needed the caffeine fix before going home for some sleep. I'm back on days tomorrow,' he explained, savouring the hot, reviving drink.

What he didn't tell her was that he'd been doing extra shifts to avoid having to go home. Things were becoming more and more untenable with Rebecca and he didn't know what to do about it. They had grown further apart than ever. He had tried to encourage her to get out of the house, to take up some kind of voluntary work or hobby if she didn't want to get a job. Anything to give her something else to focus on instead of sitting at home working out ways to try and persuade him to change his mind about having a baby.

He wasn't going to change his mind. Ever. What he hadn't told Rebecca was that he had once teetered on the brink of fatherhood—unknowingly and no more willingly as that may have been at the time. He took another drink, his gaze fixed on Megan. Since talking to her and hearing once and for all that her baby had been his, he'd been able to think of little else.

Hearing in words the reality that he had held his tiny, lifeless son in his hands had hit him far harder than he had ever expected. And it had only made him more certain that having a baby with Rebecca was the wrong thing to do in so many ways, for him, for her and, most importantly of all, for any resulting child.

Setting down his mug, he folded his arms and leaned on the table, watching as Megan spread honey on a granary roll. 'How's Jess?'

'A bit sore. Very upset about the newspaper report. That beastly man,' she growled, echoing his feelings and those of everyone he knew.

'Poor Jess. No one needs that kind of thing.' He shook his head. 'I think people are more stunned at discovering she's a qualified doctor and saved that boy's life than anything else.'

Megan licked sticky honey off her finger, a simple gesture but one that nearly stopped his heart and brought a wave of all-too-familiar desire—the same desire he had always felt for her and her alone.

'Megan...'

'Don't, Josh, please. I—' Her words snapped off, her expression changing as she looked beyond him. He sensed her complete withdrawal, but before he could ask what was wrong, she spoke again. 'Your wife is here.'

He swore under his breath, looking round and seeing Rebecca standing just inside the entrance of the canteen. As always she looked picture perfect. Expensively dressed, polished, outwardly beautiful...and completely out of place.

'Megan,' he began again, returning his attention

to her, not at all sure what he wanted to say, still so confused and churned up inside, knowing only that he resented Rebecca's intrusion.

'Just go, Josh.'

After a moment of indecision he rose to his feet, spurred into action as Rebecca spotted him and began to close the distance between them. After an inadequate word of farewell, he left Megan and worked his way between the tables towards Rebecca and the exit.

'What are you doing here?' he asked, taking her arm to steer her out of the canteen, irritation shooting through him, compounded by the tiredness of two long night shifts.

She made her customary pout. 'You said the garage wouldn't have your car ready until this afternoon, so I thought I'd surprise you and pick you up.'

'I told you there was no need.'

They walked in silence towards the exit. A silence that spoke volumes about the physical, mental and emotional distance between them. They had nothing to speak about, nothing left in common. They didn't talk any more. He wondered if they ever had. One thing was certain…he could never share with her the jumble of emotions that continued to rage within him about Megan and about Stephen, their lost son.

'You! Ms Carmichael. Or Dr Carmichael…whatever your name is!'

Leaving Intensive Care after visiting Will, who was making good progress, and having been thanked by his grateful parents who had seen the newspaper report but were just relieved that their son was alive, Jess halted.

Her stomach churned as she turned to face the man whose angry voice had bellowed her name.

She'd been overwhelmed by the support she'd received from colleagues, many of whom had made a point of stopping her on her walk from A and E to Intensive Care. Now she was forced to encounter someone who sounded far from friendly.

The man was short and stocky with a ruddy complexion and a receding hairline. His heavy footsteps pounded on the floor as he strode determinedly towards her. Nervous, Jess heard the familiar ping that announced the arrival of one of the lifts, accompanied by the soft whooshing sound as the door opened. Unfortunately the lift was too far away for her to use it as an escape route.

'It's outrageous that you are allowed to walk around this hospital so close to vulnerable patients,' the man stated loudly, making her cringe with embarrassment. 'I don't want you anywhere near my wife.'

As the man continued his tirade, his language becoming ever more abusive, Jess was very aware that they were drawing a crowd. People walking the corridors stopped to see what was going on, while others emerged from nearby wards and offices. No one intervened. She was on her own.

Alarmed and humiliated, Jess stepped back, only to find her path blocked as she came up against something solid and strong and warm. Before she could even draw breath and absorb the fact that Gio was really here, one of his arms wrapped around her, across the front of her shoulders, drawing her against his familiar frame, making her feel protected.

'That is enough, sir.' Gio didn't raise his voice and

yet his words rang with such authority and steely command that her detractor at once fell silent. 'You have no business abusing any member of hospital staff at any time, and even less so when your information is wrong and you are speaking from ignorance.'

'But—'

'But nothing. Jessica is a highly valued and respected colleague. Her status is no one's business but her own and she poses absolutely no danger to anyone else,' he stated firmly, his hold on her tightening as she relaxed into him, drawing on his strength. 'Yesterday she saved the life of a young man who would have died had she not been there. For her courage and her selflessness she deserves gratitude and praise, not the ill-informed comments and judgemental attitudes of people who do not know what they are talking about.'

Jess remained speechless with amazement as Gio launched into his defence of her, declaring his support of and belief in her. But even when the man who had challenged her had been silenced and walked away by Security, she discovered that Gio had more to say, uncaring of their audience of colleagues, patients and visitors who remained.

'I am so proud of you, Jessica, and so sorry that I was not here for you when you needed me,' he declared, gently turning her round and cupping her face in his hands. She stared into intense blue eyes, every part of her shaking. 'I love you. I want to marry you and spend the rest of my life with you…if you will have me and forgive me for being so stupid this week and letting you down.'

Jess barely heard the gasps of delight and whispered comments from the people around them. All she could see, all she could hear, all she cared about was Gio, the man who had changed her life in such a short time, who believed in her and accepted her and who had just announced his love for her to the world.

'If I'll have you?'

She didn't know whether to laugh or to cry! So she did both. At the same time. He was everything she wanted. All she wanted. After the last few days of pain and uncertainty, thinking she could never have more than his friendship, she could hardly dare to believe this was true. For now, a wave of love and joy swamped the doubts that still lingered within her. Uncaring of where they were, of her painful side and throbbing leg—even of providing more gossip fodder for nosy Rita—she wrapped her arms around his neck, welcoming the instant response as his own arms enclosed her and held her close.

'I love you, too,' she managed through her tears.

As he swept her off her feet and into a passionate kiss, she dimly heard the whistles and whoops, the calls of congratulations and the spontaneous round of applause. She kissed him back with equal fervour and with all the emotion, love and thankfulness that swelled her heart.

After what had seemed the longest of days, and when he finally had Jessica to himself, Gio could not banish the flicker of unease that nagged at him. Concerned for her well-being and her injuries, he had brought her home to her cottage and insisted she rest while he cooked them a meal. She had eaten it, but she had grown quieter and quieter as the evening progressed. Now, as she paced the living room, her limp evident, he could bear the suspense no more.

As she passed within reach of his armchair, he caught her hand and drew her down to sit on his lap. A deep sigh escaped her and although she didn't pull away from him, she was far from relaxed.

'What is wrong, *fiamma*?' he asked, scared that she was having doubts and changing her mind. 'You are so restless. Talk to me.'

'I can't thank you enough for what you did today. It was horrible and I didn't know what to do.' For a moment she hesitated, her gaze averted, then she sighed again and looked at him, revealing the shadows in her olive-green eyes. 'Then you were there and made everything right.'

So why did he suddenly feel that things were now wrong? His heart lurched in fear. 'Jessica…'

'I won't hold you to it. I'll understand if it was something you said on the spur of the moment because of the circumstances,' she told him in a rush, her voice shaky.

'You won't hold me to what?' he asked, genuinely puzzled.

Long lashes lowered to mask her expression and her voice dropped to a whisper. 'Marrying me. You don't have to.'

'You don't want me to?'

'Yes. No. Not if you don't want to.'

She frowned in confusion and he felt bad for teasing her, but now he could see to the root of her worries, it felt as if a huge weight had lifted from his shoulders. He understood her doubts. He deserved them after the way he had behaved. But this, he hoped, he could deal with.

'Look at me.' He cupped her face with one hand,

drawing her gaze to his. 'It is true I had not planned on asking you to marry me in such a way, with so many people listening. But at the time a public declaration seemed right.' Uncertainty remained in her eyes. 'Can you pass me my jacket?'

'OK.'

He held her steady as, her frown deepening, she reached out to retrieve the jacket of his suit, which he had discarded and left draped over the arm of the adjacent sofa.

'Thank you.' With his free hand he checked the pockets until he found what he needed. 'The timing and the setting may have been unplanned, but I meant every word I said.'

He heard her indrawn gasp of surprise and she looked at him with a mix of warring emotions in her eyes. 'Gio?'

'I'm not surprised you doubted me. I deserve that after the terrible way I behaved last week,' he told her, pressing a finger to her lips to silence her protests. 'It needs to be said, *fiamma*. I was wrong. I knew how badly other people had treated you and yet I allowed my own momentary fears to rise up and my withdrawal, timed with my trip to Italy, must have felt like another rejection of you. I am so sorry.'

'Don't.' She caught his hand, their fingers instinctively linking together. 'I understand. And I don't blame you.'

'You should.'

She shook her head, her loose hair shimmering and dancing like living fire. 'No. You went through so much with Sofia. I knew you were scared of going through anything like that again. And, let's face it, the odds could be less good with me.'

'I do not care about odds, Jessica, I care about *you*,' he insisted. 'I never imagined that I could fall in love again, that I would ever know happiness and peace again, but my life changed for the better the moment I met you. Thanks to you I stopped existing and started living again.'

'Gio,' she whispered, her eyes bright with unshed tears.

'Please, I need to say this.' He drew her hand to his mouth and kissed it. 'I hate that I hurt you, that my withdrawal left you so lonely and uncertain. You deserved so much more from me and, if you will let me, I'll spend the rest of our lives proving to you how much I love you and that I'll never let you down again.' He paused a moment, sucking in an unsteady breath, his heart thudding against his ribs. 'I came back from Italy knowing what an idiot I had been and knowing what I wanted and needed to do. Events overtook us, and my plans went awry.'

Eyes wide with disbelief and hope, she bit her lip, her fingers clinging to his. 'What plans?' she managed, and he could feel the tremble running through her.

'My plans to be with you alone, like this, to beg your forgiveness and to ask you properly to be my wife.' Holding her gaze, he released her hand and reached into his pocket once more, drawing out the box. 'I bought this in Italy. For you. I meant all I said this morning, I just meant to say it in private! So the timing may have been wrong, but the question was heartfelt and genuine, not something I made up on the spot.' He placed the little box in her hand. 'Jessica, I love you. I want to spend the rest of my life cherishing you, being your friend and your lover. Please, will you make me the happiest and luckiest of men and marry me?'

'Yes. Yes, yes, yes!'

Jess felt as if her heart had swollen so full of love and joy that it would surely stop beating. All day doubts had nagged at her, but now her fears had been allayed as Gio had laid his own heart on the line for her. Again. Her vision blurred by tears, her fingers shaking so badly she could hardly make them work properly, she did as he encouraged and opened the jeweller's box.

'Oh, my,' she gasped. 'Gio!'

'You like it?' he asked nervously, and she laughed through her tears that he could doubt it.

She gazed down at the gorgeous ring. Set in platinum were three stunning olive apatite stones that exactly matched those in the earrings her grandmother had given her and which she wore every day. The three stones were set on a slight angle with the shoulders of the ring overlapping each side, each sparkling with a row of tiny diamonds. It was the most divine ring she had ever seen. She didn't dare imagine how much it had cost but it was not the monetary value that mattered, it was that Gio had chosen something so special, with such care, knowing what it would mean to her and giving it to her with love.

'It's beautiful,' she murmured huskily as he took it from the box and set it on her finger. 'Perfect. Thank you.'

'You are perfect and beautiful.'

He cupped her face, bestowing on her the gentlest and most exquisite of kisses. Jess sank into him, wrapping her arms around him, wondering how she had ever been lucky enough to know such happiness. As the passion flared between them, healing the past, uniting them heart and soul and full of promise for the future, she gave thanks for this very special man.

'I love your home,' Gio told her softly as they lay in bed later that night, replete after the physical expression of their love and togetherness. 'I feel at peace here,' he continued, filling her already overflowing heart with new joy as his feelings mirrored her own. 'Any day the fences will be ready and our menagerie will come home.'

'I thought maybe you'd arranged for that to be done so I'd leave your house and move back here,' she admitted softly.

'No!' He sounded so shocked she couldn't help but laugh, secure now in his feelings and her own. 'That was not why at all,' he insisted. 'It was to make you happy but also, selfishly, because I wanted to come here and to care for the animals with you. Can this *be* our home, *fiamma*? Can we bring this beautiful shell back to life together and make it ours for ever?'

'Yes, please!'

Snuggling into his embrace, she smiled into the darkness, knowing that they shared the same vision, not just for this place that would be their home but for their future. However long they were blessed with they would share together. And with the friends and colleagues who had shown them so much support and understanding.

It was not just the cottage that had been a shell that would be brought back to life. She and Gio had been shells, too. They had each been alone, rocked and ravaged by the events that had turned their lives upside down. But fate had brought them together…two people who had needed each other so much. They had found their place. Had found each other. And together they had found the sunshine, new hope and a fresh joy of living.

Safe in Gio's arms, Jess felt truly at peace, secure in a love, a friendship and a happiness that neither of them had ever expected to know again. They had been granted second chances and they had found their rightful place in this special part of Cornwall.

It had been a difficult journey but, finally, she was where she was meant to be…with Gio.

LET'S TALK
Romance

For exclusive extracts, competitions and special offers, find us online:

- **f** facebook.com/millsandboon
- **𝕏** @MillsandBoon
- **◉** @MillsandBoonUK

Get in touch on 01413 063232

MILLS & BOON

THE HEART OF ROMANCE

A ROMANCE FOR EVERY READER

MODERN

Prepare to be swept off your feet by sophisticated, sexy and seductive heroes, in some of the world's most glamourous and romantic locations, where power and passion collide.

HISTORICAL

Escape with historical heroes from time gone by. Whether your passion is for wicked Regency Rakes, muscled Vikings or rugged Highlanders, await the romance of the past.

MEDICAL

Set your pulse racing with dedicated, delectable doctors in the high-pressure world of medicine, where emotions run high and passion, comfort love are the best medicine.

True Love

Celebrate true love with tender stories of heartfelt romance, from the rush of falling in love to the joy a new baby can bring, and a focus on th emotional heart of a relationship.

Desire

Indulge in secrets and scandal, intense drama and plenty of sizzling hot action with powerful and passionate heroes who have it all: wealth, statu good looks…everything but the right woman.

HEROES

Experience all the excitement of a gripping thriller, with an intense romance at its heart. Resourceful, true-to-life women and strong, fearless face danger and desire - a killer combination!

To see which titles are coming soon, please visit

millsandboon.co.uk/nextmonth

JOIN US ON SOCIAL MEDIA!

Stay up to date with our latest releases, author
news and gossip, special offers and discounts, and
all the behind-the-scenes action
from Mills & Boon...

 millsandboon

 millsandboonuk

 millsandboon

t might just be true love...

MILLS & BOON

MODERN

Power and Passion

Prepare to be swept off your feet by sophisticated, sexy and seductive heroes, in some of the world's most glamourous and romantic locations, where power and passion collide.

Julia James

REGNANCY SCANDAL

MILLS & BOON
MODERN

Jennie Lucas

Chosen as the
SHEIKH'S ROYAL BRIDE

MILLS & BOON
MODERN

Kim Lawrence

A WEDDING at the
ITALIAN'S DEMAND

MILLS

Sharon Kendrick

The
SHEIKH'S SECRET BABY

MILLS & BOON
MODERN

MILLS & BOON
True Love
Romance from the Heart

Celebrate true love with tender stories of heartfelt romance, from the rush of falling in love to the joy a new baby can bring, and a focus on the emotional heart of a relationship.